THE WOLF BOY

The Wolf Boy

A novel
by
SAM OSHERSON

BOOKS

Adelaide Books
New York / Lisbon
2020

THE WOLF BOY
A novel
By Sam Osherson

Copyright © by Sam Osherson
Cover design © 2020 Adelaide Books
Acknowledgement: to Adele Osherson

Published by Adelaide Books, New York / Lisbon adelaidebooks.org
Editor-in-Chief
Stevan V. Nikolic

For any information, please address Adelaide Books
at info@adelaidebooks.org or write to:
Adelaide Books
244 Fifth Ave. Suite D27
New York, NY, 10001

ISBN: 978-1-951896-59-1

Printed in the United States of America

Contents

Cast of Characters

Major Characters:

Gisgo—Commander of Hannibal's infantry.

Hannibal Barca—Carthaginian general who led invasion of Italy during second war with Rome.

Hanno The Great—Leader of the anti-Barca faction of the Senate in Carthage.

Hamilcar Barca—Late father of Hannibal, leading Carthaginian commander during first war with Rome.

Hamilcar the Younger—Son of Hannibal.

Hasdrubal Barca—Hannibal's younger brother, commander of Carthage's army in Iberia.

Imre—Hannibal's wife, an Iberian princess.

Jonaz—Squire to Hannibal.

Marhabal—Numidian Prince, commander of Hannibal's cavalry and childhood friend.

Nahatum—Orphaned child captured by Hannibal. The Wolf Boy.

Sappho—Nahatum's lover, descendant of the poet Sappho of Lesbos.

Solyphos—Greek scribe to Hannibal, formerly his tutor.

Minor Characters:

Alazne—Nahatum's mother.

Archimedes of Syracuse—Great mathematician and inventor.

Alexander the Great—Macedonian King, conqueror and military genius.

Barnabar—Great Chief of the Celtiberians.

Pacuvius Calavius—Nobleman of Capua, major Italian city allied with Hannibal.

Fabius Maximus—Roman Consul opposing Hannibal, 217-216 BC. "The Delayer."

Lady Busa—Italian landowner who provided refuge to Roman survivors of Cannae

Magalus—King of the Boii (Bologna) tribe in Italy, ally to Hannibal.

Marcellus—Roman Consul, conquered Syracuse, died in skirmish with Hannibal's Troops, 208 BC.

Marcus Atillus Regulus—Roman Consul, defeated Carthage in first Punic War.

Phillip V of Macedon—Enemy of Rome, flirted with alliance with Hannibal.

Rantan—older boy, leader of the wolf pack.

Scipio—Roman Consul Publius Cornelius Scipio, defeated Hasdrubal in Iberia, victor at Battle of Zama, 202 BC.

Tenalakis—Bookhunter and bookseller, lived in Ierapetra, Crete.

Thucydides—Greek historian and General.

Xenophon— Greek historian and soldier.

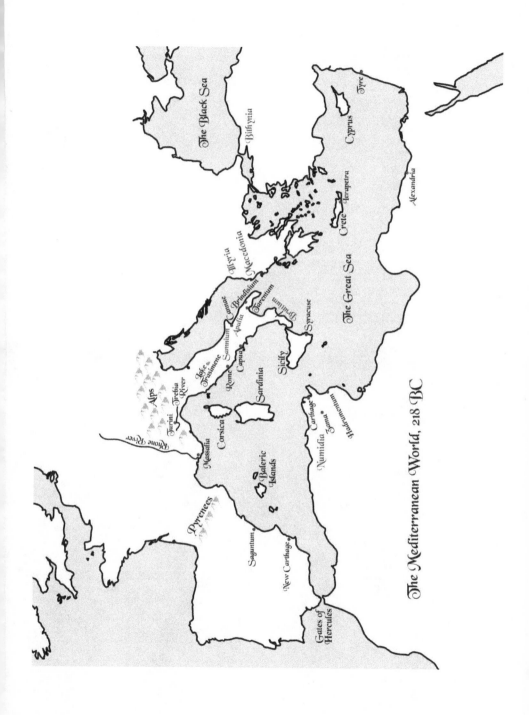

The Mediterranean World, 218 BC

Preface

Before there was a Roman Empire, before Julius Caesar, before Cleopatra, before Christ, two city-states were locked in a sprawling, brutal, century-long struggle for domination of the known world. Rome was an emerging military power dominating Italy. Carthage was the powerhouse of the Mediterranean, a trading and mercantile center with a busy, imposing harbor near what is now Tunis, on the northern coast of Africa. Their pivotal, world-shaking series of clashes came to be known as The Punic Wars, lasting from 246 BC to 146 BC.

Carthage was older than Rome, and far more illustrious—a cosmopolitan, multicultural city. Which city would determine the course of Western Civilization? By most logic the strategic balance in this struggle should have favored the more populous, aggressive, and ambitious Romans. However, Carthage had one advantage: the military genius of the Barca family. The name, Barca, means lightening or thunderbolt in Punic.

The fierce patriarch, Hamilcar Barca, had been an illustrious commander toward the end of the first war. Despite Hamilcar's bristling opposition, the Carthaginian Senate—its treasury exhausted—finally ordered him to negotiate a peace treaty with Rome. In an effort to restore Carthage's fortunes—and his own reputation—Hamilcar eventually left Carthage for Iberia, with its rich forests and reserves of silver and gold, taking his nine year old son, Hannibal, with him. Over the years, the father raised Hannibal to fulfill his legacy: defeat Rome.

As Hamilcar expanded Carthage's empire in Iberia, relations with Rome stretched to the breaking point. Then Hamilcar died, tragically, during a military operation. Twenty-five year old, untested Hannibal was elected by popular acclaim to command the army.

There was a second war with Rome coming, and it was his war now.

Prologue

The sand stung the back of Hannibal's neck in the hot early morning wind. He surveyed the field of the coming battle, bathed in golden sunlight reflected off Roman helmets: a long sandy flat plain, devoid of water, except for a small river on the far end. This is what he wanted, what the plan demanded, offering a slim hope of victory against the supposedly invincible Roman army. In the far distance lay the little town of Cannae.

The Romans were lining up for battle across the plain. They'd raised the largest army Rome had ever put in the field and the older and cautious Consul Fabius, The Delayer, his nemesis, had been replaced by two Roman commanders eager to burnish their reputations by defeating the great– and deeply feared– Hannibal. The Consul in command that day was spoiling for a fight; he'd mocked Fabius on the Senate floor for avoiding a climactic battle with the perfidious Carthaginian.

Ninety thousand Roman soldiers lay across that plain, facing his polyglot army numbering, maybe, forty thousand. There were so many Roman soldiers it was as if all of Rome itself had come to attention, flags waving, legion upon legion. Hannibal's horse whinnied at the distant sound of trumpets calling units to their place, anticipating what was to come. From the slight rise looking over the dry, sandy plain, Hannibal could just see the river Aufidus coursing through. If all worked according to plan the Roman army would die in sight of all that water, useless to them.

Behind him, he could hear the boy, Nahatum, breathing, clearly trying to take in the immensity of the sight in front of him. The boy—his lucky charm, his devoted, hard-working servant, now scribe– had brought him here, to this: a flat plain on a hot summer day confronting a Roman army finally willing to fight him. Or was it two armies? It was enormous. Brought here to test him, to test the strategy that he had been thinking about since a young boy with his father who had died so many years ago opposing the Romans.

He looked at Nahatum, now more young man than boy, a strapping sixteen years old, his dark hair waving in the slight hot breeze. The Wolf Boy—that's what they'd called him when his guards caught him trying to steal from his tent two years ago back in Iberia, this war not yet even born. An orphan living by his wits. And wits he has, that's certain, Ba'al be praised.

For a moment, Hannibal permitted himself to think of all that might have gone differently that morning in Iberia. If he'd been out inspecting his troops. If the guard had simply killed the boy. If he hadn't walked out of his tent. If he'd not been so inexplicably charmed by the boy as to do something so illogical and preposterous as to make him his servant. The smallest difference in the events of that day, and all that followed would never have happened.

"Has there ever been an army as large?" Gisgo, the burly veteran commander of his infantry, muttered, adjusting the bridle on his horse. *A good question. The Persians were supposed to have massed a million men to invade Attica, but surely that is simply legend.* Their army at Marathon was perhaps fifty thousand. *And Alexander? He took thirty thousand Macedonians in his conquest of the world.*

And here the Romans had massed three times that number. He ought to be honored that they would only fight him now when they were certain of victory. Who could defeat such an army?

And the Romans were confident, he was sure of it. Hannibal remembered his father's words: *let the enemy think he has the advantage and use their advantage to destroy them.*

Hannibal turned to answer Gisgo's question. "Yes, it's a large army. Yet, consider, my friend: in all that enormous number of men there is not a single one named Gisgo." That produced a laugh from his infantry commander, a sound reminiscent of boulders thundering off canyon walls. The huge man did nothing small. The boy standing slightly behind also laughed. *Good. Most of all we need confidence. And some luck.*

The boy was his luck. Hannibal had barely time to meet his own infant son before sending him back to Carthage when the war had begun. He couldn't escape the thought then that perhaps Nahatum, the Wolf Boy, was more a son than his own son.

For a moment Hannibal thought of his father, powerful Hamilcar, and those many nights in front of the massive stone fireplace—flames dancing— at their estate in Iberia, debating the question they would face in the inevitable war with Rome: how do you defeat an enemy army numerically far superior and better armed than your own? *Have we answered that question, my dear father?* Then another flooded in: *will I today avenge your death and restore Carthage to its place in the world?*

He had convinced the Gauls and Iberians and all the rest of his polyglot army that the plan would work despite protests that it was reckless, foolhardy, and "bewitched by the demons of death," as one Gaulish chieftain had yelled.

We shall soon see.

All around, Gauls shouted, danced, and shook weapons at the assembled Romans across the field. Near Hannibal, three naked Gauls waved their tall, thick wooden pikes over their heads at the Roman line as they danced. All had piled their long reddish- blond hair, heavily greased, onto the top of their head. The effect was to make their massive bodies look even taller, more like bear- men.

A Gaul nearby—naked from the waist down– wore only the tunic of a dead Roman officer, streaked with dried blood, the gold epaulets clearly visible, seized in earlier battle. Past him, several others—red faces bulging– screamed taunts ("your mother is my whore") and threats ("your skull will become my drinking goblet") at the Romans, waving a ripped, bloody battle standard seized from a Roman legion destroyed last year at the battle of Trasimene, a mere ambush compared to what they were attempting this day.

How amusing, almost comical, if you didn't know what was about to happen. Hannibal could see the looks on the assembled columns of Romans standing, watching from across the dry plain, swords and shields at the ready. Legion standards rippled in the breeze. *They hate us. They hate me. All the better: an army that is enraged is an army that is not thinking.*

And then came the peal of Roman trumpets and the enormous line of men across the field started moving toward them, lances extended, armor glistening in the noonday sun, their distinctive metal helmets making them look more beast then men...

Chapter 1

Hunger

"The soldier promised you a meal if you cleaned his mule– and you believed him?" Ranton said, eyes wide in disbelief.

Nahatum nodded at the older boy. "Yes," he answered, miserable, visions of beans, rice, a piece of meat, dancing in his head, torturing his empty stomach. "And now he's disappeared." Nahatum stared at the skinny mule, washed and scrubbed, tied to an old tree, chewing slowly on the scrub grass. The blanket he'd half-heartedly beaten to get the fleas off was neatly draped over the long-eared animal's back.

Ranton shook his head. "You're always thinking, Nahatum, but sometimes there's more fleas in your head than on that mule's blanket." Ranton picked a flea off the blanket while the other boys laughed, all of them abandoned children born of the women who followed Hannibal's army of Carthage in Iberia. They were called "wolf children" by the soldiers.

The mule chewed contentedly. Nahatum considered eating some of the thorny, sticky scrub to quiet his stomach, but he'd tried that once and it had come back out his mouth almost as soon as he'd swallowed it.

"You've been tricked," Ranton said, which only confirmed what Nahatum already knew. "Come on, let's go and find this lying soldier."

Maybe you need to think a bit more, Ranton. "How are we going to find him?," Nahatum asked. "There's even more soldiers here today than yesterday."

"Well, we'll find something," Ranton said. "Something to eat, something to steal." Anything to eat, one of the younger boys pleaded. They were always hungry.

"Wait a minute." Nahatum leaned closer to the mule and spit on the flea- infested blanket three times, which everyone knew invited death to its owner. "OK, let's go."

All eight of the boys walked down the ragged, muddy lanes of the army camp, past blacksmith forges hammering out steel swords and shields, past healers with clay pots of herbs for sale, artisans crafting powerful charms and amulets from the silver, copper, and tin brought from the rich mines to the south and east.

Camp followers had set up food stalls and women stood in front of rickety huts where other hungers of the soldiers could be met. Nahatum's eyes lingered for a moment on the women– that familiar, furtive search for his mother. Then a longing again in his chest, pushed away quickly by the thought of food, an emptiness that might be filled.

So many new arrivals filled the rough paths– Persians in felt caps, armed with short spears and battle axes; Greeks carrying sheathed swords with ornamented handles, sturdy wicker shields lashed to their backs; Iberian warriors with iron-studded wooden clubs on their shoulders and thin, carved jav-elins hanging from leather straps.

Why, Nahatum wondered, were so many strange new warriors arriving in the army camp, changing familiar byways, speaking in strange tongues, cutting encampments out of the forests?

The boys stayed together, near the middle of the pathways. A polyglot of ages, Ranton the oldest at fourteen, Nahatum next at twelve. They walked quietly, no laughter, little talking. Nahatum always remembered to be careful, to stand up straight when he walked around the army camp, just as his mother had shown him before she disappeared, like he knew exactly where he was going, as if he was already in the service of some powerful chieftain, not like the wolf child he was—an orphan who was a robber, a scavenger without standing or protector, hardly more than a wild animal.

Nahatum knew, they all knew, that any one of them could disappear into a tent to become a man's property or be whisked away– suddenly a slave sent to the distant mines to carry back the wooden baskets of gold, silver, tin, the Carthaginians coveted so fiercely. That was the fate of boys like him. Nahatum remembered watching once from the woods when the long caravans came into the camp from the far away mountains, snaking lines of dead-eyed children weighted down with the heavy baskets on their shoulders. A thin, stooped boy had died right on the trail, his limp body pushed into the woods by the guards. When night came, the wolf pack had fought over the dead boy's rotting sandals. While the others were grabbing at the sandals, Nahatum had poked and touched the lifeless skin on the boy's face. What had taken the life out of it, he'd wondered, made it stiff and cold to his hand?

Just past the rough supply sheds filled with the remaining animal feed from the long winter—rotting apples, hay, moldy grain— all carefully guarded by armed soldiers, more alert than usual, Nahatum heard one of the younger boys say, "Warriors arrived yesterday who are born of long-haired skunks."

"Soldiers born of skunks?"

"Yes, they walked right past me near the gates, hair down their backs to their feet, and smelling worse than a rotting auroch in the swamp." Then the boy lowered his voice. "They looked very dangerous, so many of them, with long woven slings hanging over their shoulders. They claim to have come from islands far out in the Great Sea."

"Have you ever even seen the Great Sea?" Nahatum asked. Everyone shook their heads, except Ranton, but Nahatum didn't believe him. The older boy had claimed to do many things that turned out to be just stories.

Thinking about the Great Sea—imagining water without end—calmed Nahatum's hungry belly. He wondered if these dangerous Islanders were formed like him or if they lived partly in the water, half fish, maybe with scales instead of skin.

A long line of swarthy horsemen came thundering down the muddy byway, scattering the boys and everyone else. These men wore long, red robes that flashed in the sunlight and rode fast horses unlike any Nahatum had ever seen—small, muscular beasts that clearly could outrun gazelles.

The boys walked on, with little hope of finding the lying soldier or any food atall to steal, past the encampments of Iberian tribesmen, past the stables and up a hill onto an unfamiliar plateau, more wooded.

Then everything changed.

"Do you smell that?" Ranton said, his voice low. Nahatum, all the boys, smelled the aroma of roast meat thick with spices, garlic, and olive oil that seemed to spread everywhere in the forest. Beyond the trees they could see a large clearing that opened up in front of them.

"Where are we?"

"Let's go back," one of the younger boys said in a shaky voice. "We should not be here."

"Wait," said Ranton, holding out an arm to still everyone, as he stared out from behind a tree at the clearing. Whole lambs turned slowly on spits above fiery coal pits. In front of large dark-red clay ovens the cooks laid out platters of freshly-baked bread and roast meat to cool in the warm early spring sunlight. A single, large tent stood nearby.

Several guards with shining chest armor and polished swords at their sides kept watch in front.

One of the boys whispered, "Are we near the gates of a King's Palace?" The boy next to Nahatum was shivering, though the day was warm.

"Look at all that food," said Ranton, though that was all Nahatum could look at.

His mouth watered.

"We can surprise one of them when he brings food in a wagon to the soldiers below." Ranton's plan: hide down the trail, then spring out, all of them. "It'll just be a cook, probably by himself. Maybe we can get his boots and pants as well." As he spoke, Ranton looked at Nahatum, who realized then that the older boy wanted his opinion. *I don't always have a head full of fleas, do I?* Nahatum doubted the value of Ranton's idea; he'd gotten them all in trouble before, so he kept still, thinking about a better plan.

An argument sprang up about whether the cook might be armed. What if he had one of the long bread knives with him, edged with more teeth than a hedgehog?

"What do you say, Nahatum?" Ranton finally asked, cuffing one of the younger boys slow to quiet. All listened.

"What if we try a trick?" Nahatum outlined his plan as they all stood, mouths watering, amidst the trees, so close to the meat treasures and the fragrant flatbreads, watching the cooks and guards go about their work. Ranton smiled and nodded and that cinched it: the others went along as they always did.

Three boys burst out of the trees, yelling and running toward horses tethered toa wagon on the other side of the cook ovens, while Ranton and Nahatum charged directly into the campsite to snatch whatever food they could.

Ranton knocked aside an old, toothless cook, grabbing several loaves of flatbread. In a flash the wiry man had a carving knife in his hand and almost skewered the boy, but Ranton was quick. Quicker than Nahatum.

As Nahatum ran behind him toward the tables with the roast meat, the heat from the fiery coal pits slammed into his chest, turning his legs to mud. The rich smell of the cooked lamb so close made his head cloudy. He stumbled. Someone grabbed his arm; he spun around while tall Ranton, legs churning, kept going right out of sight with several fresh-baked circles of brownish-gold under his arm, taunting the guards as he disappeared: you're slow as mules!

The guard's belly and leather chest armor avalanched into Nahatum. The curved killing knife glinted in the man's hand. Nahatum tried to pull away, but the guard's grip might as well have been the jaws of a lion. The guard twisted the boy's arm deep into his back. He kicked out frantically, blinded by the shaft of pain climbing up his shoulder. A sharp smell of sweat and roast meat attacked him.

From all around, Nahatum heard shouts: He's mine! No, mine. He'll make a good slave boy! A sharp hand dug into his elbow. The boy bucked and kicked, now a bull auroch from the forest deep, eyes wide with fury, wanting to crush his tormentor. Foot found knee. The burly guard bellowed in pain.

Yet he held on. One foot anchored in the gravelly soil, the wolf child twisted and pulled for his life toward the far trail at the edge of the clearing, narrow and so dark it could have been the entrance to the Underworld.

His elbow, shoulder, were on fire. "May death curse you," he spit at the guard withthe lion's grip.

"What's going on out here?" A commanding voice, yet not loud. The pressure on Nahatum's elbow eased. All the noise and activity stopped, like the silence of field mice when the hawk appears in the sky.

The guard bowed, without letting go. A man in a green tunic emerged from the flowing folds of the nearby tent, followed by several others, one of them a hairy giant. The guard pushed Nahatum toward the one in front, who stared, running a hand through his short black hair. The push sent another flame up Nahatum's back. He squirmed to straighten himself in the man's grip, and, he resolved, that no matter the pain, he would not cry out.

Nahatum stared at the black- haired man. Shorter than the giant, but tall nonetheless. At the edge of the clearing, the trees huddled, moaning in the morning wind. The blood raged through his sore elbow.

"Who are you?" The man addressed the wolf child directly, surprising everyone. He spoke in the rough Iberian dialect— Nahatum's language- common to the area. Sun- browned arms contrasted with his light green tunic. He had an angular face, no beard, gray eyes.

Nahatum knew that he should stay silent, and hide himself away in muteness. But since he was already dead-- like all men, these were merciless— he refused to die silently, like the startled deer in the forest who stands there stupidly while the hunter aims his bow.

"Who are *you?*" the boy spit back. And prepared himself to die.

"Foul wolf boy," the guard hissed, wedging Nahatum's arm tighter still, almost knocking him over. The giant in back growled through his beard. Through the burning in his arm, Nahatum heard him say something that sounded like, "just a boy…To the mines." Then he heard it clearly: "…eat our dead." Nahatum's teeth started to chatter.

To everyone's astonishment the man in the tunic ignored the giant and again addressed the wolf child.

"A spunky boy." The sun- browned man's mouth spread into a slight smile, wrinkling his cheeks. His green tunic rustled. "I am Hannibal."

Nahatum clenched his jaws to stop his jittery teeth. He wanted to bite something, tear at it, crush bones between his jaws, as he'd seen lions do to deer carcasses in the forest. He considered the man standing in front of him claiming to be Hannibal. The boy had of course heard the name many times. Everyone spoke of Hannibal Barca, commander of Carthage's army in Iberia, with such awe and mystery– he is taller than the great Black bear, and his war cry makes stalking lions flee; he charms awful Thunder Beasts from the Underworld to fight alongside him in battle, creatures so huge they crush men underfoot— how could this man really be him?

"And I'm Hannibal's son," the boy scoffed.

Hannibal Barca, first-born son of one of the most illustrious families ofCarthage, felt the corners of his mouth tighten. *Impudent boy*. He wondered why he had even stepped outside the tent. He'd heard the cries of so many young boys. Slave children, noble children, wild wolf children—if he reacted every time he heard a young cry of pain, he'd get nothing done. He knew he should walk back into the tent and continue working to convince his commanders, who were now standing right behind him watching this scene, about the worthiness of his war plans. Gisgo, behind him, blowing wind through his teeth impatiently, was right: he should send the unruly boy to the mines and get back to work.

Hannibal was about to turn away when suddenly an oath rang out. "Spawn of a hyena!" His guard's face was contorted in pain and he clutched at his knee, where he'd been kicked again, harder this time. The boy was half-way across the campsite heading toward the trail into the woods. Two other guards ran after him, their chest armor clinking in the still air. They had to pull the boy's clenched arms from the trunk of a nearby oak tree and drag him back, kicking furiously, dumping him on the ground at Hannibal's feet. Looking up at Hannibal, the boy's eyes widened.

Something tugged at Hannibal about this boy. Defiant. Trying to look brave when really so frightened. Cocky kid. A bit like himself at that age.

From behind came Gisgo's deep, rumbling voice, muttering about this waste of time. "My Lord, a wolf child... The mines." He heard murmurs of agreement from the men clustered around.

But, it was the boy's face that captured Hannibal. The look in his eyes: fierce and sad at the same time. He didn't look down or away, as a thieving boy might.

With a single, sweeping gesture, staring into the distance across the meadow, Hannibal stifled the voices around him, then returned his gaze to the boy.

"Well," he said directly to the wolf child, surprising even himself, "No sooner do I say good-bye to one child, when another arrives at my tent."

Nahatum had no idea what the man was talking about. He couldn't stop thinking about the fact that the giant who wanted to eat the dead also wanted to send him to the mines. And, as he looked up at the man who claimed to be Hannibal, he remembered all the soldiers he'd seen speaking gibberish before, walking down the muddy lanes of the camp, especially those with only one arm or leg or missing ears, even noses– men with all the hair burnt off their heads, or with curdled patches of beet- red skin that looked like some demon lizard gripping that spot. Now he wondered if all soldiers spoke nonsense, even great generals.

"Give him some food," the man instructed. "Afterward wash him. Then trim his hair." He paused a moment, again staring into the distance, toward the trail the boy had just tried to reach. "After that, bring him into my tent."

No. A flame of fear ignited in Nahatum's chest. He kicked out at them all, but the two burly guards holding his arms lifted him up off the ground, shaking him, then slammed him down so hard it left him dizzy. He heard a rumbling protest from behind Hannibal, who glared back at the giant. The protest stopped.

The guard he'd kicked gave an awkward bow, favoring his knee. Hannibal turned on his heels and walked back into his tent, followed by the giant and another, smaller, man in a flowing white caftan that glistened in the sunlight. The boy, still in the grasp of the guards, stared at the cruel, curved knives each carried at their waist. The saffron tent opening flapped apart, snapping against the side, then quickly shut, a moment of light, then darkness. Something awful awaited him in there, the boy knew. Then he could think of nothing but the sweet, dark, warm chunk of roast lamb thrust at him.

Gisgo stared down at the map spread out in front of him, frowning as if Hannibal had just put a talking three- headed miniature cow on the large table.

"My Lord, I don't understand...."

The sound of the screeching wolf child being dragged down to the river to be washed almost drowned out bull-throated Gisgo, the battle-hardened, no-nonsense commander of Hannibal's infantry, the thousands of mercenaries—a polyglot collection of fierce, proud Iberian tribesmen, impassive, turbaned warriors from India, regal black Africans, Persian fighters with painted faces who knew a dozen ways to kill– plus his purebred, haughty Carthaginian veterans.

Massively- built, with powerful arms well- tested in combat, Gisgo wore the knife scar on his face snaking up from beneath his thick beard as other men might wear medals. His hair was long and unkempt, increasing the bear- like aspect. Years older than Hannibal, Gisgo was Carthaginian-born himself. As a young man, he'd been a foot soldier in Hamilcar's army when Hannibal's father created the well-trained core of soldiers that his son now led. No easy task, Hannibal thought, commanding a man ten years older who has worked his way up the ranks under your father's tutelage.

Hannibal looked across the carved mahogany table at the third man in the tent: Marhabal, the Numidian Prince– Hannibal's childhood friend—who'd brought his incomparable desert horsemen by boat across the Gates of Hercules from their homes in north Africa, thousands of them, the best riders in the world, like liquid fire in their flowing red caftans streaking across the ragged Iberian meadows. Lean, a bit shorter than Hannibal, Marhabal—dressed in a white caftan, as befitted his Numidian royalty– stroked his carefully trimmed beard, deep in thought as he sought to grap the enormity of what his friend was proposing.

No help there, Hannibal realized as the dark-skinned Numidian stared at the map.

Concentrate. These are the men most loyal to you: you've got to convince them of the worth of your plans. You can't order their allegiance, you've got to earn it.

"My Lord, this map....I've never seen anything like it." Gisgo pointed a thick finger at the papyrus sheet in front of him. "Italy is here....and we are here on the coast of Iberia." He looked up. "Usually maps are smaller, telling you how to get to where an enemy is camped, we draw them ontheground. Perhaps the Numidian understands this...." Gisgo scowled at Marhabal, who shook his head. Gisgo looked like a mountain sitting across from slender Marhabal. "I didn't think a Numidian would....You don't need maps in a desert."

In a minute they'll be trading insults again. "Indeed some of the details remain to be worked out. I am still gathering information. There is so much to know. This is a journey like no other." Hannibal leaned over the the map that covered the entire long table to show the two men the route he proposed. "We march north and cross the snow- capped mountains into Gaul—I've sent emissaries in secret to several of the Gaulish tribes and they promise us safe passage –and then through the forests of Gaul to the Endless Mountains, as they are called, which block us from Italy."

He moved his hand quickly over the empty areas on the map, the places where there were no clear routes, where no traders or mercenaries—or fools—had yet gone. He spoke in eager and confident tones, making his voice a bridge over all that remained yet unknown. "We will find passage through those mountains, with the help of rebellious Gaulish tribes there who are very worried about Rome's ambitions. We will find our way into.....here, Northern Italy. We will catch the Romans entirely by surprise."

"The distances…" Marhabal murmured.

Gisgo cleared his throat. "We don't even know exactly the route we will take.

War is coming. Let us fight the Romans here in Iberia where we have allies."

The sides of the tent snapped tightly in the afternoon breeze. Hannibal felt a weariness in his shoulders. "We need to strike quickly and directly at Rome. The key is the element of surprise. The conquest of Rome in a sudden, lightning invasion of Italy."

He felt a renewed energy. "How many victories did it take for the great Alexander to destroy the Persian empire?"

"Three," replied Marhabal.

"Granicus, Issus, and Gaugamela," added Gisgo quickly, as if refusing to allow the Numidian any advantage in knowledge.

"Exactly," confirmed Hannibal. "Three smashing victories and Alexander destroyed the vast Persian empire, far more powerful than Rome. I tell you, three such victories on Italian soil and the Roman federation will collapse."

"That presumes three smashing victories. Against well-trained Roman armies on Italian soil, where they enjoy advantages in re-supply and reinforcements "Gisgo's voice trailed off.

Gisgo didn't have to continue, Hannibal knew. *He's really asking what I have accomplished to warrant such confidence. Burnt down Saguntum, a minor city a few miles up the coast with ideas of allying itself with Rome and I compare myself to Alexander the Great?* Hannibal considered the burly man, battle scars visible on both arms. *Gisgo will support me up to a point out of loyalty to my father, but to what point?*

He tried to envison what awaited them in those mountains, across the uncharted forests of Gaul, but the blank areas on the map stared up at Hannibal like the dead eyes of an ambushed soldier.

Marhabal looked up from the map, seeming not to have been listening to Gisgo. "The last war went on for twenty-three years."

"Carthage was exhausted, surrendered before we really needed to," Hannibal added. "No more wars of attrition, by the grace of Ba'al. Rome must be defeated quickly. Once they have their teeth into you, they don't let go."

"Cut off their head, like we do to snakes." Gisgo said. His deep voice made "head" sound like "dead." He ran a hand through his bushy beard. "Well, then, how about the navy—ferry troops across to Sicily. Or directly to Italy?"

"Gisgo, you and I have been in Iberia so long we forget that Carthage no longer controls the seas, as in the old days."

The Cothon at Carthage, the city's great protected harbor, a mile wide, where their vast war fleets had once been docked, was now almost empty, the great ships burnt on the beaches in front of the city as required by the humiliating peace agreement years earlier. The one signed by his father, at the orders of the Senate.

"A land invasion, coming from out of nowhere. Catch the Romans entirely by surprise." Marhabal said, his eyes bright with energy. "I like that."

Hannibal smiled at his old friend. *Ah, cavalry commanders like Marhabal, always impetuous, savor risk. Infantry commanders are different. A veteran like Gisgo wants to think about the difficulties.*

"Forty thousand men, ten thousand cavalry. The supply wagons. Lord Hannibal, how will we feed this enormous army in a strange land ruled by foreign gods? And forty war elephants. They will cross these mountains?" Gisgo fell into silence, tracing the proposed invasion route with one enormous finger extended over the map table, as if trying to feel the distances involved through his very skin.

"And Solyphos," Gisgo asked. "What does the old Greek think of this plan?"

Hannibal looked at the empty chair at the map table, Solyphos' usual place, where he'd sit with his patient smile, carefully gathering the sleeves of his robe before setting to write, offering words of wise counsel. The man's presence had always calmed Hannibal; it'd been true since the day years earlier when his father Hamilcar had hired the Greek warrior and scholar to come to Iberia and be his young son's tutor. But now he was sick, still in his tent, Hannibal explained. A disturbing question formed itself in Hannibal's mind: did Solyphos' absence betray his tutor's doubts about the war plans?

And who knew what the native Iberian chiefs—with their thousands of wild-eyed tribesmen– coming to council in a few weeks will say? Hannibal knew that if theydidn't join, he had no army.

"Rocky soil in those mountains, " Marhabal said. "It will be hard on the horses' hooves."

"Who cares about your horse's hooves," thundered Gisgo. "My men have to march across these barren lands. We will need leather to replace their shoes. Every cow, sheep, and goat that we slaughter will need to be skinned. And our supposed Gaulish allies will need to supply us with whatever animals we cannot herd along on the march."

Marhabal ignored Gisgo, speaking directly to Hannibal. "My men are ready, our horses are strong. We can do this, Hannibal."

"We are going to need thirty tons of grain a day to feed the thousands of men during the march," Gisgo interrupted. "About the horses, I can't tell you how much hay they'll need." He looked across at Marhabal, skeptically: "Hopefully the Numidian can tell us that." Gisgo went on with the list. Two quarts of water per day per soldier. They'll literally drink some rivers dry along the march, he pointed out. Onions, beans, grains, figs, dates, chicken eggs, smoked gooseflesh, oranges, salt, thyme and other spices. One hundred head of cattle, plus assorted chickens, goats and sheep. The line of march will stretch for dozens of miles. Dried meat, biscuits, sour wine.

"Which reminds me," Gisgo said, a smile unexpectedly brightening his face. "The Balearic Islanders arrived, quite fragrant in that mastic oil they douse themselves in before battle. We will need them; the volleys with their war slings are a very effective weapon, if used correctly." The thought of battle, Hannibal noticed, seemed to relax the infantryman. "But their odor! Worse than skunks. " The infantry commander laughed so hard he showed teeth: "The Romans will smell us coming, even if we never get there."

Some wine would help focus our attention. A call for young Rabilan, his servant. *Ah, no, that boy died of the coughing illness during the last moon.*

Instead, in came Jonaz, Hannibal's squire, his attendant on and off the battlefield, the one always close behind him in combat, carrying his extra battle shield and swords, still walking with a distinct limp, courtesy of the wolf boy's swift kicks to his knee.

Stout, though not as massive as Gisgo, and clean shaven with a black tattoo—several lines and dots– on his upper lip. A narrow face and broad, pronounced nose.

Gisgo made no effort to restrain a smile at the sight of the squire's limp, nor a jab: "Were you reciting your prayers to Ba'al Shammon, Jonaz, when you should have been holding that thieving wolf child tighter?"

Ba'al's breath. That wolf boy again. Hannibal knew that everyone expected him to have sent the rude child to be a slave, to work in the mines with the rest of them. He hoped that this didn't make him look weak in front of the others. *Well, horse farts to them: maybe this boy could make something of himself, given a chance.* He needed a new servant. Hannibal pictured all the nobles' young sons prancing through their sword work in the fields, children of some of the same Senators who'd betrayed his father in the last war. Any one of them, he knew, would die to become Hannibal Barca's servant. *Let them rot in the Underworld.* Perhaps this wolf boy– raw, hungry, living by his wits– was made of tougher stuff. He'd see what this spunky wolf child could do. A plan formed in his mind.

Hannibal dismissed the forlorn squire. *Forget the wine. Focus.* His commanders were again arguing. Hannibal returned to the discussion just as Gisgo was advocating his plan for eating their dead as a way to solve their supply problems through the frozen mountains.

Hours later, the guards threw the boy into the tent like a sack of potatoes. His hair was shorn, and he was still wet all over and cold from the river, clad now in scratchy clothes that made his skin prickle.

"Just sit there and be quiet—no rudeness," this strange man, Hannibal, instructed, again in the very dialect that Nahatum had known all his life. The awful giant seated near Hannibal, boulder- jaw– more hair than a black bear, tumbling over his head and down around his shoulders, curling on his arms– glared at Nahatum. The boy quickly looked away, but not before noticing that the man was holding some small thing in his bear-paw hands. He ripped into it with a fearsome bite, tearing it apart.

A fig.

The tent seemed dark to a wolf child more used to the bright dome of early afternoon blue sky. Nahatum checked his scalp, worried that the guards had hacked off all his hair. He found a hand's length all around, reaching over his ears. His skin itched without its coat of dirt, scraped off by the guards in the awful washing. He pictured a tethered goat, cleansed before the sacrifice, then its throat slit, as he'd observed from the woods on feast days. These men delighted in burning goats, sheep, oxen, for thepleasures of their god Ba'al Shammon, whom they believed lived in the burning fire of the sacrifice.

The boy tripped on the woven rug, pleasingly soft under foot. Sitting in achair seemed unthinkable, so he squatted on the floor next to it, knees pulled close to chest, trying to figure a way out of this hopeless situation.

Through the open flap of the tent, Nahatum could see the orange clouds of the setting sun. The hairy giant's enormous back was just a few steps in front of him. Then at the bottom of his vision, an ant appeared on the sandy carpet at his feet. Nahatum balled his fist and brought it down hard on the insect, crushing it. He pounded it to be sure. Then he ate it, as they often did in the forest. And he felt a little better.

He recalled more of what he had heard in wandering the muddy byways of the army camp: Lord Hannibal has jagged teeth filed sharp like knife blades. He burnt an entire city to the ground when they resisted his demands. Everyone had talked about that. Saguntum. Even when the people there surrendered, Hannibal ordered the townspeople thrown into the flames. In battle, he makes his soldiers disappear, then reappear where you least expect them. He is a shape shifter, taking different forms– a scorpion, a poisonous snake, a leaping cougar, killing people from behind, in the dark, from the shadows.

Be careful here, find a way out. The boy strained to see the sharp murderous teeth in the gloomy light, but when the man spoke all he saw were orderly rows of white peeking from behind his lips.

Something poked into his foot where he squatted. Pine needles on the rug. A good omen, he decided. Pine needles reminded him of the last day with his mother. Before she'd disappeared, her body wracked by coughs, she'd taken Nahatum deep into the dark forest, down trails softened with pine needles, holding him close as they talked, singing to him when she'd had the breath, and she'd left him with the other boys in the wolf pack, entrusting his safety to them.

What, he wondered, would she make of the fine animal skins strewn across the woven rugs, gold and silk everywhere, and the booming voices of men arguing in their strange language. Sometimes the men lapsed into the local patois. He pieced together arguments about crossing vast snow- covered mountains, impossibly high, ruled by strange gods. The giant and the other one– his white caftan had a gold trim that sparkled even in the dim light—seemed worried, perhaps even scared.

Nahatum's mother had told him about the tents where soldiers lived, often returning to their cave in the woods with a treasure from a visit to the camp, a piece of carved wood or a shiny stone or, best of all, some food—a chunk of chicken or goat roasted in cumin, or a ripe fig, or a mouth-watering paste made from chickpeas and put on stale bread. Once she brought back the spirit world itself, holding up a glowing, twinkling rock that filled the darkness of the cave with a pulsating light, some glow-stuff that lived in the hearts of fish and had been painted on the rock. She'd explained that there were spirits alive in the fish as there are within all the world, spirits that shine and sparkle. Even as she coughed so much that she sometimes had to stop, she instructed her son to remember this glowing when the world seemed at its darkest.

In this gloomy place different from anything he'd ever known, Nahatum remembered the bright light of that fish-painted spirit rock, the way it bathed his mother's face in its blue-green shininess. And he was warmed by the secret he had told no one else: his mother was coming back for him someday. He knew this in the very bones of his boyhood. He searched for some sign of her in the tent– her woven shawl, her cotton dress, the comb she wore in her hair when she'd go into the camp.

In a far corner there was a sleeping pallet held off the ground by large stones, with black and white zebra skins piled on top. An enormous, thick bearskin lay rolled in a corner. He wondered if there was a way to steal it and bring it back into the forest. The dense, leafy, bee- filled, pine-scented forest, the only place where he really felt safe. A bright yellow-and-black gazelle skin decorated one side of the tent. Several spears leaned against tent poles, handles brightly painted, sharp edges visible in the afternoon sunlight shimmering through the tent. He considered seizing a spear and sticking it into the back of the giant in front of him but imagined that the creature would likely pull the bloody spear out of his own back, laughing as he stabbed Nahatum to death with it.

He rocked on his haunches looking for something to crush. He found a small spider in a web just behind him on the wall of the tent. Silently, he grabbed it in his hand and balled his fist as tightly as he could. When he opened his palm he considered the smashed little thing, a mangle of pulp with a lifeless leg sticking out. He thought how big he was and how small the dead thing was. Nahatum knew then that he could bear whatever came toward him. He was a match for the giant– faster, smarter. Even tougher, yes he was. He'd survive. Then the giant grunted, muttering something to Hannibal, and the feeling popped, like a frothy bubble in a stream, and Nahatum again knew himself as a little boy trapped in a tent with deep-throated men and he was scared.

The boy found nothing that reminded him of his mother, nothing she had ever told him about. Still on his haunches, he cradled his still-sore elbow in his hand. He thought about his mother's cough, that rumbling sound from deep inside that made her stop and put an arm on a tree or his shoulder when they'd walked. By the time she'd taken him to the pack, her smell had changed too; no longer a deep mossy fragrance. His mother then smelled of sweat and she had the sharp odor that comes from the inside of a broken, decaying tree.

He felt sleepy, but through the drowsiness heard Hannibal's voice, hard and insistent. Then more voices– gruff, low, questioning– around the table.

Darkness began to fill the tent. Movement, rustling. The boy nodded awake.

Now several candles glowed on the table, filling the tent with dark shadows and gloomy shapes. The men were filing out quietly, walking slowly. a few murmured words.

Then they were alone. Hannibal turned back from the entrance and kicked one of the low stools next to the table. Not hard, just enough tip it over. He watched as it fell, then stared at it. The candles fluttered on the table as the tent entrance flapped in the insistent night breeze. The boy considered bolting for the entrance, but the man was too close. And there were guards outside.

Hannibal ran his hand down his sharp, hawk-like nose to his cheek and stared down at something long and thin and crinkly that lay open on the table. There were several stacked one upon another. The boy watched Hannibal flick the flat-thing with two fingers, which made it growl-crinkle. The man paid no attention, turning instead toward Nahatum, as if just remembering he was there. The boy sprang into alertness, the way sleeping cats do when they sense danger. If he was going to die in this tent, he'd put up a fight. He searched for something to use as a weapon.

Hannibal dragged a low three- legged stool from the table over to a spot nearer to Nahatum, who cringed away. A musky, woody smell accompanies the man, a mixture of smoke, mossy ground, tree bark, the coolness of the evening. He looked right at Nahatum, rooting him to his spot with those gray eyes. Nahatum wondered if there was a hint of merriment in them.

Again in the local patois, the man said, "Your name is….? And this time, tell me your name."

"Nahatum," the boy breathed out, resting his arms in front of him on his legs.

Hannibal nodded. Small popping noises came from above their heads. Hannibal looked up. "It has started to rain. The bright day has given way to a rainy night."

Unsure what to reply, Nahatum decided that the best thing was to stay silent. "You are one of those wild boys who roam the woods and steal what you can from us.." He looked right at Nahatum, attentive as he sat. Then, shockingly, he asked about Nahatum's parents; words no one had ever spoken to him before. He wanted to know about the boy's father. Mother? Nahatum's eyes watered slightly and he blinked, looked away. His foot twitched, his fingers curled– again, the urge to crush something.

Hannibal cleared his throat in the silence.

He stood up and walked right over to the spears stacked against the wall. The boy balled his hands into fists and tightened the muscles in his chin–– no matter what happened he didn't want his mouth hanging open in death, like one of the stupid, lifeless fish the white-bearded demon man who lived alone in the far meadow hung from the sides of his tent to dry in the sun.

Hannibal looked up from the spears. "I'm not going to hurt you. Relax." He examined several spear tips, wiping them off. One of his knuckles looked battered. He lifted a spear up, hefting it in his hands, then put it down.

"Who knows what my squire will say about this behind my back. By tradition, the son of a noble becomes the commander's servant. Are you perhaps noble- born?" Hannibal laughed as Nahatum's eyes widened. "I presume you are not." He paused, sighed. "I may regret what I am about to do, but I am the commander of this army, am I not?"

All these questions were more than had been addressed to Nahatum in the total of his life. His head swirled. He did have the presence of mind to nod to this last question, though he didn't understand much else of what the man said, except that he, too, agreed that he was not noble-born. Whatever that meant, he knew he wasn't. How much nonsense, he wondered, did this supposedly great General speak? And if he has sharpened murderous teeth that can kill, where were they?

"I'm looking for a boy to become my servant. You will do this for me." There was silence.

"Will I get food?" the boy asked.

A slight smile. Hannibal nodded. "As my servant, you will help the cook prepare meals. You'll eat well. There'll be no need of stealing to make up for any lingering hunger."

"Where will I sleep?"

Hannibal laughed, seeming more amused than irritated at the idea of a wolf child negotiating with him. This very fact made the boy curious. After all, the man could have had him killed in the whisker of a moment.

"Outside, near my tent, or, on very wet or cold nights, you may sleep inside in the corner." He pointed to a space across the tent from his pallet, near a small low table with a large clay brazier next to it. He waited a moment. Then, an eyebrow cocked: "So, you understand?"

Maybe. Yes, he nodded, playing the warrior for time, what a story to tell the pack. Especially if he could steal that bearskin and bring it back with him. Deep down, though, something unfolded within the boy. He shocked himself by wondering if he might really become something called a servant to this strange, scary, yet inviting man.

"Good." Hannibal clapped his hands together, rubbing them as if deeply pleased, then sent the boy outside to sleep among the cooks. The next day, he instructed, Nahatum would begin to learn what he needs to know. Jonaz, Hannibal's squire, would teach the new servant his chores. Hannibal chuckled: "Assuming he can still walk after those kicks you gave him today."

In the moonless evening chill, someone thrust a blanket into his hands, a thick one, almost new. The first blanket Nahatum had ever touched without holes and mildew all over it. Like a bearskin of his own. He wrapped himself in it and lay down on the ground, near the dancing warmth of a campfire, surprised at how easy it was to find such a valuable spot. Tonight he'd sleep well, tomorrow he'd run away. The rain had stopped. He soon fell into a fitful sleep, twice startled awake by the sound of his mother calling his name.

The boy had barely left as Hannibal turned back into the tent. *What a strange day.* He poured himself a goblet of wine and sat down at the table, running his hand over the rough surface of the precious maps. His mind drifted back to the morning and the screeching wolf boy he'd encountered outside the tent, scared, but acting brave.

The boy had even tried to run away down the very trail to the port where only a few days earlier he had sent his wife, Imre, an Iberian princess, and his young one-year- old son, to be put on a navy boat to Carthage. *It was the safe choice.* The son was his heir. His wife needed to be in Carthage for what lay ahead; it was simply too dangerous to leave them behind in Iberia. He pictured the wagon creaking down the trail taking them away, his son looking back, watching him until they could no longer see each other.

Would he ever see his son again?

Th-wack. The back of the squire's hand hit Nahatum again, sending him stumbling into Hannibal's swords. The boy regained his balance against the side of the General's tent. If only the man—this Jonaz– had kept using the horsehair whip he'd just put down—it was softer than the thick bony hand.

He knew he should have run away at the first light, but the smell of breakfast, followed by all the food he could eat, well… And then Jonaz had appeared and had practically thrown him into Hannibal's empty tent.

"Yesterday you kicked me good, foul wolf boy. Today is my turn. I'll teach you how to be a servant." With his narrow face and pronounced nose, he might have been one of the cave hyenas that the boy had once barely escaped.

This time there was no escape. The man hit him again, harder, the copper ring on Jonaz's finger catching on the boy's cheek, pulling across his mouth. He tasted blood.

Warm, comforting. Did the squire intend to kill him?, the boy wondered. He looked toward the tent flap as if his mother might walk in to help him, a rock in each hand, hurling them as she did to protect them from cave bears, smashing one right into the man's head, her aim so true and fast.

Hannibal's swords were almost within reach, but what would he do with one even if he had the strength to grab it? The boy licked his lip, stayed sprawled on the rug, a better place, while the squire loomed over him.

He had to figure out what he had done exactly to provoke the beating. His mind raced: it had something to do with the coal brazier in the middle of the tent. He'd picked up some sticks, thoughtlessly imagined actually starting a fire on the chilly morning— what a wonderful thing, a fire to warm you, when you want. The squire's face had swollen in rage. That's when the real beating began, the boy realized. Just because he wanted to start a fire?

"You wolf children are no better than animals. Lurking around, stealing. Ruled by your animal hungers." Nahatum scrambled to his feet. Jonaz took a step closer, still limping slightly. The boy's leg twitched; he ached to lash out again, his foot like one of his mother's rocks—hard and true in aim. Let the foul hyena limp with both legs.

Before, between punches and lashes with the whip, the squire had shown the boy how to use a broom, whisking the dirt off the woven rugs that covered the floor. How to fold the General's clothes and place them in the carved mahogany chest in a corner of the tent, though the first time Nahatum had touched his master's clothes, the squire had hit him with the whip.

He'd hit him when Nahatum had gone to move the odd construction of sticks and strings—like a child's version of a hut– on the table by Hannibal's bed. "Do not touch that, wolf child, it was made by Hannibal and his little boy before the child left for Carthage." He'd hit him when he'd gone to arrange the bearskin coverings on Hannibal's bed. Then as if nothing happened, he told Nahatum that when they were on the march with the army, Hannibal preferred to sleep outdoors, along with the infantry. "He prefers to share the burdens of the soldiers, just like his father did. That's why the army loves him so."

Now the squire ordered him closer still to the large coal brazier in the center of the tent. The boy approached carefully after what'd happened when he'd picked up the sticks a few minutes earlier.

The man sighed and shook his head. "I can't believe I'm explaining this to a wolf child. Fire is where Ba'al Shammon lives." As he spoke the name, Jonaz slowlytapped the tattoo on his upper lip: several straight black lines with three dark dots above them.

The boy'd seen similar on some of the priests in the camp. They tapped like that when they prayed.

Speaking carefully, the boy asked, "Who is Ba'al Shammon?"

The squire, hyena- face set firmly, considered the boy from a great distance, as if looking at something very small.

And offending. "Great Ba'al Shammon is the god of Carthage, by whose grace and mercy my city prospers and survives. That is why we make our sacrifices in fire, as we did in the old days."

The boy shuddered, remembering the sacrifices. The pack used to watch, hidden at the edge of the forest. Goats, pigs, oxen, slashed and bloodied as he was right now. The priests with their feathery headdresses, muttering in their strangelanguage.

"You wouldn't understand. We need the glorious power of Ba'al Shammon for us to succeed in the coming war."

He explained that a servant started the fire in Hannibal's coal brazier every morning. "This is a problem, since how could you, a wolf child, be allowed to chant the prayers while making a fire? That would be offensive to our god."

"I will make the fire exactly as you show me, even if I cannot say the prayers."

"You must approach the fire with the knowledge that our great god Ba'al reposes in the flames. Respect is the key. Don't be too eager when it comes to making a fire."

That must be what I did done wrong before, what provoked the beating. Nahatum guessd that he hadn't shown the proper respect, insulted the man's god, hurrying to make the fire. But how was he not to? What a wonderful thing—to actually make a fire! Of course he'd eagerly grabbed at the lighting stones and kindling. Since his mother left so long ago, he hadn't been as close to fire as he'd been the past day, and he'd never, ever, made one.

"Watch me." The squire put kindling wood into the squat clay burner, scraping the sparking stone, adding coals, gently tending the flickering flames, saying the appropriate prayers to welcome Ba'al and his consort Tanit into the sacred space.

The boy was careful to stare into the budding flames, to look for some sign of the gods. He stood straight and tall, which he hoped made him look appropriately respectful. He ran his tongue over his cut lip, tasting the warm blood and relaxed a bit. And he kept an eye out for another punch.

The squire turned away from the fire, toward the boy. He again tapped the tattoo over his upper lip– the three dots appeared to quiver. "Ba'al Shammon choose Carthage alone of all the cities of the world to know the awe-filled secret of fire."

"Secret?"

Jonaz raised a hand as if to strike the boy for questioning him, then stopped. "Fire is the gateway to the real world." The flames sparkling before them were a sundering of the false world and a door into the divine world of Ba'al and his consort Tanit, where loyal followers spend eternity in a land of a thousand pleasures. "Fire consumes our physical body and releases the spirit," the man explained. "I knew this to be true since I was a young child helping my father, the Grand Priest in the great Temple to Tanit in Carthage, to light the sacred fire."

Nahatum strained to see this other world in the flames, some sign of the gods, while the squire rocked and muttered, gaze fixed on the flames. For a moment, Nahatum considered kicking him again and running out of the tent, but now the possibility of actually seeing a god held him in place. As well as something else, something he couldn't quite identify but knew it involved Hannibal.

As the flames gathered, they lunged forward and up, hungry and fearless. To the boy, the fire was a sleeping animal suddenly brought to life by the presence of prey. How fast and intent it was. How powerful. The boy stepped back, speechless, the flames alive, a lion-fire that might spring right at him.

The squire nodded. "Yes, be afraid. Be awed. That is Ba'al Shammon and his power. The very power we will need for this war that lies ahead." Then he sighed again, and banked the fire, reciting another prayer. Nahatum watched the flames disappear.

"Now you need to show me you can make a fire for Lord Hannibal when he commands." The man's hands twitched. "I cannot believe…."

The boy braced for another blow. Instead, the squire—his narrow face contorted in lamentation—explained how to arrange the kindling, how to pack the coals, how touse the sparking stones.

He stepped back. "Now you do it."

Nahatum concentrated on the task, the exact way the man had placed the wood, the coals, the very motions he made with the sparking stones.

"All right, that's correct." The man sounded more disappointed than pleased.

Nahatum barely had time to admire what he'd done—everything correctly!—when the squire's hyena eyes locked onto him.

"Hannibal's father—the great Hamilcar, may his name always be remembered— would never have taken a wolf child to be his servant." Jonaz shook his head. "A boy without standing, without parents, without a city—it violates the natural order of things for one such as you to serve Hannibal. I hope your presence is not a sign of some weakness in our young commander." Jonaz shook his head. "We lost the last war because we lost our devotion to the gods."

Watch this man carefully. Always. Keep enough distance to get away if need be.

The squire picked up the leather whip. "Enough of this. Take that wicker basket in the corner, put all these clothes in it and follow me down to the river to wash them."

Jonaz exited the tent as if pursued by jackals. *Yes jackals, indeed.* Nahatum resolved to rip some fur from a dead jackal along the trail then stuff the powerful charm inside one of the squire's sleeping blankets to encourage fear and cowardice in the man.

All the way down to the river, Jonaz badgered the boy. "Perhaps you can wash yourself clean, scrub off the stain of being a wolf boy without parents. Not even good for a sacrifice." The boy's shoulders and arms ached and the whiplashes burned as he hauled the heavy baskets down the steep, rocky river bank. He was heartened at the squire's words, "You carry the heavy basket well...", but then his chest quivered: "...perhaps you will do well in the mines."

As they passed out of the underbrush near the river's edge and half slid down onto the gravelly shore, Jonaz hissed: "Unless, wolf boy, you can escape. Sometime when I am not looking, take your accursed spirit out of our camp."

Then just like that the squire turned and marched back up the hillside, leaving Nahatum alone with the basket of clothes. He looked into the weeds and bushes for the presence of death. This was the part of the shore where he once came upon a rotting auroch carcass, the skin blistered and swollen and infested with beetles. From that, he had learned that death worms its way into our bodies through the skin, turning what was once warm and whole into something lifeless and festering.

Nahatum ran his tongue over his mouth; the cut was starting to close. No more blood, no more warm comfort. The boy beat the clothes until his hands were numb from the cold river water. A few soldiers bathed further downriver. He could have dashed across the shallow river and into the inviting forest on the other side. Find the wolf pack. He held a dark green shirt of Hannibal's to his nose, smelled the man's sweat, his hair, his skin, the Iberian dust, a sharp, quickening odor. The smell clung to him, rooting him to his spot. He kept washing the clothes.

Eventually the squire returned, sweating and puffing in the afternoon sun, emerging from the thick overgrowth at the riverbank. He looked disappointed to find the boy still there. Nahatum realized that his leaving had been a sort of test; clearly the man hoped he'd be gone. "Did you finish the clothes? I see not. Hurry up." He sat on a rock, watching, while the boy folded the clothes back into the heavy wicker basket. "Slow at this, aren't you? You'll learn to work harder, that's for sure. And maybe we'll find some other use for you."

Some other use? The squire's tone made the soft hairs on the boy's arms tingle as they did in the forest when there was something on the prowl just beyond the trees or lying in wait, unseen, in the tall grass.

By the time Nahatum had wrestled the basket of wet clothes back up the hill, the cooks had begun carving roast goat for lunch. The aroma of smoke and cooked meat hung in the air. Terra cotta platters filled with dates and figs and apricots and boiled cabbage and chickpeas and roasted artichokes and nuts and cooked chicken spread across several long tables; scattered among them were ochre red ceramic tureens of stew, thick with meat and tomatoes.

The boy's knees buckled. He'd been starving all day despite breakfast anddespite stealing a further chunk of bread after that off the tray of food he'd brought to Hannibal in his tent that morning. He'd grabbed it right as the man emerged from beneath his bearskin covers, like some forest beast. Clearly this General isn't nearly as clever as everyone claimed, Nahatum concluded. And he surely didn't have sharpened teeth, that much was pretty clear already.

The boy stuffed a piece of sliced goat into his mouth, the sweet, warm meat giving way as he chewed. Fat and bloody meat dripped on the old brown woolen pants and tunic that were now his.

The toothless cook who'd kicked him awake that morning handed the boy a carved wooden tray with three bowls of stew on it. He gestured with his head toward Hannibal's tent, which now had a purple, gold-fringed awning stretching from it. A table was set beneath it, and Hannibal, the foul giant, and the wiry man in the white caftan were seated around it.

"Take this lunch to the General and his friends." Tomatoes and chick peas and thick chunks of roasted goat floated in the steaming, fatty mix. "Don't spill any, wolf child, or you'll get beaten good."

The air was pleasingly cool underneath the awning. The boy set the bowl carefully in front of Hannibal all right, but his hands started to shake as he movedcloser to the others at the table: The man-beast next to Hannibal glowered before continuingto speak. He ignored the slender third man entirely. They were talking in that strange language—Punic—that sounded to Nahatum a bit like music when Hannibal spoke. When the giant man-beast said something it sounded like boulders tumbling down from rock walls, as they did in the quarry near the army camp.

Still, Nahatum listened to the sounds, trying to make out words, as he often did when around the cook and the guards. He already had learned the sound for "plate" and such important things as "bread" and different kinds of meats and a few fruits. And, he'd memorized "knife" and the wooden thing– *kafta* – that these men used to both spear meat and vegetables and to convey soup to their mouths.

The one who looked like the fearsome hairy auroch was arguing with the slender man who reminded the boy of a fox, quick and clever. He could tell that they were arguing from the way the Auroch pounded his fist on the table and the impatient look that Fox gave him. When he stopped pounding, Auroch reached for a fig from the bowl near him.

The tomato-goat stew sloshed in its bowl as the boy leaned in toward the Auroch, who up close seemed to have even more hair than skin. The knife scar winding along the side of his face was clearly visible. The man would slash his throat, the boy was sure, if he spilt any on the man's purple tunic. Then after he was dead, would he eat him?

The Auroch moved the folds of his sleeve aside with a sharp claw- like movement of his hand. The arm was marked with slash lines from his wrist to past his elbow. A thick, wine-red scar wound down into the palm of his right hand.

Nahatum bent toward the table, the overfull bowl wobbling in his hands, burning his thumb. He barely stopped a wave of stew from surging into the man's lap. The boy managed to retain the balance of the bowl, but the clay seethed heat. His hand shook.

The Auroch's deep voice boomed. He smacked one large hand in the other, and his elbow jostled the boy's arm. The bowl teetered drunkenly. The boy righted the treacherous thing with a desperate tilt, but spilt some of the boiling stew on his own arm. He stifled a scream. Hannibal said something to the Auroch in reply. Nahatum bit his tongue and placed the bowl down in front of him, then withdrew, breathing deeply to still the hummingbird beating against his ribs.

Auroch glared at him and made a rumbling noise that Nahatum realized was their strange sound for the wooden flat-bottomed, spear-thing thing they used to eat soup with. *Kafta*. The man wanted one. Nahatum hurried outside to the water bucket to cool his arm then found three of the kafta-things. He hurried back into the tent and gave one to each of the men. Hannibal looked surprised as he did so. Auroch took one, stared at the boy and muttered more boulder-words. Fox surprised Nahatum by smiling at him, an odd gesture, then slid his chair slightly back to allow him to put the stew easily on the table.

Nahatum took a step back to survey the table and felt satified by what he saw. All three bowls found their place on the table. Not a drop was spilled on any of the three men. All had their kafta- spear things. Pretty good, for a wolf child.

Why not end with a bow, as he'd seen the guards do? Then Nahatum found a place in the corner under the awning to squat and rest, keeping the Auroch's mountainous back in front of him. He concentrated on hearing the unfamiliar sounds and every now and then the boy picked out a word— he thought he may have learned from the way Hannibal addressed them that the Auroch's name was "Gisgo" and that the Fox was named, "Marhabal," and he listened carefully to make sure he was correct.

How did the boy know which utensil to bring us just now? Gisgo had spoken to him in Punic. Hannibal considered the boy squatting in the corner looking well- pleased with himself. *Odd. Well, sort that out later.*

"Lord Hannibal, we must be realistic about what happens when you go to war." Massive Gisgo turned to the Numidian across from him– resplendent in his gold-trimmed tribal caftan, denoting royalty–shaking the table as he did. The infantry commander spoke slowly, as if to a child, as he addressed Marhabal, who listened, elbow on table, hand stroking his trim beard. "You probably don't understand what a protracted war is like, do you?"

Gisgo had directed his venom at Marhabal, but Hannibal wondered if the man really felt it for his commander. The invasion plan had given pause to this experienced veteran of many wars. The difficulty of what he had proposed again pressed heavily on Hannibal. He stretched out his right leg against an incipient cramp.

Before Marhabal could respond, Gisgo again pounded the table, "Eating our dead is the answer. Many will die along this journey, before we reach Italy. The priests can say the rites, bless them till our Lord Ba'al Shammon is happy. It'll be like a sacred sacrifice, like in the old days…" The man's voice trailed off. He reached for another of his figs, brought directly by fast ship, along with olives and dates and chickpeas, from the rich farmlands that ringed Carthage.

"Old days?" asked Marhabal in his elegant, highly educated Punic. He watched Gisgo carefully peel a fig, then reached for one himself. Gisgo said nothing, more attentive to the fig than the Numidian. Hannibal could see that his old friend had some trouble understanding the coarse infantry commander's thick, vernacular Punic. He turned to Marhabal.

"There were human sacrifices in the old days, long ago. In the great temple on the Byrsa, the hilltop citadel at Carthage. Some misguided people even think we lost the last war because we had abandoned the practice. They think Ba'al is angry, so is punishing us. We don't really talk of such things any more. Eating our dead? This kind of sacrifice we do not need to ask of our dead….or our living."

Marhabal chuckled, Hannibal smiled. "Thank you for coming all this distance, my friend. It is good to have you here."

Gisgo sighed, his body heaving as though breaking bands of iron with his chest. "Relying on desert horsemen where we are going...."

Marhabal interrupted to allow that, though there was some fear, his men were excited at the idea of conquering the snow mountains.

"Have you ever seen snow? Ridden through ice?"

Focus. You have got to get some control over this meeting. Hannibal took a spoonful of the goat soup Marhabal's confused expression gave way to understanding. "Ah, no. But my men are eager to make the journey...This will be an adventure."

"Spoken like a true goat herder. You think you are going for a jaunt across the desert to some oasis? We are going to unknown lands ruled by strange gods."

"Strange gods rule all lands, Gisgo." Hannibal considered what to do about his two unruly lieutenants. He could order both men to stop the bickering, but then the simmering resentment—was it competiton?—between them would only go underground. Gisgo turned to him. "How much can we trust the loyalty of the Numidians, Hannibal?

They've changed sides before." Marhabal replied that he had no need for advice from old infantrymen. "Particularly one who looks like he couldn't ride a horse further than the nearest town to plunder."

Gisgo's chair thundered backwards, landing in front of Nahatum. The boy skittered backwards like a startled cat, but Hannibal noted that he didn't run. Gisgo, knife in hand, loomed over Marhabal, across the table. Marhabal calmly glared back at Gisgo, a knife suddenly in his hand, too. "Hannibal need have no doubts about my loyalty to him."

Wonderful: My two essential lieutenants are now going to kill each other fighting about snow, which neither has ever seen. Hannibal could feel his chest tightening. Would his guards or the cooks over there at the cooking pits spread word through the army of this unruly scene?

And there was the boy, back on his haunches, watching all this, apparently unafraid. *How nice, to be able to watch without having to act.* Hannibal took a deep breath. *You are the commander, stay calm.*

Hannibal continued to slowly spoon soup from his bowl. He deliberately blew gently on the spoon, as if he had all the time in the world, then tasted it while the two remained motionless, standing, looks of hate on their eyes. The silence continued until both men relaxed into their chairs as if they were in a dance, eyes on each other.

"I want my commanders to cooperate." He hoped his tone was both serene and authoritative. "Stop this, both of you. Your loyalty is to me. I have no doubts about either of you. What I want is your allegiance to my invasion plan. No more arguing. Understand?"

Marhabal nodded, eyes still on the infantryman. Nahatum scurried back to his place just under the awning behind Gisgo, more frightened puppy than wolf child. Gisgo shook his massive head, affirmatively. "You have my complete allegiance in these plans, of course, Lord Hannibal, but your father...."

"My father!" Hannibal put down the spoon. "My father is not leading this invasion. He is dead." Hannibal's chest wanted to collapse into itself. He pictured sitting with his father— alive– at their grand villa in New Carthage all those evenng in front of the huge fireplace discussing the audacious invasion plan: sharpening it, honing it. His plan, their plan.

"My Lord, I meant no insult..."

"No, of course, no insult taken," Hannibal murmured through another spoonful of soup. Sometimes the real virtue of eating, he contemplated, is that it shuts your mouth, preventing you from saying what you'll later regreat. Yet he felt some rebuke in the comparison. The man served with Hamilcar. Served him well. Everyone asked what his father would have done. Ba'al's hindquarters: he did the same. Would his father have burnt Saguntum, miles to the north, to the ground? Killed all those people? Hannibal remembered the ragged line of survivors fleeing the burning city, the thick plume of smoke rising from the shattered buildings. He shivered a moment; he hated sieges. They turned everyone into animals—it was all about brute force, both sides fixed in their positions trying to outwait the other, like two stags with horns locked in place. No strategy, no surprise, no expanse of territory in which to outwit your enemy. Maybe his father would have been more patient. Starved them out. Maybe he would have been more skilled with his words and charmed them into ending their allegiance to Rome. Yet they were arrogant people. They rejected Carthage's ambassadors. They negotiated with Rome in secret, thought Rome would come to their aid. He had to move quickly. Set an example.

Gisgo seemed to have read the unspoken thought. "Lord Hannibal, your unhesitating actions against Saguntum made Rome—their supposed ally– look weak."

"Which is why Rome wants my head. They have a delegation in Carthage right now demanding the Senate renounce me, turn me over to them."

Marhabal turned to Hannibal and was about to say something when Gisgo interrupted him. "That will never happen. Not to the son of Hamilcar Barca. The Senate knows the city would revolt. That is how much your father is revered."

Hannibal wanted to ask Marhabal what he was about to say but his anger overtook him. "Revered? Except by those who would blame our fate in the last war on him. What a soil pit the Senate is…." *Concentrate. Your father is no longer here. The mantle of the Barca family has fallen to you.*

Gisgo loudly drained his bowl and said, "You must be aggressive and move quickly. Solve the supply problems. No hesitation, as you showed in the way you dealt with Saguntum."

"We have to convince the Gauls to join our cause. This whole thing rests…"

"You will convince them. Ba'al Shammon smiles on the Barca family. He will bring good you good luck."

Marhabal had been quietly eating his soup. Now he leaned in toward Hannibal. "You know when to strike, when to seize the advantage, Hannibal. You will bringyour ownluck."

"If we had luck my father would be alive right now. He knew never to depend on the good will of our beloved Ba'al Shammon. The god is a trickster. The best way to obtain a god's fortune, he always said, was to have a better battle plan than your enemy."

The three men sat in a companionable silence, Hannibal aware of the boy rocking gently on his haunches in the corner, watching, curious. What did he see? What did he understand? He's clearly a smart lad, Hannibal concluded. And, a cheering sight, really, amidst these brutal plans.

"Ah, Gisgo, we shall see whose gods have power in the frozen mountains. And we will not be eating our dead, either."

After lunch, Hannibal walked with Marhabal across the meadow toward the fields where the Numidian cavalry grazed.

The muscular, fast Numidian horses whinnied and snorted as their riders—red jellabahs sparkling in the bright sunlight—groomed them; they looked eager to start the march. They're smaller than Roman horses, Hannibal noted, though clearly quicker. He wondered if they would be strong enough for the thousands of miles they would be asked to ride. Used to the desert sand of North Africa, how would their hooves fare on the hardscrabble, rocky soil of Gaul and the Endless Mountains?

They continued walking toward the wooden stockade fence surrounding the stables.

"Back at lunch, Marhabal, you seemed about to say something about my father and the Senate."

"Ah, yes, but I thought it best if I let Gisgo—that human sandstorm—bluster along and kept what I had to say to myself."

"Well, Gisgo is not here now."

Still, his friend looked reluctant to speak, studying the horses in the pasture.

Hannibal could see bare spots and whole areas with sparse grass. In the few weeks the Numidians had been there they'd already overgrazed this meadow. They will need dozens of wagons of hay from the spring harvest and will depend on the Gaulish tribes to supply them more while on the march.

"So, Marhabal, there is something on your mind. Out with it."

The Numidian turned toward him. "I have news from Carthage, sent by my father via letter just yesterday."

"Yes, what is it?"

"You remember Hanno the Great, Hannibal?"

A sour taste came into Hannibal's mouth. "You mean Hanno- the- So- Called Great? The ineffective general my father replaced, with great success, before Carthage decided that a humiliating peace with Rome was better than the demands of winning the war? The same so-called Great One who never forgave my father and tried to bring a tribunal against him?"

Marhabal smiled. "Yes, exactly. Your father's old nemesis." Again, a hesitation.

"Well, what about the despicable man?"

"My father writes that the Senate is quite angry at Rome's demands and will never turn you over to the Romans. Still, Hanno has been making fiery speeches claiming that the Barca family is setting up their own empire in Iberia. He says that Carthage should be devoting its resources to its African territories, to turn away from Rome andthe Great Sea and expand into Numidia and down into Africa."

They were on a slight rise. Marhabal stopped under a tree and looked out at the pasture, as if unsure whether to go on.

"There's more, isn't there. Well, I want to hear it. Tell me."

Marhabal looked apologetic as he spoke. "Hanno calls Iberia a 'Barca empire' and claims it is larger than Carthage's territories in Africa. The man thunders from the podium in the Senate, implying some nefarious Barca plot to seize resources for your family's own use. He says you are more Iberian than Carthaginian, that you've lived most of your life far from the city."

Hannibal studied the frisky horses in the early spring Iberian meadow alive with wildflowers. They looked so content, as if they needed nothing else in the world than some grass to eat and sun to warm them. To the south he could just see the city of New Carthage, the capital of Carthage's empire in Iberia, fortifications barely visible in the distance. The army base had been strategically placed to protect New Carthage from any attacks from the north; Hannibal had expanded it to provide the space he needed for the huge army he was gathering. The Iberian sun glistened off the imposing sun-bleached white walls of the city. Is that light, Hannibal wondered, different from the blue-golden light that bathed Carthage itself? He could feel his distance from the city of his birth. Would he ever see it again?

They were at the stockade fence that surrounded the cavalry's stables. Marhabal reached over the fence and took the reins of his own horse, a formidable gelding, stroking its muzzle. The horse leaned in toward its master. "Hanno says that the city cannot afford to overextend its treasury. He is constantly reminding the Senate about what happened with the Mercenaries War. Hamilcar, he claims, promised his soldiers money that the city didn't have. Remember the horror of the Mercenaries Rebellion? He blames that on your father and now he cautions the Senate about providing too much power to you, whom he calls 'another Barca general.'"

"He is bringing up old charges. My father refuted all that years ago." His words sounded steely even to Hannibal. If he could have burnt this Hanno alive right then, he would have.

Marhabal patted his horse. His silence seemed to echo into the stillness.

"Are you suggesting that you agree with him, my friend? That I am overextending Carthage's resources?"

A broad smile emerged from the handsome Numidian. "Not at all, Hannibal. I am ready to leave as soon as you give the command. Rather, I am suggesting that we be aware that little in the way of supply and reinforcements can be expected from Carthage. We will, truly, be on our own once this invasion starts."

The cook's blade flashed in the late afternoon sun as it dug into the peppers, slicing them into thick wedges with astonishing speed. Nahatum watched as another cook did the same with carrots, while a third took apart several goat haunches using a thick blade and a wooden mallet.

There seemed no end to the work in the camp. All afternoon he'd been cleaning the wooden bowls and metal cooking pots, hoping some day to be able to use a knife like these men. Not for cooking, but in battle, to slice into the red mud of a man's chest as the toothless cook carved into the shank of a goat.

He kept his distance, wary around them all, and listened carefully as the cooks and the guards talked among themselves. Some spoke Punic, some the local patois. He picked out a few more word- sounds in the strange but not unpleasing Punic. Bread. Eggs. Wine. Whores.

He was so busy that he forgot about Hannibal until Jonaz, sneaking up behind him, slapped him hard on the shoulder with the leather whip.

"Hannibal wants to see you. Stop what you are doing."

Nahatum stared across the clearing at the solitary tent, darker now in the twilight. "Go now. You don't keep Hannibal waiting, wolf child." The squire pushed him forward so abruptly that the boy stumbled crossing the solitary clearing, feeling the eyes of the cooks on him.

He slowly pushed aside the tent opening, so as to have the opportunity to run if need be. Hannibal was alone, sitting at the table where the crinkly things were spread out. A rush of warm air brushed past Nahatum into the cool evening.

"Ah, boy..." Nahatum's chest tensed. The man's gaze had a sort of heat to it. "...Naha..."

"Nahatum."

"Nahatum." The sound of his name spoken by the man made Nahatum hesitate where he stood.

"Light the charcoal brazier."

He felt Hannibal watch him as he worked, careful to remember the order and arrangement of kindling and coals as Jonaz had shown him. He wondered if he should mumble some attempt at a prayer as he struck the sparking stones, but he didn't know any and mindless muttering seemed just too stupid and dangerous.

Hannibal said nothing about prayers. The fire came to life the first time the sparks hit the dry leaves. Hannibal nodded and Nahatum relaxed and added more coals.

Hannibal stared into the blazing twigs. The flames illuminated his gray eyes and made a faded but distinct reddish-black burn mark dance on the man's wrist. The boy stifled a gasp at the unexpected scar.

"Your first day learning your chores."

He wondered if Hannibal had gotten reports on his work, his attentiveness, or lack of it. The hummingbird beat again, trapped inside the ribs of his chest. What had the squire, the cook, said? What an unsettling feeling, Nahatum considered, to be worried about what this man thinks of him. He'd never felt anything like that before. He wanted the man to approve of his work.

"You didn't spill any soup at lunch." Hannibal smiled. "I was waiting to see if Gisgo would wind up with a hot bowl of it in his lap. That would have been quite a sight." Then he laughed. A deep bubbling laugh. The boy smiled too, despite his nervousness. He liked the man's laugh, wanted to hear it more. Hannibal leaned back, glancing over toward his bedside table at that rough hut- like construction of bare wood and string that had provoked a beating from Jonaz. Then the man stared into the fire. "Spilling soup. That should be the extent of our worries in life. I hope I do not make a bigger mess in the coming days."

"Sir?"

"Nothing…."

Then Hannibal held up the flat-bottomed, spoon utensil. He asked what it was called in Punic. The boy made the sound, *kafta* as the cook did, as Gisgo-Auroch had.

"How did you learn that?"

"I listened, Sir. Have I done something wrong?"

"Hmmn. No, not at all." This time he didn't stumble over the name. "Nahatum…"

"I know other words, too." He made the sounds he'd just learned. Bread. Eggs. Wine. Whores.

The General's eyebrows shot up toward his black hair. "That is impressive. You learned all those today?"

The boy nodded.

"Well hopefully you will find that last one useful someday." Then that slight smile, a more serious tone: "You did well today."

The boy's chest warmed.

"Now, please bring me my dinner."

The boy hurried out, then returned with a plate of roasted goat, a small bowl of the chickpea paste, and a platter of roasted eggplant and basil. The general had put some more coals into the brazier.

"Thank you. That is all."

The boy turned to leave.

"One more thing. Where's the bread?"

"Bread, sir?"

"Yes. The piece you held in reserve for me from my plate this morning. When you didn't think I was looking." Hannibal's eyes seemed aimed at him, mouth set, flashing no teeth.

Nahatum's cheeks got hot. This man had powers to make him blush, smile, warm his chest. And to scare him. His cheeks continued to roil their unpleasant heat. Nothing like this had ever happened to him. He didn't like it.

"You can go out to the cook and find it, or a twin, and bring it back to me. I'd like it now." Before Nahatum could escape, Hannibal added, in a tone that seized the boy, "Do not steal from me again."

As Nahatum hurried out, almost tripping over a chair, suddenly clumsy, Hannibal's hard stare nipped at his heels, as if he was barely fleeing the jaws of a lion.

Later, the boy wrapped himself in his blanket on the ground outside Hannibal's tent. The forest, deep in darkness, gave off warm, honeyed scents. The sounds of the night darkness surrounded him: an owl hooting, rodents rustling in the stand of spruce past the campfire, tree toads calling. He wondered if they were lonely, calling to each other from far away. In a soft wind, a branch fell, something floated, wings fluttering, through the leaves. The moon rose, clouds passed, the moon returned. There are spiritsall around us, his mother had told him, spirits of the trees and the woods, and the spiritsof the dead, wandering in the nighttime forest, their lives unfinished, their endings abrupt.

Nahatum turned and pulled the thick Carthaginian wool blanket over his head. Six winters, spring, summers, autumns, had passed since he'd last seen his mother. He worried that he was forgetting what her face looked like.

He startled awake in the silent darkness, but knew not to move, not even to open his eyes. Something was there, close. Huge and dark, looming over him. Was this Death come for him? All he could hear was the low hiss of the dying fire. Peeking through almost closed eyelids, the thing was caught by the dim light of the embers.

The thing was Gisgo staring down at him, leather chest armor flickering red in the fire's embers. He held a massive sword in his hand. Abruptly he growled, an animal sound, and walked over to several of the guards posted on the edge of the glade. The men had been asleep. Gisgo yelled at them, his voice like thunder.

The terrified men straightened up tall, put their bronze chest armor back on, picked up their swords and spears. Enraged, Gisgo lapsed into the patois: they were guarding Hannibal's tent. Did they think they were all safe just because they were not yet at war, because they stood there sleepily in their own encampment?

"Fools," he roared. "Hamilcar Barca taught me never to take anything for granted. The moment you think you're safe is the most dangerous. Never assume. That is true in Hannibal's army as well."

Yes, sir, the men stammered as Gisgo stamped down the dark trail, sword in hand, yelling that he was going to check on every one of the guards posted around the encampment.

Then there was only the hooting of the owls, the sound of a cracking branch deeper in the forest, some animal—not, death, the boy hoped—on the prowl. The guards stood rigidly at attention, as if turned to stone by Gisgo's thunder. The boy rolled himself tighter in the blanket, trying to calm himself, but sleep did not come.

In the bare light of the flickering fire he found a stick, poked the flames back into life. He reached toward an ember, felt the burning heat, withdrew his hand. He stared at the blinking red coals. Then Nahatum reached a hand toward the glowing embers andlaid his wrist on a burning coal, the same spot where he remembered the ugly red burn mark on Hannibal. The scream rising in his throat stopped as a shock of pain flooded him. The pain was followed by calmness. He pulled his wrist back, examined the burn. The hummingbird had stopped beating in his chest. Holding his aching wrist close, the boy fell asleep.

A restless sleep claimed him for the next three nights. One night he dreamt bears attacked the rough hut in the forest where he and his mother lived, huge cave bears with long snouts and boulder jaws, covered in fur, roaring death at them. His mother drove them away, hurling rocks with savage accuracy. He decided the dreams were a good sign and woke each day unexpectedly alert, sensing his mother's presence. Not close, still faraway, but soon to come back for him.

And then, two days later, he saw her.

Late in the afternoon the heat of the day still lay heavily on the trail back from the river, and the heavy wicker basket of Hannibal's wet clothes fought him for every step.

Suddenly, a long caravan thundered down upon him. He scrambled to one side, just avoiding the horse's hooves. Horsemen on their polished saddles galloped by, followed by mules pulling sleds filled with clothes, animal skins, swords and spears and shields, some with baskets of winter vegetables and slaughtered deer, goat, sheep, strapped to the wooden pallets. Women, some brightly clad, walked slowly along among the animals, carrying packages and baskets.

Several more riders passed by, their hats waving in the breeze. Then, he looked on the most remarkable sight: a wooden platform carried on the shoulders of four stout men. He wondered if he was in a dream. The platform had low sides and some cushions, and a woman lay inside, propped up by pillows.

She was coughing, a deep, familiar cough. He stared at her light brown cotton dress, with the thick green woolen shawl draped over her shoulders even in the heat of the day. She briefly smiled at the boy staring at her, than put a cloth to her mouth, masking her face. Her chest heaved. She looked as if a frantic animal was trying to claw its way out of her chest. Nahatum wondered if he had thought the same so long ago when he walked alongside his mother through the forest pines.

He ran alongside to keep up with her, to get a better look. This was not easy; the four men trotted along at a good pace. If he slipped and fell between the thick wheels of the accompanying wagons, no one would stop. For the briefest moment her eyes followed him from behind the cloth, as if pleased by his efforts. Then more coughing, her skin pale, eyes staring into the distance.

The basket he still carried wrestled with him, blocking him, tripping him, massive, a stupid thing between him and his mother. Sharp wicker dug into his hand, making the blister from the days- old burn on his wrist ache. He let the thing fall away.

Hannibal's pants, shirts, tunics, scattered along the ground, but he couldn't be concerned about clothes right then, even if some slid into the muddy ruts under the wagon wheels. He must catch up. He would.

But the platform was soon far ahead. Chest close to bursting, he watched the woman's back fade away into the busy camp.

He cursed the clothes, Hannibal, the evil wicker basket, which now lay half- broken at his feet. Nahatum kicked it and watched it roll into the road, where a wagon's wheel crushed it, almost snapping the accursed thing in half. Then he was in the road, smashing the wicker, cracking its bones, a lion clawing open the chest of a deer.

He knew that Jonaz, that foul hyena, would beat him for what happened to the clothes and the basket. He wondered if—please, no– Gisgo would hear of it.

Yet what did any of that matter now? His mother was back, he told himself. He knew then what had happened to her: after she left him, she'd found her way out of the forest to a powerful warrior chieftain who had made her his bride. She'd returned, finally, to find him, carried by her servants. She was now somewhere in the vast army camp looking for him, he became convinced. Just then on the trail she'd coughed too much to recognize him. He'd have to find her himself.

And that, he resolved as he skittered up and down the hillside collecting the scattered, mud-stained clothes to take back to the river to wash again, was exactly what he was— somehow– going to do.

Chapter 2

Lizard Skin

Mediterranean Coast of Iberia Spring, 218 BC

For days, Nahatum tried to sneak away to search for his mother in the hidden alleys and muddy lanes of the camp, but there was so much to do. If Hannibal didn't have a chore for him, then Jonaz did. Jonaz no longer did his own clothes, having given them to the boy to clean. And he'd seemed almost pleased when Nahatum returned with the ruined basket, beating him with his horsehair whip while mumbling some prayers to his god.

The boy's calloused hands turned a deep red from pounding clothes against the rocks in the cold river water. They ached at night sometimes too, and for him that was a further sign of her return: she'd spoken bitterly to him about cold river water when she'd return from a day of washing clothes for the soldiers; said it contained evil spirits that made your fingers ache. And now he'd seen her.

He didn't care about the sharp, short knife the toothless cook had shown him how to use, letting him chop the peppers and potatoes for the enormous cauldron of stew they were preparing. He cut and sliced frantically, as if each cut of the blade could bring his mother closer.

"Wolf boy, come here." Jonaz walked over from Hannibal's tent across the clearing. His limp was gone. The boy kept chopping. "Wolf boy," louder this time. There was a smirk on the squire's face, which made Nahatum want to kick him again in the same knee. "Gisgo wants you."

Gisgo. All thoughts of kicking the squire disappeared, swallowed by the buzzing inside Nahatum's chest. "Why?"

"Rude, you are. Don't ask questions, just go." Then, with that hyena smirk: "Likely he wants to send you to the mines."

Run. Nahatum's terror was interrupted by the old toothless cook, looking over from stirring the bubbling stew in the iron kettle. "He's not going to send you to the mines, Nahatum. We need every able-bodied man we have, what with all the activity in this camp. And Ba'al knows with all you eat, you are clearly becoming a stout boy." Laughter from the assembled cooks. One of them, carefully stoking the fire beneath the kettle with more logs, added, "Yesterday, I saw my cousin from south of the Guadalquiver river, he arrived here with all the men from his tribe, hundreds of them. Hw says Hannibal has big plans for a war with Rome, there'll be a lot of treasure for the taking. I told him he still owed me for the horse I gave him when I joined Hannibal's army last year. He said in a few weeks, he'd pay me with Roman gold. His chief is going to a big meeting with all the other chiefs tonight." He gestured toward Hannibal's tent.

Mention of the far-away Guadalquiver river froze Nahatum in place. His mother had spoken of it; she was from somewhere near there in the south of Iberia. Now she was close by, returned to him, the proud wife of a great chief, he was certain.

"See," said the toothless cook, looking at Jonaz rather than Nahatum, "Ignore our friend the squire here, who thinks he can speak with Ba'al Shammon himself. Gisgo needs you here more than in the mines. Now, go, he's at the stables. Don't keep Gisgo waiting."

Nahatum hurried down the narrow path, filled with men bartering, arguing, pushing past one another, the camp now resembling the river marshes where fiery herons, eagles, osprey, cormorants screetch and jostle in the shallows and on the sandbanks. The lanes of the encampment had turned to mud as hundreds of horses' hooves thundered through, then were churned to a thick soup by the men on foot. The camp was a river overflowing its banks.

When Gisgo saw Nahatum walking down the dusty trail, the morning already hot under the sharp spring sun, his eyes narrowed, as a hungry bear might squint at a tethered goat.

"What are you doing here, wolf boy?," His deep throated growl made Nahatum feel smaller than he was. "I sent for Jonaz to help with this work party. We are going to cut down trees to make an encampment for some new arrivals."

"Jonaz told me to come here, Sir. Said you wanted me."

"Ba'al's butt. I told him...." This was followed by some more muttering and oaths from the man-auroch. Then: "All right, it's late. Hurry back to the cook's area and get a tin ladle."

Nahatum ran like one of the Numidian's stallions. A tin ladle. He'd never seen such a thing and insisted the cook teach him the correct way to name it in Punic: *malekeh.*

When he returned, Gisgo instructed the boy to hold onto the wonderful ladle— their *malekeh*– and to walk near the water wagon. "We'll need this on such a day. Keep an eye on it. Fresh water's gotten scarce in this camp. Some of these tribesmen would steal the whole thing if you give them a chance."

So Nahatum was in the rear, walking alongside the creaking wagon as the work party of Iberians and Berbers threaded its way through the busy main byway of the camp. They made two groups; Nahatum part of neither. The wild-haired Iberians from past the Tagus river wanted nothing to do with the regal Berbers of Africa in their red, green, ochre headdresses and colorful Jellabhas. Nahatum trailed a few steps behind. Gisgo was far ahead in the lead, parting the crowded lanes like a three-oxen plow.

When Nahatum heard her, it was unmistakable.

The cough—though faint amidst the bustle of the market-place—was as familiar as if he'd heard it not just days before, but every day since that time so achingly long ago when his mother was near him, alive, talking, singing to him. He teared up at the sound. He stopped to listen for where it came from.

The cart creaked along so slowly he had time to walk in one direction, then another, even to walk down a muddy al-leyway as he strained to hear the sound over the buzz of unfa-miliar words, the barking of dogs, calls of the merchants, the whinnying of horses.

The boy turned off onto a dusty lane, away from the bustle of soldiers and merchants, winding cautiously amidst tents decorated with green and red and brown ribbons, passing goats tethered to tent poles, stepping carefully over rivulets of foul water draining nowhere. He followed the sharp hacking sound. Louder, insistent and repetitive. A thin woman lay on a low wooden pallet outside a tent entrance, covered by a blanket despite the heat of the day. There was a tethered dog, sleeping in the noonday heat. An old, torn green shawl was just visible under her head, the fringes lying in the mud. The lady he had seen on the trail. Chickens clucked and pecked at the dusty ground.

Years had passed and the boy knew that his mother would have changed, aged.

The angle of her nose, the way her mouth moved. Different than he remembered. He tried to dictate to his memory: *this is her!* But a boy knows his mother instantly. And in that moment Nahatum admitted the truth to himself. This was not his mother.

His shoulders felt heavy and his stomach turned. He kicked at the dog, who growled back and moved out of his way. Surprising himself with his quickness, Nahatum grabbed a chicken at his feet, determined to pull the head off the stupid, squawking thing, when the woman spoke to him.

"Water."

She'd barely gotten the word out when a cough seized her and she shook as though tossed around by a giant's hand. She brought a cloth to her mouth, then rolled slightly toward the side of the pallet and spit a vile brownish blob onto the ground.

Smaller than he remembered his mother, her hair was very reddish, not his mother's rich black. The odor was familiar: sweat and decay. She half- rose with effort from the pallet, her breath coming in gasps, her mouth twisted awkwardly. He wondered if her mouth was always in that half-moon shape or if the coughing had permanently twisted it. He was so close he felt heat rise from her pale, waxy skin. It was the skin that focused his attention. He touched her arm, drew away. The drained color and the dryness, death forcing its way into her.

She opened her eyes and looked up at him, at first without recognition, then the droopy half-moon was replaced by a slight smile. Amidst his misery, the boy was warmed.

"Water," she repeated, this time in a sort of moan. In all the mud and wet there was nothing to drink. Nahatum leaned down and lifted the edge of the lady's shawl out of the mud, restoring it to the pallet.

From within the tent a man emerged holding an empty wooden bowl. He cursed, then dipped the bowl into a muddy rivulet flowing near their feet. He ignored the boy. His long white headdress hung down over his hair and back. He had a craggy, weathered face with bushy white eyebrows and a great beak of a nose. His long robe, white and red and gold, brushed the pallet. His left hand had no fingers, giving it the aspect of a club.

Kneeling beside the woman, he put his left hand under her head and carefully lifted her toward the foul liquid in the bowl. Brownish pellets freckled the woman's cheek, and he gently wiped them away with the fringe of his robe. He wouldn't let her drink, though she strained to take the bowl to her mouth. "Unclean." He cursed, then wiped the dirty water on her face, neck, patting her, trying to cool her burning skin.

Nahatum turned and ran down the narrow lane, into a busier one, trying to remember the turns that would put him back near the work party. He found it, several of the Berbers just ahead, the wagon straining forward, pulled by an old mule. He took the long tin dipper hanging from the side and drew out a full ration of still-cool water.

Cradling the dipper in both hands, careful not to slosh water out, he ran back, kneeling by the lady. The man with the club hand was nowhere to be seen. He held the dipper forward to the sick woman, who nodded and leaned in, putting her hand firmly on his to steady the metal container. He felt the touch of her hot skin. She drank all of it, greedily, then lay back down. Her sudden movement knocked the tin ladle onto the ground.

The man looked out from the tent, this time staring at the boy. He pushed aside the tent flaps.

"What are you doing?"

Nahatum picked up the ladle and backed away. The man stepped forward and grabbed the metal dipper from Nahatum's hands then put it to his lips, tasting the remaining drops of fresh water.

"Who are you?" The man's eyes were hard and narrow.

The boy turned and ran, legs kicking high. He ran as he'd often done before, blind as a rabbit, whose survival lies in its speed. Rabbits ran to get away from, not to get somewhere. So Nahatum ran till he could no more and when he slowed and looked around, Craggy- Face was nowhere to be seen.

He recognized nothing, had no idea where he was. Just tents and warriors and a muddy byway. Dark, late afternoon shadows spread over the tents and the alleys, and people's hands grabbed at him.

Rabbit, run, run.

On their way back from the afternoon cutting trees, with the setting sun behind them, it was the long-haired Iberians up front (who'd refused to walk near the useless Berbers who barely knew how to swing an axe and had loafed the whole time no matter how much Gisgo had yelled at them) who were the first to spot an exhausted Nahatum standing in the lane amidst merchants' tents, looking lost and confused.

When Gisgo bellowed out that "the little thief" would pay for what he did, Nahatum started to run with what little energy he had left. The fleet Berbers came to life, running the wilted boy to ground and pinning him until Gisgo thundered up.

"Where have you been?"

Nahatum had no idea exactly where he'd been. And he would not tell Gisgo what he had been doing; he would never talk of his mother to any of the men around him. He swayed, dizzy in the still- hot Iberian sun. He was so thirsty.

"Where is the ladle?"

The ladle, Nahatum then realized, was gone. Which made him sadder, and dizzier, still.

"So, stealing from us. Trying to run away. A hammered tin ladle could fetch afew coins, if you bartered smartly." Gisgo ordered the Berbers to search the boy's pockets but of course they found nothing. Which only seemed to confirm Gisgo's suspicions.

"You spent it already. Did you buy some roast chicken? Did you lose it gambling?"

"I didn't sell it."

"Of course." Gisgo stroked his bushy beard. "Unless, there was some other purpose to your disappearance. Something else you were doing." His auroch eyes narrowed. "Tie him up. We will bring him back to Hannibal."

That tent is too small. Hannibal peered out of his own tent across the clearing to where a phalanx of men were at work setting up the special meeting tent, bringing in exquisite woven carpets and even some tapestries direct from Carthage.

Where will all the chiefs fit? He had the beginnings of a headache. He hadn't slept well. Long nights poring over supply manifests, half-drawn maps, re-reading accounts of Alexander's lightening war of conquest all the way to Persia. How, Hannibal wanted to understand, did the great General keep his army intact through such a long campaign?

He turned back into his own tent. *Stop this right now: did Alexander the Great worry if a meeting tent was big enough?*

Besides, there's enough room in the tent. He had set his men to bringing in more tables, benches, fine chairs, some covered with leather and zebra skins and gazelle hide. Peacock feathers sprouted from elegant pottery vases fired in the kilns of Phoenicia. The damn tent was so fancy the whole thing reminded Hannibal of the grand dining hall in the hilltop citadel, the Byrsa, back in Carthage, where at that very moment one of the presiding Suffettes might be entertaining important Senators. He sighed. *Or, the Roman delegation now demanding my head.*

He stared down at his maps, key to everything that was to happen, and scratched his right wrist, his sword hand, feeling the familiar burn mark on the wrist, the sign of his ultimate devotion to his father. He had been five years old when his father took him to the the stone temple on their vast estate outside Carthage, just the two of them, where they both had sworn eternal enmity to Rome. Young Hannibal, overcome by the sacred fire, the slaughtered goat, the prayers to Ba'al Shammon, had thrust his wrist right into the hot coals, burning himself in a sign of his devotion to his father's desire. The burn mark always there, always a reminder.

He knew he must convince the chiefs that night. It was already late spring.

A yell at the door, guards stood aside. Gisgo. Why, Hannibal wondered, was Gisgo pulling some bound animal behind him by a rope? A panting, sweaty, bloody and beaten wild beast.

No, Hannibal realized with a shock, it was the boy, Nahatum. Arms lashed to his sides by thick ropes. Face and shoulders raw and bleeding. Behind him followed a stern looking Jonaz.

"Apologies for interrupting you, my Lord, but I have difficult news."

Hannibal tensed: Gisgo was speaking the local patois, not their native Punic—the infantryman did that when agitated.

"Go ahead."

"Your Lord, I fear the wolf child is not what he seems. I fear he is a spy…"

"Ridiculous. Gisgo, calm yourself."

The man bowed.

A seed of doubt bloomed in Hannibal's mind. *Wouldn't that be just like the Romans, to send a little boy into my camp? And what wolf child would know so many Punic words? What if this is a Roman- educated boy, trained to penetrate the camp and learn what he could? The map table! If the Romans found out his plans, all surprise will be lost.*

Gisgo explained about the work party and the boy's disappearance. "At first, Lord, I thought he had simply fled with the tin ladle, to sell it for what he could get. But when we re-captured him we were in the area where the newly- arrived tribes are camping. What if he ran into an alley to report to a chief? A spy…"

Hannibal glanced at the papyrus pile on the table. He lifted several scrolls.

Nothing missing.

Gisgo turned and struck the boy about the shoulders and head with a leather whip. "Where were you? Where did you go? Who were you talking to?" The blows pelted the boy's head and shoulders; he hardly had an opportunity to respond. Hannibal had seen hardened warriors cry out after fewer blows from powerful Gisgo.

"Stop that, Gisgo."

There was a slight tremble in the boy's lips but still he looked at Gisgo with fiery eyes. Resolute. If they loosened the ropes would the boy kick the infantry commander? The fatigue worked at Hannibal's eyes, dug into his forehead. He didn't have time for this, just hours before the chiefs assembled for their grand meeting. But he knew he must deal with it: if the boy was a spy, he had to find out what he knew and whom he had been talking to.

"In Carthage, we crucify spies," Hannibal threatened the boy directly in Latin as a test. "A horrible death is in store for you."

The boy looked back at him blankly, with none of the alarm that would betray someone who understood the language of Rome. Gisgo nodded and Jonaz looked mightily pleased at the mention of crucifixion. The squire, Hannibal imagined, might even favor crucifying the boy several times.

The boy was likely not Roman. Yet he could be in their employ. The boy looked up, as if studying Hannibal. Hannibal wanted to look away from the directness of the boy's gaze.

"Untie him." Hannibal ordered, wondering why he did so. This was a time to look strong and decisive, not weak and uncertain, he told himself. Again he was aware of Gisgo watching, evaluating his leadership. The boy twisted himself when freed from the ropes, shaking his whole body like a wet cat.

"Nahatum, tell me what happened."

"I'm not a… spy." The boy stumbled on the word. "Someone needed water." Gisgo seemed to spit as he spoke. "Is this a joke? Yes, someone needed water. The men in the work party who were heavy with thirst from working in the fields cutting down trees. The whole water wagon might have been stolen…And, what did you do with the ladle I entrusted to you?"

Nahatum shrugged. This boy could be maddeningly stubborn and controlled, Hannibal reflected, even when his life was at stake. Impressive.

Both Jonaz's hands were curled into fists; he looked about to hurl himself at the boy. A sort of heat emanated from Gisgo. Hannibal thought of baying hounds running a bloodied young buck to ground.

"Which tribe, who were you consorting with?" Gisgo demanded. Nahatum looks confused. "I don't know..."

Gisgo rumbled with impatience. "Lord, let me take this wolf child away."

He should, Hannibal knew. In one way, that'd be easiest—and probably most politic—to just order Gisgo to crucify the boy along with the thieves, deserters, unlucky losers of some rivalry with a chieftain, and occasional hungry, foraging lion, that lined the roads out into the countryside to serve as warnings to others, humans and beasts. The thought, though, of passing the boy's broken body hanging from the cross, being picked clean by crows every time he rode out in the country, made Hannibal's chest ache. Besides, killing him right now would be a stupid strategy. If the boy was a spy—and he could be—Hannibal had to figure out what the boy knew and, more importantly, who he had given that information to. It could be any one of the chiefs.

Yes, that's it. The meeting tonight. Who does the boy talk to? How does he behave? "Not now, Gisgo," Hannibal ordered. "We have the chiefs arriving shortly and we must focus on the meeting tonight. The boy can serve wine." He charged Jonaz to keep an eye on him at all times. Then he sent the two away, telling his squire to stop hitting the boy. In fact, to apply herbs to the cuts and bruises. "I don't want my servants bleeding through their tunics at the meeting."

Alone with Gisgo, he stopped his infantry commander in mid- protest. "We need to know which of the chiefs may be disloyal to me, who may have a secret alliance with the Romans. We will watch the boy carefully—if he is a spy, whoever is employing him will surely be at the meeting tonight. You watch carefully in the room, see if he talks to anyone or tries to give one of the chiefs or his lieutenants any information."

Gisgo smiled, nodding agreement. "Let him think he is free, but use him to our ends. A strategy worthy of your father. Then we will crucify him."

Hannibal's mind was already on another subject. He asked if his scribe will be at the meeting and Gisgo told him that, yes, Solyphos was feeling better.

"Here, wolf boy, take this with both hands. Pay attention. Carry it into the big tent where the meeting is going on. The one with all the noise and yelling."

The toothless cook handed Nahatum a groaning platter of meat, olives, figs, roasted vegetables. The platter lurched in his hands; he almost dropped it. He had no energy; just wanted to go to sleep.

Luckily, the cook put out two hands, holding him by the shoulders to steady him. He flinched at the cook's touch. The man's tone softened as he stared at the wounds on the boy's shoulders and face. "Great Ba'al…"

The boy didn't care. He knew he was already doomed. He hadn't understood everything that was said a few hours earlier, but he knew he was in deep trouble.

Hannibal had told him weeks ago to never to steal from him, and now they all thought he had stolen the ladle. The idea that he'd disappointed Hannibal was most painful. The way the man looked at him as he sent him from the tent ripped something out of the boy's chest.

"Wolf boy, look at me." The cook slapped him, which helped, woke him a bit. "Don't drop anything tonight, child, no matter how hurt you are."

Nahatum nodded, and ignored the pain in his shoulders as he carried, as if in a dream, the clay platter piled high with delicious food into the noisly, crowded meeting tent set up in the center of the clearing, within sight of Hannibal's tent.

The tent was a wild stockade of yelling, laughing, drinking men. The smells of sweat, wine, incense, candles, cooked meat, made the boy's knees weak. The sound of different Iberian accents and inflections swirled around him, changing and disguising familiar words.

Men jostled each other, clustering around Hannibal's familiar table, now moved to the large tent. Hannibal sat at the head of the table. He did not look happy. As the boy approached, Hannibal said to no one in particular, "The chiefs are hungry....and thirsty." Several pounded their bronze mugs on the table, making their silver and gold wrist bracelets jingle. One burly man placed his mug on top of the crinkly piece of papyrus with dark marks on it spread out on the table. Hannibal moved the mug off the papyrus and for a tense moment the stout chief glared at him, but the mug stayed where Hannibal put it, away from the crinkly stuff.

Hannibal turned to Nahatum. "More wine. And hurry." Eager to do something right, Nahatum tripped over a tent pole on the way out, much to the laughter of the assembled chiefs. The toothless cook outside mixed carafes of wine with water ("these Iberians won't notice the difference") and Nahatum hurried back trying not to bump into one of the chiefs—his face distorted by a missing eye– pissing outside the entrance, a wine mug hanging loosely from one hand. The man pushed the boy aside and stepped back into the tent. Nahatum followed him. Hannibal pointed at various men and Nahatum refilled mugs.

A big man wearing a leather vest stood up and reached over to the wooden platter in front of Hannibal, who had referred to him as Barbabar, Great Chief of the Celtiberians. The man's vest had long claws woven into it. Bear, lion, badger. In one hand he held a woven sack that click- clacked as he ran it between his fingers; with his other hand he picked up an entire joint of roast goat. Chewing on the meat, he yelled at Hannibal, "you want us all to become birds and fly over the mountains." He imitated a bird flapping its wings, the goat meat waving in the air, flecks of juice and spit flying. Several of the chiefs roared with laughter, and pounded their mugs on the table, their hands big as steel axe- heads.

"We will find the summer passage through the mountains," Hannibal replied, pointing to the crinkly leaf-stuff spread out on the table as if that meant something. The General's voice sounded calm. The chiefs paid little attention. Bear- bearded Barnabar fiddled with the sack in his hand, tossing it in his hand, making those clattering sounds. For once, Nahatum was relieved to see Gisgo, chewing deliberately on a fig, standing behind Hannibal. The giant stood several hands taller than Barnabar, and his eyes followed the sack that Barnabar tossed in the air, which, Nahatum concluded, was better than staring at him, as Gisgo had been doing all night. As had Jonaz, that vile hyena of a squire, standing on the other side of the tent, against a wall. Behind Gisgo lay two large, carved wooden chests that Nahatum recognized; he'd been told that first day not to touch them, and he hadn't, despite his curiosity.

And then in the corner, Nahatum saw the old sorcerer. This was the one Hannibal called Solyphos and for the boy there was no scarier sight in the whole tent. The flask of wine he was supposed to be pouring trembled in his hand. Ancient, whispy white-haired, the man sat on a little stool next to a small table where he was casting spells and throwing charms,

using a long owl's feather that scratched out black lines on
more of the crinkly stuff that the boy now knew everyone
called papyrus. Nahatum had heard the rumors: the man steals
people's souls with the black marks he makes using feathers
from birds whose songs he has plundered.

Hummingbird beat its wings deep in Nahatum's chest.
*Get out of the tent, away from the evil sorcerer. Run for the woods.
No, stop, the guards outside will kill you if you do that.* Outside,
though, he could at least breathe.

Yet Nahatum could see that Hannibal was in trouble in
some unknown way inthis meeting. With great effort, Nahatum ignored the sorcerer and the rattling in his own chest
and renewed his effort at making the chiefs happy with more
wine, with platters of roasted meats, cheeses, sweets.

The sorcerer kept gesturing toward the boy with his wine
mug. Finally, the boy walked over with his flask. There were those
dark black lines and the evil feather right in front of him, and
when Nahatum tried to pour from his carafe, his shaking hand
betrayed him and he spilled wine right onto the table where the
socrcerer's magic lay. The man cursed and pushed Nahatum away
with his disgusting bony hands, then used his tunic to wipe up
the wine. Some of the lines lay blurry, though Nahatum remembered not to look too closely for fear of losing his soul.

Several drunken chiefs stood muttering and laughing near
Nahatum. One of them, the scraggly whiskers of his beard
hanging down like branches of an old pine tree, yelled toward
Hannibal. "We made a treaty of loyalty with your father, Lord
Hannibal, to resist the Romans here, in our lands. But now,
with your father's death, things have changed.

"None of us want the Romans to dominate, but we never
agreed to leave our forests and our families and our crops to
march across wild lands and endless mountains. For what?"

A man near to the drunken group adjusted his headdress. Nahatum looked more closely in the dim light. That familiar craggy face, bushy eyebrows, the weatheredlook: the one who'd confronted him at the tent of the coughing woman. He leaned wordlessly against a tent pole, arms folded on his chest, looking sad, as if only half-listening to the argument. The scary club hand was not visible.

A chief whose face was pitted and scarred like a dried riverbed cleared his throat. "What of the terrible Thunder Beasts, Lord Hannibal, will you drive them over the mountains too?" Hannibal nodded. Then the chief spoke of Hannibal's father, Hamilcar, with great respect, but said that Hannibal's proposal was too dangerous. Like some sort of thunder beast himself, Barnabar bellowed, "The accursed beasts will resist their handlers; they have more sense than those who try to lead them." He continued to play with the noisy sack in his hand, then took a swig from his mug and wiped his mouth, his fingers almost disappearing into his beard.

Gisgo's hand tensed on his knife, but Hannibal stilled him with a hand on his arm. Barnabar emptied the sack from his hand to the wooden table– teeth spilled out, clinking and clattering against each other. They were not animal teeth.

Nahatum forced himself to move around the crowded room, filling mugs with wine, while the argument raged. Suddenly, a new voice dominated the room.

"You! Boy." There was such command in the voice that the room became silent. Nahatum looked up from his pitcher of wine. "Stop." The man's eyes stared deep into him from beneath the thick white eyebrows.

Every muscle in the boy's body urged him to flee, but he could not. He faced the craggy- faced chief.

The chief, his white headdress carefully folded around his neck, walked up to Nahatum, studying him. "You are the boy who brought water to my wife, she who is sick with the coughing plague. Are you not?"

"I am." Nahatum whispered in reply, though he held the man's gaze.

"I almost didn't recognize you with all your wounds and bruises. Did a pride of lions penetrate the camp?" Laughs and shouts from the crowd. Craggy Face waved his good arm sharply, as if he regretted his joke. "No matter. I did recognize you."

The man looked from the boy to Hannibal. Then he reached into the folds of his elegant caftan and drew from his belt the tin ladle. He held it up as if displaying something regal, a trophy. "I have brought this tonight to find out which of my fellow chiefs I am indebted to for their kindness."

There was silence.

"Who is this boy?" He pointed the end of the ladle toward Nahatum Hannibal replied. "He is… my servant."

"I see. And you sent him with water this morning. For my Queen. Thank you. Your graciousness is most appreciated, Lord Hannibal. We are not used to Carthaginians with such appreciation for the rules of courtesy and respect." He handed the ladle to Hannibal. "The boy dropped this in his haste to carry out his duties."

Hannibal remained silent a moment, considering Nahatum. Gisgo, behind him, forehead furrowed, looked as if he'd just seen pigs dancing.

Finally, Hannibal replied, "A great chief deserves the respect of Carthage."

"Our fathers may have fought against each other, Lord Hannibal, but now seems the time for us to join forces." The chief turned to the crowd of assembled chiefs in the tent. "Hannibal is right. Rome wants to subjugate all of our tribes.

One at a time. We need to unite in his army and end Rome's attempt to make us their slaves."

The argument started again but this time Hannibal's words had renewed force and there were more nods of agreement among the chiefs. Finally, Hannibal raised his arms.

"This is about trust and respect. It is also about riches. This is what awaits all who come with me!" Hannibal's voice seemed to deepen. There was silence in the room, and everyone was now on their feet.

Hannibal walked over to the two large carved wooden chests. A guard next to them stepped back. Using a brass key, Hannibal opened the first ornate chest. He pulled out a large handful of gold and silver engraved coins. He tossed them in the air; the precious metal glittered in the candlelight. "This is from Saguntum, the town five days ride south that allied itself with the Romans, and which I conquered last winter– Roman coins and jewels. Plunder!"

The room buzzed, as if the sorcerer had charmed all the bees in the forest into the tent. Chiefs pointed as Hannibal ran his hands through the treasure. All the different intonations of the Iberian patois, a river of sounds, streamed through the tent.

Hannibal slammed closed the top of the smaller chest and turned to the large wooden chest. Another key, and the top opened easily in Hannibal's large hand. He reached in and pulled out a flashing handful of color—the blue of sapphires, red of rubies, green emeralds, sparkling diamonds, golden and silver coins with ornate, glistening engravings. "From the great treasury of Carthage, a sign of our respect foryour worthy tribes. To be distributed to all who joinus."

There was a gasp and the room went silent. "This is but a token. Riches beyond words await us in Italy!" The room filled with the sound of wine mugs pounding the table. The skeptical chiefs sat down. No one left. All eyes were now on Hannibal.

He pointed at his table, explaining, convincing, one thick arm jabbing the air, the other extended down. The large red-black burn scar on his wrist was clearly visible. This time the chiefs looked on carefully, whispering to each other. The talk went on long into the night. Nahatum dozed in a corner of the tent.

Then he was awake, a hand suddenly shaking his shoulder. He moved quickly, anticipating another blow from Gisgo or Jonaz. Instead there sat Hannibal, looking at him. Gisgo sat behind, brow furrowed, elbows on his knees. A few threads of young daylight broke through the tent opening.

"Nahatum," Hannibal said. "That was well-done yesterday. Whatever you did… So. Now I want to know exactly what happened yesterday."

Nahatum explained about the lady and the coughing. That's all, nothing about his mother. "I saw she was thirsty and ran back to…to…" He remembered what Gisgo had said about water in the camp and figured that would be useful to add: "..to bring her some clear water, since they didn't have any."

"Clear water?"

"That you can see through, without all the mud and bugs in it."

"Ah. I see." Again that warming smile. If Hannibal smiled, would he now still send him to the mines? Water rose in the boy's chest and around his eyes and he bit down hard on his tongue to stop this uncomfortable force from gaining strength. "With the *malekeh*," he continued, remembering the cook's word for ladle in Punic.

"You don't speak Punic, do you, Nahatum?"

"What is Punic, sir?"

"The language of my homeland, of Carthage."

"Not yet, Sir. I would like to."

"You are a smart boy, Nahatum, perhaps you will learn." The General contemplated him for what seemed like hours. Then: "We have underestimated you, Nahatum. Your intelligence, your depth, your energy. These are things not often seen in a boy such as you."

Behind Hannibal, Gisgo was shaking his head. "My Lord, we still don't know… I mean, what if…." Hannibal cut him off. "Enough, Gisgo. This boy can be of real use to us."

Hannibal explained that the craggy-faced man in the white headdress was a chief of one of the largest tribes in the north of Iberia. He had brought thousands of warriors with him. "For his men to join us swells our army and also provides us passage toward the Snow-Capped Mountains that lead to Gaul." Sadly, the man's wife—queen of the tribe—was very ill and needed water and healing herbs.

Was he still to be punished? *Speak. Find words.* Nahatum had gone to the mines so many times that night he hardly cared any more. "May I see her again, Sir?"

"Ah, yes. The Queen." Hannibal's eyebrows came together. "Not many women where we are going." He thought a moment, then smiled. "That might be a good idea, indeed. You will see more of her. I want you to take some fresh water and healing herbs to their encampment every day this week. Yes, you'll see more of her." A pause, then: "When you have time. We are preparing to leave, in days, and there is a lot my servant needs to do."

His servant? He was not to be cast out. Was this true? Nahatum looked right at Hannibal, who held his gaze and was there even perhaps the hint of a smile? This was not a trick. He could breathe again. He could stay, with Hannibal. Sleep near his tent, beside the fire. He would find his mother. She would also be a great lady. Perhaps the Queen would even lead him to his mother. His chest skipped. He would have to hurry if the army was soon to leave.

The mysterious crinkly things on Hannibal's table made a rustling sound as Nahatum swept off the rugs the next day. He considered the stack of them: they looked like long rolls of smooth tree bark, three piled atop one another, held flat with rocks, and a knife stuck through one corner. They looked to the boy like enormous leaves from a giant's tree, each covered with black lines—straight, curved, round– that reminded him of frosted meadows in the early morning light, when all the animal tracks are clear to the eye.

The night before, Hannibal, along with everyone else, had been so intently focused on those things, everyone arguing about them as if they were the juiciest, tastiest pieces of meat. Nahatum lifted the old wooden broom—better to keep a safe distance– and poked at the stuff on the table, which rustled and quivered, like a bat fluttering into the night sky. Another poke with the broom and the top one fluttered again. He waited warily for it to get up and fly away.

"Be careful there…." Hannibal pushed aside the saffron curtains and walked towards Nahatum. The boy jerked the broom stick back.

A ripe, musky animal odor that the boy didn't recognize accompanied Hannibal. Nahatum's duties had yet to take him to the sprawling stable area where all manner of animals were kept. The General walked over to the table, surveying it. "Help me off with my shirt and pants." His pants were caked with dark, dried animal dung—not horse, not goat, not cattle– and his tunic peppered with brambles.

As he put on the clean shirt the boy held for him, Hannibal said that he'd spent all day at the new stockade being built on the far side of the animal pens. "More elephants arrived. All morning I listened to Indoi, their keeper, tell me the troubles he's been having: getting the new ones to mingle with the older ones, keeping the males from tusking each other to death over the females, worrying how they will do in the vicious cold of the mountains. I assured him that he will receive an extra supplement of large blankets for his beasts. He told me he worries about the giant one, Sirus, whom all the other elephants follow. He wants to keep Sirus happy as we cross the mountains and so here I am, the commander of the army, talking with this fellow from far-off Indi, past Persia even, about his elephants and how to keep his lead elephant happy and," Hannibal's voice rose, "who really is the leader of this army: me or an elephant?"

"You, Sir." *What was an elephant? Best not ask, this is not the time.*

Hannibal smiled. "Thank you, Nahatum."

His commander sat down on a bench at the strange table and studied the unrolled stuff, touching the top one. Again, a rustle. The boy picked up a half- eaten apple off the ground left over from some meeting. Broom at his side, the boy studied Hannibal. Then, without looking up, Hannibal extended his large right hand into the air and commanded the boy toward him. He told him to toss the rotten apple into the bucket. "Ever seen one of these?"

"That? What's it for?"

"What does it look like?"

"A drawing?" Nahatum made a motion in the air, as if poking with a stick in dirt.

Hannibal laughed, that sound like a large bird swooping through a blue sky, then he slapped the table with his hand.

The boy could see the thickness of his teeth. "In a way, yes, I suppose it is a drawing. One I've paid dearly for. Plying spies and allies with treasure for information, suffering fools, promising the world to those who will help me fill in these voids." Hannibal explained that the papyrus-stuff was something called a "map" and he swept his hand over the unrolled thing.

He patted the polished wooden bench. "Sit here. Next to me"

"Me, Sir?"

"Yes, you. Who else is here?"

This was the closest he'd ever been to the man. Hannibal's odor mixed with the heat of the day to make a pleasing pungent smell not unlike that which comes from the burnt wood inside a full- grown tree after lightening has hit.

"A map," Hannibal explained, "an accurate one, is like an eye that runs ahead of you far into the distance." A picture of the world that makes for victory, showing you where to march, where you might find an ambush, the best ground on which to meet your enemy. "The key to any battle, to the life of any army is to find the ground that will work to your advantage. It matters not the size of your army or your enemy's or what gods they fight with, or even what gods accompany *you,* if you can determine the best ground on which to fight. My father showed me how to seize the high ground and how to find the hidden ground, where to hide an army to achieve surprise."

Nahatum yawned.

"The point is, I've been working for years to gather the maps I need." Hannibal's hand moved just above the papyrus, not touching it. "Do you know what *these* are?" He pointed to a mass of squiggles and marks. The boy saw clouds and a deer; one looked like a bear.

"Animal designs?"

Hannibal smiled. "They're words." Hannibal then made a claim that truly confused Nahatum: the black marks *meant* things. He didn't understand.

What was clear, though, was that Hannibal was sitting next to him, talking to him as if it mattered. This led to a renewed effort by the boy to pay attention, with some success. The words were about places and people in the world. The papyrus "maps" were made on "scrolls." Strange word-breaths: both short, snappy bursts of sound. Maps. Scrolls.

Hannibal untied a leather strap and laid out another scroll, pointing at lines and rows of squiggles. Words were things written down on papyrus scrolls, stories about the world and the people in it. This made no sense to the boy. Did words trap things on papyrus like a fly stuck in hot wax? Another kind of deep, very scary, magic. He studied the way the lines curved and dipped and flowed. On the open scroll on the table, the boy saw a snake, a cloud, a tent, an animal claw, a fang. He stared intently, trying to conjure words, but could not.

The General chuckled. "I'm a good tutor, after all. I ought to be—I had a great one. Solyphos."

Nahatum wanted to ask about that word—*tutor*—but he was already awash in things he could barely understand. Hannibal pointed to places on the map-thing and intoned mysterious names: Carthage, Rome, Greek- land, Tyre, Judea, Egypt. The man seemed to have the world entire captured on this piece of papyrus in some spirit- laden bit of magic. Hannibal pointed to a spot on the map, talking about some people called "Jews."

"Odd people. They believe their god speaks to them." Hannibal rubbed his scalp, making a scratching sound. Then, laughing: "Imagine believing that a god wants to have conversations with people. Although," he added, "it can be very helpful to your army's morale to spread rumors that the gods come to you in dreams, assuring you of victory in the coming war," He shook his head. "They are fierce fighters, those Jews. I have some in the army." He stopped and looked at Nahatum, his right eyebrow cocked slightly. "What do you suppose a god's voice sounds like?"

"Like yours."

A slight recoil. Hannibal was silent a moment. Then he laughed, but with less of a lilt this time. "I doubt that." He shrugged, stood up, sat down again. "Back to work Nahatum."

The boy returned to sweeping while the General rolled up several scrolls, then unrolled some others. After a few moments, the general cleared his throat.

"Have you taken water and herbs to the Queen yet today?"

"No sir, I had planned to do that later, after cleaning." Though it would be dark then, Nahatum realized, when there's greater chance of being stolen away by a drunken warrior, disappearing into a tent. Hannibal nodded, as if understanding what was unspoken.

"Take this with you." Hannibal strode over to the large mahogany cabinet containing his clothes. He returned with a long rich purple sash, gesturing for the boy to stand before him.

"When I send you into the encampment on errands, wear this." He looped the sash over the boy's shoulder and around his waist; it felt soft against Nahatum's bruises.

"Carthaginian Purple. The royal color of the city. A sign that you are in my service. You will have no trouble now."

The bright material tugged at Nahatum as if in greeting.

Maps are drawings! Words are animal designs on papyrus! Hannibal considered this as he walked alone down the forested

path toward the horse stockades. *Could be, actually. Clever boy.*
The set of Nahatum's face back in the tent stayed in his mind.
The boy's furrowed brow. He was trying very hard. *Maps actually are drawings, aren't they? Remember that. You can see things that are not there, and you can leave out things that are.*

The boy drew out such unexpected feelings in him: warmth, even playfulness.

And now he'd given him a new purple sash, as if he was Carthaginian-born? The boy had better deserve it, or Gisgo would not let him forget that. He needed to be careful here, not be overcome with feelings hardly understood. *You want your enemy to be in the grip of mindless passions. You don't want to be doing that yourself.* Hannibal ran his fingers over the burn scar on his wrist. *Remember your purpose. Keep a clear mind for what lies ahead.*

Each of the next three days, Nahatum went to the craggy-faced chieftain's tent after his chores, bringing water and medicinal herbs. Each time, he saw the lady on her pallet lying outside in the sun. She was weak and had difficulty rising, once waving aside the herbal mixture the boy brought. Each time, though, she smiled, recognizing him. The boy found that if he kneeled to lean in, holding the goatskin bag of herbal mixture close to her mouth, she would eventually drink some.

Nahatum knew it was the powerful magic of the herbs that was helping her recover, but still, it was almost as if he was himself making her better, defeating whatever spirits were at war inside her, making her whole body shake and tremble. When she rose toward him from the pallet to drink down the mixture, Nahatum remembered his mother, the way her skin had become a sweaty, smelly thing, scary to touch, and he'd hold the sash Hannibal had given him, hoping it had the power to drive away the spirits trying to take over the lady's body, spirits that could change her skin from something soft and cool to the ugly thing it'd become: clammy and stiff, like the lizards in the swamp.

The chief nodded when he saw the boy, telling him to convey his gratitude to Hannibal. The third day he also ordered the boy to tell Hannibal that his men were ready for the journey ahead.

As their departure came closer, so did the boy's anticipation of his mother's return. She will see him with his sash and he remembered exactly what Hannibal had called the color. He will tell her that first thing. "See, what I'm wearing? It's called 'Carthaginian Purple.'"

On the afternoon of the third day, Nahatum found Hannibal at his writing table, brow furrowed in concentration. "Wait here, Nahatum. As soon as I'm finished, I want you to take this letter to the traders camped near the blacksmith forges. They will take it back by ship to my wife in Carthage."

Nahatum tended the coal brazier thinking about what Hannibal had said about words, trying to understand this idea that they *meant* something. As he wrote, the general spoke aloud, as if trying to shape his thoughts. The boy sensed a connection between what Hannibal said and the lines that appeared on the papyrus.

The boy heard Hannibal apologize to his wife for sending her—an Iberian princess– to his family's estates outside Carthage against her wishes. He reminded her of the dangers the war brought and gave her advice on crops and management of the vast family estate. He told her to instill values of duty and loyalty in their son while he was gone ("the time allotted in this world between fathers and sons sometimes seems so short.").

The thin reed in Hannibal's calloused hand looked to Nahatum like a stork's beak as he dipped it into a jar of black liquid, pecking away at the papyrus as if searching for insects.

Then suddenly: "Nahatum! Go to Solyphos and tell him I need more papyrus."

"Who, Sir?"

"My scribe."

"I don't understand, Sir."

"Come, come, Nahatum. You remember Solyphos, who was here during the meeting with the chiefs, taking notes." The hummingbird began pecking in Nahatum's chest. "Don't stand there with your mouth open, boy. He's the white-haired Greek who lives in a clearing in the forest on the far side of the river. Now, run, get me more papyrus."

The sorcerer. No. Nahatum grabbed his waist sash and ran down the trail toward the river. He passed Iberian tribesmen laughing as Persian mercenaries with painted faces kicked a pig's bladder among themselves back and forth. There was the clink of coins being exchanged.

And then Nahatum almost ran right into Ranton, the older boy from the wolf pack. Nahatum at first didn't recognize who it was pulling the heavy sledge; Ranton, meanwhile, had stepped aside at the sight of the figure wearing the Carthaginian purple sash hurrying down the path.

There was a quick embrace and laughter. Nahtum asked about the other boys.

Ranton told him that two had been nailed to crosses for stealing, where they died. Several others had found work in the service of one or another chief.

"You are Hannibal's servant now? Come on, Nahatum, you are making up stories." Ranton considered him, and his eyes got wider. "Yet here you are wearing that sash that all those Carthaginians wear. Did you steal it?"

"Hannibal gave it to me."

Ranton shook his head. "OK, perhaps this is true." Nahatum expected to be asked stories about Hannibal. Instead, Ranton asked, "What do you steal? Who do you sell it to?" Pointing to his sledge, he said, "These knives and swords are hardly the equal of what the Carthaginians have. Steal us some and I'll make us both rich. My chief will pay well for good weapons." He looked more hardened than Nahatum remembered. There was an edge of worry around his eyes, which darted here and there as if to make sure no one was sneaking up on them.

"I don't steal from Hannibal, Ranton."

"What do you do?"

"Right now I'm on my way to the sorcerer's tent to get Hannibal more papyrus."

Ranton's eyes got wide. "The man rules the wasp kingdom. They are people he has trapped in insect bodies. I've seen it happen, Nahatum. One day before you came to the pack I saw him lure birds down from the sky—he plucked feathers from them to use in his conjuring, then he commanded their spirits to fly away though the birds were no longer alive."

Nahatum's teeth began to chatter; he bit on his tongue to stop them. Ranton's voice became a whisper. "The sorcerer casts spells for Hannibal with feathers and black lines of forbidden shapes that reveal the future."

"I... spilled wine on the sorcerer's conjuring." Nahatum tried to boast, but his voice faltered as he spoke.

Ranton stepped backward. "If you look at the black shapes, they steal your soul."

"Come with me."

"No," the older boy yelled. "I have to get back or else I'll get beaten. Besides, why would I want to go there? See if Hannibal can protect you from the sorcerer's spells."

And with that Ranton resumed pulling the heavy sledge down the trail.

Soon Nahatum found himself in front of a large, billowing tent that stood alone in a small clearing dotted with spring wildflowers in bloom, close to a line of pine trees.

Wasps hovered around the entrance, and rows of fish with dead eyes hung from racks on the side of the tent in the morning sun.

The boy tried to ignore the awful wasps at the tent entrance, black heads and long brown bodies, eager to sting. He whispered Solyphos' name. His throat was dry and his voice didn't sound like his own. The boy put his hands on his purple sash, thrusting it forward so the wasps knew who was his protector. Finally, he repeated the conjurer's name, louder.

The tent folds parted. A stooped, white-haired man thin as a spider's leg squinted into the bright sunlight.

"Yes?" His strange accent made the words sharp, barbed. Nahatum hadn't realized the man was so tall. This gave him an even more mysterious air, as if his height was further evidence he wasn't really human.

"Ah, Hannibal's boy," he said, not unkindly. Then: "The one who spilled wine all over my papyrus."

"Hannibal..." Nahatum started to say, then put one hand into the other to stop the shaking. "...needs more papyrus."

Solyphos nodded impatiently and disappeared behind the blue- green cotton folds. Several of the wasps followed him.

"Well, come in!" he ordered the boy "Don't mind the wasps. They are most interested in the gall nuts I use to make my ink, and will pay you little attention. Just walk slowly and mind your own business."

Piles of nut shells lay on one long table that ran along an entire side of the tent.

Clay bowls were filled with open and unopened nuts. The tender nut meat lay discarded, on the table, on the ground. Nahatum reached for a nugget, but found a large wasp sitting on it, and jerked his hand back.

"Leave all this alone!" Solyphos warned, sweeping his hand over the table, moving several glass and clay jars filled with black ink– each like a tiny moonlit pond– away from Nahatum. Other jars were piled high with deep brown mounds of the nut meat, looking like scat from the black bear or wild bull. Evil- looking scrolls were rolled up on the table. An open one, partially covered with squiggles, sat on a small table near a worn wooden chair with a knitted pillowed back. Nahatum blinked his eyes shut, not to have his soul seized by the sorcerer's markings.

The tent was so different from his master's. There was a table with wooden pans of water filled with what looked like long sheets of very thin flatbread. And weapons? They filled Hannibal's tent, but all he found here was an old but well- polished sword leaning near the entrance.

"Stop rubbing that sash of yours, you'll wear a hole in it. Servants need patience.

Then maybe they won't spill wine."

"What do you do with all these nuts....?"

Solyphos sighed. "Ink, I said. No one listens anymore. For the papyrus I'm making." He pointed to the long pans of water, then added, the pride unmistakeable, "Papyrus made exactly according to the Egyptians' specifications."

The fragrances made the boy's nose wrinkle—the pleasing scent of the gall nuts and the musty smell from the large pans of water, and the sharp perfume of the ink.

Nahatum sneezed.

"So, Hannibal wants more papyrus," the man snorted. "I have tried to teach him since he was a little boy—write slowly and write in small characters. Concentrate on your writing. Papyrus is hard to make." Solyphos seemed amused as he spoke. There were dark lines underneath his fingernails, and the skin on the tips was stained black. He scooped up a pile of limp fish with both hands from another table and thrust it at Nahatum. They were not fish, but fish skins—eel, pike, trout– dried and firm to the touch, all the meat scraped carefully away from the side. The inside was pink and smooth, the touch similar to the papyrus Nahatum had poked on Hannibal's map table.

"Tell Lord Hannibal that papyrus is in short supply, given our plans. I can't make more papyrus while we're marching, where we're going. If he wants me to write the record of our epic journey, we will have to do with fish skins for our letters." He pursed his lips, biting on his lower lip. "If we *have* an epic journey. We may hardly need papyrus, with Hannibal bringing this disorganized group into the teeth of the Roman army, on their own soil."

Solyphos looked at the sash on Nahatum's chest, then at the boy. "The man has some hard decisions ahead. He can't be doing odd things like making servants out of wolf children." Nahatum blinked. A softer tone returned to Solyphos' voice. "Though maybe if they are hard-working and learn not to spill wine on hard-won papyrus."

Nahatum waved wildly as a wasp skimmed past his hair, as if on patrol.

"Now go, young servant," Solyphos suddenly ordered, clapping his hands, "I have work to finish."

The sorcerer might as well have clapped lightening right into the tent. Nahatum bolted out, past the guardian wasps.

Back at Hannibal's tent, his general took the fish skins and nodded. "Solyphos is a demanding teacher," Hannibal sighed, turning to complete his letter.

The next day Nahatum watched dust clouds recede into the distance as Marhabal led his Numidian cavalry ahead of the main army, to scout as far north as the snow – capped mountains of Iberia they were very soon to cross. The horses' hooves seemed to spark as they galloped away.

From his perch on the slight rise, Nahatum saw long rows of giant boulders lined up on the practice fields below him. He looked more carefully. Not boulders, these were the Thunder Beasts. What Hannibal called, "elephants." He was thankful to be so far away, able to watch from a safe distance. He tried to make sense of what he saw.

Enormous, wrinkled heads and wide mouths, from which sprang two long white, rounded, pointed bones like giant's spears, and then a long, gray snake that extended down, snorting and rooting along the ground. Nothing he had ever seen even resembled them.

Suddenly several of the elephants raised that enormous snake into the air and bellowed to the gods, and Nahatum watched the well-trained Numidian horses in the neighboring stockade go wild with fear, trying to throw their riders. What Roman soldier, Nahatum thought, could possibly stand up to animals as fearsome as these?

He turned to leave and there in the furthest field were the sling throwers from the Balearic Islands practicing their ways of battle: using long whip- like slingshots to hurl rocks with astonishing accuracy, breaking off branches of trees far across the field.

Nahatum pictured the branches as Roman heads, smashed to pieces.

"Yes, pack those," Hannibal ordered Jonaz, pointing to fur boots, leggings, and a bearskin cloak.

"Yes, sir, though may I point out that it is still late spring and not yet even summer?"

"Summer lasts but a short time where we are going, Jonaz." He didn't add what he was thinking: *and we are leaving weeks later than I'd hoped.*

"And Nahatum, pack that in a separate little box." He gestured— casually, he hoped, not wanting to seem to make too much of it—at the little wooden hut construction he'd made with his son days before the little boy left with his mother. "Yes, that. Pack it carefully now."

Then Hannibal stepped outside the tent to read the letter that had arrived from his wife, Imre, on elegant parchment, written in the careful hand taught to her by Solyphos at Hannibal's direction after their marriage. Their letters must have crossed in passage, he thought, assuming his wasn't lost to storms, pirates, or hostile Roman ships. She wished him to know that she was well and that his son was well. Then she wrote:

> "... I am your eyes and ears now in this city and I must tell you that vile Hanno the Great has called for Carthage to accede to the demands of the Roman delegation here. The Romans want the Senate to apologize for the destruction of Saguntum, to make reparations, and to give you over for trial.

"Since there is clearly no support for giving you over to the Romans, Hanno has called for you to be banished from the city, like some common traitor."

Not just banished, Imre wrote, but banished so far away that Hannibal's name would never be spoken in Carthage again. She went on:

"This awful man was shouted down in the Senate, which is nearly unanimous in support of war with Rome. However, you should know that there are those who await any misstep on your part and who will pounce like a vulture on a wounded lion if such should occur. So, my lord and master, be careful…"

Hannibal thought of his wife's deep green eyes, the way they flashed against her black hair and dark skin. He re-read the letter. *When you go to war, there are two wars— the one against your enemy and the other in your own city, against those who would use the war to further their grievances.*

He remembered Alexander the Great. It took three victories to bring the entire Persian empire to its knees. Three victories on Italian soil and the Roman federation will collapse. The past will be fixed, the debt paid to his father.

Later, he coaxed one piece of papyrus from Solyphos and wrote:

"To my dear wife: You will be my eyes and ears, and you have my heart as well. I carry you and my son—my heir– with me on this journey.

When I return, Carthage's future will be restored
and our son will inherit the Barca name with pride."

He wanted to write something of the uncertainty he felt,
how he missed her and longed to see his son, about the vast-
ness of what lay ahead, but wasn't sure what to say. Or even if
he should say it. So he sealed the letter, thinking: *three victories,
then home.*

There was so much preparation—they were to leave the next day
with the rest of the army– that Nahatum scarcely thought of his
mother, nor did he notice that several days had gone by without
his bringing water or healing herbs to the coughing lady.

He didn't think about either until he stumbled upon a
procession while coming back from an errand for Hannibal far
from his tent, so far that he had taken a short cut past that dark
place where the dead were burnt or buried, depending on the
custom of the mourners. Various tattered pieces of cloth, often
ripped from a shirt or tunic, hung limply from bare tree limbs;
pitiful reminders of the dead in the day's drizzle.

A group of men crossed the foggy, cold meadow. They
seemed to be carrying a white log on their shoulders and when
Nahatum stopped to look more carefully, he recognized the
richly beaded woven headdress of the chieftain with the club
hand, walking slowly alongside an older, white- bearded man
in robes. Several men with shovels had been digging a hole
in the ground, their green and red Iberian tunics dark with
sweat even in the cool day. The boy stepped closer. Several men
scowled, but the chieftain clearly recognized Nahatum, seemed
almost to have expected him.

The coughing lady's body—waxy, lifeless face exposed–was wrapped in the white cotton and lay on the ground next to the dark hole. Her green shawl was tied at her waist around the cotton, as if it were a sash. She looked relieved from her pain, and Nahatum was thankful for that, but her face no longer seemed her own.

He became dizzy, took a step to feel the ground beneath him. She was no longer the woman who had smiled at him from her regal platform, carried by attendants, on the trail so many weeks ago. For Nahatum, she was now the possession of the spirits and demons that had raged within her. And that even now inhabited her. Yes, he saw– he was staring not at the women, but at the very creature that had killed the woman, and taken possession of her body, that had driven the life out of her body.

A name for this demon formed itself in his frantic mind: Lizard Skin, death from the Underworld that roamed the earth and turned living bodies into waxy, terrifying, leathery husks. His stomach threatened to come up through his mouth and for a horrible moment the boy feared collapsing on the ground.

"Her shade is at rest." The scraggly white-bearded man chanted. He turned to the craggy- faced one, embracing him. "Her shade returns to the Underworld in peace." Several men lowered the body—that thing– into the ground, then shoveled dirt on top while others chanted in their heavily accented Iberian. Crows cackled in the trees across the meadow, mocking the chanting. The chief dropped onto his knees, ignoring the mud on his woven pants and tunic, and piled rocks on top of the muddy ground above his wife's grave.

A hole opened, too, inside Nahatum and he gripped at his stomach. He knew then that his mother had died, a long time ago, taken by Lizard Skin. She was never coming back. *Stupid wolf child!* Accusations raged in his mind: She had died alone, uncared for, in the dark forest. Those who die uncared for cannot have a spirit at ease, a life completed. Their shade wandered the earth, uneasily. His mother had said as much when she was alive. Was there something he could have done?, he wondered Was there some way he had failed this woman who had tried to protect him to the very last?

The Iberians trailed away past him, the pile of stone complete. The drizzle turned into a steady rain. Nahatum picked up a rock and hurled it at the bevy of crows in the far- away trees. Then another. Crows startled, cackled protest, flew into the air. Rock after rock. He was a Balearic sling- thrower, smashing Roman heads. He was an elephant crushing helpless bodies beneath his massive feet.

Then the crows were gone. He was alone. The rain pelted him, the wind whipped at his face. He was a slingthrower no more, just a boy—cold, nose running—standing in the mud. The sky had filled with black clouds. The fury would explode him. He reached down, picked up a sharp stick, pushed it into his arm, near the burn mark that reminded him of Hannibal. The pain calmed him. His arm ached and he quieted as the storm washed him in its merciless rain. His mother dead, her shade angry at him, her unreliable son. Lizard Skin roamed the world.

He began to run. Hard, fast. To his only refuge: back to Hannibal's army. To the enormous elephants. Even to giant Gisgo. To the thousands of fighters with their many weapons. And most of all, to Hannibal. Hannibal would protect him. Hannibal was a force—the only force that could defeat the very Underworld itself.

He couldn't wait to leave. A part of this army. Near to Hannibal.

Chapter 3

The Emperor of Snow

Iberian Pyrennes, Gaul, Swiss Alps
Late summer- fall, 218 BC

Some images from the first days of the march north that Na-hatum would remember years later:

Climbing into the back of a supply wagon and scrambling atop wooden crates and sacks of flour, beans, dates, oranges. The sweet fragrance of peaches mixed with the tartness of lemons and burlap's bristly smell. The crack of the driver's whip as the wagon jerked forward and the march began.

In the light of the setting sun, a last look at three women with long knives carving a dead goat into pieces. A piercing thought of his mother.

The elephants, swaying gray giants, forty of them, filling the road ahead of the army. Walking as close as he dared to the massive, rippled legs, as if dodging tree trunks. Their eyes. a rich dark brown, illuminated with a flickering light, like flames. They would flap their ears at times, some silently, some with a sound like hands clapping. Walking near them, he felt a throbbing in his chest as if his body could hear the rumbling from their stomachs, like echos inside a dark cave. Once an elephant's tail brushed across his face, the great animal's rippled hide reddened with Iberian dust.

Egyptian infantrymen, each with a single long braid falling from his shaven head to his shoulders, charcoal smudge under their eyes to protect from the searing sun. Coal black African warriors who seemed to lope rather than walk, long spears held at their sides. Iberian tribesmen, dark hair to their shoulders, round wooden shields lashed to their backs, long wooden staffs moving as they marched.

The Egyptian warriors rubbed their hammered bronze necklaces from time to time, mumbling in their strange language. Listening, Nahatum picked out the word, "amulet." Amulet: he imagined their gods sitting on carved wooden chairs, pleased by the soft sound of fingers stroking metal.

The Iberian plain spread out ahead. Rocky, dry soil interrupted by patches of tall brush.

He remembered, too, the day an exhausted horseman— dusty sash of Carthaginian purple around his chest– caught up to the army with a message. War had been formally declared. Carthage had refused to hand Hannibal over to Rome. Standing in the Senate at Carthage the senior member of the Roman delegation had held out two fists, one for war and the other for peace. Which did Carthage choose? Defiantly, the *suffete*, the chief magistrate of the Senate, replied that it was Rome's choice. "We choose war," the Roman replied. "And we accept it," the Carthaginian senators cried out.

A mob of soldiers at a narrow river bridge, yelling at each other in a dozen languages about who would cross first. Hannibal rode up and, from atop his grand horse, created an orderly march. "Enough arguing! We fight as one or we all die alone." The crowd cheered.

As they approached the foothills of the mountains, whiskered mountain goats perched in the low branch, their heads reaching up with greedy teeth to rip spiky leaves from the higher limbs.

The dark-haired slingthrowers from the Balearic Islands walking along the side of the road, hefting rounded chunks of granite and shale, dropping some, storing others in long woven sacks dangling from their waists. One man quickly stood, sling spinning gracefully above his head, the brown blur whirring like a swarm of bees. A sudden snap of the hand sent the rock speeding toward a goat far off across the meadow, standing in a low tree. The rock smashed into the goat's head and it fell heavily to the ground, enough food to last for days.

Hundreds of snow geese filled the sky one day—enormous birds with broad wings, long necks extended, white bellies lined with black obsidian stripes that ran along the underside of their wings. Looking down the rugged switchbacked mountain trail, the line of the army extended as far as he could see. All of life seemed to be moving north toward Gaul.

Solyphos, the old Greek, wandered off the trail into the oak trees, collecting gall- nuts, tattered cotton bag at his side.

And, finally, after weeks of threading their way through the mountains, a cheer came from way ahead as the boy labored with the cooks and wagons up a steep, narrow embankment toward a rocky ridge. He scrambled forward. At the top, men embraced, pointed, or just stared ahead, a long, ragged line of jubilant soldiers along the ledges and atop tall boulders. To the north, the distant snow-capped peaks glittered in the bright sunlight above the mountain pass before them. To his south, the Great Sea crashed upon a rocky, cratered shoreline. Tiny gulls swooped low over the frothing, deep blue water.

Behind them lay the vast plains of Iberia. Ahead far below stretched the massive green forests of Gaul, and the boy thought for a moment that the entire world was covered with trees. The soft white morning clouds created floating dots of shadow among the color, so that the land itself looked like the speckled fur of a huge, sleeping animal.

Damn helmet!

Hannibal grabbed for the ridiculous plumed helmet, just managing to keep it on his head. He sat precariously atop tall Sirius, the massive lead elephant, as they lurched through yet another Gaulish village. His thighs burnt from clutching the elephant's neck and he was in dismal danger of sliding right off the beast. Another bump; his hands found the leather strap circling the animal's shoulders. He grabbed at the holstered mallet that held the pointed metal stake used to stop runaway elephants in battle. The only way to stop them: pound a stake through their heads. He was tempted to do so to Sirius right then. Why, he wondered, had he agreed to have Indoi, the elephant's handler, walk alongside rather than ride on top as well? Solyphos had insisted: no cushioned litter to sit in, no handler. Just you atop the elephant will be the most dramatic, the old Greek assured him. *Well, how dramatic will it be when I fall off in front of all the Gauls I'm trying to impress?*

The elephant's massive gray body slouched and shook along the narrow forest trail. The beast never stopped, just kept moving. Hannibal shifted on the broad, rippled back, this time hand grasping wiry hair thick as straw. His back hurt. He hadn't been on an elephant for years. His father had insisted he learn to ride them. Hamilcar had wanted his son to understand how they dominated the landscape, how archers atop the animal could shoot at will in all directions, why undisciplined fighters would break and run at the sight. *To appreciate their use, father, is one thing; to actually ride the beast is another.*

Still, the effect in Gaul was undeniable. Ferocious village guard dogs bred from wolves howled with fear and cowered in the back of their pens when the elephants marched through villages. The Gaulish tribesmen— stout red-haired men with skin white as egret's feathers— ran away when they saw regal Hannibal astride Sirius at the head of the army. They kept referring to him as King Hannibal. He'd also taken Solyphos' counsel and worn a thick woven cape of royal Carthaginian purple edged with white fur along with the helmet adorned with peacock feathers sprouting from the top. He thought that he looked like one of those preening nobles in the Senate at Carthage, lolling in the marble corridors with hats woven of bird feathers of iridescent green, blue, yellow. He only put it on when Solyphos reminded him that Alexander the Great had worn a uniform of similar design when conquering Persia.

The Gauls might be terrorized by elephants, Hannibal reflected, but they'll be worthy fighters, if he could instill some discipline in them. They already feared the greed of Rome, so it had been easy to negotiate safe passage. There had been many toasts of eternal friendship between Carthage and these proud, warlike people over the past weeks, as spring turned to summer. Thousands of Gaulish warriors joined the army, adorned with eagle, owl, osprey feathers of their own, with bear and lion claws dangling from their necks, armed with thick pikes and long spears hacked from tree limbs.

Another bounce and he was almost airborne. *Feathered, yet not a bird.* He patted the elephant. *This is really happening. After all these years of planning. A war plan that Alexander the Great himself would have envied.* Hannibal allowed himself to imagine the grand history of the campaign that Solyphos would write. The Greek's work would go alongside that of Herodotus and Thucydides, books the old scribe had taught him. Solyphos could title his history, "Hannibal's Wars" or "The Wars of Hannibal."

Sirius lurched. Hannibal cursed and grabbed for the nearby elephant ear, huge as a war galley's sail.

"Boy, come here."

Nahatum ignored the sorcerer's scratchy, thin voice. He continued to walk along the trail with the rest of the army, concentrating on the raucous late afternoon sounds of the Gaullish forest—ravens, jays, the far off call of hawks, the occasional bear roaring from deep within— trying to identify familiar sounds. Every call he recognized reassured him. Even after weeks, he still felt uneasy in this strange place.

There had been spring rains, which had finally stopped, though the day remained cloudy. Ahead, he could just make out Hannibal's brilliant peacock feathered- helmet, his master atop the great Sirius.

Then, sharper this time, insistent. "Boy! Here." The stooped old man handed him a large cloth sack, half- filled. "Carry this over your shoulder."

"What is this?" Nahatum didn't want to look directly at the magician for fear of enchantment of some sort, but he wasn't going to carry a bag without knowing what was in it.

"Gall nuts, of course. Keep an eye out for them along the edge of the trail."

He'd walked a few feet when the wasps found him, buzzing around the collecting bag, bouncing heavily against his hip. He swatted a big one away and tried to assess if it was bigger, faster than the ones in Iberia. He told himself that the wasps were after the gall nuts, not him. He hoped.

Whenever the old man saw an oak tree, he hurried over, cloak flapping in the breeze, thin legs fluttering. It was late, it had been raining for days, Nahatum could feel his tiredness after tramping all day down muddy forest roads, and now Hannibal was getting further ahead. Nahatum fumed and hurried to catch up.

"Stop, boy, wait for me." The man was haggling trailside with Egyptian archers from the army for the plumage of the birds they had killed while hunting for meat.

Bundles of dead crows, hawks, owls, geese lay tied to long sticks. A treasure of meat for hungry soldiers, but the man wanted only the feathers. All five of the Egyptians wore bronze amulets around their necks, each with a different form and design.

Wasps, amulets. Nahatum knew he was around too much strange power. He wanted to get away, back to Hannibal and the mighty elephant he rode.

Solyphos sorted through a handful of crow feathers. "No good." The man threw the shimmering blue-black back feathers of a crow on the forest trail in front of the astonished hunters.

The argument continued. "I want thick, strong feathers." Solyphos told the hunter who spoke the Iberian camp language that he'd only pay for feathers from the goose, owl, swan or eagle. He wanted them to go back into the forest and bring back better feathers. The hunters shook their heads, fingered their amulets and gestured into the dark, overgrown woods.

Nahatum agreed with their fear. There was something about those woods that was different from what the boy knew back home in Iberia. He felt it particularly as the day's twilight gathered. Darker, wetter. Rotting, fallen trees, wormy soil. Forest of theDead. Could his mother's body lie somewhere in that dark place? That was an odd feeling to him: he'd always felt at home in the woods. Notthere.

He was convinced that there were unimaginable beasts in this foreign land, ready to spring at him. He wasn't sure if even the elephants—mighty Sirius– would be their equal. He hoped so. Nahatum looked at the sorcerer, haggling, and wondered how strong his powers were in this strange land.

The Egyptians kept fingering their amulets and repeating a strange word– "khatts." Solyphos sounded angry, telling them there were no "khatts" in the woods and the Egyptian who spoke the polyglot insisted that they were not going back in the darkening woods. Nahatum waited for an angry Solyphos to turn the frightened men into wasps or fish skins but all the old man did was shrug and buy two red wing feathers of a hawk. Then he turned and walked back toward the long line of march, clearly expecting the boy, and his baggage of gall nuts, to follow.

The boy hesitated to address the sorcerer, but a terrible question formed in his mind and he stuttered it out: "Sir. What are... khatts?"

Solyphos cursed. "Foolish men. I have to be so careful with my quills, with all the writing I have to do, because those men are scared to go into the woods at night. What rubbish….." Solyphos stopped mid-sentence, turned around and asked if the boy spoke Egyptian.

No.

"Then where did you learn that word?"

"I listened. Those men spoke of khatts and they rubbed those metal things around their wrists and on their necks. Amulets, they're called."

"Wolf child, you have the ears of a bat. About your eyes, I can't say, since you are always looking off into the forest or staring at the ground when you talk to me."

Solyphos explained that khatts were the Egyptian spirits of the dead. The men, ignorant and superstitious, were scared to go into the woods at night, or even as darkness slowly arrived, because they imagined the entrance to the Underworld was somewhere in these strange forests, where the spirits of the dead wandered, carrying the living back into that awful place.

Solyphos stared into the misty darkness. Nahatum barely heard the man say that there were no such things as khatts. The boy stumbled over the gall nuts that scattered where he'd dropped the sorcerer's bulging bag in his haste to flee.

Hannibal. I have to find him. Night was falling. The boy pushed past crowds of Egyptian, Iberian, African warriors rolling out blankets, men collecting damp wood for fires, an army slowly finding places to sleep for the night. He knew then that his worst fear was true: that his mother's shade wandered this shadowy, bleak land. All the way back to Hannibal the terrorized boy worried that he would trip over the rotting bones of his mother.

And then an old man on a donkey, a trader from who knew where, led his pack of mules, clanging with pots and pans and goods of all sorts, into the army camped alongside the trail in western Gaul. He let it be known that he brought news for Hannibal and was willing to sell it for the right price.

"Bring him over here," Hannibal instructed the guard who came hurrying along the trail to inform him of the arrival. "And tell Gisgo and Marhbal to leave what they are doing and join me."

"Whatever this peddler has to say better be worth my leaving my men," Gisgo announced when he joined Hannibal and Marhabal. "I was training the Gauls. They have no idea how to fight as a unit. They run forward, paying no attention to their battle line or fellow fighters, every man for themselves. The disciplined Romans will wipe them out if they try that."

Hannibal sighed. "Keep working at it, Gisgo. We have time before we meet the Romans." Gisgo nodded at Hannibal, completely ignoring Marhabal.

Just then a thin old man in tattered cloth pants and shirt, an ancient gold silk scarf wound around his neck was led up to Hannibal, guards on either side.

The threadbare gold scarf caught the sunlight, giving the trader the aspect of an exiled, wandering priest. The man looked very nervous, and stared at the ground in front of Hannibal.

How many fools have I had to entertain to get the information I need for this invasion? And here we are again. "I am told, esteemed trader, that you bring news for me."

Silence.

"Ah, I have forgotten my manners," Hannibal said evenly. "Travelers with news should be properly entertained." Wine and food were brought in and the old man came to life, putting heaping portions of the roast duck on his plate. "Jonaz, bring us some of that strange brew the Gauls are so fond of, what they call beer." Hannibal didn't like the taste, but carried kegs of it, gifts from the chieftains whose territory they passed through. The trader poured himself a beaker full; Hannibal was glad to get rid of it.

"King Hannibal, your wisdom and might is known throughout the land and I am honored to be in your presence." The trader wiped his mouth with his coat. "I am sure your strength is only surpassed by your wealth and some token would be welcome in return for the news I bring you today."

Gisgo, leaning backward against a tree, stared at the old man with eyes that beamed disdain. Hannibal murmured to Jonaz, who hurried off and soon returned with a small purse. Hannibal reached in and produced a gold coin. "I am sure, worthy trader, that the news you bring is worth itself in gold."

"You are a wise man, King Hannibal. This news, if used correctly, is worth itself in gold AND silver."

Gisgo sighed, a deep rumble. "Give him to me for a few minutes and we can save ourselves all this trouble. And the gold."

Hannibal reached in the purse and produced a small Carthaginian silver coin. "Your information better be very valuable."

The man pocketed both coins, took another piece of duck, then said: "The Romans are but a day's march from here and they are looking for you."

"What!" exclaimed Gisgo, leaning forward.

Hannibal re-filled the trader's beaker of beer. "Tell us everything you know. Spare no detail and there will be more silver for you."

The trader told them that the Romans were frantically searching for Hannibal's disappeared army. They had first sent an army to Iberia, not knowing that Hannibal was already in Gaul. Now they had apparently landed an army on the coast, but were unsure if Hannibal was really there. The trader saw a fleet of Roman trimeres in the harbor at Massilia, Rome's ally, but a day's march away. The city was flooded with Roman troops. "It looks like there are several legions there."

"Well, well."

"Hannibal this is an opportunity for us. A surprise attack on Massilia, an easy victory," Gisgo said. Marhabal interrupted him. "My cavalry would welcome a chance to engage the Romans." Gisgo interrupted Marhabal. "This could be a test of our army. See how they do in a surprise attack, give them an early victory to build their morale. Perhaps a taste of the Romans will help the Gauls understand the importance of our fighting as a unit." Then: "This is just the kind of advantage Hamilcar would welcome."

No, he wouldn't. My father would know that an attack on Massilia would waste all the element of surprise in the invasion. By the time we arrive in Italy, the Romans will be ready for us. Still, Hannibal could feel the pressure to do something, and quickly, to strike out at the Romans, after those weeks of marching and boredom. He knew that there was no better break from boredom for a warrior than to sack a city.

A commotion interrupted the talk. "The Romans are at Massilia!" Pushing aside a flustered guard, Barnabar, the great chief of the Celtiberians, walked up the trail to where Hannibal and the others sat. "Let us go quickly now, Hannibal, and destroy the sleeping Romans." He tossed his cloth bag of teeth from one hand to another, as if anticipating filling it with Roman contributions.

Hannibal dismissed the trader, dispatching several of Marhabal's cavalrymen to ride with the man a day north, to insure that the sly old trader didn't now ride south to sell his news about Hannibal to the Romans.

Then he turned to the new problem at hand: the peddler's news had spread through the army with the speed of a leopard, and a hasty gathering of chiefs had arrived trail-side behind Barnabar, pressing Hannibal, wanting to know how soon they would attack the Romans.

The chiefs were drunk with the promise of the plunder they'd find amidst Massilia's storehouses of grains and cheeses and wines, their silversmiths and craftsmen. Hannibal surveyed the scene, the wine and beer being poured, Gisgo and Marhabal eager to test their men, the excited and boisterous chiefs, Barnabar gleefully tossing that awful cloth sack in the air, further stirring passions.

Hannibal knew what he had to do, and he hoped he could do it. *You have to put a stop to this celebration and tell these men that there will be no attack on Massilia.* He held his father in his mind—the formidable Hamilcar, staring down his enemies– as he rallied himself.

"Jonaz, Nahatum, pour no more wine, nor beer." He stood to his full height, surrounded by the noisy throng, which grew eerily silent when Hannibal told them his plans. The army needed to avoid a battle now at all costs. "Attacking Massilia could cost us this war. Only a decisive defeat of Roman forces in Italy will bring real victory." The scowl on Barnabar's face grew deeper as Hannibal spoke. "We must encourage the Gaulish Italian tribes and hill villages to leave their alliances with Rome and join us," Hannibal reminded them.

Again he had to bend a cluster of chiefs to his will. He knew he was speaking hurriedly and he heard his voice shaking slightly, that awful moment when a foreign god seemed to take over his words, but he kept going. "Surprise is the biggest ally we have. The Romans don't know where we are and we are not going to let them find out."

Barnabar stood against a tree, tossing that sack, and he wasted no time before speaking. "With all respect, great Hannibal, did not your father promise his army great plunder and pay during the last war and did he not fail to provide it? Did not his army rebel because his promises were not kept?"

Stay calm. Here is where passion must be controlled. What he wanted to do was to take that cloth sack of teeth and stuff it down the man's throat– let him suffocate on those he has killed. Yet a fight now in the army would be a disaster. It all could come to an end right there. He saw the murderous look on Gisgo's face, who would eagerly defend his commander's honor. Perhaps Barnabar's yelling had a useful side: Gisgo would support Hannibal if he saw him threatened by this rude tribal chieftain.

Be careful here. Turn this meeting your way. Hannibal yearned to consult Solyphos who was somewhere further back along the trail, yet he knew what his old tutor would say, what his father would say: *lead this army. Keep yourself together. Don't be swept away by your passions.*

"Illustrous Barnabar, you are chief of a great tribe, and I value your counsel.And, you have wisely advanced my point: we cannot take a small reward now and forego great riches later."

This confused the stupid man, as intended, Hannibal was pleased to note. While Barnabar was speechless, Hannibal spoke to the whole group. "One lesson I have learned from my father is to have no mercy on those who mutiny. They will die a horrible death." The sack stopped moving. "A disciplined army like ours will find all the plunder it wants in Italy. Great Barnabar does not need to take a pittance now as a reward, wasting time plundering a small town like Massilia when great riches await every man here in Rome. That is what we have come for: the plunder of Italy."

The army cheered at that. Perhaps less so than in Iberia weeks earlier when everything seemed possible, but cheers nonetheless. Gisgo and Marhabal nodded; they would follow their commander. As would the rest of the army. *I've done it. Now all I have to do is find our way to Italy.*

The next day they marched north—away from the Romans at Massilia, along the banks of the broad Rhoneus river and towards the vast wasteland known as the Endless Mountains.

That night, Nahatum startled awake from under a tree near where Hannibal slept.

He heard something out there, rustling in the woods. An owl swept across the trail, gliding silently as if right for him, so close the boy ducked, his hands protecting him from razor claws and a knife-like beak. A sharp hoot as it passed, wings spread like a dark shadow over him, and then it was gone, followed by an animal's piercing death cry, held in claw to be eaten alive on a nearby tree branch. The boy yelled out in response, a rock rising from his stomach to throat. He felt the presence of his mother's angry shade.

He picked at the burn mark on his wrist with a fingernail, a familiar scar now, to calm himself. He dug until there was blood, and the thickness in his chest began to loosen.

The Rhoneus river—broad and fast-flowing—stood in front of them after days of marching. "Truly the widest river I have seen," said Marhabal, standing on the shore next to Hannibal, studying the deep, swift current, fed by days of rain. "Faster and broader even than the mighty Wadi Mejerda, don't you think?"

Hannibal smiled at the mention of the majestic river that flowed out of the mountains and down to Carthage. A thick mist rose from the water.

They'd need rafts, cut and fallen trees to float men across. Hardly any of the men, he wagered, could swim. He was a strong swimmer himself. Marhabal's cavalrymen and their horses were at the water's edge and, further down, the elephants were enjoying themselves in the shallows, spraying showers of water over their bodies with their trunks. Crossing should be a straightforward, if time-consuming task.

A ruckus broke out on the far shore, just visible across the broad expanse of water. Loud, surly tribesmen were gathering, shouting threats, shooting arrows, waving spears, and pounding on drums. These are the Volcae, "a foul people," one of their guides informed Hannibal.

"And not too bright, wasting arrows that fall harmlessly in the water," intoned Gisgo. The man, Hannibal knew, would hurl himself at the Volcae if he could get at them, tossing those poor villagers aside by the handful. "I wouldn't want to try to cross while they are shooting at us," Hannibal suggested. "They are making a point." Arrows splashed mid-river like dying swans.

Soon, thousands of the men of the Volcae tribe had gathered to oppose them.

Then a boat appeared out of the mist, carrying what looked to be three elders—each wearing a foxskin fur hat– and poled by four stout tribesmen. The fur of the hats extended loosely down over their ears, creating an appearance of large bushes sprouting from both sides of their heads.

Hannibal welcomed the emissaries graciously. They announced, grandly, that they have brought demands to insure safe passage across the river.

"Well, let us talk this over with the respect and courtesy my visitors deserve," Hannibal said, though he noted that the elders displayed none themselves. They nodded curtly, and followed Hannibal from the river's edge, approaching the food and drink quickly being laid out for them under a large tent as if it was simply their due.

There was little talk, besides a growing list of demands. The elders drank the wine, ate the food, and barely spoke to Hannibal, as common courtesy and respect would have required. Their demands were substantial and the amount—of silver and gold, of weapons, of grain, of butter and cheese, things the army hardly had in their supply wagons– kept going up as they saw the size of the army and the endless line of wagons and the number of men marching down the trail toward the river's edge.

The fact that these men wanted as much from him as they could get wasn't a shock to Hannibal. Yet as he sat under the tent awning, looking out at the river, watching the three elders consume his meat, olives, an entire bowl of Gisgo's beloved figs, a full cask of the foul Gaulish beer, Hannibal felt a rising anger, one that he didn't resist. He offered them a purse of gold shekels– princely tribute. They wanted more. They wanted more gold, and spears and shields and fur clothing and....the list seemed endless.

He concluded that he would give these people nothing. And worse.

He called for Jonaz, who hurried up to the tent. With a flourish, he said to his squire, "Have the cooks arrange a grand supper for us all tonight. We will have a celebration to assure our safe passage." He listed the fine cheeses and wine and smoked meats that the Gauls had provided along their route. Smiling at the elders, he announced loudly to Jonaz: "I want to give these people a time they remember."

The elders smiled back.

While the feasting was going on that night, Hannibal stepped outside the tent, where Marhabal was waiting. "At first light tomorrow, take a picked force of your cavalry and ride several miles upriver. Camp there tomorrow night. The next day you are to ford the river and remain on the far shore. When you see a bonfire from this shore, fall upon the Volcae men assembled against us."

Marhabal smiled in the evening darkness, his olive skin illuminated by a campfire outside the tent. He clearly welcomed the assignment. "I don't need a large force to scatter these people. Perhaps one hundred riders."

Laughter and merriment came from inside the tent; the Volcae elders, having drunken mugs of the Gaul's beer, were singing a song.

Hannibal had no smile to return his friend. "Take five hundred riders and kill as many of the men as you can. Spare only the women and children."

"Are you sure?" Marhabal asked, the smile disappearing.

"I want this rabble to know what happens when they try to force tribute from us. And besides, it will do your men some good to have a chance for spoils and looting. They can keep whatever they find of value in that village, as long as the women and children are not hurt; make sure of that. Some spoils will help morale and spur the army to cross faster to join in on the looting. A small gift after turning away from Massilia." He gestured toward the drunken elders in the tent. "Make sure to remember those arrogant ones in the fur hats."

Marhabal smiled—grimly this time– and nodded.

The next day, the emissaries, clearly tired from their night of partying, had not budged in their demands. Hannibal told them that he needed to think about how best to provide them the tribute they deserve. "I will see you receive such before tomorrow is out." He sent the emissaries across the river back to their homes. "Rest safely in your beds, and tomorrow you will have my answer."

As the day dawned, the Volcae on the opposite shore cheered, beating their drums and hooting and hollering at the sight of the bonfire being built by Hannibal's men. Then came a deep, rising, pounding sound. Hoofbeats, hundreds of them. The Volcae first pointed up the riverbank, then some fled, into the forest, down the riverbank, into the river itself, where they flailed in the deep water.

"I gave them a choice, did I not?" Hannibal observed to Gisgo, as they watched across the river: "Those who choose not to drown, choose to be cut down by the sword." Marhabal's cavalry broke upon the panic-striken tribesmen like a terrible thunderstorm, the horses in full stride, their legs extended, the horsemen with swords out, swinging in the air.

Gisgo watched the performance of the Numidians carefully, saying nothing. Even at that distance, the two of them could see mounted Numidian archers drop their reins at full gallop, aiming with great accuracy into the panicked mass of tribes men.

"Impressive, the Numidians, don't you think?", Hannibal finally asked his infantry commander.

Gisgo shrugged. "Against lightly armed, disorganized tribesmen, my Lord. We'll see how they do when confronted by a Roman Legion."

The boy watched the destruction on the far shore with hungry eyes. He recognized the red caftans of Marhabal's cavalry as the men fell upon the Volcae. The pounding of horse's hooves. The trampled people. Flashing swords slicing off heads, arms.

Spears, arrows poking out of fleeing people. This was what it was like to deliver death. To be the conveyer of death, not the one who feared it. He feasted on the sight.

This is the power he had been waiting for. Hannibal's army displaying its might.

What force. Hannibal magic: the power to destroy whatever was in his path. The boy couldn't wait to get to the other side to see the dead up close and stayed close to Hannibal.

The army streamed eagerly across the river in endless clumps of men balancing awkwardly onto makeshift rafts. While a few poled along, the others clung tightly to their conveyance. The horses were led into the river, better swimmers than their riders. The cattle, too, swam, and the supply wagons were carefully floated across.

Further down the shoreline the elephants posed a distinct problem. Nahatum heard them trumpeting, announcing their refusal to wade into the wide and fast- flowing water. Their handlers coaxed and beat the animals, all to no avail. The enormous beasts stood stolidly, and did not move. He hurried along after Hannibal who ran down the shore, eager to get the animals moving.

Hannibal ordered elephant- sized rafts built. One for each elephant, to guard against animals moving and tipping the raft. Logs were lashed together; handlers waited on each raft for their elephant, to pole them across. Still the elephants balked, refusing to leave solid ground to walk onto the wobbly constructions.

Gisgo observed the scene from nearby where he was supervising the infantry crossing. "I can bring some men with lances to force them on those rafts," he yelled to Hannibal.

Hannibal shook his head. He called for Indoi, the lead elephant handler. "Sirius is the lead elephant, correct? All the others follow him."

The little turbaned man nodded his head.

"Bring Sirius forward. Now, cover all the rafts with deep layers of grass and dirt while they're anchored tightly to the shore."

Soldiers fell to the task. When Sirius walked onto his raft and contentedly nibbled at its carpet of fresh grass, the others soon followed onto theirs. Forty rafts, forty elephants, were soon being poled across.

Hannibal magic, the boy knew. Nothing defeats him. Finally, with the bulk of his army on the far shore, Hannibal stripped off his clothes and handed them to Nahatum, telling the boy to carry them across on a raft. After Nahatum poled across, Hannibal dove in and swam effortlessly across with powerful strokes.

At the far shore, Nahatum awaited with dry clothes and a towel. Dead bodies everywhere, faces frozen in panic, dead fish eyes. Flies had arrived and seemed to prefer the eyes. Then Hannibal emerged from the river.

For a moment, they were alone on the shore; it seemed like everyone, including Jonaz, was searching through the dead bodies for whatever plunder they could find.

Hannibal toweled off, looking back at the river. Droplets of water clung to his dark chest. "My father drowned in a river like this," he said, and Nahatum wondered if his master was talking to him. "Carried away by the current while my brother and I stood helpless on the shore, trying to fend off an ambush by an arrogant, rebellious tribe that wouldn't negotiate."

After a day of looting and feasting, the march continued. Towering granite cliffs scraped the sides of the lumbering wagons as the army headed north along the river.

Flowering vines draped the cliffs, filling the air with succulent, warm fragrances. Some days they passed through ravines so narrow that they splashed along with one foot in the river.

Nahatum liked the feel of his new pike in his hand as he walked. Thick and sturdy, it made a satisfying click- clack as it hit river stones with every step.

He'd decided that it would be good to have a weapon. Borrowing a knife from the cooks, he'd carved a thick branch in the style he had observed among the Gauls, decorating it with a cormorant feather. The pike, he reasoned, would bring him good luck—or at least the ability to defend himself—if he met a khatt at night in these strange forests.

It was not only khatts the boy feared. Every day the boy watched Jonaz invoke Ba'al Shammon's love and mercy to provide the army safe passage. The boy had tried to ignore Jonaz's impatience and anger.

Yet much now seemed to be the fault of "the wolf child": when the army made slow progress, the summer days starting to wane, Jonaz lost no chance to remark that "the wolf child" had brought them bad luck. When the hunters brought back less and less fresh meat, Jonaz complained to the cooks about the curse that the wolf child had brought to the army. The toothless cook sometimes defended Nahatum, but the truth was that food supplies were shorter now, the cattle almost gone. There was a constant search among soldiers for omens of good or ill. "The wolf boy's presence has angered Ba'al Shammon," Jonaz said over and over, his face trembling with outrage. He never said this within Hannibal's earshot, of course. But the boy heard. Yes, he concluded, good to have a weapon.

They smelled the Endless Mountains before they saw them. A cold, lifeless scent that mingled with the airy nectars of the hill country. Far ahead, the mountains seemed to cover the sky. Thick fingers of ice reached down from the peaks into the higher valleys. The ice glistened blue-white in the morning sun, clawing at the life in the warmer valleys below where mountain flowers bloomed and animals breathed their hopes of finding prey, their fears of becoming prey.

Tempers were short and the men now marched with increasing hunger. In those mountains there was no one to forage from, or even to sell them wheat or cheese or meat. They passed few villages, only the occasional wooden hut built several feet off the ground on thick stone foundations so as not to be buried in the winter snow that piled up higher than a man's head.

Rumors abounded in the army predicting early snows, cloudy days bringing the winds of winter, freezing temperatures. Even the reassurance of the native guides did not reassure the jittery soldiers, who noted that all of the guides had brought sturdy bearskin robes with them as well as boots lined with wolf fur. Who was to say that the snow would not come early as punishment from whatever gods ruled these mountains? The Egyptians spent all their time on the trail muttering in their strange language and rubbing their amulets.

Further on they marched. The land itself seemed twisted and inhuman, all jagged angles, sudden drop-offs and ravines. Thick mist arrived and shrouded the trail, only to disappear in sharp sunlight. Blink while walking and you could be mid-air. At night the wind moaned through canyons, by day the army marched past strange rock formations– a horse, a bear, a lion, a badger, an auroch, trapped in rock.

The story sprouted in the army that this inhuman land was inhabited by strange beings different even than the Gauls, who were themselves strange enough, with their torrent of odd sounds and their white skin and red hair, as if spawned from different seed than the warriors from Africa or Egypt or Persia. Soldiers reported seeing misshapen beings darting among far canyons and high up on mountain ridges, beings twisted into strange shapes, perhaps humans whose souls had been stolen and imprisoned in the rocks of the mountains themselves. Nahatum became convinced he'd actually seen Lizard Skin several times, though he told no one. He kept his pike close and hurried back after helping Solyphos with his bags in order to stay close to Hannibal in the march.

The boy was determined to be ready whenever whatever accursed thing it was that lived in those mountains revealed itself.

Hannibal's feet ached. He marched on foot now, the elephants far behind. It was important to demonstrate that the army's fate was his as well. Besides he'd never ride an elephant through these mountains– the beasts swung so far over the edge of rocky trails that their bellies hung right over drop-offs so deep he couldn't even see the bottom. *Yet the elephants followed their handlers, Barnabar be damned.* Hannibal chuckled. The enormous beasts' thick, jointed feet were extraordinarily nimble.

I wish my men were as nimble along these mountain trails. We are moving too slowly. He could feel the chill in the August air and he hoped his maps and his guides were trustworthy. *Are they?* He had hired the guides as he marched through Gaulish villages; the chiefs who sent thousands of their warriors also vouched for the guides they provided. Yet could the guides lead him into some blind canyon, only to then have the Gauls themselves turn on him? A pang seized Hannibal's chest. *I could be leading this army into the greatest ambush in history, greater even than the one that befell the Egyptian king Ramesses the Great in his war with the Hittites. What a terrible fate to be known for.* The guides could sell his head to the Romans. What a price they'd pay.

He became aware how immensely far from home he was. How different from Carthage, this land of cold canyons, sheer cliffs, fierce peaks that defeat the very sun itself. In Carthage, the sky formed an azure blue bowl over the land. The golden sunlight spread over the furrowed farmland that stretched miles from the city. And what was his wife Imre is doing at this very moment? And what of his son young Hamilcar, named after Hannibal's father, now six months older?

More than once he'd noticed a stone formation that reminded him in shape of the Byrsa, the great central citadel of Carthage, built of yellow-flecked Numidian marble; the marble glowed like wildflowers when it caught the morning sunlight. *If you remember correctly. It's been years since you've been there and now you're homesick?* Often visiting Carthage as an adult, he'd felt almost foreign-born, as much– or more– Iberian than Carthaginian.

So, who was he? Where was he? He was lost, that is what—and where– he was. If lost means not knowing where you are, then he was lost. Forty thousand men and ten thousand horse and forty elephants and fat Barnabar, king of his Iberian tribesmen, who would turn on him in a flash—eager to add teeth from the "great Hannibal" to his cloth bag.

Hannibal stopped so abruptly on the trail that Jonaz practically walked into him. Further behind, the boy stood patiently, holding that ragged pike he had somehow found for himself. Hannibal ordered his squire to go to his supply wagon and fetch the box with his maps.

They set up a little table in an outcropping just off the trail and Hannibal sat in the carved wooden folding chair studying his maps, just to be sure. He rubbed his hands together, rubbed the parchment, running his hand over it, careful not to smudge any of the carefully drawn lines, as if testing its validity by feel. The three guides came running from ahead on the trail. The tallest one, the most experienced, sat with him, explained.

We are here, we will be there. Hannibal studied him, looking him in the eye. The man did not blink, but his eyes betrayed nervousness. Nervous because he hid a secret or because Hannibal, the great King, was studying him?

The army hadn't entirely forgiven him for avoiding the Romans near Massilia and there was talk that he was afraid to fight them. Hannibal's heard the rumors: he can destroy a Volcae village, but he marches away from the Romans.

He yearned to be back on flat ground, where he knew what to look for when a fight was at hand, where he could figure out the best terrain for battle. In these mountains, he didn't know really what form an attack could take, nor exactly where it might come from, and he didn't like to be such a target, known to his attackers, without the attackers known to him.

Across the trail, the boy was poking at the limestone wall, watching him. "Nahatum, come here." The boy hurried over. "I see you have found a pike."

"Yes, sir. Not found. I carved it myself." He stood about a head lower than Hannibal and looked thinner than when they started. *Still, when full grown he will be solid.* He considered asking if the boy was hungry, perhaps finding him some dried meat from the supply wagon, but that would only make his life harder. Jonaz would never forgive the boy for that.

"I see. And, you are ready for a fight? If one should come upon us here in these mountains."

"Yes, Sir. This is a thick pike." He held it forward for Hannibal to see, pointing to the rough carvings he had made in to the wood. They appeared to be birds, and was that a feather scratched out in the grain? Hannibal wanted to smile at the sight; something lightened.

"We continue our march." The assembled men in the rocky outcropping jumped to their feet and set off. Quickly down the dusty trail, Hannibal urged them. We will catch up with the forward guard, find our dear friend Marhabal. He laughed now to himself as he walked. *What a wonder: the boy's readiness to face whatever comes upon us in these mountains. Try to do the same.*

For days they marched through curving canyons. The elephants moved in their swaying long lines, trunks sometimes holding the tails of the one in front or resting on another's back. When they stood, waiting, in the line of march, they flapped their ears, making that sound like hands clapping.

During a day of rain, the boy watched an elephant stand patiently on the mountain trail, head held high, ears flat against his neck, as the rain pelted his back and ran off his wrinkled hide in little rivers. The rain had soaked the animal's ruddy skin to a deep purple. Carthaginian purple, the boy insisted to himself. A cold rain, a harbinger of snow, one of the Gauls claimed. At night it was cold enough that the boy, along with everyone else, clustered around flickering campfires. The boy's search for gall nuts had long ago been replaced by a daily search for firewood. But where to look? The timidity of their fires was a constant source of complaint, and Jonaz even beat him once for returning with nothing but scrawny scrub wood to burn. They had marched way past trees worthy of burning.

The cold began to leech into their bones.

Gisgo was unhappy. And gloomy, Hannibal noted. Not a good sign. "These strange shapes and forms...."

"What are you talking about?," Hannibal asked from across their campfire.

Gisgo kicked at the tiny flames with his leather boots, as if a beating would make the fire burn warmer. Without answering, Gisgo turned to the boy, leaning against the canyon wall: "Can you not find some firewood somewhere amidst all these rocks, some bent, malformed tree in these accursed mountains?

He pushed the boy past Solyphos, sitting and staring into the embers, and out into the dark, as if there was a forest of dry wood just beyond the flat platform of rocks behind him. More likely, Hannibal guessed, he hoped the boy would fall off a ledge, as several men had this week, standing up to piss at night, walking a few feet from their blankets, and disappearing into the abyss. Just yesterday Gisgo complained about how slowly the boy brought lunch on a stop along the trail. As if everyone wasn't hungry and tired.

Hannibal kept an eye on the boy, who seemed able to find his way. He wanted to ask again what strange shapes and forms his gloomy infantry commander was talking about, but the cold sapped his curiosity.

The boy returned, clutching an armful of dung bricks and arranged them so as to burn most easily in the fire that remains. He had mastered the skill of making fine bricks out of horse, cattle, elephant manure, every day collecting, then drying, whatMarhabal's horses and Indoi's elephants had produced. The cattle were now gone.

"We are making fires from shit," announced Gisgo. He kicked at one of the smoldering bricks. "And the smell is particularly foul."

The infantry commander, Hannibal noted to himself, was perhaps the one most experienced in this matter. Making fires from dung bricks was an old trick; Gisgo had used them before, on campaigns in Iberia and North Africa. Gisgo's smelled shit, as it were, all over Carthage's empire, fighting for Hamilcar and now for Hamilcar's son.

Something else was bothering the veteran and Hannibal studied the man to figure out what that was.

"What kind of dung is this?" asked Marhabal, picking up a brick, sniffing it. The boy, who seemed to have become an expert on the subject, examined one and proclaimed it manure from the elephants.

"Camel dung is far superior for making fires." Marhabal adjusted his woolen Numidian djellabah, a long, loose-fitting, hooded robe well-suited for the cold mountains, and extolled the virtues of sweet- smelling, long burning camel shit. Gisgo's mouth looked as if he would grind his own teeth into dust. Solyphos suggested that there might be problems with the digestion of the elephants, as well as the horses, given how meager their diet is up here. "Rotten hay, rotten manure."

The boy worked hard at the fire, poking and blowing and coaxing it. The bricks finally caught, giving off their smoldering heat and light.

"Some of the men wanted to use a supply wagon for fire-wood yesterday," observed Marhabal. "Chop it up."

"Your Numidians…" snorted Gisgo.

"Actually, they were some of your infantry. They'd approached my men to destroy one of the wagons carrying the remaining hay for our horses."

Gisgo made a rumbling sound, looked apologetically at Hannibal. "I'll march with the men tomorrow, keep an eye on them." He scanned the far cliffs as if also keeping an eye on something else.

"What shapes?" repeated Solyphos, looking at Gisgo. "What signs were you talking about before?"

Hannibal felt gratitude for the presence of the wise Greek.

The fire gave off some light now, and the boy leaned back looking satisfied, then scurried over to his usual place several steps behind Hannibal.

"All around," gestured Gisgo. "Look there, does that not look like a horse entrapped in the rock." He pointed at a rock formation. "See, there. The rock top of that granite boulder is a horse's head, and there are the stone ears and its hideous distorted face, there, as if the animal were in pain." Gisgo pointed to two protuberances that resembled a horses' front legs, "the whole thing twisted, as if the poor beast was trying to leap, kick, free from the rock."

There was an uncertain nod of agreement from Jonaz.

Solyphos squinted into the darkness. "Can't see anything in this light." He wrapped a bearskin around himself, and stood up, waving away Hannibal's efforts to help. He walked over to the cliff face and tapped on it with his knife, chipped off a few pieces. "Limestone. All around us. Not a horse to be seen."

Gisgo snorted. "I don't care what you say the rock is made of. I have seen horses, bears, cattle shapes in these rocks. What if this stone trapped the spirit of animals....and people? Ate their spirit." His voice dropped even lower, more ominous. "What if there are beings entombed in these rocks?"

Jonaz looked around hastily and Hannibal noticed the boy clutching his pike.

Marhabal looked as if he wanted to laugh out loud.

"Nonsense. There is a physical cause for these shapes..." Solyophos sat down slowly, heavily, with a sigh, and it was impossible now for Hannibal not to see him as an old man, gaunt and withered. Back in New Carthage his tutor once was vital and robust and could throw a javelin farther than Hannibal was ever able. When he taught Hannibal and his brother Hasdrubal Greek and Latin the young Solyphos had insisted that his privileged students read the plays of Sophocles and Euripides, the philosophy and science of Aristotle and the histories of Herodotus. There were times when the youthful Hannibal had confessed to his tutor that he wished he had been born Greek (and had Solyphos for a father, though young Hannibal never said that part) and Solyphos had kindly told him that the wondrous white city of Carthage was the envy of the world. He had much to be proud of, Solyphos reassured his adoring student.

With a shock, Hannibal thought: *this expedition will kill Solyphos.* If not these mountains, then Italy. Solyphos must know he cannot survive and, oh, how Hannibal wanted the man to. He wanted Solyphos to write the histories.

Hannibal's arm began to itch. The nights were so cold. He missed the orange trees of Iberia and the fragrant eucalyptus of Carthage.

Jonaz's spot was empty, but the squire soon returned with a bag of dried meat and a sack of wine. Gisgo reached into the bag. Jonaz read his mind: "Figs are gone." Gisgo stared at

Nahatum as if that too was the boy's fault. The wine was passed around in its goatskin.

Jonaz spoke, hesitantingly. "If I may say, Lord, the men are wondering if their dead relatives are entombed in these rocks, whether we are marching closer to the entrance to the Underworld."

Solyphos sighed. "You sound, squire, as if you have already been sipping from the goatskin."

Jonaz's face tensed. "You can mock me, but yesterday I saw rocks up on the heights that were shaped and twisted into a form that might well have been my dead father."

Solyphos stared at him. "Perhaps the air of these mountains has interfered with our thoughts and concentration," the scholar- scribe finally replied. Then he wrapped himself in two blankets and turned away, as did Hannibal, each seeking whatever troubled sleep they could find.

The guide, tall and unusually thin for a Gaul, stared ahead into the mountain valley, squinting uncomfortably into the wind, like a spindly, useless mountain tree. Nahatum, standing behind him and Hannibal, wished he could know exactly what he saw.

To the boy, the valley ahead looked hardly different than all the others they had marched through, as strange and otherworldly as any of the others, the trail lined with low, spiky outgrowths huddling against the granite cliffs. Above them, high ledges promised more wind and gravelly plateaus leading to where exactly? He could hardly tell one place from another in this land without markers or boundaries.

"This is the territory of the Allobroges." Useless Mountain Tree's voice was low, grave. "The mountain people. Sullen, unfriendly. An evil land."

Still they marched– the thousands of them– men, horses, no more cattle or sheep and just a few remaining goats, and the elephants, trunks swinging rhythmically as they walked, as to signal their quiet determination. Silver ribbons of water rushed through deeper canyons far below. A thin, endless string of an army. With all the loops and bends in the trail, those in the vanguard often lost sight of the main body, which usually could not see the rear guard.

The boy, up near the front, ready to respond to Hannibal's needs, contemplated the unseen Allobrodge. Were they formed like him, with a head, two arms and two legs? Or, were they misshapen and evil, like so much of what they've found in these mountains, like the prickly bushes and strange rocks that Gisgo and Jonaz and the others talked about every night at the meager campfires? The boy was sure that the rumors were true, that the dead did return to these mountains, that somewhere very close by lay the entrance to the underworld.

He stayed very close now, keeping a careful eye on the General.

The next day the Useless Mountain Tree guide was gone. Hannibal raged, though careful investigation revealed that the desertion was not betrayal, but rather fear. Gisgo placed the infantry on alert, but there was no ambush, no sign of collaboration between the guide and a hostile tribe. Gisgo made a point of asking the wolf boy directly if he knew anything about the guide's absence. Hannibal watched as the boy stammered out the truth: he knew nothing.

Marhabal would now ride along with the remaining Gaullish guides, taking along several of his own Numidian scouts.

"Ah, yes," scoffed Gisgo, "the desert goat herders will lead us out of these mountains."

Hannibal ignored his infantryman. "Ride as far ahead as you safely can, Marhabal. See if you can find the location of the final pass out of these mountains into Italy. My map indicates it's within a few days march."

The Final Pass. Nahatum heard this phrase repeated as a prayer, the men gripping their amulets along the nervous army's line of march. Tired soldiers spoke of the final pass, where they would look down on the fertile plains of Italy— with its bountiful fall harvest—as they did months earlier on the rich forests of Gaul from the ledges of the Snow- Capped Mountains leading them out of Iberia. Some imagined that from there they'd see the very walls of Rome in the far distance, shimmering with gold.

Nahatum even heard it from Ranton, his mate from the wolf pack, when he stumbled into him as he collected horse dung far down the line of march. His old friend looked so thin to Nahatum, hardly as he remembered him.

"Nahatum, they say we are almost at the final pass, tonight or tomorrow. Is this true?"

"I don't know, Ranton. Maybe. Does your chief feed you?"

A bitter laugh. "Yes, after he has fed himself and all his fighters. Have you some food in that bag you can give me?"

"All I have is shit from the horses, Ranton."

"Hannibal is eating horse shit now? Your great commander has led us to this?"

"No." He explained about dung bricks for making fire, but the confused older boy seemed not to understand, shivering and asking again about food.

"I have no food with me, Ranton, but here, take this." He handed the older boy the woolen blanket from his shoulders.

"Thank you, thank you." Ranton grabbed it and put it over himself, hurrying away. "I can trade this for some horsemeat that will last me until we reach the final pass tomorrow."

Then Marhabal and his scouting party disappeared.

They simply did not return from the next day's scouting. Two days passed without a sign of them. The talk among the cooks and servants was that the Numidian and his scouting party were all dead, probably dragged into the underworld by the invisible Allobroge.

A slingthrower from the Balearic Islands claimed to have seen belching fires erupt from the canyon far ahead. No one else could see it, no matter how high they climbed on the ledges. The Persians prayed to their god Ahura Mazda to protect them from Ahrima, the Evil Spirit determined to destroy this world and all its inhabitants. Several Egyptians found Hannibal to tell him that someone had stolen their amulets right off their necks while they slept. The khatts of their relatives would haunt the army if something was not done about this desecration.

After much searching and yelling, two Gauls were brought forward, accused of selling the amulets for food and gold and silver.

Standing in the middle of the trail, Hannibal demanded: "If so, who has the amulets?"

Confused expressions, finger pointing. No one knew. There was talk that Barnabar was involved in those transactions, but he yelled and cursed and claimed no knowledge.

Hannibal ordered the two thieves held for the night while he considered what to do. At dawn a Gaullish warrior was found dead with an Egyptian knife in his heart. The Gauls vowed revenge if something wasn't done. The Egyptians vowed further revenge if the amulets weren't all returned.

An hour later, standing on the edge of a yawning precipice, Hannibal ordered the two Gaulish thieves brought to him bound at the hands and legs. "Throw them off," he ordered. Down they went, screaming, into the mountain abyss, to the cheers of the Egyptians.

Their screams had barely faded when Hannibal calmly said, looking directly at Barnabar and the assembled Gauls: "You have until the noon high sun for all stolen amulets to be returned or…." Hannibal pointed at the abyss. "… more of you will go over that cliff."

By the time the sun was high in the sky, all amulets had been miraculously returned. Marhabal, however, still had not returned. Three days they had been waiting.

Nahatum was worried: he could see that his master was not right. It wasn't just the anger, everyone knew about that. All the servants and cooks and the guards were careful to do just what they're supposed to. The cooks were not even taking an extra bite of the already thin soup nor any of the remaining cous-cous. Besides, everyone was short- tempered.

No, his master was preoccupied; there was a dark cloud over him. Nahatum saw the empty, far- away look in the General's eyes, as if he was searching for someone, something not there. The boy wanted to help, to do something. He remembered the simple wooden and string construction back in Hannibal's tent in the army camp in Iberia, in the hurried days just before the army set to march—the way Hannibal looked, and a tone in his voice— when he ordered the boy to pack it to bring along.

The supply wagon would have that wooden thing. He didn't have an easy time finding the supply wagon, having to thread past and through the stalled line of the army, men camped along every narrow level spot, waiting for some word about when to move forward, had their scouts arrived back with word of the final pass?

When Nahatum did find the wagon, he had to search for that unusual box.

Holding it it firmly in both hands, the boy walked right up to Hannibal, sitting morosely beside a dung campfire and handed it to him without a word, for he had no idea what to say.

"What is this? Why have you brought this?" The General stared down at the wooden box as if he didn't recognize what it was.

Nahatum felt a buzzing rise in his chest. He had made a terrible mistake.

Then Jonaz was standing over him. He could feel the man's hot breath even in the day's chill. "It is the box with your boy's little house or whatever in it, Sir. The wolf child had no business ferreting around with the supply wagon. I will take him away and teach him manners."

An impatient gesture from Hannibal, still seated, still staring at the box, silenced the squire.

"Boy, tell me why you brought this to me."

"Did I do something wrong, Sir? I am sorry. I thought you might want it."

Hannibal stared at the boy, which made him very uncomfortable. "Well, just put it back. I have no use for this now. We might as well burn it for the little bit of flame it will produce.... no, don't throw it in, just take it back to the supply wagon."

The boy almost dropped the thing walking numbly away. "No, wait." A strong command. "Come back here."

The General carefully opened the box and stared into it for what seemed to Nahatum like an entire moon-high night. The construction was barely visible in the low light. Finally he closed it, sealing it carefully. He stood up and handed it back to Nahatum.

"Thank you, Nahatum, for bringing this to me. You may return it now safely to its place in the supply wagon."

Shouts. Running. Hannibal was out of his blanket and on his feet. *Ambush.* The sun had barely risen, just breaking over the far peak. *Think, prepare.* A perfect time for an ambush. Gisgo must have checked the guard details as usual. They'd slow down an attack, buy us time.

Jonaz ran up, out of breath. "They're back." Marhabal and his party appeared behind him. *Ba'al, you trickster, be praised.* Hannibal felt relief flood his body. Weary men leading exhausted horses appeared out of the dawn haze. Solyphos and Barnabar joined the group greeting the returned scouts.

Marhabal explained that they had camped the past night not a quarter-league away, but didn't know how close they were, so winding was the trail. They'd lost the trail two days ago and couldn't find their way back. "We lost a man, walked right over the edge in the mist." By now that was such a common experience that all it did was provoke muttered curses from the assembled group. "We had to walk the horses, the trail is too steep and rocky, and the drop-offs spooked them." They'd lost their way in canyonlands around the distant peak. "But we have found some well-used, promising trails." Marhabal's face broke into a smile—the handsome Numidian clearly relishing his discoveries–as he suggested to Hannibal and Solyphos to call for their scrolls.

"Maps," Barnabar exclaimed, the bear claws on his vest shaking. "What good is all of your papyrus and your ink and your quills and this old Greek, whose hand shakes so, how can he draw a map? We are following the shaking of an old man's hand."

Marhabal's voice, tired but firm: "No. The map is accurate." The Numidian pushed aside the sleeve of his caftan and planted a finger on the scroll. "We are here. Four days march to the final pass."

The march continued, renewed. Four days. They could do that.

Oddities. This is a time of oddities. Hannibal walked along the trail, avoiding some large rocks. Marhabal, his friend, had disappeared. The boy appeared with the fragile toy he and his son had made and wordlessly handed it to him with such intensity and eagerness. Then his friend reappeared with the news they are almost there.

The boy is a good omen. Hannibal felt some connection he could not quite discern between the behavior of the boy and the return of Marhabal, a connection real nonetheless. So, he turned to Gisgo, walking alongside him, and announced: "The boy is a good omen, do you see, not an omen of darkness." He slapped the man on his back, a moment of camaraderie he hoped the grizzled veteran felt as well.

He couldn't quite tell about that. Gisgo smiled but remained silent.

So, they followed the twisty trail Marhabal found, bypassing a coiled limestone peak that looked to Nahatum as if a cruel god had carved it from the earth with thunderbolts. There were still no signs of the whereabouts of the Allobroges. No huts, no villages, no summer meadows with grazing cattle, sheep, goats. He wondered who could possibly live in this land and longed for elsewhere. He was sick of the wind. He was cold. He was hungry. If Solyphos wasn't handing him chunks of his ration every day, he'd have starved by now. He hated that the old sorcerer came up to him on the march and quietly handed him a piece of bread, dried meat, rotten fruit, when no one was looking.

The boy always took it, his empty stomach would not let him do otherwise, but he vowed to figure out soon what plans the dark sorcerer had for him.

The next day, the Allobrodge revealed themselves. The army passed through narrow canyons and low trails with hundreds of large, strange, furry beings lining the ledges and ridges, many holding staffs, poles, pikes. Some said the beings were merely clad in fur, but Nahatum tended to agree with those who claimed that on the ledges were stranger creatures whose entire bodies were as hairy as the low-land black bears the hunters used to bring back to camp.

The creatures watched as the line of elephants passed, the infantry, the long string of cavalry, the supply wagons. None moved or waved, none yelled. They only watched. Mute beings. Were they alive? Made of limestone? Were they human?

Nahatum had slept poorly for nights, sometimes hardly at all, being awakened repeatedly by the moans of the dead imprisoned in the rocks, the screech ofentombed animals—half-eaten—rising from the bouldered canyon where they had made camp. He'd dreamt that a curved limestone column with knarled sides had erupted, the surface of the earth gashed open, spewing forth a hideous bony-leather claw bigger than an elephant, reaching for him.

The rumor began along the line of march, starting among the more devout Egyptian warriors, that the Allobroge lining the cliffs were their dead relatives come to life. Nahatum marched quietly along and listened to Gisgo telling Jonaz—the infantry commander and the squire now oddly friendly– that he'd seen his dead father up on the ledge. He feared, too, that he saw one of the men he had killed in battle, looking down at him. Jonaz replied that he yearned to see his father again, the man who had raised him and taught him proper respect for the gods. He strained upward, looking for a stout, heavy-bellied figure wearing his favorite red felt, conical hat.

As he marched along the rocky trail, Nahatum, too, searched the figures lining the ledges, hoping to see his mother again, brown shawl flowing over her shoulders. When they'd left Iberia that was the only shawl he knew, faded and ragged, but deeply beautiful to him. Since then he'd seen so many shawls and dresses amidst the Gaulish villages. He tried to picture his mother's shawl, the exact look and feel of it, and hated himself as it blurred in his mind.

Hannibal, too, contemplated the ragged line of Allobroges far above and the rumors about them. What, he wondered, if his father was indeed up there? His mother? He'd barely seen his mother since age nine, and he'd been not much older when she died unexpectly back in Carthage, neither the doctors nor the priests able to save her from the wasting illness that periodically swept around the cities of the Great Sea.

His father, on the other hand, would be watching his dream come true, alive in the hands of his son. The invasion of Italy, right to the heart of Rome. *What would my father say to me if he was up there right now?* He couldn't imagine. Then it came to him: *he would say that those people up on those ledges would love to pillage your supply wagons.* That's what they're after. Even depleted as his army was, they had enough gold, silver, tools and weapons to make these people rich.

Hannibal's mind started to work. Plan for the possibility of an ambush, and quickly. He remembered without looking that their maps indicated– and Marhabal had confirmed– that tomorrow they were to pass through particularly narrow canyons lined with gorges and steep fall-offs. Reorganize the line of march. Have Gisgo follow behind the supply wagons with 100 picked armored infantrymen to protect against any surprises from the Allobroge.

Dead relatives, indeed. *Protect your supply wagons.* That's what his father, wherever he was, would say.

When the attack came, it seemed as if from nowhere.

No one had slept the night before. The wind with its eerie calls, the fierce darkness of the rushing cold air. An early start— but, as always, at Hannibal's insistence, not before the army was fed breakfast, even if just moldy bread and water. Then onto the march, wagons creaking, the trail threading through a deep gorge on a thin trail mid-way up the north side.

Gisgo's stout veterans, long spears at the ready, clad in their leather and metal chest armor, swords dangling from their waists, were scattered among the supply wagons, as Hannibal instructed. The gorge they'd entered was so deep that the vaulting rock walls blocked the morning sun. The Allobroge lining the high cliffs had disappeared, much to the dismay of those soldiers who'd yet to see their dead relatives.

The trail along the sheer cliff face was barely wide enough for the creaking wagons. Rivulets of cold water flowed down the rock wall. The other side of the trail dropped off straight down to a fast- flowing river, strewn with boulders large enough to see even from the height. A royal ibex watched from the sloping far side of the gorge, nibbling at green poking out of the rock.

Somewhere near the head of the line of wagons Hannibal marched, but Nahatum could not see the metal of the General's battle helmet, as he was wedged between two wagons in front and back with no room to walk alongside. The roar of the river below almost drowned out the curses of the wagon driver ahead who had to whip the tired horse picking her way over the unforgiving trail. Whenever a horse stopped, the rest of the march behind stopped too.

The boy envied the blinders on the young mare just ahead, preventing her from seeing the near drop-off. During a brief stop– some animal ahead needed either encouragement or whipping to go on—he patted the mare's snout, murmuring low tones to calm her. The driver flicked his reins above her ears. Pots and pans jiggled and the wagon bumped ahead.

The trail widened. A winding side canyon joined the trail, the opening flat and dusty before it curved out of sight.

Then Nahatum heard a loud rumble overhead; at first the startled boy imagined thunder. The boulder– larger than the boy– landed a few feet in front, rolled, then disappeared over the edge. A second smashed into the wagon right behind him. He heard the mare's whinny and turned. Her eyes were wide, seemed almost to glow, as she struggled against the pull of the wagon pushed toward the abyss. Wagon and rider and horse lurched toward the precipice. The rear wheels of the wagon slipped over the edge, slowly followed by the rest of the wagon, taking along the driver and the mare. The driver screamed. The mare made no sound, pawing desperately at the trail with her front hooves. Her eyes seemed to focus on the boy and he noticed they were a deep green.

As he stood there frozen, he heard the boom of more boulders but ignored the sound, peering over the edge. The smashed wagon and horse and driver—small broken figures far below, lay unmoving as the river water washed over them.

Allobroge emerged from the side canyon. They crowded the trail, now littered with boulders and broken wagons and dead soldiers and those pinned by the fallen rocks. They didn't attack, but ran to loot the wagons. Fur- clad beings rummaged amidst smashed wagons, emerged carrying sacks and crates, a sight that was almost comical to the boy standing there unsure what to do. An armored infantrymen ran his spear through a man stumbling to carry an enormous crate. He fell over and didn't move, blood dripping out of his bearskin onto the slats of the crate.

An Allobroge– he suspected her to be a woman creature from the way she ran– hurried past, clasping a large burlap bag to her chest. The boy swung his pike at her, off balance, just missing. Holding the pike with two hands, he moved up the trail toward the side canyon and caught up with an Allobroge staggering away, one of the few remaining goats draped over his shoulder. Nahatum planted his feet and swung wildly, hit- ting the creature so hard in the stomach the boy expected the being to burst. The creature collapsed forward onto its knees, dropping the goat. The boy used his pike to butt him in the head. He melted onto the ground and lay still. That blow was as powerful and satisfying as anything the boy had known—here was something solid and real and true. He wanted to feel it again, he wanted to roar like a bear.

Another of Gisgo's men slashed at an Allobroge and cut off his arm at the elbow. Nahatum swung at a lumpy Allobroge running past and caught him in the chest with the spear point of his pike. The man-creature bounced off the cliff wall and staggered ahead into the side canyon.

The boy caught up with one man and smashed him— it— across the back. The boy's teeth rattled. He heard a squeal of pain as the Allogbroge fell over and lay there. The boy followed several of Gisgo's infantrymen, legs pumping, feeling so alive, in pursuit of the fleeing Allobroge.

He was carried forward by the hope of finding those spirits that had taken his mother. He'd find his way to this dark Underworld with armored infantrymen at his side, no longer a scared little boy, but now a warrior from Hannibal's army. Allobroge skittered around the corner of the canyon in full flight. A wild- eyed man on his right threw a rock, just nicking the boy. He pursued the creature, the salty taste of blood on his lips.

There were calls from behind, familiar voices, but he ignored them. *Faster, catch them.* Here, the boy was convinced, lay the very lair of those beings who took his mother so long ago. He would finally confront Lizard Skin himself.

The boy ran around one twisting granite corner, down a short distance and past another into a wide place, room- like, with sharp rock walls. The trail continued at the far end down another narrow corridor. In front of him, though, frantic Allobroge were pawing through crates, throwing clothes on the ground, fighting over a cooking pot and several long knives. Other Allobroge, panting hard, ran to join them.

But Nahatum was alone. He extended his pike. Advancing on them, the creatures turned and drew their knives, picked up their poles, and spread out, tight- lipped, eyes intent. Ten of them formed a semi-circle around him.

Nahatum gripped the hard wood of his pike and for the first time heard his heart beating.

Then there was a loud noise from behind. He dared not take his eyes off the creatures in front, but their eyes widened and mouths dropped open, as if struck dumb. Several turned and ran. The boy felt something grabbing at the back of his tunic– a large, hot claw just below his neck. He screamed as he was lifted right up into the air, legs kicking. He could barely hold onto his pike as the rest of the Allobroge fled.

Then he was thrown over the back of a horse, Gisgo's huge, muscular stallion. All he could see were the dusty, sandaled feet of armored infantrymen, spear tips clearly visible. They were running after the remaining Allobroge.

Gisgo released his hand from the boy's back. "Servants stay with their masters during a battle, unless ordered otherwise!" The words echoed in the boy's ears like rocks bouncing off a canyon wall. "I only came because I was ordered. A direct order. 'Take a horse, get him back,' he yelled to me. All to save a disobedient servant boy."

The horse's tail brushed across his face. He dug his fingers into the animal's flanks. By the time they were back at the trail, Nahatum was in danger of falling off. So many Allobroge lay along the trail. The female one with a spear in her back. Another groaning on the ground, one arm missing. An Allobroge sat propped up against dark stained rocks, his face almost white, blood pulsing from his stomach in thick gulps. A black stream flowed aimlessly into the dirt.

These are beings just like me. They are made of red mud. They are like any of the men in the army. This was confusing. He'd thought of them as Creatures, evil and dirty and dark. He wondered where was the entrance to the Underworld. Somehow he had gotten things all wrong.

The boy slid off the horse onto the trail. His master stood beside a wagon missing a wheel, at the entrance to the little side canyon which had spawned the Allobroge ambush, his helmet pushed back on his head, sword in his hand, the blade dark.

Hannibal's voice was jubilant as he congratulated a group of infantrymen for the way they had reacted, the discipline they had shown. "You fought well. Good work, good work. The damage could have been much worse."

He spotted Gisgo and gestured with his right arm. "The men did well fighting in terrain they had little experience in, caught by surprise. You have done well in training them."

Gisgo nodded and looked disdainfully at Nahatum, walking slowly behind. Hannibal saw him. "Never run off again like that in the middle of a battle. Servants stay with their masters. We lost my own supply wagon, but the damage could have been worse."

Nahatum nodded, head down, again that empty feeling inside when he had disappointed Hannibal.

Hannibal and Gisgo walked off, discussing the possible future uses of a side canyon for the purpose of ambush.

Nahatum looked around. Flies dotted bloated faces. One dead man had an arrow sticking out of an eye. Or where the eye should have been. Another looked asleep on his back on the trail, fur leggings and vest providing him cushion, but for the gaping sword wound in his chest. The boy knelt beside him and lightly touched the wound with his finger, sending protesting flies into the air. The blood was sticky and red, like his own. He pressed the skin with three fingers. Soft, hairy, yielding. Not leather, not limestone, not the scaly substance of some other world.

The boy walked over to the ledge beside the trail and stared down at the river, now swollen with smashed wagons, smashed bodies, smashed horses. He searched in vain for Hannibal's supply wagon with the little toy wooden construction that lay somewhere amidst the ruined wagons.

Half- way down, on a narrow ledge, Nahatum spotted a body, lying face upward, arms askew and eyes open, staring up at the sky. Likely knocked off the trail to his death in the first cascade of boulders. Something was familiar to Nahatum about the face, the hair….Ranton. A long sword was holstered in a fancy scabbard, undrawn. Had he stolen it from some unsuspecting soldier? Nahatum sank to his knees. Ranton was dead and he was alive, saved by Gisgo himself, sent by Hannibal—"all to save a disobedient servant boy."

He knew then that he owed his life to Hannibal, several times over.

A shout distracted him. Something cold and wet flew right into his eye. He looked up. White specks floated down from the sky. An elephant snorted and stamped its feet. A wagon driver cracked his whip at the small, hard flakes twisting downward, then opened his mouth to let them land on his tongue.

It had begun to snow.

Blankets became an even more prized commodity. Fights broke out that day and the next over who owned which old, ragged blanket, and more than one soldier died of knife wounds to settle disputes. Wind- whipped rivers of snow skittered against the rocks at the edge of the trail, taunting the army as it marched.

Barnabar was heard to refer to Hannibal, out of earshot, as the Emperor of Snow. "The man's not interested in fighting the Romans at all," the chieftain snorted, "everyone is going to die in these mountains beyond understanding."

The army had to keep moving, or all was lost. "We know the pass into Italy is ahead," he reminded Gisgo and Marhabal, "tell your men to spread the word down the line of march. We are close. Keep moving."

Hannibal hurried ahead, walking quickly then to keep warm, eyes on the thick dark clouds that had still not, Ba'al be praised, released a blanket of snow upon them. The steep trail narrowed as it wound between rock walls, veins of snow burrowed into thin crevices.

His progess was halted by a crowd of soldiers milling around on the trail. Ahead, an enormous boulder– gray with black streaks, pocked and grainy– sat in the middle of the narrow trail, between two steep mountain walls, like a cork in a bottle. Men, wagons, animals had all drawn to a stop.

Gisgo caught up. Hannibal stepped off the path to make room for white- haired Solyphos who also arrived, walking slowly. The boulder was huge. If they didn't move it, they were trapped. Hannibal could feel the blood drain from his face. A reedy Egyptian warrior pointed a gleaming bronze cat amulet at the boulder, his mouth moving in supplication.

From somewhere nearby, a familiar voice boomed out: "We're lost, Hannibal, and now can't even move forward." Barnabar stalked toward Hannibal from the crowd. "The mountain spirits are punishing us still." Cloth bag of teeth clattering and swaying around his neck, Barnabar bulled his way to Hannibal. The bag had grown. He scraped at the rocky soil with his foot. "Someone has to tell you—it is time to go back to our homelands in Iberia."

"We keep going." Hannibal ignored the Iberian chieftain, who called him the Emperor of Snow right to his face—and sent for turbaned Indoi, the keeper of the elephants. "Bring the great beasts forward." The great bull Sirius and another enormous elephant swayed past, chain mail battle armor clinking on their heads and shoulders.

The cold ground churned under the elephants' feet as they dug into it, pushing forward, their foreheads butted up against the massive boulder. The muscles in their backs and shoulders flexed, tensed, released, then the sinews hardened again and again, reminding Hannibal of the rising and falling of storm waves from the Great Sea itself.

Indoi's barbed whip picked a trail of blood across Sirius' shoulders. The rock remained in place. Finally, the elephants refused to move forward against it.

"Take them away," Hannibal ordered. A great emptiness engulfed him. The wind whistled through the silent rocks. A collective wail seemed to rise from the men huddled along the trail. Barnabar began to say something but Hannibal turned on his heels and walked away. Gisgo followed closely behind, his eyes on the crowd, a hand on the sword at his belt. Any assassin would have to get past Gisgo, an unlikely event.

"We camp here along the trail tonight," Gisgo announced, his voice more a growl than a command.

You can only toss pebbles against a rock wall for so long before the noise becomes a sort of torture. "Gisgo, you can stop that now," Hannibal said.

No one had slept that night. Gisgo sat with his back against the rock wall, facing the trail, his leather armor lit by the low light of the early morning sun just breaking over the taller mountain peaks. From where he sat next to the infantrymen, Hannibal could see the rest— Marhabal, Jonaz, even the boy—lay wrapped in blankets with weapons by their sides. He'd had the boy retrieve his battle shield and several knives from the supply wagon that survived the ambush. He refused to wind up like Alexander: killed at the hands of his own army.

The boy sat huddled, watching the lower trail, his pike beside him. Even Solyphos traced shapes in the cold dirt with the tip of his old sword.

"There must be a way past that boulder, scholar, teacher."

Solyphos looked up from his work in the dirt, coughed. Then: "Remember your Aristotle, Hannibal?"

"Of course. We read him when you taught me Greek." He worked his jaw against the hard layer of breath frozen on his cheeks, lips, mouth. Solyphos coughed again, wrapped the blanket more tightly around himself. Then:

"Aristotle wrote about the effect of hot and cold in rapid succession on substances. He claimed that all objects were composed of tiny substances, which he called 'atoms.' Heat, he suggested, makes these atoms move very fast and cold slows them down."

Hannibal sighed. *The cold has addled the old man's thinking.* Sad. "How does this help?"

Solyphos sneezed, further evidence that the old man was in the grip of an illness. *So, we are to die here in these mountains and one of the saddest pieces is that I have led this fine old man up to his death. As I've led thousands of others.* There was not even a fire to warm Solyphos as he coughed to death. *This is unbearable.*

All night long, they'd heard the sound of axes being taken to the remaining wagons and Hannibal had not intervened. Let the men occupy themselves with the useless gesture of making their last remaining fires; better they took an axe to thewagons than to him. Still, he regretted not ensuring that some of the wood be brought to where they have slept so that a fire might warm Solyphos. And, Hannibal noted, the boy's lips were a distinct blue.

"Extremes of hot and of cold applied to the boulder may excite the atoms and cause it to break apart into smaller pieces."

What? Ah. Yes. Hannibal stared at his old tutor; their eyes met. Solyphos' mind still burned brightly. "Crack the boulder," Hannibal whispered. Frozen snow and ice for the cold. For heat, Solyphos suggested boiling their casks of vinegar. "Aristotle claimed that more sour liquids have greater heat properties."

Solyphos' voice, clear and insistent, filled Hannibal with an unexpected joy, even in this dire moment. "Firewood, now," he announced. "Ba'al be praised. We must gather all that remains of our wagons."

Hannibal inched forward on the cold ground, tossing his blanket from his shoulders, Solyphos now at his side. Gisgo joined them, moving forward on his knees. There was a fierce energy between them. They were speaking quickly now. How many wagons were left? Enough for a bonfire, if we move quickly. We need a large cauldron. Hannibal's mind sped on, hoping this was not madness. Men will have to be sent down trail to the cook's wagons. They will roll the largest cauldron they can find right up to the base of the boulder. The casks of vinegar. Thank Ba'al we've brought several casks for barter, for taste. How much was left? No one knew. Bring it all. We need men to gather piles of snow, buckets of it. Marhabal had joined them now, eager. He suggested the buckets used to feed his cavalry horses. Find them, get them.

Hannibal stood, wanting to give out a roar, a lion roused, instead clapped his hands, kicking at one of the soldiers sleeping in the shadow of the boulder, pointing and poking with his sword. These were his loyal men, Carthaginian-born. He sent them down the trail, armored and weaponed, to bring back all the wood they could find. To get the cauldron. To bring the vinegar. And, yes, to gather more snow. "Tell anyone who can hear that we are building a bonfire. Now. We're going to destroy this boulder."

This roused even the boy, who spluttered to life and hurried down the trail, telling whoever would listen that "Hannibal has powerful magic. He is going to use it. Hannibal has magic to destroy the boulder."

Perhaps the mountain air has gotten to me, Hannibal thought, because that struck him as so funny he laughed out loud.

The warmth crackling from the roaring fire gave the boy's skin a painful tingle. Men huddled all around it. He was filled with a restless energy so he joined the line of men passing wooden buckets of bubbling vinegar hand- over- hand to the very top of the boulder. Several men standing there dumped each one down the sides.

The stench was overpowering— thick and rancid, attacking his nose. He was close to choking and retched, afraid he would vomit, though there has been no food for a day. He didn't stop, though, thinking of Barnabar yelling at the General, of the frozen pain in his feet. He passed heavy buckets upwards until his shoulders ached. Boiling vinegar, snow and ice, boiling vinegar, snow and ice. Clouds of choking steam engulfed Gisgo, Marhabal, even Barnabar standing further away, watching, shaking his head, surrounded by his evil-looking men, their breath frosty in the mid- morning chill.

The boy could see Hannibal pacing next to Solyphos, who had his hand in the pockets of his woolen pants. Hannibal always kept a sword now strapped to his side and a knife in his belt. He wore chest armor as well. The boulder hissed, seeming to leak angry liquid from its very insides.

Solyphos leaned over and whispered something to Hannibal, who handed a flat- headed steel axe to a towering Gaul. The man climbed to the top of the boulder, passing right by the boy, still hauling buckets. The Gaul, shockingly, tossed off his shirt in the cold air, planted both feet, and swung the heavy axe over his head as if it were a light stick. The crash of steel on stone made the boy's teeth ache. Dark clouds hissed from the boulder and trailed away into the air.

"Yet again." Hannibal bellowed. More vinegar, more snow. The boy's legs and back ached, and his palms were cracked and bleeding. Bucket after bucket traveled over the steep rocks, all the men working wordlessly, never dropping one, the boy aware of only two things: Hannibal standing, hand on his sword, and Barnabar, further away, watching, shaking his head as if they were all fools.

A shout from Hannibal to the Gaul atop the boulder. Another fierce, thudding blow. Then a terrible cry hurled from inside the boulder, an anguished screech that made the skin on the back of Nahatum's neck stand up. The massive thing cracked in two. The boy threw his right arm up across his face, elbow out, to ward off furious, clawed spirits, flying for his eyes, throat, heart.

What the boy did see was that Hannibal embraced Solyphos, who smiled and patted the General on the back, the only time the boy had ever seen anyone do that. Gisgo and Marhabal congratulated Hannibal. Barnabar walked carefully over to the broken boulder, gingerly inspected it, then peeked down the trail that was now open and extended into the distance. Their way forward.

The boy followed Hannibal at the proper distance for a servant. Soldiers hurried by, some using pieces of leather to carry warming coals from the bonfire as they marched. He heard some of them talking, adding to what will now be said about Hannibal. "Yes, indeed, he has great magic. His power can smash solid boulders to pieces."

Nahatum passed the steaming remnants of the once mighty boulder and he contemplated what he had just witnessed. His mind was chewing on something. Who really held the magic that split the boulder? Yes, Hannibal, but someone else, too. Not the powerful Gaul with the steel axe. Not the bubbling brown vinegar nor frozen blue- white snow. Not the mighty elephants. Something else, some power deeper than any of them.

Solyphos. The power had something to do with him.

A soldier pushed him into a rock, yelling at him not to bump into people.

Solyphos held the magic that split the boulder. His power came from this man Air-E- Stotle, a wise Greek who was dead– judging from the talk last night, when his teeth were chattering so much he could hardly sleep– but whose spirit was alive, honored and happy in the words written on the papyrus that Solyphos had read and had long ago made Hannibal read, and which Hannibal had forgotten but Solyphos had remembered.

The boy couldn't say it exactly then, but the power to move unmoveable boulders somehow lay in words written on papyrus. This was a puzzle, one he vowed to devote some thought to.

Shouts ahead. The view had opened up. Nahatum ran past cheering men, Hannibal's black hair guiding the boy forward to a rocky ledge. Thousands of feet below, the broad, fertile plains of Piedmont. Italy lay before them. They had been this close to the final pass. There were no cheers this time, as there were when they had crested the mountains from Iberia leading into Gaul. This time there was only exhaustion.

Barnabar nodded to Hannibal. And then Hannibal stared into the distance, chin held lightly in his hand. To the boy, the man seemed incomprehensibly tall and wise and unconquerable. Hannibal held aloft his shield and the prowling lion glistened in the morning sun. He was pointing that lion in the direction of Rome. Perhaps the Romans already could see the glint of sunlight coming from it and were afraid.

Hannibal's gray eyes blazed, as a lion when he spotted his prey. And the boy burned with desire to be a lion too, to make his master proud.

Chapter 4

Solyphos

Northern Italy
Winter 218 BC- Spring 217 BC

Hannibal's legs ached from the long descent down the mountain. He could see a village in the distance, a wooden stockade of felled trees sharpened at the tip. When built correctly such wooden walls were effective at repelling marauders and robbers. *Ah, the Gauls and their wood, their admirable forests. This is what Carthage needs. There's enough marble, we need more great trees.*

Yet there was a limit to what wood could withstand. He could see that the distant village was not that impressively defended. What he didn't know was how these Italian Gauls would react to his arrival.

Smoke drifted from some of the small huts visible beyond the stockade, chimneys in use on the cold afternoon. They'd caught the townspeople by surprise, some perhaps still having their mid-day meal. He could imagine the worry among those few people on the parapets: thousands of men streaming toward them, strange men, tattooed men, black Africans, fearsome beasts.

Hannibal tried to imagine how these townspeople saw his cavalry. Swarthy men in their strange hooded dejallabahs, on their exhausted horses. Gaunt men waving their desert swords and yelling at them in a strange tongue. What did these people make of them? Foreign demons? Strange beings from the Underworld?

Weathered amulets of wood, bronze, clay, hung down from the top of the stockade– charms and spells to repel devils and demons, supernatural and human.

Marhabal—of course, Marhabal—was already far ahead with his Numidians, the cavalry in front of the town gates and massed along the spiky logs of the stockade fence.

Hannibal admonished himself: he should have sent some of the Gauls ahead, perhaps they would have seemed more familiar. Yet would anyone in his army have seemed familiar? Still, he should have planned for their first arrival in Italy instead of straggling out of the mountains like an unruly mob. His army was still arriving. Tired, hungry men walking alone, in twos, in small groups, threaded down the mountainous trail.

How we arrive matters. You should have planned this more carefully. He had to obtain the good will of these very people. His father would have thought of that. Why didn't Solyphos advise him of this? Solyphos, who now coughed so much that he couldn't advise anyone. Solyphos, who needed to make the journey down the mountain in one of their few remaining creaky wagons after he'd fallen on the steep trail. Getting the scribe to ride in the wagon was about as hard as getting the lead elephant, Sirius, to cross the Rhoneous river. It took a lot of persuasion. He'd ordered the wolf boy to ride along in the wagon, just to make sure.

They were behind him then, still sitting in the old wagon, and Hannibal walked over to it.

"That is Taurini," Solyphos suggested, arm resting on the wooden slats of the wagon side, looking out at the distant village. "I think I shall get out and walk now."

"Stay awhile longer in the wagon, my tutor. Let us see what develops next. We need them to open their gates to us."

Not likely. The townspeople had shut their gates and were yelling taunts at the cavalry massed in front. When Barnabar arrived at the gates, he began yelling something, shaking his arms at the townspeople of Taurini, who just stared back, uncomprehending. Barnabar was his lead negotiator? Not a good sign. His Gaulish recruits were yelling swears at the townspeople on the ramparts.

The Numidians held a prisoner near the gates, some unlucky town shepherd or herdsman likely, yelling up at the people looking down. One of the Numidians ran the prisoner through with his sword. They hurled the body up against the gates. *Oh, no.* This was how they arrive as liberators from the Roman yoke? Spears were being thrown.

Arrows shot. Another man looked to be dead in front.

Hannibal sent Gauls familiar with Taurini to stand in front of the gates and tell these people that he meant them no harm.

His emissaries had to retreat under a hail of stones and arrows.

I hate this! He cursed the stubborn, ignorant people who would not be wooed.

Didn't they understand the threat that Rome meant to them? More arrows from the townspeople. Their aim was terrible, Hannibal noted. His hungry army was spread around and in front of the town.

Now his curiosity was aroused. How would this army do if they had to invade a town? They repelled a vicious ambush in the mountain, one that might have destroyed a less disciplined group. What would happen now?

The men were all looking back at him. He couldn't stand there thinking all day.

This was a very hungry army, the men liable to do anything in their desperation. Better to aim that desperation at those stubborn townspeople than at him. Bring up the elephants.

He could feel the will of his men, the entire army aimed at this little village. *I came to liberate you. We meant you no harm. Open your gates.* Did he really mean that? Well, he did and they didn't listen. Barnabar, Gisgo, Marhabal, Solyphos, even the wolf boy, his good luck charm, were all looking at him. There was an energy to leading an army. A tension rose inside him, a muscle poised to do something, to release, to smash. Every man in the army felt it. He raised his arm. Trumpets sounded.

"To the town! Take it!"

The men bellowed in response, a sound deep and strong, a huge wave of sound, and suddenly there were thousands of men running toward that stockade. The war elephants, thin and haggard as they were, joined the raging river, their handlers atop, whipping them on. Hannibal watched. He wanted to understand the effect there.

And the effect was this: the mass of men and elephants smashed into the fence like the huge wave from the Great Sea he once saw as a little boy at Carthage, washing over the sea wall protecting the city. Some had said Ba'al Shammon was angry at the city, others swore they heard a convulsion under the land before the water hit. And now the enormous wave that was his army smashed through the sad little stockade that once protected Taurini.

We had come to liberate you.

The wooden stockade lay shattered, like a row of battered teeth. Nahatum leapt over the prickly sideboard of the wagon. Then he was past the town gate, on his own in the gathering darkness. Hannibal was nowhere to be seen. The mule driver wrestled on the ground with someone, a long loaf of dark, grainy bread caught between them.

Nahatum was so hungry, and tired, too, but there was something new and different, so much energy in the air, so much to see. Orderly rows of what must be houses, rows that spread out of sight, big houses, not the huts he'd seen in Gaul, thatched roofs sprinkled around the countryside. He ran past—what?—he stopped, looked down into it, hands on the low wooden sides, into the deep darkness, he saw a bucket and rope– a village well, with a wooden roof over it, and benches around it as if people sat there and did what?, he wondered.

There were people shouting and the sound of smashing wood, the sharp odor of burning thatch and smoking pitch. The neat dirt lane kept going but there was anotherone off to his left and ahead another path to the right. The one on the left scared him a bit— no voices, no people. Empty, except a scream from that direction. No, he kept going straight ahead.

People were running in all directions, from all sides. A soldier ran past in a woman's skirt, ripping bites from a loaf of bread, followed by a black warrior, laughing, wearing a horse's bridle over his shoulders, a carved wooden figurine in his arms.

Nahatum almost tripped over several dead bodies. Down another street a group of men push several women into a house with a smashed door. Everyone seemed to have someone else's clothes on top of their own, women's hats on men, a wild-haired Balearic Islander running in thick leather boots he hadn't even bothered to tie.

What sights! He ran down the straight muddy pathways so different from the crooked lanes that wove so haphazardly between the tents whenever they camped.

Flames leapt from roofs. Dancing shadows played around him in the evening twilight.

Then he found himself lost, at the end of a small dark street. He wound up with a goatskin of wine, no memory of how he got it, yet he kept squirting it into his mouth.

There seemed no bottom to it. He was a tribal chieftain back that night in Iberia, pounding his fist on the table in Hannibal's tent, demanding more wine. His head swam. The flames continued their strangely beautiful, multicolored dance across the walls and roofs of houses. He could see into some now, doors splintered, walls cracked in. Men clustered inside a broken down house around a table, a dog barking atop it, the men hopping, as if doing a strange dance. The boy laughed. He heard Gisgo's voice down a street somewhere, bellowing something he couldn't understand and which he ignored.

Everything was starting to spin around. Where did that wineskin go? He steadied himself on a doorpost. A broken door hung loosely on iron hinges, smashed open. Just inside was a kitchen table set with plates of cheese, a bowl of honey, a loaf of bread.

Someone had set out a meal for him.

He stepped inside and reached for it and then—where did they come from?– there were several other men—long-haired, faces painted in the Persian fashion—standing near the table. One grabbed the loaf of bread, then another reached to knock him over. The boy snatched half the loaf away and smeared soft white cheese on it, then dipped the whole mass into the honey bowl. Before anyone could stop him he shoved the entire thick, chewy thing into his mouth. The taste overwhelmed him. How long since the fragrant touch of honey had blossomed on his tongue?

Except that then his stomach tried to come up and out through his throat and it did: the bread, the cheese, the wine, covering the table and the remaining food, just missing his Carthaginian purple sash looped around his waist. His eyes ached.

The Persians stopped moving. One of the men, eyes wide, red paint covering his forehead and down his cheeks, pointed at the boy and laughed. He was holding a mug, smelling of wine, which threatened again to coax his stomach to come out his mouth. The sound of pissing on the floor was distracting. Behind the man pissing, several smashed chairs lay in front of a hearth with a dead fire. There were sleeping pallets along the walls, and two smaller pallets in one corner. A small broken toy wagon and several smaller carved animals—a cow, a fearsome bear in mid-roar, a goat, complete with chin hair hanging down—lay sprawled atop one. Women's clothes were scattered across one of the pallets.

He was woozy, but the strange sight drew him toward it. Little wooden animals. There had been that strange toy hut of Hannibal's, something to do with his son. Now that lay in the bottom of a river in the Endless Mountains. On the march through the villages of Gaul the children had sometimes held little carved pieces of wood, but they'd run away when he'd approach them. The carved animals now on the sleeping pallet were so carefully done, he could see the roar of the bear, the moo of the cow. Someone spent time carving them, the kind of time Solyphos spent over his papyrus conjuring the things he called words, the kind of time Hannibal spent over his maps, seeing far into the distance, the sort of time he'd spent bent over his lost pike carving a cormorant feather into the side.

Whoever carved it had done that for a child, for someone not all that much younger than him, Nahatum. He wanted to hold a small carved animal in his hand, to tower over it and squeeze it in his palm, to hold it there and make it feel safe. He knew that the tiny animals felt very scared, with all the strange men around them, breaking things, making so much noise. He really didn't want them to be burnt to ash in the fires all around, the smell of burning thatch in the air. He was about to stuff them into his pocket where they'd be safe, when one of the men behind him slammed down his mug on the table. The boy jumped, turned around, arms at the ready so that when the man reached for him, Nahatum smashed him with a broken chair leg, hitting him so hard the swine fell heavily against the table, cursing the boy. Before anyone else could move, he was outside.

The darkness was now so complete he could hardly see despite the flames that seemed to be everywhere. Gisgo's voice again, yelling at someone to stop throwing torches onto the thatched roofs. "We need the huts for ourselves." More bodies in the street. How long was he in the house? He never took the carved animals. Who cares?, the boy resolved, he didn't need one of those, he wasn't not a child anymore, if he ever had been. A rider- less horse thundered by. The boy ran toward the sound of Gisgo's yelling, that deep booming voice calling him as never before. He turned a corner and…there was Solyphos standing in front of a fireplace inside a collapsed house with just one wall standing.

"Pillaging," the old Greek spat out. "I've seen enough of it in my life. Make me a fire." The boy lurched backward, which added to the pounding in his head. His stomach was both empty and angry, yet the idea of food threatened more vomit.

He wanted to go to sleep. Solyphos coughed, though it sounded more like a bark.

The wall offered some shelter from the wind, but the night was so cold. The fire smoldered, giving off wisps of smoke. He put his hand over the warm ashes. Who had made the fire now in front of him? He imagined a family—the children with little carved animals in their hands, perhaps—just hours earlier, settling down for a peaceful night with another day to come.

Solyphos sighed and sat down on a low stool. The boy bent to his task, poking at the embers with a long stick, arranging the logs so conveniently stacked—by someone else—next to the hearth.

"Well, you have found odd accommodations. Two walls, no roof. Nice flat floor, though. Warm fireplace, too. " Hannibal walked in out of the dark. Gisgo, who had somehow acquired an enormous bearskin cloak, warmed his hands by the fire.

Solyphos looked up at the two men, then back at the fire. "A commander fit to fight the Romans will not lose control of his troops, letting them sack a town which might yet become an ally of ours."

Hannibal's chest tensed. "We're working to restrain the men and put out the fires. I've talked with the town elders. They're more hospitable now, said they misunderstood who we were."

Still, Solyphos was right, he knew. *I've lost control of my army. We've become a bunch of maurauders. In one night.* He had to get control back. At the Rhoneus river with the Volcae, here in Taurini—he had left his passions get the better of him. Barnabar was nowhere to be found. What was to hold them together? Some of the fighters could simply go off on their own; there's plenty of plunder for bandits armed as these men are. If that happened—marauding robbers from Hannibal's army—none of these Italian Gauls will have anything to do with him.

To Hannibal's annoyance, Gisgo wanted to argue with Solyphos, Ba'al help him. "The fools wouldn't let us into their town. They thought we were a band of robbersfrom the mountains."

Solyhos pursed his lips, impatiently. "Well, they've learned otherwise: a band of robbers from beyond the mountains?"

Gisgo looked at Hannibal for help. None was forthcoming. Still, he renewed his efforts. "Nothing wrong with a little reward for one's efforts. Besides, a little fear will do wonders to bring these Italian tribes over to us."

Solyphos shook his head, stroked his wispy beard.

"And the boy asleep in the corner there," Hannibal said, eager to change the subject. All heads turned. "I hope my servant has kept an eye on you and served you well, Solyphos. Are you feeling any better?"

"Yes, Hannibal, the boy has done an admirable job helping me. From the time I fell coming down the mountain, he's watched over me, never left my side. Thank you."

Gisgo stared at the sleeping figure slumped over in the corner, then walked over and kicked the boy. "Get up, you are supposed to be attending to Solyphos." The boy moaned, protested with a hand. Gisgo looked like a bear attacking a goat. "He doesn't look to be in very good shape." The infantryman half held the moaning, struggling boy in the air. "He smells of vomit."

"Nonsense. The boy worked on the fire, collecting wood and keeping me warm through this cold night. He's tired. Let him rest."

"Good," Hannibal said. "I want you in a warm house. Even if it has no roof. Keep the fire going and tomorrow please start writing down what we have accomplished. My father was right—a Carthaginian army can reach Italy by crossing the Endless Mountains. There is a summer passage. I want the world to know of this. Let Nahatum continue to attend to your needs right now."

Hannial said this, but he suspected Gisgo was right. The boy smelled of vomit and looked like he'd been doing a lot more than attending to Solyphos. And, too, there was the matter of Solyphos' hands. The man kept wringing them as if he was in pain.

Something is not right here.

Nevertheless, Solyphos nodded. "It will be good to get back to my writing. It will take me several days to set up my supplies."

"You don't have that. We're at our weakest—exhausted, starved. We need to be on the march soon—I want to find the Romans before they find us. We rest a day or two and then head south. It's all about surprise now."

Solyphos didn't disagree, to his relief. *Act like you're in command and maybe the rest will follow. Buy yourself some time.*

Nahatum's head throbbed. Worse, he wondered if he had now become Solyphos' servant. Would he no longer clean Hannibal's tent? When Hannibal hurried out, Gisgo lumbering along at his side like a dark shadow, he had not been ordered to come along. The boy's stomach sank. He could barely reach up to fashion the woolen blankets he'd retrieved into a sort of tent for Solyphos in the ruined house.

The town had gone strangely quiet. The moon was journeying toward the Underworld. Solyphos wanted him to rub his body, complaining of pain in his fingers, hands, wrists. Why did he complain about this to him, a wolf boy, yet the old man had said nothing about any of it to Hannibal?

Solyphos handed him a jar with some paste he said was made from a plant and would relieve the ache in his joints. He almost dropped the glass jar, his stomach seemed so weak, and his head—oh—and all the old man could do is scold him. Don't drop it, rub it into my hands, my back, my shoulders.

The sight of the old man's sagging, wrinkled skin sickened Nahatum. There were dark spots all over the man's arms and back. Solyphos may have some sorcery– no, that's not right, it's not sorcery exactly— with words and boulders and that smart Greek Air-E-Stotle, some power, but not enough to keep the Underworld away. Lizard Skin was creeping into the man's body. The boy gagged as he began to massage the plant oil into the man's back. Layered folds of mottled skin encircled Solyphos' waist like the flecked hide of an aged elephant.

Next morning, Marhabal was sent south with a thousand riders to scout the area as far as the river Ticinus. Solyphos was up early, too, rummaging inside a supply wagon displaying considerable nimbleness, declaring it a miracle that several chests of papyrus had survived the journey and enough gall nuts to make ink as soon as the army had found winter residence.

The day revealed the extent of the destruction– the burnt houses, the bodies being carried away, dead horses, goats,

livestock in the street, some half- butchered by the hungry soldiers. Somewhere down one of the ruined lanes was the house
with the little carved animals. Which one? The boy wouldn't
have been able to find it even if he tried. But he didn't.

Instead—headache gone, stomach calm– he carved a new
pike to replace the one lost at the ambush at the Gorge from
the fallen branch of a rugged pine tree. He made it a head
taller than himself, roughly the same size as the ones the Gauls
carried into battle.

There was even time later that day to practice pike work
with some bare-chested Gauls in the meadow just past the ruined stockade wall, the frost from the chilly night still clinging
to the tall grass.

When he returned, Solyphos sat on the ground in front
of the blanket-tent sorting through a pile of feathers. When he
saw Nahatum's new pike, Solyphos took it in hand and held
it up, tried to spin it, grimaced, stopped, then hefted it in the
air. "Sturdy. Well- balanced. Carve it yourself?"

"Yes."

"Can you use it?"

Yes, he could. He told the old man about the Gorge and
smashing an Allobroge so hard in the stomach that the man
fell over, writhing. "I practice with the Gauls."

Solyphos nodded, licking away spittle on his upper lip.
Patches of skin were visible through his thin white beard, like
a pond slowly drying up in the summer heat.

"Seen any owls?"

His eyes seemed to float in water, and he went on about
bird feathers again, this time claiming that the two outer
feathers on the left wing of an owl make the best quills. Nahatum didn't ask what quills were; the whole topic smelled of
dark magic and sorcery.

Then: "That pike of yours needs decoration. Every weapon needs to have its owner's spirit. It helps in battle." He said his own sword—old as it was— had the image of an olive tree from his father's fields back in Greece carved in the silver shaft.

"Well…What is your spirit, young wolf boy?"

"I am Hannibal's servant." The purple waist sash proved that, no matter what.

Someday Hannibal would call him back, the rotting old man be damned. "Yes, that you are. Is that your spirit entire?"

Was the old man mocking him? He, a wolf boy, had no city, no tribe, no family name, no father, and his mother was dead. Surely this old man reeking of Lizard Skin had heard the strange word that the Greek mercenaries called him: "Hey, Apotide." He'd pieced out what the word means in their language. The one who has no standing: Noone. That's not all they called him, he knew that. A hex, a carrier of bad luck, spawn of the Underworld.

"I am an apotide."

Solyphos' hairy eyebrows rose. "How did you learn that word?"

"I listened to the Greeks, the cooks."

"You listen well. Hannibal told me that about you. You have an ear for words. Perhaps an eye for them, too." A small red dot floated in the man's left eye. "I know a few things about Greek-land." A crow squawked in the trees somewhere. "You need to find one, young Nahatum." His name spoken aloud startled the boy.

"A feather?"

"No, a spirit. All your own. Everyone has one."

"I like the cormorant." He remembered the feather on his lost pike. He wished he still had it; his mother would have loved it.

Solyphos nodded. "Worthless for quills but admirable creatures nonetheless.

Patient and watchful. Is that you? They strike unexpectedly: their fishy prey hardly see them as they're swallowed. Hannibal would like that."

Hannibal. Where is he? Again, that longing. Still, it'd become clear that Solyphos was not mocking him. "Is the fire strong enough, Sir? Another log?"

"Yes, that would be wonderful. I will return to sorting my feathers, while you restore our fire."

Later, there was time to get a small knife from the toothless cook, the one not from Greek-land, and to sit near Solyphos in the ruined house carving the black feathers of the cormorant near the pikes's sharpened end. May the hunting skill of the bird guide his pike.

As he carved, he pretended he was conjuring those strange things called letters, odd shapes that he hoped would give his pike strength.

"You nailed him to a cross?," Hannibal yelled, reaching up to adjust the blue cotton fez his outburst had disturbed.

"The swine deserved it," Barnabar replied, tossing his sack of teeth high in the air. "He was protesting the tribute I demanded."

I'd like to reach right across this table and snatch that intolerable sack right out of your stupid hands. Hannibal contemplated the wooden walls of the fine Taurini house the elders offered him for use as his lodgings after he'd gotten his men to stop the looting and established some beginnings of order. The pleasing grain of the cut wood, the careful way the timbers were fit together. Whatever you want, Great One. Please, our houses for you to use. They'd begun calling him King Hannibal.

Still, he hadn't really stopped the looting. Just that morning, Hannibal had to order Jonaz to stop taking Taurini sheep and sacrificing them to purify the land for Ba'al Shammon. Now Barnabar. *They're acting like it's every man for himself. This is how armies fly apart. You've got to reestablish some discipline.*

"Two fine cows, ready for slaughter. The foul man kept saying he needed them for his family, but he only has two small children and a fat wife to feed. We are hungry, all of us."

"No. Get that poor man off the cross. Now."

Barnabar stared at Hannibal. "With respect, Lord Hannibal, why should I not demand tribute? We have all suffered in our journey across the mountains." He stared at Hannibal. "Suffered greatly."

The wooden walls of the house seemed to press in on Hannibal. *Tribute. The man acts like the new ruler of this town.* Hannibal took a deep breath. He turned to Gisgo, standing behind him. "Take several of the infantry and get that man off the cross. Apologize to him. And give him this." Hannibal took a gold shekel from the purse on the table in front of him. "Tell him it was all a misunderstanding."

Barnabar started to protest but dropped the cloth sack of teeth onto the floor,then silently picked it up. *He's nervous now in my presence. Good.* "I'm going to tell you what we need to do, Barnabar. The army needs to put this town back intoreasonable order, even rebuild a few homes before moving on, so as to encourage otherGaulish tribes to join our army. Do you understand? We need them as allies. Otherwise we will face the Romans with hardly an adequate army."

"But we came here for spoils and plunder." The man sounded genuinely disappointed.

"And for allies. We have to work together, not act like we are just rabble coming to plunder the lands of the very people we need as allies." Barnabar nodded slowly.

Hannibal had already met with emissaries of the far Boii people who were in active rebellion against Rome. With luck their thousands of fighters would join his army. And somehow he had to teach these people how to fight together, as an army, not as a bunch of separate tribes. Discipline, discipline. *You're responsible for this. You gave the order to storm the town. What did you think would happen?*

Just then Jonaz flung the door open and leaned into the room. "Marhabal has returned." This announcement was followed by Marhabal himself striding into the room, his djellabah covered in mud and stained with blood clearly not his own. Behind him, several of his men pushed two prisoners, both Roman army officers.

"The Roman cavalry fight like they're riding goats, not horses." The Numidians had defeated a large force of patrolling Romans just north of the river Ticinus, who had themselves been looking for rebellious Gauls.

His friend had not even changed out of his muddy, dark-stained caftan in his rush to report back. "We cut right through them."

"And who have we here?" The two men were standing awkwardly in the corner, surrounded by guards. They were bound tightly together by the wrists with thick rope, in the fashion customary with prisoners among the Gauls. Tall, well-fed, both wore bronze chest armor that likely just that morning had been polished by a servant, though now mud streaked the metal. And the ribbons dangled down like peacock feathers. They stood uncomfortably, off- balance, bound together as they were, as if unsure whether to pull away or move closer to each other.

Hannibal sighed. "Untie those men."

Solyphos walked in, followed by the boy. Good: Hannibal wanted his tutor to hear this, to see the Romans. The boy stood there staring at the prisoners. He looked improved over his sorry state the other night.

"Nahatum, get Solyphos a chair."

Through this all, Hannibal had been studying the prisoners. One might have thought that two Romans surrounded by unkempt, dejallabh-clad warriors, plus Gisgo, resplendent in his fur coat, looking more beast than human, would feel some awe, some willingness to grovel. Not at all. The Romans stood there breathing disdain.

When Hannibal turned to the older of the two Romans—even more peacock feathers dangling from the chest armor—and asked him, still speaking in the Gaulish patois—which Roman army he was from, and who was his commander, the Roman ignored the questions and replied:

"What tribe is this? What ransom do you want?"

He spoke the patois haltingly, as if the words tasted foul in his mouth. His eyes scanned the room as if looking from a great distance.

Marhabal shrugged, amused. "They think we are from this area, part of the Northern Italian Gaulish revolt."

This is what you forget. This Roman arrogance. The haughty disdain. Did they speak to my father this way during the surrender? "I am Hannibal Barca, commander of Carthage's armies in Italy." Something broke through him. The skin on his neck bristled as he spoke.

The Romans laughed. Both of them. Then: "Ah, an educated Gaul. Do you think us fools? There are no Carthaginian armies in Italy. Ridiculous. I ask you again: what ransom do you bandits want?"

Let's try Latin and see what happens. "Listen to me. Carthage is at war with Rome. This is an invasion army. If I can, I will be at the gates of Rome before the next winter."

Ah, ha. The Romans' mouths dropped in unison, as if they were trained monkeys. Then Hannibal spoke in Punic: "So now you understand." The sound of his native tongue resonated in the room. He wanted to yell at them in the language of his father: Now do you understand! Instead, he said, "Too bad, these men don't speak Punic." He repeated himself to them in Greek. Another Roman silence.

"Nor Greek," Solyphos laughed, clearly amused at the Roman ignorance lurking just beneath their disdain.

So, they conversed in Latin and the Romans, regaining their arrogance, claimed that there were two Roman armies just to the south. They would put an end to this "uprising, invasion, whatever it is." Their advice: set a ransom and return home any way you can.

The news of two Roman armies—well fed, well-armed, no doubt—panicked Barnabar, who proposed finding a secure base in Northern Italy for the winter and returning across the mountains to Iberia with their plunder in the spring.

Hannibal ignored this. "We march south tomorrow, to find these Roman armies."

Barnabar protested, slamming his hand against the wall, the gold bracelets on his wrists clanking. Marhabal interrupted Barnabar. Gisgo interrupted Marhabal. All three yelled at each other. To the amusement of the Romans, who stood there with mocking smiles on their faces.

"Quiet." Hannibal stood, balancing himself with a sword in his right hand, tip digging into the wooden floor. He would have liked to dig it right into the eyes of the smirking Romans. "We are all in great danger. A minor success is the poison of a great victory. Marhabal has simply won a cavalry skirmish. That is all. We need a decisive victory over a Roman army and soon." So, he concluded, "we march south tomorrow to find the Romans."

No one moved. Solyphos sat rubbing his hands. The boy just stared at the Romans, eyes wide. That wolf child, so clever and perhaps even now thinking to somehow use things to his advantage. *Do the same, Hannibal.* But how? *The prisoners: use them.*

A plan formed in his mind. A way to use the prisoners to teach his quarrelsome army about discipline and the importance of fighting together. Not with these two officers. What he had in mind was too barbaric for them. No, they of course would be ransomed back to Rome, as honor dictated. But Marhabal had brought many more prisoners; Rome- loving Gauls who'd been captured fighting alongside the Romans. Yes, they would do.

The strength of Solyphos' grip on his arm surprised Nahatum. He could hardly bear the feel of the ancient, flaking skin. When Hannibal had startled the group arguing in the house by ordering an assembly of the entire army in the fields just past the village gate—Now, he'd demanded, clapping his hands like thunderbolts—Solyphos had stood up from his chair with a grimace, put his hand on his lower back for a moment, then reached out for the boy's arm.

They joined thousands of jostling, shouting men lining the low sloping hills just outside what remained of the village stockade. Solyphos insisted that they stand near the front, near to where Gisgo, holding a rough cloth bag, and several well-armed guards surrounded a forlon group of Gauls.

And there in the middle of the sunny field stood Hannibal. He paced, tall and alone. The crowd grew silent as Hannibal came to a standstill, staring at the prisoners. He held up a length of rope, then ordered that all the prisoners be bound at the wrist in pairs.

"Great soldiers of the Carthaginian army! Numidians, Iberians…"– his voice gained force as his words were relayed by dozens of translators calling out in the polyglot of languages among the thousands of men–…"Celts, Africans, Islanders, Carthaginians, Moors, Egyptians, Persians, Greeks." He was shouting now. "All of you. Watch closely."

Hannibal turned to the anxious group of prisoners. "I give you each a choice. Two pairs of you will fight to the death. The winning pair will be given their freedom and a horse and weapon and be allowed to join the Carthaginian army." Those who refuse to fight, he went on, will be given over as slaves to "my new, esteemed allies."

Hannibal bowed toward two men wearing woolen cloaks dyed red and purple. Gaulish chiefs from further south in Italy, in revolt against Rome. More fighters for the army. The men solemnly returned the bow.

The prisoners' faces drained of color. Two men, newly bound with rope, twisted their wrists till they bled, trying to free themselves. Both were sweating and red-faced. Others stared mutely at the ground, tethered to each other like horses waiting for their wagon. Solyphos shifted at the boy's side, leaning now on his staff, moving his feet, his hand—the same one that had once performed its mastery over the papyrus now more like a claw than anything else– still gripping the boy's arm. The boy moved awkwardly a step away, relieved to put some space between them.

One pair nodded, their shackled hands making a slight jerky gesture to volunteer.

The two stumbled forward, out of step with one another. Helpless. Or not? One was a stout bearded man and the other was taller, long-haired, wearing a sheepskin vest.

Hannibal offered a barely perceptible nod. Guards pushed the two forward into the center of the field, and the men stumbled again, pulling awkwardly at their wrists.

Then another pair—both shorter and more muscular— moved forward clumsily. A long, half-healed scar trailed down one man's cheek. Nahatum saw a quick glance and nod between them; they understood something.

Gisgo stepped forward, reached into the bag and carefully handed a dagger to each of the four men.

"Ah, a *pugio*," Solyphos observed. "Captured from the Romans at the cavalry skirmish. An evil weapon for close fighting. Made for stabbing."

The pairs circled each other warily, awkwardly, pulling and pushing at their partners, each man waving his blade in the air with his free hand. Nahatum could see sweat forming on the brows of several of the men, though the day was not warm.

Thousands of men watched in total silence, waiting for someone to die. The stout bearded man seemed to be breathing in gasps, his dagger moving awkwardly side-to-side. He looked terrified and kept tugging his bound wrist as if to free himself. The shortest man suddenly slashed low at the stout bearded one, who jumped away to avoid the blade, pulling his long-haired companion off his feet. Long Hair yelled in desperation as he stumbled, fell, struggled to get up. The other pair sprang at the fallen one in coordinated fashion— that's what they had understood, how to move while bound together— stabbing him over and over in the chest. Their daggers made tearing sounds pushing through dirty sheepskin, muscle and bone.

The butchered long haired man lay heavily on the ground, as his bearded partner stood frozen watching the awful scene, his breath now coming in thick gasps. A thick, dark stain poured over Long Hair's chest– a slashed wineskin emptying.

His bearded partner, standing off- balance, tilted sideways by the binding, finally came to life as the other two turned towards him, daggers at the ready. He cursed, tried to run. Ah, that was the worst thing to do, Nahatum saw immediately. The man pulled frantically at the twisted leather that anchored him to his dead partner, motionless on the ground. The other pair moved forward. Each man stabbed him, one in front, one in back.

They pulled their bloody daggers out and each stabbed him again. And again. He fell like a tree over the body of his partner.

The blood pulsed in the boy's chest, arms, neck. He joined in the roar of celebration. Behind him came the chinkle of gold coins changing hands.

Gisgo, long sword now in hand, led the winners away, to continued loud cheers. Two more pairs came forward. Now the boy leaned forward in anticipation as the crowd began this time to yell encouragement at the desperate pairs, hoping for a good show.

"Come, boy. I've seen enough." Solyphos's hand pulled on his arm. The two pairs of men circled each other warily in the center of the field. Solyphos pulled harder on the boy's wrist. *No! I am not bound to you like some prisoner.*

"I wish to return to my work." A sharp jerk pulled Nahatum off- balance.

"No. You are not my master. I serve Hannibal." He righted himself and pushed the old man's arm away.

A big Gaul swung a dagger at his opponent, who slipped and soon found the dagger in his throat. He lay pinned to the earth like a beetle forked on the cook's table. The fight ended quickly, with two more dying men on the ground. Then another. Then another. Some pairs fought well together, others slashed thoughtlessly, ignoring each other, stumbling, kicking at their dead or wounded companion. They were soon killed by their more skillful opponents, who learned to work together. Some very big Gauls were killed by much smaller opponents, while some men who looked fast were slowed and died because they ignored the binding at their wrists.

In one fight, one of the men was gravely wounded rather quickly, slipping on the muddy, blood-soaked ground. Nahatum expected the fight to be over quickly. But, no: the other pair rushed in too soon for the kill, too confident of victory. With a quick move, the Gaul defended his partner and killed both their opponents. Hannibal applauded loudly for that pair, and called for his doctors to tend to the wounded one.

Dozens of dying men writhed on the ground like fat worms. Dozens of winning pairs were escorted off the field, to have their wounds tended to and to be welcomed by Gisgo into the army. None declined the offer.

The field was a muddy sea of blood. With each confrontation the boy couldn't wait to see what happened, to watch the flash of the dagger in the sunlight. Each fight seemed new, fresh. Which of the men would be cut? Whose stab would find flesh? The gristly sound of knife ripping through muscle made him grind his teeth in a way that was, finally, pleasurable.

How long had they all been standing there, cheering? Finally, a moment to sneak a glance over his shoulder. Solyphos was nowhere to be seen. Who cared, who knew, where the old man was? This was where he should be, right here, watching Hannibal. His master—and he, Hannibal, not the old man, was his master– knelt on one knee watching, hand under chin. He was the one who defeated death.

The sun was low in the sky. He was exhausted. Hannibal was walking ankle deep in the blood-mud. You could hear his boots being sucked in and out of the sticky ground. "So, men of the Carthaginian army—you think I have been providing entertainment? That I gather you here for sport?" No one spoke. The boy's breath came in heaves, as if he had been through a battle himself.

"Listen well to me. We are all prisoners too—prisoners of this country. We have no choice: the way back is blocked by winter snows and hostile peoples, the way forward by the Romans. We must defeat Rome or die ourselves in this land."

Hannibal seemed to be speaking directly to him, looking right at him. "We must depend on each other in the coming battles, as these men have." He gestured to the surviving pairs, bloody and wounded themselves, but still alive. "Those who fought without supporting their companions died. Those prisoners who fought together wontheir freedom. It matters not where you are from. It matters not who was your mother or your father. It matters only that you are brave and will support those who fight alongside you. Remember: if any part of our battle line breaks, we are all doomed."

A cheer rose from deep in the ranks. It started slowly and low and gathered force, mingling accents and intonations. Nahatum heard his own voice, mixed in with all the others. Hannibal!

He knew then that he was something, that he had a spirit for the first time in his life, and that he was a part of something much bigger than just himself. He wanted to yell out his master's name. Hannibal!

Hannibal held his arms up and waved them triumphantly in the air. The strange burn mark on the man's right wrist was clearly visible to the boy. Nahatum waved his own arm in return, with his own burn mark right there on the wrist, dancing then in the manner of the African warriors he could see across the field, chanting their strange sounds and moving their bodies wildly, as if possessed. They were all bound to Hannibal now. The boy's wrist tingled.

"Hannibal!," he screamed, even louder.

Two days later, Hannibal stood on a hillside in the late afternoon darkness after marching south past fields empty of livestock, empty of farmers, apples dangling unharvested from trees, wheat rotting on the stalk, the local men all having had joined the invading army or off fighting with the Romans.

The two Roman armies had combined into one that was but three leagues away, camped just beyond the thick forest on the other side of the shallow but swift-flowing Trebia river. Hannibal stared down at the cold, rushing water, Marhabal at his side. The Numidian slapped at his chest, sending his djellabah billowing out.

"Are you practicing for flight, old friend?," Hannibal asked. "Launch yourself from this hillside to soar like the eagles of Djebel Babor? Remember how we used to hunt when I visited your family in Numidia?"

A hearty laugh, the satisfactions of memory. "We're hunting something much bigger now, aren't we, Hannibal?" Then: "It's cold. I can feel the wind coming off the river."

"Ah, finally the Numidian feels cold. I won't tell Gisgo you said that. He warned you."

Marhabal laughed and opened his djellabah to reveal a woven Roman cloak. From the small front pocket he produced a palmful of desert sand that sparkled in the morning light. "From my homeland. I carried a small box all the way over the mountains and now it is the pocket of a dead Roman's battle cloak. I am ready for battle. So, what is our plan? You always have a plan. Even when we were hunting those eagles, you'd be ordering me around, telling me how to sneak up on the birds. In my own country."

What is my battle plan? A plan was forming in his mind, yet the cost of the journey through the mountains washed then over Hannibal: he'd lost almost half his army from hunger, sickness, the ambush by the Allobrodge on that twisting trail in the gorge.

Ten of the war elephants had died along the way. The Romans were rested and well- fed and outnumbered them. However, he'd learned something back in Taurini when talking to the arrogant Roman prisoners: they'd revealed that their commander—Consul Sempronius —was impulsive. Those haughty Roman officers had tried to threaten him— "He is not a man to let some rebellious marauders deal him a defeat. He will come after you, and quickly"—but all they'd done was give him valuable information about their commander's temperament.

So, Hannibal thought standing on the hillside looking down at the river, we must draw out this impulsive commander and use the terrain to our advantage. *As you always said, father: pay attention to the water. Water instills fear– fear of losing your footing and flailing helplessly against your enemy, of chaos in the battle line, of drowning under the weight of your own armor.*

They faced a well-disciplined army, twice their size. They must weaken it. He wanted the Romans cold and hungry, hurrying into battle.

"Marhabal. In the morning, just as the sun is coming up, you will attack the Roman camp. I want them to see clearly who you are and which direction you have ridden from. Attack and then withdraw."

"Withdraw? Marhabal's forehead furrowed in frustration. "We've already seen these Romans can hardly ride. Let me penetrate their camp, strike quickly for this Consul Sepronius' tent. This time we capture him."

Well, the Romans are not the only impulsive ones. Maybe you have to be rash to be a great cavalryman.

"No, we need to be careful now. Winning a small cavalry skirmish—I'm sorry, my friend…" He put a hand on Marhabal's shoulder…"does not provide the strategy for defeating—no, destroying—a large army. I want you to poke at the Romans, like a boy poking a stick into a bee's nest. Attack and then retreat. Make it look even like they are driving you off. Flee back through the forest and across the river, this way. Make a lot of noise."

"Retreat." He sounded so forlorn.

"I want the Romans to pursue you at first light, in haste, without planning, when the day is coldest and most importantly, when the river is coldest. I want you to splash your way back across that river and up the hill, right to here." He swept his arm in front of him, at the crest. "We will be waiting with a few surprises for the Romans."

Yes, I've learned something from that unpleasant mountain ambush in the gorge: the value of hidden troops in a side canyon, like the one just down river.

Marhabal was to ready the cavalry for their early morning ride, while Hannibal would find the cooks and talk to them directly. "Why are you talking to cooks?," asked the surprised Numidian. "To make sure our secret weapon is ready, first thing, before battle. Secret weapon?" Yes. Hannibal loved this, he was so glad his friend asked:

"Breakfast before battle."

The large wooden bucket of oatmeal hanging over each shoulder weighed heavily on Nahatum as he walked through the dark, cold early morning mist. *Am I again Hannibal's servant?* He hoped so. Hannibal had ordered him directly to the cook's area. The thick leather straps dug into his neck, the skin already prickly from the frosty air.

The boy lurched around the campsite, ghost-like, past men readying their weapons for battle. He was entranced, his tired shoulders strengthened with the power of what was happening around him. He knew the men were each summoning up whatever charm, enchantment, spell, or power they knew to protect them in what lay ahead. Private rituals and personal worship, preparations that they prayed would blunt their opponent's sword, lift the arrows over their heads, keep them from the thousand gruesome deaths— or worse, injuries– that awaited on a battlefield. Men bent over flickering campfires, swords on their laps, lovingly sharpening the blade with a pumice stone.

He passed a Numidian cavalryman weaving horsehair into his own braid, as if to become one with the animal. The elephants were already prepared for battle. Yesterday, he'd watched the turbaned Mahouts–elephant handlers who speak the Indoi language, men so lean their ribs showed through their skin— as they sharpened the long tusks of their elephants, polishing the white ivory to spear- sharp points, talking gently to the enormous beasts, soothing them. Then they fitted the tusks with sharp iron tips.

Battle, not breakfast, was on everyone's minds. The boy walked timidly among the warriors, buckets swaying. Even the cooks had protested last night after his master had called him and all the other servants together and told them to collect all the buckets they could find. They were going to give out oatmeal before the birds even called the day into song? He'd never heard the toothless cook even talk to Hannibal before and, astonishingly, the man lost himself and objected: "You're supposed to have a feast after battle to praise the gods who've given you victory, not breakfast in middle of the night."

The cook might rely on the gods, but the boy knew hunger and the desperate things it made people do. He hardly needed to hear Hannibal's words to the cooks, urging them to get to work: "Let the Romans come into battle cold and hungry, not us." Still, the cooks grumbled when Hannibal was out of earshot: "It's up to the gods, not oatmeal." Nahatum thought long and hard about that: maybe a stomach full of oatmeal was more powerful than the gods.

Now he fingered his sash for courage as he wobbled at this unnatural hour among the fearsome Balearic Island slingthrowers, buckets knocking into him, and them. The Islanders sat around their campfires, readying themselves, amidst their rocks. And their stench. What was it Solyphos said yesterday? The Balearic slingthrowers smear the foul oil of the mastic tree on themselves before battle. How did the man know so much? They brought the oil with them in little pouches.

The god of Fear, Solyphos had said—they believe it terrorizes their enemies.

Well, it certainly terrorized Nahatum then. Wordlessly he held a ladleful of the steaming oatmeal in front of several men, slings dangling from their belts. "From Hannibal himself." Grudgingly, they reached up their battered tin cups and he filled them. He dared to stand there and makes sure they ate, his free hand on his Carthaginian purple sash.

Chalky rocks lay scattered at their feet, mixed with black granite shale. One man had a leather pouch stuffed almost to overflowing in front of him, another hanging from his waist. The man next to him bent over a rock, using black ash from the fire to draw a sacred design on it.

The boy moved on with his buckets. And without his pike. He would not fight that day. "You are not ready to engage with Roman legionnaires," Hannibal had instructed earlier, while Jonaz helped his master put on battle armor. "Stay with the supply wagons." And again, there it was: "You can assist Solyphos while he takes notes on what he sees."

"Oatmeal," Nahatum told the next group of soldiers. "Direct from Hannibal, take some, his orders. I come directly from Hannibal."

Crows—those black harbingers of death—squawked high in the trees. Hannibal walked over to the crest of the hill, peering down at the bend in the river. The leather battle armor pulled at his shoulders as he leaned against his sword. Since Saguntum, back in Iberia, he had developed a habit of resting it, tip first, on the ground before battle. The sun began to peek over the top of the tall pines. He waited for Marhabal to return, bringing the Romans in pursuit, if he was lucky. Or unlucky.

A peal of thunder from across the river. No, hoofbeats! An uncountable number. Their pounding—dull thuds—filled the air. The crows took to the sky. A mass of riders— Marhabal's Numidians, djellabhas flying— poured out of the woods and splashed across the river. Once, back in Iberia, he'd seen desperate men fleeing a forest fire. His next thought: *where was Marhabal?*

"Jonaz."

"Lord?" Came the reply from behind, his squire holding his battle shield and extra swords.

He and his squire hurried along the ridge behind the thousands of massed Gauls— the center of his battle line—arrayed along the hilltop, looking down at the steep embankment. The thudding of the hoofbeats came closer. And then there was Marhabal, his djellabah a rich red in the early morning light, his horses' hooves digging into the soft spring soil of the hillside, the man's head low and close in to the horse's mane.

Marhabal's riders followed closely behind, horse's hooves kicking up bursts of spray in the busy river.

As they approached, Hannibal yelled orders to the battle line of Gauls: let the riders pass, move aside, then regain your place. Marhabal seemed to ride right toward him, then they all swerved away at the very top and disappeared into the woods behind the Gauls.

The frosty silence returned. The crows settled back onto their branches, silent this time as they waited to see what would happen next.

The boy sat miserably on an empty wooden crate, feet kicking at the slatted sides, in the deserted cooking area. He stared at an empty, slimy bucket of oatmeal in his lap.

There was a pile of buckets but no one there to clean them— the cooks having been pressed into battle. *I won't do it. I'm Hannibal's servant, not the cooks'.*

How Jonaz would mock him: the wolf child, the hex, the crow who brings us bad luck, cannot even fight to defend the army. On the orders of Hannibal. Useless.

The cooking area lay behind a slight rise, away from the hilltop where the army was massed, waiting. Even from there you could hear the distant thunder of hoofbeats approaching. Closer, closer.

He sprang forward toward the battle line just in time to see Marhabal's cavalry emerging over the crest and then disappearing into the forest behind them. Where were they coming from? Why did they ride away?

The boy edged closer still. Hannibal didn't specifically forbid him from watching, even if he was forbidden from fighting. The Gauls were lined up closest to him, holding their wooden pikes. They began to sing and chant, swaying, chests naked despite the morning cold, long red hair draped over their shoulders and down their backs. A familiar odor. Ah, yes, there were the sling throwers lined up in rows, three deep, slightly back from the crest. So, the Romans wouldn't see them standing there until they reached the top of the hill. Each man's long leather sling was filled with a rock. Hannibal was nowhere to be seen.

Nahatum's foot couldn't find a pebble or stone to kick, no way to dig the toe of his sandal into the usually sandy soil, the ground packed hard by men's feet.

A rustle of fabric on his arm. Solyphos' tunic waved in the wind. The boy, startled, ignored the man, watching the line of dancing, singing Gauls. Feathers, charms, amulets waved atop each man's thick wooden pike.

A far-off noise. A deep rumble, different from the pounding of hoofbeats. These were not horses. The crows again squawked away into the sky. Tearing, splitting sounds. Branches cracked and broke in the woods on the other side of the river. The smaller trees swayed in the pink dawn light. The Roman army, five men abreast, came hurrying down the forest trail. He saw a thick, worm-like monster slithering toward him through the woods—all leathery flesh and sharp, pointed metal spear-horns, taller than Hannibal's African warriors, wider even then his elephants—knocking aside the very forest itself.

He stepped backward. "Steady, young Nahatum." Solyphos' hand rested on his shoulder and this time the boy didn't push it away. Across the river, men poured out of the forest. Metal men with glistening helmets covering their faces, waving iron spears and steel shields, snorting smoke from their noses and mouths. Their skin looked black in the low light.

He heard Hannibal's voice—where was he?—off to his left. Calm, low, commanding. "Slingthrowers. Ready." There he was, striding now toward the Gauls on the right flank of the hill, magnificent in the armor that Jonaz had put on him. Again, calm words. "They are crossing the river. Let them crest the hill, give the slingthrowersa clear volley."

Hordes of Romans climbed the hill. The boy crept closer to get a better look.

Their legs and tunics glistened wet with cold river water. He wished he hadn't looked— he saw an angry wave about to smash into him. A line of the demons crested the hill and ran toward the singing, swaying Gauls. He knelt low behind several of the biggest Gauls and could just see through their legs.

The Romans were only about ten running steps away. Some wore leather helmets almost like bowls over their heads, others had metal ones. One helmet, shining so that it must have been bronze, had a thick metal finger extending down over the man's nose. A spike protruded from the front and for a moment the boy wondered if the Romans had horns. His chest seemed to have become ice and he couldn't make his legs work. No matter: Solyphos' hand on his back kept him from running away.

The bronze helmeted Roman ran with a stolid gait, like a boar or pig, sword extended and shield held high toward, then over, the crest of the hill, right into the center of the Carthaginian battle line.

Why don't the Gauls do something? Nahatum's mouth went dry and his legs felt nailed to the ground. He couldn't make them move.

A whirring sound filled the air. Arms high above their heads, the slingthrowers spun their pouches, then released the rocks, stones, shale, granite. They'd talked of rock avalanches all the way through the Endless Mountains, but the boy had never seen one. Now he did. A rock smashed into the face of the helmeted Roman and he fell like a tree, backwards into the man behind him, who held up his sword, as if to command the rocks to stop. A shield was a better idea. The dull thud of rocks on shields—Romans huddling behind and under them— was followed by a sharp whizzing sound, like that of angry bees. A rain of arrows—the archers must have been lined up behind the sling throwers— descended on the Romans.

Roman bodies lay everywhere at the crest of the hill, yet still they came. The sling throwers kept up their barrage, but the Roman swords and spears were relentless. All the boy could see was Gauls holding this part of the battle line. Where had Hannibal gone? Where was mighty Gisgo, with the armored infantry? The Romans ran past, and over, the fallen bodies of their comrades. How grateful he was, really, that he was behind the Gauls, that they stood between him and the Romans with their slit-like mouths and cruel eyes. Then the Gauls raised their pikes over their heads, yelling curses at the Romans, and ran toward them, leaving the boy where he knelt, nowhere to hide, staring at their backs.

The line of Gauls collided with the Romans. One of the Gauls directly in front of the boy fell over, the point of a Roman spear sticking out from his back. Another Roman ran through a break in the line, directly toward the boy. A Gaul confronted him, his carved wooden pike pushing back a steel Roman sword.

The boy turned. Solyphos was gone. He was alone. From the slight rise, he could see that beyond the cook's wagon the old man was running into his tent. Nahatum bolted then, too, hating himself for seeking shelter with a coward. All he wanted was to get away from the Romans. They would soon overrun the whole camp. He had to hide.

Somewhere. In the forest. He knew how to disappear in a copse of wood, in the hidden spaces of a pile of boulders.

Almost past the tent, he bumped into Solyphos coming out. "Help me with this armor, boy." He slowly thrust freshly-oiled but old and worn leather armor at Nahatum, almost falling over as he did. Frantic as Nahatum was, the sight of the armor calmed him, made him think of Hannibal just a few hours ago looking magnificent in his own armor. Well-stitched leather patches strengthened worn spots and sword gouges. "These Gauls need help. I can't stand around and watch, no matter what Hannibal said." The boy stood there, holding the armor, staring at it. Solyphos yelled at him. "This is also not the time for panic. Come on." He slapped Nahatum on the side of the head.

The boy lashed the armor on the old man, forcing himself to focus on tying the knots so they would not come undone. That was the worst thing, Jonaz once told him in a quiet moment: to have your master's armor come undone in the middle of battle. He didn't want that to happen to Solyphos. But, then, what would happen to Solyphos? The man could hardly walk, and now he was going to battle the Romans? All the boy wanted to do then was stay in the tent, hide there. Instead, he ran for his pike.

When he returned, Solyphos had begun to walk with unsteady steps toward the battle line. He looked so thin and frail compared to the tall, bulky Gauls in the distance.

The boy quickly caught up to the old Greek warrior-scribe, who suddenly bent over, trying to catch his breath. "I am not myself, I tried to run too quickly." The old man used his sword more as a staff than a weapon; it seemed the only thing keeping him upright. Nahatum, leaned over to support him, but Solyphos pushed him away. "Go, boy, do the best you can, that battle line will not hold much longer."

Nahatum's legs felt made of mud as he walked toward the fighting, men stabbing and thrusting and killing and dying all around him. A Gaul with a bloody slashed throat lay dead on the ground, eyes cold and fish-like, staring at Nahatum.

Suddenly there was movement to the boy's right: a Roman ran toward him, sword extended, wearing one of those awful helmets. Nahatum watched as if in a dream, knowing then that this was the day he was to die. Then off to his left he saw an enormous Gaul, long red hair past his shoulders, ram his pike deep into a Roman's soldiers gut; the Roman fell like a tree. The boy realized he was not fighting alone.

His pike was longer than the sword of the Roman coming quickly toward him. He swung it in a quick, low arc underneath the Romans' weapon, as the Gauls had showed him during those long days of practice in ruined Taurini. The Roman took the full weight of the pike against the side of his knees and collapsed to the ground in pain.

A snarling sound from behind. With the stub of his pike, a wounded Gaul, blood dripping from the wound on his arm, was trying to parry a Roman whose sword had smashed his weapon into pieces. Quickly, Nahatum thrust out his pike butt-first and caught the Roman full-on in the stomach. The wood struck deep into the man's armor plate and he gave out a gasp and stumbled, tripping over the lifeless body of another Gaul at his feet. The wounded Gaul grabbed the Roman's sword, found the break in the Roman's chest plating, and drove the metal deep into the man's ribs. He fell and didn't move.

A bird flew past the boy's ear. No, a knife. The Roman whose knees he'd just shattered threw it from where he lay. Furious, pike over his head, Nahatum brought the heavy wooden thing down full-force, smashing the man's head. On the ground in front of him lay a bloody mess, mouth agape, metal helmet pushed into the man's eyes, bloody fist of flesh where his nose was. The boy bellowed in triumph.

Gaulish fighters were shouting and moving backwards. Their line was breaking.

Nahatum wanted to run back to Solyphos, a thin, lone figure he could just see further back standing near the cook's tents, to get away from the relentless river of Roman soldiers still cresting the hill. Then a deafening bellow erupted from behind. Not trumpets. A familiar musky smell. An elephant thundered past, trampling two Gauls not a wagon length from the boy. More bellowing. He whirled around. Several drivers, legs straddling the elephants' necks, feet behind their floppy ears, were whipping the animals toward the Romans. Blood dripped from the elephants' backs and legs as long, barbed lashes dug into their skin. Leather battle armor covered the animals' heads and shoulders. Archers sat atop, raining arrows down on the Romans. One elephant swung an iron ball attached to his trunk; with one powerful stroke he beheaded a Roman. Lizard Skin himself would bow before that sight.

A Gaul pulled Nahatum back by his collar as another elephant rumbled past; they'd as likely kill either of them as kill a Roman. An armored legionnaire stood frozen about ten paces away—eyes wide, nostrils flared, mouth grimacing. The boy recognized that look. Terror. Now the Romans knew that Hannibal could unleash monsters. The Roman stepped backwards, as did several other legionnaires. The Roman battle line wavered, starting to break apart under the elephants' brutal charge down the hillside. The boy charged forward, screaming and yelling, behind the elephants' swaying backs, surrounded by angry Gauls eager to kill Romans. They were inspired. The boy was swept into the solid phalanx of sweaty, bloody men pushing the exhausted Romans down the hill toward the cold rushing waters of the Trebia.

The water was so cold, yet he splashed forward, barely feeling it. The Romans were trying to form a battle line in the freezing, onrushing water almost up to their knees. More yelling. Hannibal's African warriors appeared from somewhere upriver, he could see them off to his left. And than there was the Carthaginian armored infantry, somehow behind the Romans, who were now surrounded.

How did Gisgo and his men get there?, the boy wondered, then he was splashing toward the disorganized Romans, swinging his pike.

As the sun descended, Nahatum stood exhausted at the edge of the chilly shallows, Solyphos was beside him. The scribe was still in his old battle armor, holding his sword, having picked his way slowly down the hill in search of the boy. Solyphos flexed his fingers and wrung his hands to keep them from freezing. The Roman army was no more. The water flowed over the dead and the dying. The sounds of the dying mixed with the sound of rushing river water flowing over the river rocks and gravel, creating a strange, almost melodious effect. Then it was broken by a loud clatter, metal on rock. The boy whirled around, pike ready. He found Solyphos staring down at his sword lying where he'd thrown it in the rushing river.

"Are you wounded? Hurt? Sir?" Nahatum was surprised to feel so tenderly toward Solyphos.

No reply from the old man. He looked so tired. Was he disappointed that he'd tried to fight and couldn't? And now to have treated his sword with such disrespect; most soldiers treated their weapons better than themselves. The boy stooped to pick it up and handed it back to him. Solyphos wiped the sword off, tenderly, on his shirt and returned it to the leather scabbard on his belt, all the while shaking his head. More moans from the dying Romans in the river. "What are they saying, Sir?"

"They're calling for their mothers. Dying soldiers often call for their mothers. I've heard it before, in many languages. I promised myself I would not participate again. Now here I am."

The boy stifled a laugh, not sure what he found funny, except the old man could be spouting crow-talk for all the sense he was making at the end of this great victory, and with Lizard Skin himself on the loose, crawling into men's bodies and making them his own. How could he listen to nonsense when his head felt like it was about to drift off into the leafy branches above their heads?

The boy kicked at a Roman lying belly down in the stream, the stump of his arm draining pink in the water. Bubbles trickled from his mouth. His legs twitched twice as the boy's foot found him, then stopped. Soon the bubbles stopped, too.

Solyphos clenched his fingers, as if reminded that his hands barely worked. "This cold casts a spell on my joints."

Where was Hannibal? The boy hadn't seen his master since the battle began. He ran up the hill, toward the crest where men milled around, talking, staring into space, tending the wounded and dying. He searched amidst all the activity, all the warriors, aware for the first time that Hannibal might be wounded, or worse. That was impossible to imagine, yet he did. The worst thing in the world. The lightness in his head drifted down into his chest, hollowing it out.

Then he saw him, standing outside his tent, the leather battle armor so clean this morning covered now in red streaks and dirt stains. Beside him, Jonaz was shooting arrows at the vultures circling overhead. He had a deathly fear of vultures. He believed that Mot, the Carthaginian God of Death, took the form of a broad-winged, beady-eyed vulture who carried away the dead. Hannibal turned and told his squire to stop wasting arrows.

Hannibal. Gisgo. Marhabal. The three were laughing and talking. They'd learned something from that mountain ambush: Gisgo and the armored infantry had been hiding in a side canyon, ready to spring on the rear of the Roman army and cut off any escape. "You are a magician, My Lord," Gisgo said. "The Romans had no idea where we came from."

The boy recalled what he'd heard about Hannibal so long ago in Iberia: In battle, Hannibal makes his soldiers disappear, then reappear where you least expect them. He is a shape shifter... Then Hannibal saw him. "Ah, boy, come here. You have some blood on you? Well, good, not your own, I see."

"Sir, I...." He yearned to tell Hannibal that he had killed a man in battle, that he did what any good soldier would do, but then he'd have to admit that he didn't stay behind at the supply wagons, and that neither did Solyphos. What was this?—he felt an odd loyalty to Solyphos. No matter, Hannibal interrupted before he could say any more.

"Not now. Help me with this armor. It needs cleaning."

The boy ran toward him, vision still blurred by the pesky water in his eyes, but his heart full.

The army marched triumphantly southward through boggy farmland and swampy forests toward their winter encampment in the town of Bologna, the home of the Boii, a powerful and rebellious Gaulish tribe which formed an alliance with Hannibal after his great victory.

Hannibal, perched once again atop Sirius, rode along among—and above– his victorious men, calculating: thirty-five years since Hamilcar Barca had surrendered the armies of Carthage to Rome to end the first war. Thirty- eight years since a Carthaginian army had defeated a Roman army. *Father, I hope your spirit finds relief.*

He tried to get the image of what he'd seen at that river out of his mind. *The water actually ran red with blood. A river of blood.* He had done that: lured the confident Romans into an elegant trap and destroyed them. Thousands of men who had awoken that day with lives—hopes and plans—were now dead because of him. You are a magician, Gisgo said. A magician of death.

He wanted this war over, soon.

Still, such thoughts drifted away as Hannbal analyzed the effectiveness of his strategy: the coordination of the cavalry and the infantry, Gisgo's side attack that led to the rout. His battle line held, except for a small number of Romans who cut through the center and escaped—the Romans are formidable when they are fighting straight ahead.

Their armor, that is a problem. What will he do about that? And their ability to maintain a central, interlocked battle line. The Gauls fight so independently and loosely, they still don't know how to fight as one.

There was much to do, much to take care of. One victory— no matter how decisive– does not win a war. But a second one?

Bologna was a place of wonder. Nahatum wandered daily through the vast Boii village, which stretched over the hills and almost out of sight. The houses—set so close together that he could hardly see between them– had walls and floors of rough, thick pine, cut into boards that revealed the wavy design of the grain.

The inside of the houses, formed of the forest, smelled like the forest and reminded him of his own forest home. The thatched roofs would bend under the weight of the winter snow but would not yield. The thickly piled snow, Solyphos informed him, served to help keep warmth from the fireplaces in the houses. "Which is good," Solyphos added, "given how wet and damp this place is, surrounded by swamps and bogs."

Not that Nahatum noticed. He slept in the small barn attached to Hannibal's house, among the pigs and chickens who became the meals for his master and friends and the many visiting Gaulish chiefs. What did it matter that everywhere was wet? They'd marched through large swampy fields that grew the rice that he'd learned was a specialty of northern Italy. The small chewy bits reminded him of ants that he'd eat on hungry days back in the forest. Why not just eatants?

A winter encampment provided more free time. There was only so many times you could clean your master's swords and shields, sharpen his weapons with the whet stone, or wash blood off clothes. After so long on the march, always moving and always hurried, the boy had time to linger at the animal pens after bringing slop from the kitchens to the animal troughs.

He particularly liked to feed the elephants. He studied their movements, remembering how they were able to thread themselves—their huge bulk– along narrow trails that gave grown men pause. Their massive feet were padded; he observed them walk on their four huge front toes along the rocky trails. These were the very beasts that had terrorized the Romans at the Trebia, that led the charge that restored the army in the face of the Romans' might. Almost all now had wounds– bloody shoulders and cuts and scars on their trunks and legs, their massive heads. The elephant's histories were slashed on their bodies. Long scars, gashes, sad places with pustulence running down their sides. The animals were so brave in their treatment of the wounds, allowing him to rub in aloe and other herbal remedies. On wet days the rain splashed off their back so that they shone like ebony carvings.

There were fewer in the pen than he remembered in Iberia. He'd heard that a number of elephants had died of the cold in the mountains, but had not seen any of the deaths and with all that was happening, he had pushed the knowledge out of his mind. Until then.

One day Nahatum walked up to an elephant and put his palm right up onto its hard folded skin, so tough that it could withstand Roman arrows and spears, yet also oddly soft to the touch. The elephant was shivering in the unheated barn. Later, the boy brought a blanket from their supplies and covered the beast.

Solyphos was always asking him to bring more wood for his fire and rubbing his hands, elbows, knees, as if to set them ablaze like kindling. The boy, though, had the barn, with its warm hay-bed to sleep in at night and Hannibal's fireplace to tend during the day. He couldn't ask for more, serving both men, happily.

And, finally, he had killed a man at the Trebia. He smashed in a man's head with his pike. Sometimes he had unpleasant dreams of the man's shattered face, that bloody mess, that one eye that poked out from the smashed helmet, lifeless, dead, looking right at him.

Still, he was proud that he killed a man; now he could be one of the soldiers, no longer just a boy. He'd not told Hannibal. In fact, Hannibal was so busy that Nahatum only saw him when bringing in wood, food, drink during meetings. There was the laundry, cleaning the house, helping the cooks, every now and then helping Solyphos (who seemed to have recovered his strength and eluded Lizard Skin), taking the slop to the animal pens.

He planned to tell Hannibal soon that he knew now how to kill. That he was ready for battle. This was what a man of value did, someone who was not, that Greek word, an *apostide* without worth. He would be a valued warrior.

He waited for the time to tell Hannibal because he didn't want to seem to be reaching beyond his station. Yet when Nahatum was honest with himself the boy knew that what stopped him from telling Hannibal that he was ready for battle was his fear that Hannibal would laugh at him.

The thud of his boots on the wooden floor irritated Hannibal, putting him in mind of Carthage—the polished marble floors inlaid with precious stones. *Boots on marble don't make an incessant thump when you walk.* His left eye ached.

He paced in the second- grandest house in Bologna, given to him by King Magalus, a not unpleasant fellow. There was the scent of old wood throughout. The King had joined the war, and sent messengers hailing Hannibal's arrival throughout the countryside. *You are in fact now the master of Northern Italy. Be pleased at this.*

Yet the wood continued to annoy him. Floors, walls, ceiling, stockades. The Gauls loved their wood—houses of wood, pikes of wood. They insisted on going into battle at the Trebia with wooden pikes and of course Roman steel cut right through it. They've refused the swords and spears collected from the dead Romans at the river. A treasure trove of steel weapons. No interest. They'd taken the cloaks and some of the leather hats and helmets, but even then they said they would wear them for warmth in the winter, but not into battle. They claimed that their pikes contain powerful tree spirits that will carry them to victory. To fight in Roman clothing rather than naked would sap them of their power.

Ba'al's breath. These Gauls' love of wooden pikes is going to cost them dearly in the coming battles. The Romans understand the value of steel: they're fighting for empire in Iberia partly because of the iron from the mines there. Their Roman killing sword, the *gladius*, was a fearsome steel weapon. Well, better that the Gauls paid the price than his Carthaginian veterans. So many more Gauls. Still, he was going to have to think about how best to use them in battle, their wood against Roman steel. Despite the massacre, a few Romans escaped at the Trebia.

He rubbed his left eye, couldn't get rid of the pain.

He didn't like this longing for Carthage. He could feel the smooth marble floors there cool to the touch on the very soles of his feet. In Iberia, his father built an estate that rivaled what the family owned in Carthage, with beautiful onyx marble brought over directly from Oued Abdallah. He'd run across the polished granite floor in Iberia and slide towards his father who would catch him and throw him high into the air. His brother Hasdrubal was there somewhere, probably trying to slide after him.

Some people thought of his father Hamilcar as brutal and single-minded, but they didn't really know him. Or, maybe he was, but that wasn't all he was.

He needed to stop wondering, too, about his little son back in Carthage, and whether he ran along the marble floor of their villa. Maybe he would be back in time to catch him sliding across the marble and throw him into the air. First he had to defeat Rome. He was almost there.

Concentrate. You have a lot to think about, with the meeting tonight in the Boii's grand meeting hall.

If he could only get the blurriness out of his left eye. The cold and damp, had been bothering the eye for weeks now.

That night, Gisgo kept talking to the bleached white skull in his hand as he walked back with Hannibal from the meeting at "the Convenor"—the Boii's massive gathering hall, walls more than a spruce high, floor wider than two lowland pine trees set head-to-head. Hannibal could see that his infantry commander was in a good mood.

Gisgo held the skull in front of him almost at eye level. Was he talking to it or taunting it? A cold wind blew from the hills down onto the dark, foggy lane, as they walked back to Hannibal's house, trailed by Nahatum carrying a torch.

The infantryman kept repeating to the skull the toasts the visiting Gaulish chiefs had exchanged with the two of them. The smell of the thick honey-scented wine had filled the warm air of the big room, driving out the odor of damp clothes and soaked skin. The Boii and Umbrian chiefs had passed the ceremonial goblet now in Gisgo's hands— the bleached, gold-lined skull of a Roman Consul killed years ago in a great Boii ambush of a Roman army—and pledged fealty to "our brothers from across the mountains." Hannibal's prophecy had been fulfilled: Gauls on both sides of the Alps had put aside their differences and flocked to him as a liberator from the Roman threat.

The dark lane was nearly empty. They passed houses of thick, hewn logs built high off the ground, in the Gaulish fashion, above the snow. Gisgo had asked their hosts to borrow the skull to allow him a similar ceremony among his infantrymen. "Soon every man will have his own Roman skull to raise in praise to Ba'al Shammon," he'd told them. The Gauls had looked confused at this reference to the Carthaginian god, but no matter.

Gisgo was so pleased with the skull and their success that evening that he clearly didn't hear Hannibal grunt, then stumble, half-falling. The infantryman just caught him by the shoulder, preventing a bad spill.

"I thought something ran between my legs. My left eye's no use now. It constantly deceives me. If I close my right eye, everything is fuzzy." The constant ache, the endless fog and mist, when it was not actually snowing. *Tonight the eye is worse. Do I say anything?* He can see nothing out of the eye. He turned to Gisgo, and the boy now standing beside him also holding his arm as if he were an old man.

"I seem to have gone blind in one eye."

"Saffron, My Lord, will heal your eye. The potency is increased when mixed with lentils." The bearded Carthaginian doctor—trained in the medical school in Alexandria— placed several small ornate, carved boxes on the large table in Hannibal's residence, along with a number of silk bags. Working slowly and cautiously, the doctor took each ingredient with a small silver spoon and placed it in his wooden pestle, crushing the mixture into a thick paste that tasted awful.

Two days passed without any improvement. The priests arrived to call on Ba'al Shammon's help, followed by Boii healers and masters of forest herbs. All crowded into Hannibal's house. Remedies, amulets, charms, cat's eyes. Visitors poked at Hannibal's eye, staring at him, muttering prayers and holding up the red- spotted yellow-brown skin of the Egyptian sand snake, bathing the sick eye in the soft blue light reflected from Syrian crystals. An Egyptian doctor bled Hannibal four times while the boy poked through the thin, berobed man's large dirt box gathering the slippery leeches. The next night the priests rubbed the entirety of Hannibal's sleeping pallet with garlic, which they claimed had powerful properties against scorpions and evil spells. At least in Carthage.

But apparently not here in the land of the Boii. The garlic reeked through Hannibal's bedroom but had no effect on his dead eye. The boy told him that rumors spread in the army that whatever evilness had taken possession of his eye was stronger than Hannibal's magic.

Be careful here. Commanders who become ill breed dark questions. Some will ask if he had he lost the favor of the gods or if there was some secret weakness in the man. Jonaz and several others had just the day before sacrificed two sheep and two goats for the pleasure of Ba'al Shammon; he'd heard his squire had blamed Nahatum for the troubles, claiming—yet again—that the boy was a hex, displeasing the god. He'd have to speak to his squire about blaming the boy.

Hannibal dug his sword into the wooden floor of his study, gouging a deep hole. He tried to contemplate the possibility of going blind in both eyes, but his mind rebelled. He had already practiced one- eyed with Jonaz and some of the best swordsmen among the infantry, relearning his close-in sword-work. He dug the sword deeper again into the floor, gouging another hole. Two holes; one for each eye.

The boy came to the door to announce that the Egyptian doctor had reappeared, the box of leeches under his arm.

No, by god! Hannibal pushed the frightened man out the front door of the house, right into the snow, telling him that he didn't desire his services. "My right eye is good as ever. I don't want you damaging that one." As he slammed the door behind the hapless Egyptian, Hannibal called for Nahatum to summon Gisgo and Marhabal, yelling loudly enough for all in the street to hear. "Enough about my eyes; all is fine. Let us return to our plans for the Spring. I want to hear about what we have learned from our spies about what the Romans are planning."

The boy knew exactly what the trouble was. Yes, a hex, but not one of his making. As he lay in his corner of the barn, burrowed deep in hay against the frigid night blasts, he considered what happened that afternoon when he brought some frozen slop to the animal pens. The elephant handlers, the Mahouts, dressed only in loincloths under their bearskin cloaks, had given up their own blankets to cover their elephants, so unused to the bitter cold of the Italian winter. He'd stood there, watching the great beasts shivering.

"Your master is blind now, they say," muttered the young Boii stable boy. "No. His left eye is sore, that's all. His sight will return."

"It's the vapors. The Romans put a hex on Hannibal. They can make pacts with the Underworld, release vapors that can kill a man even if he be in far Boii- land. My uncle died the same way fighting the Romans."

So, Nahatum knew then that Lizard Skin had come once again to take what was most precious to him. He would not allow that to happen this time.

He woke the next morning determined that no Roman spell or vapor from the Underworld would cause Hannibal further harm. His mother had long ago fed him boiled roots when he was sick. Of mugwort? Sassafras? His mother's magic would work where the doctor's herbs failed. He hurried through his chores – this was far more important than cleaning each sword perfectly– and then rushed into the village in the sun- drenched afternoon, crawling through the snow under the raised huts, digging into frozen ground with a knife borrowed from the cook wagon. A root, any root.

Then he realized: somewhere nearby must be an entrance to the Underworld. How else could a vapor be released? He could look for healing roots and perhaps find the way into the Underworld as well.

He elbowed his pike through the snow into the hard, rippled ground, desperate to find the hidden tunnel or opening the Romans had used to entice a vapor from the Underworld into the encampment.

Nahatum's search went on for several days, taking up more and more of his time.

He hurried through tasks, finding any excuse to get out of Hannibal's house and underneath the village huts, wandering into the hills around the village, along the edges of the nearby frozen swamps. He thrust his pike everywhere, digging until his hands chaffed and ached. The Underworld was clever, of course, and hid its opening well. The frozen ground revealed no entrance, and surrendered no healing roots either to his cold, bleeding hands.

The boy remained undaunted, unbowed. Lizard Skin had come once to take what was most dear to him. Not again.

Hannibal poked at the bone around his eye socket, rubbed the taut skin, as if to prod a dead animal to life. Then he stared at his writing desk. *You can see fine with one eye. Get to work. You have more to worry about than a useless eye.*

There were letters to be dictated, and the history, the story to be told. He wanted to write to his wife, Imre. He hoped eventually for some word from her. With the coming spring it was not mad to imagine that letters might get through by sea.

And, then there was far-away Phillip V, King of Macedonia. Magalus, his new Boii ally, had said that Phillip might be interested in an alliance; the man understood the threat of a "Roman peace" settling over all of Italy. As Phillip should, a direct descendant of Alexander the Great. What a correspondence to have, with the descendant of Alexander himself! Could a letter find its way to him?

First you need to get Solyphos here. A heaviness invaded Hannibal's chest. His old tutor now wrote so slowly that sometimes Hannibal wondered if the man had himself lost sight in his eyes. *He was supposed to have been here a half hour ago.* The weariness intensified. Hannibal pictured Solyphos stooped over his writing tablet, the man's writing impossible to read.

What had happened to that beautiful calligraphy that he used to envy as a child?

The man is old, be merciful. The passage through the Endless Mountains would have killed any other man his age. *He has survived because he wants to help you. Remember that.*

Still, right now nothing seemed to be happening the way Hannibal wanted. First the eye, now Solyphos. "Nahatum, where is Solyphos?" No response from the other room. "Nahatum, where are you?" No reply. *Someone else I seem not to be able to control.*

Finally, Jonaz walked in, carrying his sword and shield, fresh from the practice fields.

"Have you seen my servant?"

"The wolf boy, my Lord?"

"Nahatum. My servant, Jonaz."

"No, my Lord. He seems around so little these days. I thought perhaps you had sent him on an important errand." The words spilled out of the man like ferrets in search of mice. "I have wanted to beat him several times for not doing his chores." *Beat him?* The boy used to be so thin. Not anymore. He was already Jonaz's height and broader of shoulder. *In a fair fight, it's not clear who'd do the beating.*

His son back in Carthage would then be almost two years old. How broad- shoulder would he become? He pictured a muscular boy, but of the Barca stock, not so muscled as to assume that is what it takes to bring victory in life. His son must be properly tutored—Greek, Latin, Punic—and he thought to write Imre about this. Which deepened his frustration at Solyphos' absence.

"Have you noticed, my Lord," Jonaz' eyes narrowed, "how slow the boy is to do his chores. Here…" he held up a woven Boii shirt the King had given him, unwashed. "And your sword has not been cleaned from your practicing yesterday…and I should say, Sir, that your sword work remains excellent, even with your injury or whatever it is....” The man's voice trailed off. He looked to be stumbling toward some conclusion. *The ferret about to pounce.* “Where is the boy going and why has he disappeared just when your eye became...troubled?” Jonaz hestitated. “If I may say....”

“Yes, please. I depend on your advice.” *Jealousy is a sort of ferret,* Hannibal reflected. *Jonaz still can't abide Nahatum, as if the boy's very presence casts a shadow over the Squire's place.* Hannibal felt a sudden sympathy for the pious man: Nahatum's place at his commander's side must be intolerable for him. The rewards of faith would claim that place for him, Jonaz. *Some praise is in order.* “You are my sturdy and trustworthy battlefield companion, loyal Jonaz. Give me your counsel.”

Jonaz seemed to relax and gestured at the sacred hearth he had set up in a corner of the room since Hannibal's eye had gone bad; one that the squire lit endlessly for the protection of Hannibal, smoke filling the room. *I may well die of that sacred smoke before anything my eye does to me.* In a consipiratorial tone, Jonaz ventured, “Might Ba'al Shammon be expressing his displeasure of a wolf child so close to his hearth, to his sacrifices, to the General himself?”

Hannibal considered how many others in the army shared Jonaz's suspicions.

Focus. Use this moment to your benefit. Turn the problem into an advantage. If the boy is seen as the source of his troubles, might that be for the better? Let them blame the boy.

Hmmn. Yet the problem with his eye is truly not the boy's fault; he doesn't want Nahatum injured. Clearly Jonaz would as soon use the boy as he would a goat for the sacrifice. That must not happen. Still, he had to do something.

“My Lord?”

"Go find the boy, Jonaz. Bring him here."

Here is the spot where Hannibal stumbled that night last week after the meeting.

Nahatum knelt to look underneath the Convenor, the great Boii assembly hall, almost waist- high off the ground. The boy sensed that the entrance to the Underworld was nearby. He crawled underneath, now a badger, a weasel, unafraid of the foul darkness lying ahead, a place of evil where no sunlight could find its way. He ignored the cuts and scrapes inflicted by the frigid, unforgiving soil, poking his pike here and there, searching for small holes that might lead to bigger ones, to tunnels. Tunnels that brought vapors to attack Hannibal's eye.

Poke, scrape, poke.

And then something had him tightly by his ankles. *Ba'al's pubis!* He kicked sharply, but it had a grip of steel and was pulling him roughly along the ground out from under. He kicked, screamed through the dirt and snow digging into his mouth, his nose, his eyes as he bumped along.

And then he was upright and in front of him stood a different demon: Jonaz, breathing heavily through his woolen shirt, knife at his waist, that ridiculous Roman helmet with medals hanging off, stolen from some dead man. And then he, Nahatum, was back in Iberia that first day he was captured, the heat of the ovens at his back, kicking, lashing out frantically, only this time no longer just a scared boy, no, he was an angry almost- man , and then he was swinging his strong arm at the astounded squire, smug in his helmet, and he connected, a fist found the man's jaw. Jonaz stumbled backward though it was but a glancing blow.

Jonaz stood there, hand on his jaw, a different kind of look in his eye. Rage. And fear.

"Hannibal wants you, wolf boy," he spit out, his mouth not working quite right.

Warily, the boy could see it. Jonaz looked smaller. Something had changed between them.

"At the Trebia, we faced a Roman army of roughly forty-two thousand men. Our force, including our Gaulish allies, totaled only 30,000."

"Wait, Hannibal," Solyphos interrupted. "Repeat that last sentence." The old man rubbed his gnarled hands together as he wrote. The quill scratched uncertainly along the papyrus.

Hannibal repeated his dictation and then went on. "By carefully slecting the terrain for battle and provoking the Romans into a rash, impulsive decision to engage us, we…"

"The last part, again, please."

We've been at this all morning and hardly made any progress. "We provoked the Romans into a rash decision to engage us and…"

"Slower, please."

"…achieved a remarkeable victory. At least fifteen thousand Romans died, with a similar number taken prisoner."

Even with the fireplace blazing in his house, still the old scribe constantly put the quill down.

This is interminable. I can't get anything done.

Solyphos grimaced, lips tight, and looked to clutch the long owl's feather more than hold it. The feather flopped, lopsided in his hand. He adjusted it awkwardly with his left hand. Hannibal's chest felt hollow. This was his once- vital tutor,

whose calligraphy was the envy of the land, as was his swords-
manship. *What am I to do now?* He blinked once, twice, unable
to get used to the blindness in his eye.

The front door flew open, a blast of cold air. In walked
Jonaz with Nahatum, whose hands were scratched and
bloodied. Jonaz pushed the boy into the center of the room.
The boy smacked away Jonaz's hand.

"Where were you, Nahatum?"Hannibal asked.

"Under the Boii's Assembly Hall, my Lord." Jonaz responded. His voice sounded slightly slurred and there was a
deep purple bruise on his right jaw.

"Let Nahatum talk, Jonaz. Nahatum, what were you doing
there?" Silence.

*I don't have time for this. The bedeviled dictation has to get
done.* Then he had to inspect his cavalry. Marhabal wanted
more blankets for the horses. They were not used to such bitter
cold. And, Indoi, the elephants' chief Mahout, complained
again about the cold in the elephant barns. There was only
so much he can do for the horses and the elephants. Only so
much straw, so many blankets. Which was more valuable, his
cavalry or his war elephants? That was the strategic question:
which could he more afford to lose? And there he stood with
a stubborn servant who didn't do his job and was in danger of
becoming the sacrifice everyone wanted so as to purify their
be-hexed commander.

"Answer me, Nahatum. Why were you under the Convenor?"

"I, I….I wanted to help you, Sir. Your eye."

Jonaz laughed. "What? Trying to find a healing herb. You
think you know more than the shamans?"

Solyphos took the boy's hands in his, inspecting them.
"You have been digging…in the frozen ground." He reached

into the leather bag at his waist. "Rub some of this herb into the skin."

Hannibal regarded Nahatum in the deepening silence. *You were trying to help me. To fix my eye, restore my sight.* Something softened in his chest. *Again, boy, we have all misunderstood you. Your courage, your caring, your wish to do something that helps.*

"Nahatum, my sight will be fine. Thank you. Sit over there by the fire and apply Solyphos' herbs to your hands."

Jonaz looked then like he wanted to gouge holes in the floor with his fists.

Hannibal considered his fuming squire. *Remember, the man's devotion to you is no less than Nahatum's.* "Well done, Jonaz." The man seemed to brighen at the praise. "Go now to Marhabal and have him assign to you as many of his men as it takes to bring whatever blankets we can find in the supply wagons down to the stables for his horses. We must keep our cavalry healthy at all costs."

They returned to the dictation. "The entire of northern Italy has come over to me as a result of the victory at the Trebia."

A curse. Solyphos had knocked over the jar of ink on the writing table, black running across the papyrus which contained all their dictation of the morning. The boy jumped up to help, bringing in some rags to mop up the table and the floor.

"I will recopy all this, Hannibal. I am just a bit tired today. The cold...."

"Nahatum, please bring us some of the Boii's excellent spiced wine."

The boy soon returned with a carafe. Hannibal waved him back to the corner, then himself poured two cups, and put one in front of Solyphos.

"Your writing has slowed, my dear tutor. We cannot ignore that any more."

"There's time, Hannibal. I will get all this written down."

The boy sat on his haunches in the corner where he rubbed the salve into the broken skin on his hands.

A bubble of bile rose in Hannibal. "How do you know how much time I have? How much time you have? This is taking too long."

"I am working as fast as I can. Your wound has made you irritable."

The eye. The pain had lessened, but the eye remained dead. "Your slowness has made me irritable. However, I apologize, dear Solyphos, for my sharp tongue just now."

"It doesn't matter how fast I write, Hannibal, if I run short of papyrus. And I'm almost out of ink."

"Well, make more." As soon as he spoke, Hannibal regretted his impatient words. The proud old Greek could barely write. He coud no longer make the necessary papyrus or ink.

Solyphos rubbed his gnarled hands again. "That's no simple task. As you say, I am no longer as strong as I once was. My hands not as graceful. Perhaps if I had a servant."

The boy. He could let Solyphos have Nahatum, with his energy and intelligence, as a gift, a true apology for his harsh words a moment ago, a sort of salve for the proud scribe.

"Dear Solyphos. I want you to take Nahatum here as your personal servant and assistant. You can use him to help you make the papyrus and ink. As to your writing, perhaps as the winter wanes and we leave this swampy land, the vapors will release your hands."

The old man nodded in assent—slowly, gently, emphatically, and with such a satisfied look that Hannibal wondered then if Solyphos had harbored that very idea when he'd first walked into the room.

Why did Hannibal send me away? What have I done wrong?

Nahatum passed a miserable week sleeping on the floor of Solyphos' hut, blankets spread under the long tables, listening to the old man snore, eating the tasteless rice gruel he demanded every morning.

A week spent building wooden pans to make papyrus, sealing the seams with thick, sticky globs of heated pine resin. Days spent splashing through the marshes behind the practice fields cutting the long reeds and tying them in bound stacks to bring back to make the papyrus. Nahatum's back ached from hunching over the pans of water on the long tables making papyrus.

Some days he carried Solyphos' burlap bag—filled with the strange utensils of his trade, the quill, a small vial of salt to dry the ink—around the camp. Other days, he cut and hammered and sealed the bins— head filled with the biting, sharp-sweet fragrance of the dark resin– while Solyphos walked over to see Hannibal and the other commanders for long discussions of strategy. Not once in that week did Solyphos ask Nahatum to carry his writing supplies to the meetings.

Those evenings, the boy watched as Solyphos bent over his writing table with his notes from meetings with Hannibal. Face contorted, the man moved the quill slowly over the remaining parchment, often stopping to rub his hands or to ask Nahatum to boil water to make a soothing soak.

A week now since Hannibal gave me to Solyphos. What is to become of me? There were several village boys who now tended Hannibal's fire, washed his clothes, brought him his dinner.

A darkness, cold as the winter day, filled Nahatum as he hurried back to Solyphos' house through the busy village streets with a heavy bucket of well water and yet another bound stack of freshly cut reeds. The water splashed his feet as he hurried, so that the bucket was only half full by the time he pushed open the door with his foot, losing more water on the wooden floor. Solyphos looked up and sighed from his perch at his writing table, quill hovering over the papyrus as if in mid-flight.

"That took long enough and now there's more water on the floor than in the bucket." Those pitch black fingers. Hair flying in all directions, as if trying to escape from his head. Solyphos stood up slowly, hand on his back. He turned to the long table across the room and stooped over to pick up the wooden tray on it. It wobbled. Water spilled over the edge.

"Hurry! Take one end." The boy jumped at the urgency in the man's voice, and took the whole awkward tray from him.

"Damn my hands. Useless." He rubbed his hand and the boy thought of vultures fighting, their twisted, hard bodies, claw-like talons. "This winter stiffness is the worst it's been. The curseable dampness here, endless cold." He talked about a wise Greek doctor, Hippoc…the boy lost the name… and the four humors of the body.

"Vapors," the boy responded. "A hex." He put the heavy wooden pan down on the table, rubbd his own hands.

"The constant wet imbalances our humors, makes the body stiff."

"A Roman curse." He took the wooden bucket with the swamp water he had just brought and poured it into the pan.

Solyphos looked at him, eyebrow raised. "A Roman curse?"

"They've hexed us." He drew his breath in to steady his heart against the sorrowful darkness inside him. His mother, Hannibal's eye, his master's giving him away. "Everyone's talking about it. I'm going to find the entrance to the Underworld, take the curse off Hannibal." He spoke slowly, carefully, the intensity of his speech mirroring the depth of his hope. *Maybe, too, Solyphos, that'll make your hands young* again, no longer vulture talons.

Solyphos looked at him, eyes deep with sympathy and concern. "Oh, poor young man. You are caught in a web of superstitions. There are no hexes. No curses."

"That's not true," Nahatum yelled. The old man had his own hexes and charms that he made with his infernal quills; how could he lie so?

Solyphos stared at Nahatum, who suddenly regretted his insolence. If the old man threw him out of his service where, he wondered, suddenly frantic, would he go then?

When Solyphos finally spoke, though, his tone was still warm and comforting. He pointed to the wooden pans, now refilled, as if that's what they've been talking about all along. "Good, Nahatum, you are learning. Now we make more papyrus. Come, I will show you."

The next day, Solyphos poured several large, mottled brown gall nuts into the boy's hands from the sack. "Here hold these." A few bounced on the floor.

"In the dish." He pointed to the table. "And get the ones on the floor." When Nahatum bent down to get them, the man sighed, as if lamenting something he had lost. Then he beat the nuts with the wooden mallet. Once, twice, three times. A curse. "I have no strength." He threw down the mallet, just missing the boy's leg.

"The body always betrays you." He flexed his fingers again. A knuckle cracked. "Here, you do it."

A resounding pounding of the mallet into the bowl, and the nuts exploded, raining hard splinters on him, Solyphos, the floor. Again, harder still, smashing the splinters into smaller pieces.

"Enough," Solyphos shouted, then gestured for Nahatum to kneel beside his seat. They each knifed the soft insides from the broken shells. Careful, pleasant work, gently coaxing the reddish-brown meat into the bowl. Then Solyphos showed him how to use the mallet to grind the nut-meat into a sticky paste. While the boy stirred the paste over a small fire in a copper bowl, Solyphos added drops of water to make a thick, dark, bubbling brew. Ink. Amazingly, the rich brown meat turned into a fiery black soup.

Another kind of magic.

By the afternoon, they'd filled several clay jars with the dark liquid. As he worked, the boy remembered stories about Solyphos, stories that once filled him with terror: he cuts his veins and conjures his own blood deathly black. He augurs in his tent with razor sharp talons and bird feathers. He tortures fish and hoards their skins for watery enchantments. *No. The stories are wrong.* How could people be so confused?

There was some other kind of magic going on, one that was visible, right in front of him, if he could only understand it.

Hannibal paced the floor in his house in the snow-ridden village like a trapped lion. Gisgo sat at the table, deep in his own thought. Snow had been falling all day. *How long till we are on the move again? This is as awful as being fixed in the siege of a city.* He was eager to carry the invasion to Rome. He wanted to write more letters and proclamations, woo the cities farther south: particularly Capua, that prosperous rival of Rome. Cities he had only heard of.

Then the door creaked open, and Solyphos walking slowly into the house, brought to him by Jonaz, Nahatum trailing behind them— trying to walk, as a proper servant should, as slowly as the scribe, and barely succeeding—carrying the bag of writing utensils and papyri. The boy set to laying out the clay pot of ink and the writing quills on the raw wooden table, then carefully unrolled the writing papyrus.

Gisgo moved from his chair near the table to a low wooden stool across the room.

Strange the power of Solyphos, the hesitation even fierce warriors show around him. Jonaz leaned against the wall near the door, watching the scribe's quill scratch across the papyrus. The man played his thumb over his forefinger to ward off evil spirits. It was a familiar gesture among those who worship Ba'al Shammon, the fingers creating a form supposedly pleasing to the god. Even Gisgo, on his crude stool across the room, fingers thick as boar's tusks– tapped thumb to forefinger three times when in the presence of Solyphos' writing. Once when he'd asked Jonaz about this, his squire had replied, "the ancient one is casting lightning- powerful spells with that feather." *Forked lightning. If only Solypos could. Or me.*

And who knew what the boy made of Solyphos? He stood near the fireplace watching the man work the quill. He hardly looked at Hannibal at all, watching the scribe instead. There was that familiar intensity to his regard; it was in his eyes. He held Solyphos' burlap bag– familiarly, close to him– heavy with rolls of papyrus, spare quills, and, Hannibal noted, the boy held an extra jar of black ink in his hand. No finger tapping. The boy was studying what Solyhos was doing.

"Let us finish our letter about the great victory at the Trebia." Eventually they might be able to send it to Carthage by fast ship. With luck, the letter could arrive before spring. It took so long, and was so uncertain. First Solyphos had to actually write the letter, then it would be sent with riders to a friendly port, along with some treasure to ensure its safe passage. Then by swift trading ship to Carthage, hoping to elude the Romans.

Still, just writing a letter brought him closer to home. "Soon we will have our own port, allied with us. We will have travel between ourselves and Carthage, reinforcements, fresh men and horses," and perhaps, Hannibal thought, a letter would come back from Imre. News of his son. "Once the Italian cities have broken from their alliances with Rome. We march south soon. One more big victory."

"I'm not sure you want to write that, Hannibal," Solyphos suggested.

"Which?"

"Either that you plan to march south or that you need only one more big victory. The first because if the letter falls into Roman hands, they will know your intent. And if it does arrive in Carthage and you say you need just one more big victory. Well, what do you think your enemies in the Senate will make of that?"

"You are right. We can't appear that close to victory. Then they will think there is no reason to send further supplies and reinforcements."

"Exactly."

Solyphos returned, slowly, to his writing. There was an evident look of pain on his face. Sitting him near the warmth of the fireplace hadn't helped. Once, that quill flowed over the papyrus like a graceful, undulating snake through sun-green meadow grass. Hannibal dictated more, and the words poured from him.

Solyphos rubbed his hands. "Slow down." He dipped the quill, massaged his hands.

"You write slowly again this morning."

Solyphos' eyes flashed. He held up his quill, offering it to Hannibal. "Do you want to write instead?" Hannibal felt a heat rise in his chest. *Such disrespect right in front of my infantry commander.* An urge to lash out at the old man pulsated through him.

What am I to do, though, write these letters myself?

"No, my tutor. Your letters are so well-formed. I've never been able to craft them as beautifully as you." There was such silence in the room that Hannibal wondered if he could hear the snow falling. "I will speak more slowly."

Gisgo shifted uncomfortably in his chair.

Solyphos grunted, nodded. Hannibal had dictated but a bit more when Solyphos abruptly put down his quill down. "That's all I can do today." He apologized. "My hands only have so much strength."

The boy organized the scrolls and jars and quills in an expert fashion and the two left. The sight of Solyphos' heavy walk toward the front door filled Hannibal with an ache that he wanted to drown in details. "Gisgo, let us have your report about the state of our army." The infantry commander cleared his throat and said that the elephants were not doing well so far from the warmth of Africa. He had taken some blankets from the Gauls townspeople for the huge beasts.

The details droned on yet the picture of old, stooped Solyphos departing his house, slow step by slow step, stayed lodged in Hannibal's mind like a sword wound that wouldn't heal.

Nahatum dropped the bulky bag on Solyphos' creaky table when they returned to his cottage.

"Can I go carve my pike now?"

Solyphos's stare took the words away. The man could paralyze a vulture. The boy had watched what happened back in Hannibal's house, the way that Solyhos had talked to Hannibal. Was he mocking the General? "Do you want to write instead? Here you take the quill."

No one spoke to Hannibal that way. And then his master…. No, Hannibal was no longer his master….Hannibal had apologized. And, he'd seen the way Hannibal watched Solyphos when he augured with the quill on the papyrus. With admiration, not—like Gisgo, like Jonaz, even himself—with fear. Hunched, frail still, Solyphos seemed a dark shadow across the room. The sharp, flinty set to his face: the ferocity of a hawk.

"Looking forward to more killing?" asked Solyphos.

"Of course." Yet the voice pulled at him, seemed to demand something more. "I killed a man at the Trebia. I helped us win the battle. This is a great war."

The old Boii chair wobbled as Solphos sat. "All the joy we take in war." An exasperated gesture with his arm, then he asked for help taking off his shirt. "All of us. The Romans, the Carthaginians, Hannibal, the Senate. My own dear Spartans, those haughty Athenians back in the time of our wars. We all love it."

"I want to smash the Romans for the hex they've put on Hannibal." Could the old man understand? Help him? " I want to find the Underworld…."

"War doesn't solve anything—it's a sport for us."

This made no sense. Had the old man gone mad? Then Solyphos said: "It feeds our thirst for more and more. It distracts us from the Underworld, whereever that is, which we all fear so much."

A bee hive seemed to inhabit Nahatum's chest. He couldn't pay attention and just wanted to get out of the man's cottage. "I can make a fire before I go, Sir. Do you need anything else?"

All this did was produce an exclamation. "Thucydides!"

Was this an oath? A spell? Solyphos slapped his knee and stood up so quickly the boy had to step back. He gestured at the wooden case across the floor, filled with rolled up papyrus scrolls. "Push that over here."

Then the old man rummaged through it, like a cat in search of a mouse. "Here it is." He held up a scroll, calling it a "book." Another new word. What was a book? Was it like a map? Then the old man was saying that this thing called a book had a name, and a long one: *The History of the Peloponnesian Wars.*

"You read this, you'd understand." The thing rustled as he waved the scroll at him. Read it? Knowing what the marks mean on the papyrus. Doing some kind of magic. Nahatum, a servant...read? The man was mocking him.

What Nahatum wanted was to lose his misery in carving his pike, on the path to becoming a warrior who would again make Hannibal proud. He was nothing, no longer Hannibal's servant, the purple Carthaginian sash lost in the mud. Now he just trailed around behind an old man, tending his fire and carrying his bag.

"Listen." Solyphos unrolled the scroll, insisting Nahatum sat while he read. "Be convinced that to be happy means to be free and that to be free means to be brave. Therefore do not take lightly the perils of war."

"Who said that? You?"

"No. The man who wrote this book." Again that name, hard to understand.

"Those are his words?"

"Yes."

"From how long ago?"

"A long time ago. The poor, confused man. He urges us to fight for our freedom, which is a good thing, of course. Be brave. But also, there is price of war—do not take it lightly. War comes to weigh heavily on those who wage it. Ah, poor Thucydides: he extolls it, but is weighted down by it. But at least he put it down in a book."

"His words are still alive."

Solyphos laughed ("yes!"), and the boy smiled back, pleased to have made him laugh in a way that was clearly not mocking him. Solyphos told him that this man, an Athenian, wrote the history of the war between the Greek city states.

"He began writing at the moment that war broke out, believing that his history would be greater than any previous history of war." Solyphos snorted. "When he finished it, he felt differently about war." He wiped a bit of spittle from his lips "You worry so much about the Underworld, young Nahatum. Here is where a spirit lives on."

The boy leaned away from the scroll and from the man, whose eyes seemed to blaze.

The old man rapped a gnarled fist on the table. "In a book."

Words keep the spirit of a person alive? Trapped on the papyrus, that scroll that the wizard was calling a book.

The bees returned to Nahatum's chest. How much better to be back in the forest, where he didn't know about such magic. Where there was no sorcerer telling him about some trickery for keeping the spirit alive, trapped on papyrus. This needed to be thought about, but not while the now-fierce old man was waving that scroll at him. "Can I please go now and work on my pike?"

Solyphos rolls up the scroll slowly, puts it back into the box. "Go."

Two days passed. A bitter wind from the frozen mountains drove an iron cold through the village. Nahatum warmed bricks in the fire for Solyphos to drag the cold humors away from his fingers. As the boy wrapped a brick in a scratchy rag, Solyphos threw his quill (owl, one of his favorites) onto the floor.

"I can't do this."

The boy picked up the quill and wiped the dirt off. He handled the quill gingerly, not entirely sure of its power. Ink had splattered on the table, and on the papyrus in front of him, leaving Nahatum nervous about that as well. What power did this dark ink have when it has escaped the jar and the quill?

"Come here. Stand behind me." Nahatum walked behind the thin, stooped man. If a stork could sit in a chair, it would look now like Solyphos.

"Lean over me."

"Sir?"

"Lean over me and give me your arms."

The boy covered the old man's back like a cloak. He stifled a gag at the acrid, vinegary smell. Age. Solyphos took the boy's right hand and placed it over his own right hand, both resting on the papyrus in front of him. The man's hand had a tremor, startling the boy, as if the quill was alive, writhing and bucking to get away. He pulled his arm away, knocking aside another quill on the table.

"Curse you. Rest your hand on mine to steady it."

Could anyone's skin be more dry and cracked? Not mottled like the elephants, their skin patterned with thick, strong ridges; this old man's skin had a pale lemony sheen. The boy tried to move away, but a backwards glance from the scribe froze him. The top of his knuckles dug into the boy's palm.

He—they—picked up the feather. Solyphos' hand moved, forming those things he called letters. The hair on the back of the boy's neck tingled. There was danger here; he could smell it.

His hand slid off the cold, aged skin. Solyphos cursed and put it again atop his hand, which looked more and more like a claw, hard and bony. Nahatum could feel the closeness of Lizard Skin.

The boy pressed down hard, half grabbing the old man's hand, and thequill skidded across the papyrus, knocking over a whole jar of ink. Solyphos jumped up, yelling.

"Your young hands work so well but you know nothing. Nothing. Get out." As Nahatum hurried toward the door, Solyphos beat the boy on the back and neckand shoulders; the claw hands leaving blows that did not hurt.

What sorry place had he come to in his life? The nearness of the ink, the feel of Solyphos' cracked skin, the sensation of movement across the papyrus as the black ink formed letters, made his skin shiver. The teeth rattled in his head. The smell of Solyphos' aged, parched skin inhabited his nostrils.

It was time to run through the town to the animal pens, to see the elephants, and feel their warm, tough skin.

A chilling wind slapped at the boy's face. Past the marsh and wetlands at the edge of the village, still dotted with snow, and then the elephant pens were in sight. He heard strange sounds—low moans, then hoarse and sharp. Crows and ravens cackled from the trees.

In the middle of the wide stockade, three of the great beasts lay on their sides. Their enormous bellies heaved, slowly, like the ground itself shaking, trunks limp. He thought of rotting logs. The raspy breathing—like something struggling to get out– was now so loud that the boy flinched, fighting the urge to run away.

The coughing illness, the hex of the Underworld vapors, had reached even here, to the most powerful of the powerful: the elephants. With the next wave of coughs, he had an urge to bite something, and his teeth renewed their clatter. He dug a ragged fingernail into a knuckle. The pain calmed him. Indoi, the elephant handler, walked nearby but one of the big bulls, standing between him and the sick ones, reared up on his hind legs, ears flared, then lowered his head and gathered himself to charge. The mahout quickly withdrew to the fence, where a crowd of Boiis had gathered to watch.

Nahatum drew closer and soon, holding a wooden bucket of winter feed– twigs, tree bark, and roots set aside by the stockade for the massive animals, he jumped the fence. He didn't dare to approach the three lying on the ground, so he brought the bucket to a healthy elephant, one of the few females, tall as a tree. While she ate, he found a second wooden bucket, filled it with the warm water heating over a fire and washed down her prickly skin.

He ran his hand along the wrinkled folds that lined her belly and shoulders, running his fingers along the intricate layers and ridges. The folds seemed to form and re- form in front of him, like the patterns and designs Solyhphos conjured on the papyrus, brought now to life. The forest of little prickers rising from her thick skin scraped against his hand. He rubbed the rough resistance. A circular scar on her shoulder, like a grayish- red eye, stared back at him. A Roman lance wound, most likely.

A rough cough from her belly. He knew Lizard Skin's ways now, and the sound filled his chest with black clouds. Her trunk grazed on the few buds of grass and leaves in the trampled mud. When he looked more closely, he saw that the very tip of that trunk had two thick fingers that she walked along the ground in search of roots. He washed the trunk with a sponge. Soapy water collected in the thick band of muscles that layer around and through the hard trunk. His hand moved over the leathery furrows ringing the trunk.

He dried the elephant, then brought a worn blanket from the stable and tossed it over her shoulders.

Further away, several elephants stood over the sick ones, snorting and snaking their trunks over the bellies, shoulders, rippled trunks of those on the ground. The sight brought the heavy black clouds back to his chest. He hurried back to Solyphos, the late afternoon sky fading red. He wanted to be inside before the sun has plunged into the river of the Underworld.

By the next day, Solyphos' mood had improved.

"You take it," he instructed Nahatum when the boy returned to the table from the fireplace, holding the warming brick wrapped in a towel. "Now, come here. Sit in my seat." The boy hesitated.

"You sigh, young Nahatum. Not easy to sit with an old man, perhaps? I will be gentler today." He stood there in front of the table, looking at him with cloudy eyes.

Nahatum sat in Solyphos' chair.

His hands were warmed by the toweled brick in his lap. Then Solyphos was standing behind him. The reverse of the day before. "Hands on the table." And then, Ba'al's breath, the old man's hands were on top of his own, paired hands resting on the table. In front of them lay an open scroll of blank papyrus and an owl feather. He could hear the man breathing.

Solyphos picked up Nahatum's hand and wrapped it around the feather.

What is to happen to me?

Nahatum tried to curl his shaking fingers around the spiky shaft of the feather. The sound of Solyphos pursing his lips invaded Nahatum's ears. He braced for the old Greek's anger again, yet instead he spoke gently to the boy. "Don't hold it like that."

Solyphos moved the boy's fingers so that the feather rested on his middle finger while the thumb and forefinger held it in place. The boy could feel the balance of it in his hand. "This is not a pike, though you need the same combination of strength and gentleness as when you hold your weapon." Nahatum imagined his pike as an enormous feather; the feather's sharp point was the very end of his pike.

He moved the feather a short distance and it twisted; except for Solyphos' firm grip, he would have dropped it. Then he moved it slightly within his hand and eases his grip. The quill stayed upright. Solyphos, keeping his hand lightly wrapped around the boy's, dipped the quill into the ink jar. He moved their hands to the empty papyrus. The scratchy sound. A line appeared, black and wild. Terror filled the boy. He wanted toget his hand away from it, as if fleeing a black, fanged snake. Solyphos' grip became iron and directed their paired hands in upward, circular movements. Where did he get his strength? Lines appeared on the papyrus, black and thick and distinct. Not a snake, nor a design.

"Aleph. The first letter in the Punic alphabet."

The man's grip was firm, but also reassuring. Nahatum relaxed against the firmness.

"You can do this."

He stared at the lines. He had done that. He had made a letter. "Let go."

The hand was gone from around his own. He was alone now with the quill, the ink, the paper. He moved the feather in a lazy way—not too tight, not too loose—and the ink made a smooth line on the scratchy papyrus. He breathed out.

"Good."

"They say you cast spells. Is that what I am doing now?"

"Don't be silly. The only pox you can put on people with a quill is to write the truth about them."

"Do you know where the Underworld is?"

"Learn to read, to write. You will find it there."

"You want me to do this? What you do? Why?"

"You will see. Learn first." Again, the hand on his, moving them both over the papyrus, the quill trailing its black line. "Aleph, again, you're written it twice."

"I don't see it." Not exactly true: he thought maybe he could.

"Practice. You will."

A sudden fear captured his chest. *He wants to make me a sorcerer, a magician like him. I will disappear into the ink. I will be hated and despised.*

A wish to get away blossomed deep within Nahatum. *Bargain for your life.*

"I will, later, if you'll let me go and carve my pike." Ba'al's honeyed breath. Solyphos agreed.

The afternoon sun was bright outside and the log Nathum sat on was warm and dry, his precious pike in his lap. The ground had no snow. How wonderful. The buzzing unrest at work in his stomach, throat, chest had flown away. It would happen—there would be no more snow, no more winter, the woods would again be bursting with green, filled with life.

I made a letter with my own hand. Conjured it. No.... wrote it.

He had done what Hannibal could do, what Solyphos did. What Jonaz could not do. What frightened the squire so. Frightened even Gisgo, who at one time seemed the most terrible creature that walked the earth.

The pike's sharp end could also be used to trace lines in the dirt, he found. How useful. Aleph, as he remembered it. And he did remember: the design appeared clearly to him. With the pike in two hands, he traced the memory on the ground with long and crude lines. He could see it, the distinctive bends and circles. "Aleph." He thought of loops and curls and curves, the deeply rutted, furrowed elephants' trunks and their skin, the splintering grain of a tree. A space opened inside him. He could do this.

"Did you practice the letters? Solyphos asked later, as Nahatum prepared stew in the fireplace pot.

"No, I worked on my pike."

Days passed, the air warming. And then there were cheering people running in the streets, now almost free of snow. Boii villagers in their bearskin leggings and green, red, yellow embroidered woolen vests streamed past Solyphos' house and the marsh toward the animal pens.

"Nahatum, go see what all the celebrating is about," Solyphos instructed from his comfortable seat in front of the fireplace.

The boy ran past the Convenor meeting hall, past the rows of tall wooden houses built up on their wooden stilts as if giants were about to step out, past the army practice fields with the roofed riding halls and enclosed drill buildings where Hannibal insisted the Gauls practice close order fighting over and over, and joined the crowd in front of the elephants' stockade. He pushed through happy villagers, laughing and pointing.

Gisgo was somewhere up front, shouting orders in his deep bull voice. A one- armed villager holding an axe jostled Nahatum, then stepped back, staring at the purple tunic Solyphos had given him just the day before. Next to him, slightly behind, was a woman with a young face, except for the skin around her eyes: a mass of wrinkles. Three thin children peeked out from behind her legs.

"Get us some," the man said cautiously to Nahatum. "What?"

The woman thrust a handful of eggs and herbs toward him. "No meat all winter.

Trade for this." He pushed away, past several men, right up to the stockade fence.

Three gray mounds lay strewn across the muddy field. The elephants. One of the mounds made the low, rasping sound that chilled his chest to his ribs. The others lay still. The early spring flies danced and darted over their massive bodies.

A large bull with battle scars on his shoulders and legs walked up to a lifeless female, scattering the flies, touching her body with his trunk from head to toe, seeming to linger over her smell. He tapped on her shoulder with his right leg, pressing his knee into her, as if trying to awaken her, to urge her up. There was no response. He slowly turned and sat silently with his haunches pushed up against her shoulder and head. Several others came up and clustered around, trunks touching the dead elephant's legs, back, haunches.

The remaining elephants surrounded the other dead one and the dying one. Sirius stood in the middle, towering over the other bulls. He grunted and pushed at the second dead female. He raised his head in the air, makes low moaning noises. He stroked the lifeless body with his trunk. Nahatum spotted an unusual grayish- red scar on the dead one's shoulder—she was the elephant the boy had washed just a few days earlier. He had rubbed her wrinkled- soft belly skin, the hard ripples of her muscular trunk. Now dead.

He wanted to put his arm around the dead elephant. To sit next to her with his hand on her trunk.

Gisgo warily approached Sirius, leading five Carthaginian soldiers holding long steel lances pointed at the beast. The big elephant wheeled and charged, huge ears flared out. Gisgo, for once, looked small. The warrior retreated several steps while his soldiers ran back to the fence. Sirius trumpeted, trunk curled high into the air.

The crowd moved backwards, seeming to doubt the safety of the stockade fence itself. Gisgo stumbled. The elephant turned back to the dead female and renewed his rumbling. He rubbed her head with his own, wound his trunk underneath hers.

The boy's eyes filled with a wetness and he bit into his lower lip till he tasted blood to put a stop to that.

Gisgo, voice like thunder, ordered the men to follow him forward. Laughter from the crowd. Then cheers. A chant rose. "Meat. Meat at the end of winter." Steel extended, the soldiers slowly forced Sirius away from the body he was trying to protect. The boy cried out to stop the sight; his words lost in the cheering.

He could not watch. He ran through the crowd, darting amidst sounds and cheers, that wetness in his eyes, an awful, sickly feeling, as if everywhere it was raining. Eerie birds screamed Roman hexes from the forest undergrowth.

Solyphos' dark hut was empty. He was alone amidst the tables and pans and papyrus. He had to regain his breathing; there was no air. He couldn't seem to control the drum that had become his chest. Rip, bite, scratch, cut. Do something. Look around.

Long rolls of papyrus dried near the fireplace. There were the long wooden pans for making the papyrus. He wanted to cut himself with the knife lying on the kitchen sink, to bring the calming blood back.

There was Solyphos' seat. *Come, sit, I will be gentle with you this time.* The drumbeat slowed. *Yes, there are the quills.* Could he see a letter? Try to make one. He wanted to buckle over. He would vomit. *No, look, now, here, see the letter Aleph. You wrote that the other day. You can recognize others. Look. Concentrate.*

Calmer. The wetness was gone from his eyes, he dried his face. He wasn't sure how he did that without cuts or bruises to still the whirling inside him. A quill—light brown, owl's feather, the one he'd used the day before?—lay on the writing table. There was a clay pot of ink.

He picked up the feather, balancing it in his hand between the fingers, feeling its lightness and the pressure it made on his skin. He dipped it in the clay pot, careful not to spill any. *Concentrate. You can do this. Make marks to make an elephant.* He scratched out some lines. The great beasts, massive and brave, gone. The female dying, coughing, rasping that awful sound Nahatum could remember still.

Things live on papyrus, like that Greek with the strange name, the confused one writing about war who lived in that book Solyphos read to him from.

He dipped the quill again in the inkpot and traced marks and shapes. He practiced the letters he'd drawn in the dirt. Again, his memory gave him a clear picture. Letters.

The air brought the smell of roasting meat. He concentrated harder. *I will become the letter, the quill is me, there is nothing else here. Aleph.* He remembered other letters— though not their names—that he'd watched Solyphos conjure. No, not conjure– write. Was writing a form of conjuring? Perhaps. Memory blessed him with images vivid and clear.

The door swung open. Nahatum leapt up from Solyhos' seat.

"Elephant stew tonight," the old man exclaimed. "Have you ever tasted it? Hannibal says it's a special delight. Made in the way of the master chefs of Carthage."

There was that wetness again. And, then, a sort of dizziness, as if from a blow to the head. And the darkness. A sense of some time long ago. The flames in the fireplace looked blurry. He thought of Hannibal's dead eye. Everything dead.

"What is wrong, boy? Do you not like the taste? Yet how could you ever have tasted the delicacy?"

He yearned to put his hand into the flames, to feel the calming, accepting pain and disappear into it. The heat of the flames drew him toward them.

"Sit down here, Nahatum." Solyphos gestured to a seat next to him at the rugged pine table. "Something is wrong. Come here. Away from the fire."

Nahatum left the flames, ignoring his wish to dig the cooking knife into his hand.

And then, as he sat on that familiar bench next to Solyphos, the rain fell from his eyes. "Sirius." Silence swallowed his voice.

"Who? Come now, tell me." The voice, so patient.

"The greatest, the bravest of the elephants." He told the old man about the sight of Sirius making his moaning sounds over the body of the female elephant, brushing his trunk up against her. This came out in a river of words, a river made more difficult because of the hated wetness in his eyes and the wetness dripping down his cheeks and even into his mouth as he tried to speak. He wondered if he would drown.

Solyphos nodded. "That is grief. What you saw from the elephant."

"What's that?"

"Grief is when you feel a terrible ache at the loss of someone you love. Elephants feel it as humans do, though some doubt that. In truth, we share that emotion."

"I don't do that."

"Yes, so I can see." A kind smile. "Though your tears say otherwise."

Tears. That's what they are. There was a word for the wetness around his eyes. An image of his mother walking away, half slumped over, down the forest path after she'd left him with Ranton and the others in the wolf pack.

He pitched forward slightly, then back. Is it raining in the house? His lips were sticky with their salty wetness. His teeth ached. He bit down on the inside of his lip, seeking blood, warmth. Solyphos was talking, though, and his voice flowed with a surprising warmth. His teeth calmed.

"It gets better. There is no cure but time." The flames warmed him. He sat there at Solyphos' workbench. "Well, actually there is no cure at all." The ancient man looked out the window. "But it does get better. A little."

The two of them sat there, saying nothing. He could hear Solyphos' breathing. Nahatum remembered once—after his mother was gone—floating on his back in the warm, muddy fast-flowing river letting the current take him until he found the shore.

"What is this?" Solyphos stared down at the papyrus on the table in front of them.

Had he done something wrong? "That is Aleph. I think." He pointed to one he felt particularly proud of. "That's another letter you write a lot." The quill: he wanted to hold it, but was that all right? Had he violated some magic?

"Bet." A hushed tone. Solyphos picked up the papyrus, examining it, then pointed to another design the boy made. "And that is Gimmel. All Punic letters."

He stood up, in that moment so lithe and quick. He did a short dance, what a funny sight, arms flailing and toes tapping. He might have been a great heron, delighted with its catch, fish firmly in mouth, wings aflutter, parading through a Gallic marsh. And then Solyphos smiled at the boy, who realized he was smiling, too. It was the first time the boy'd ever seen that: Solyphos smiling.

"I think I may be able to write some others, though I don't know their names.

Would you like to see?"

Chapter 5

The Words

Town of Bologna, Northern Italy
Early Spring 217 BC

"How large is the army that the Roman Senate has now sent to rid me from their lands?"

"About thirty thousand men, Lord Hannibal. They have raised four new legions to replace those lost at the Trebia." Gisgo paused from reporting what their spies had told them and looked around the small group assembled in Hannibal's meeting room.

Marhabal was there along with Gisgo, plus several of the Gaulish chiefs, as was Solyphos, seated at the table. Nahatum stood next to him holding the sheet of papyrus as the older man scribed notes during the meeting. The house's windows were opened for the first time that year in recognition of the warmth of the early spring day.

The warm air has helped Solyphos; his writing is firmer, more fluid. Or perhaps it is the boy. Nahatum is very attentive to him. The sight raised Hannibal's spirits as well.

My gift of the boy to Solyhos has restored him.

The word of the Romans marching against him restored Hannibal as well. Finally, they would be on the march, calculating strategy.

"Their commander— Consul Flaminius— has already caused some outrage in Rome."

"Outrage, Gisgo? What sort?"

"Flaminus was so eager to march north to confront you that he left Rome without observing the proper rituals after being elected Consul."

Solyphos held up the owl feather he was using to scribe. "The Roman aristocracy insists that all new Consuls take what they call, 'the auspices.' Their priests study the flight of birds and proclaim the favorability of success for what the Consul proposes." He waved the feather in the air, as if it was a magic wand.

"I see. So this Flaminius is in a rush to confront me."

"Our spies say that he has political ambitions," Gisgo reported. "He hopes to raise his reputation. He insists that the defeat at the Trebia was more a barbarian rebellion than an invasion, and he is eager to put a stop to it."

Hannibal felt his mouth tighten. "They'll find out soon enough what this is." The boy looked up at him as he spoke, the same look of concentration and thoughtfulness that Hannibal had seen a hundred times. "Nahatum, please bring us a jug of the Gaul's spiced wine."

The boy looked startled. Solyphos looked up from the papyrus to Hannibal, eyebrows furrowed.

Ah, yes, Nahatum is not my servant any more. That was disrespectful to Solyphos.

"Of course, I forgot for a moment." He quickly called for one of the Boii houseboys who were cooking and cleaning for him.

Solyphos whispered something to Nahatum; from a large bag over his shoulder the boy pulled out a scroll, which he carefully laid out on the large table: the map of the land between Bologna and Rome that Solyphos had carefully constructed with the help of the Guals, The Gauls described to the group Flaminius' likely location and the geography of the land between, the hills and valleys, a swamp, the large lake with itsnarrow shoreline.

"This lake…Trasimene…" Whenever possible use water to your advantage, Hannibal's father had stressed. *And it was water that killed you, father.*

The Gauls described the majestic lake bordered by wooded hills. An army passing the lake would have to march in a narrow—hence, vulnerable– line of march along a long portion of the lake bordered by wooded hills.

"How large are these hills?" Hannibal asked. Large, came the reply.

"Large enough to hide an army?"

The army left Bologna on the march within a matter of days. A hard, fast march, as though they were pursued rather than pursuer, through winter landscape just waking to the early spring warmth. The boy rode south along with Solyphos in the supply train in their own wagon, creaking but dry, passing vast marshes soon to be planted with rice. In shadowed forests, some of the ponds were still covered in dark sheets of ice.

Solyphos had used the time to teach the boy more Punic and even some Greek words. He praised the boy endlessly. Was it really possible he was good at this strange magic? When Solyphos showed him words, when he spoke them in that gruff voice, the boy could see and hear them and then—what sort of power was this?– he could hold the word in his head and bring it to life on the papyrus, even as the wagon protested and swayed its way south.

Now the boy sat crouched at daylight in a grove of fragrant juniper trees. Men huddled all around him, a silent forest of swords, spears, lances, slings. In a single night of careful and hushed maneuvers, Hannibal had hidden his entire army along the low, forested hills overlooking Lake Trasimene.

A line—it seemed endless—of Roman soldiers marched noisily along the trail not fifty paces from them. They were so close that a cool breeze from the choppy waters carried the odor of Roman sweat. Mist enveloped them.

Hannibal had told them that he wanted the advantage of surprise and that's what he'd gotten, judging by the thousands of Roman legionnaires crashing along as if they hadn't a care in the world, most half-armored, weapons slung casually over their shoulders, swords packed away. He'd found them before they'd found him.

The boy fingered his pike, felt the heat of Solyphos standing behind him, leaning forward stiffly in his leather battle armor. The boy wore only his usual woolen tunic and the Boii pants the old man had given him to keep him warmer. Was he finally to fight as a real soldier? He gripped his pike, felt its weight, practicing in his head, not words now, but sharp, killing movements, heavy blows to the side of the head, sharp jabs to the gut, the groin, the soft areas a sharp pike can find in the folds of Roman armor.

Solyphos handed him his writing tablet, wordlessly, and the boy knew: the man's hands turned into claws in the morning cold. He could not take notes about what was to happen. He wanted the boy to scratch out some of it.

No, no. He had the tablet in one hand and the pike in another and he'd have to put down his pike to take out the quill and the ink and how could he do all that while a battle was raging steps away?

Suddenly, the birds seemed to all sing at once, to bring the morning light with their calls. No, those were not birds. Those were signals. And then the trees all around seemed to uproot and hurl themselves down the hill. Helmeted men carried long lances and broad swords. An African warrior ran past, sword extended, a strange sight in his Roman armor, stained dark red and brown, taken from the dead at the Trebia. What was happening along the lake's shore? The boy strained to see past the gnarled old tree in front of them.

Roman trumpets pleaded from beyond the mist. Steel clanged against steel, a sound that put his teeth on edge. Steel thudded off wood. The urgent whinny of horses. Men shouted orders. Some just shouted. Was that Hannibal's voice?

Nahatum stepped forward to peer through the trees, put the tablet down, leaned on his pike. Solyphos was saying something, opening his cloth bag, looking for quills. The boy turned to help, his head frantic, they both were rummaging through the bag, taking out writing implements—the boy could barely concentrate on the confusing pile of quill and jars in the bag—while both simultaneously squinted to see ahead.

The mist had begun to lift. Sun flickered off lake water. Men were wrestling on the ground on the trail below, but neither Nahatum nor Solyphos could tell what was happening. A man on a horse slashed at someone. A Roman standard waved through the tree, a flashing bolt of blue and gold. The boy made up some excuse—"let me go and see what's happening, Sir"—and ran into the trees toward the lake, toward the battle, before Solyphos could say anything. And then the old man was saying something, yelling it in fact, but the boy paid no attention.

The lakeshore trail was broader than it seemed from the hill. He tripped over an arm on the ground, an orange-brown sleeve covering it. Roman. He had to climb over a pile of dead bodies, already guarded by greedy flies. Men were fighting while standing in the water. The sight of blood all around aroused something in the boy. He pushed through the bushes at the water's edge and jumped off the steep bank into the water.

He landed face- first in the water, gasping for air. He sucked in a mouthful of water, up his nose, gagged it out. Red water? Then he understood. The lake threated to drag him under. He couldn't find his footing. The biting cold focused him. He started as if just woken up. The pike floated next to him. He grabbed it, splashing, searching for the lake bottom with his feet. He dug the pike into the muddy bottom and muscled himself to his feet in the waist- high water.

Off to his left, a Numidian horseman—half-soaked djellabah clinging to his chest and legs—towered over a Roman foot soldier. The Roman's face was drained of color, his eyes wide and desperate, but he lunged forward wildly with his sword, as the Numidian and horse, as if one, easily moved aside. Then the Roman slipped slightly on the muddy bottom. In an instant, the horseman's sword flashed—the boy recoiled instinctively—and the soldier's head flew into the lake. The body pitched backward, almost falling onto Nahatum. The water turned redder still. Nahatum pushed the headless body away, watching it drift into the lake, trailing blood. The Roman's head bobbed toward shore.

A Gaul with an arrow through his chest floated by, face down. The boy looked for more Romans. None.

He had to get out of the water; he could no longer feel his feet. Scrambling up the steep bank, there was nothing to do but step over dead Romans. A trophy, perhaps? He pulled a sheepskin vest off a dead man, looked to be one of the Boii Gaul warriors, and he was about to take an insignia off a dead Roman, when he remembered Solyphos. Where was the old man? He was supposed to have stayed with him.

The gnarled tree on the hill was right where it should be. When he saw a sling- thrower, tall for an Islander, kneeling over the body, he sped up. The Islander was trying to help Solyphos get up and it was not going well. The cracked wooden stool was on its side, Solyphos' staff on the ground, the writing implements scattered. The writing tablet remained where the boy had dropped it.

Oh, no. What had he done? The odor of the Islander's mastic oil raised the boy's dread, as if a stench of doom awaited him.

Solyphos grimaced as the burly Islander tried to pull him up off the ground by the arm. "Stop."

The boy ran up, knelt down, took Solyphos' hand in his. "My hip, my leg." He closed his eyes. "I fell running toward the lake."

Don't die. Not after you fell chasing me.

And not then, just when Hannibal's voice was near...and then came Gisgo booming out, the two of them somewhere close in the stream of men passing by, carrying plunder— Roman armor, swords, jewelry, tunics. He searched around him. A man waving a golden marching standard, still on its long pole, another patting the Roman medals now pinned on his ragged shirt. An Iberian warrior's white cloak fluttered in the breeze, revealing a bloody gash from the man's hip down to his ankle, a gash he seemed not to notice.

And then he saw Gisgo, and worse, Hannibal, walking uphill in the mass of men.

Gisgo's rock-slide voice filled the air. "You were right, Lord. We drove them right into the water, where they were not able to form a battle line to fight. We broke them into pieces and cut them down. Their commanding consul's—ambitious Flaminius– has been killed and few men escaped. As many drowned as were killed, I'd say. The lake was our ally."

The boy saw them before either saw what was happening beside the gnarled tree. Hannibal, sword in hand, was breathing hard, his clothes wet, dark splotches streaking his leather battle armor. There was a hint of a smile on his face as he listened.

Oh, please, keep walking, keep savoring this victory.

Hannibal was beside them. And then he was kneeling down, putting his hand on Solyphos' shoulder. "My tutor. Are you wounded?"

The old man opened his eyes. "No. I fell. My hip's smashed, right leg's useless."

Hannibal's eyes turned steely. How could the dead eye look so fierce and still be blind? His voice was a lash. "Nahatum, your job was to assist Solyphos." The tip of his sword tapped the ground, a hunting dog on the scent, barely leashed.

"I...."

"I was clumsy, Lord Hannibal," Solyhos was speaking now, as if from the grave. "Jonaz, your goatskin." The General put his arm under Solphos' head, helping him lean forward. Solyphos coughed, sputtered, drank. Gently, Hannibal held him still partly upright.

"The poor boy did his best, but I was too quick for him. Fell right over." Solyphos smiled grimly at Hannibal. Jonaz shifted his weight behind the boy, a movement full of accusation.

"I'm sorry, Sir...I..."

Again Solyphos interrupted. "Don't add to my pain by punishing Nahatum, Hannibal." Hannibal said nothing, digging his sword into the ground as if stabbing the very earth itself. "You're still seized with the energy of battle. Harming Nahatum won't do any good." The old man rested his hand on Hannibal's arm. Hannibal released his grip on the sword, handed it to Jonaz. "Come, tell me about this grand victory," Solyphos urged. "Then we'll attend to my hip. Do you realize, my dear student, that you have just accomplished the greatest ambush in recorded history? We'll worry about writing it all down in due time."

Later, Nahatum made sure he was at the head of the litter carrying Solyphos back to their wagon. He resisted any plundering; he would not let the man out of his sight again.

Several months passed.

"One hundred and seventy farms destroyed, a thousand horse captured. Our cattle herds spill over the roads and our wagon train, filled with plunder, lumbers behind like an overstuffed pig." Hannibal looked around the dining room of the elegant abandoned hilltop villa where he stood dictating.

The Roman villas were designed to catch the breeze and protect nicely from the August sun. In Carthage, even in their estate in Iberia, there were the cooling breezes of the Great Sea, always the sea. Most of Roman Italy was hill country. Where there were not hills there were mountains, running the length of the country like a spine. A spine he was trying to break.

Beyond the window his army had pitched their tents on farmland as far as he could see. The encampment had swollen with cattle, goats and sheep, geese, even duck, and the produce of hundreds of Roman farms. Why was he not happy?

He looked down at Nahatum, hunched over the papyrus, his face tense with the effort of writing down what Hannibal dictated. Quill at the ready. The boy clearly wanted so hard to succeed at this strange experiment.

How did I let Solyphos convince me to try this? "The boy can take your dictation only until I recover," Solyphos had said. He didn't use the word, "scribe."

He, Hannibal, was suspicious—he visited Solyphos every day and the man seemed to be getting weaker, not stronger, lying flat in the back of a supply wagon. A well-appointed wagon, with a bed now placed in it, but a wagon still, and susceptible to all the bumps and bounces along the rocky Roman roads. The old man always wanted to know how the boy was doing, and he talked with Hannibal with his familiar enthusiasm. But there was a difference.

Pillaging and savaging the countryside. Is that all I have to describe? He saw the boy look up at him. "I want to describe Rome's surrender. How Capua opened its gates to us, celebrating us as saviors from Roman oppression. How Napoli welcomed our fleet into its harbor, bringing reinforcements. When will any of that happen?"

The boy, face intent, scraped the quill along the papyrus. "No, Nahtum, stop, don't write that. I was just thinking aloud." He watched as the boy scratched out what he had just written. Hannibal restrained himself. *Don't do that, you are making a greater mess of the whole page.*

This was not like dictating to Solyphos. Who knew that dictating was a dance between two people? Solyphos knew when to listen, when to write, and when he did either he did it with such attention and confidence. He gave Hannibal confidence. It was not the same talking to a mere boy, though this boy was getting the look of a man, broadening out, strong shoulders. No longer the look of a wolf cub, now more of a true wolf.

"They won't even come to battle. And that new Consul follows us everywhere, but keeps his distance." If he went over to the window that looked out on the far hills, he'd see a line of Roman soldiers watching their encampment from safety, across the valley. Everywhere he marched they followed behind, an army unwilling to fight.

His skin tightened for a moment as he thought of the Allobroge in the Alps, waiting for a chance for the ambush. He stepped over several large pieces of a smashed Roman urn—certainly not Grecian, with much less delicacy of color or design—and gestured to Jonaz to get a broom to sweep up these remains of yesterday's looting.

And what would you do if you were Rome? Three months since his smashing victory at Lake Trasimene had destroyed yet another Roman army. The Romans renamed the stream feeding the lake, the "Sanguineto"– the "Blood River." There had not been a battle since.

They understood now what they faced: there was a dragon in their midst.

A new Consul had taken command of Rome's armies: Fabius Maximus. Older, experienced, cautious. Shadowing Hannibal, sometimes in view, attacking his foraging parties when they could, but otherwise simply following him around Italy.

Not another war of attrition, like the last endless one that bled Carthage dry.

Fabius claimed they could starve him out, that he could not keep an army of his size supplied in Italy forever, that his

Gaulish allies would fade away. He had no port, no means of re-suppy by sea.

Attrition? Well, two can play that game. He would burn all Italy to the ground if he had to. And that's exactly what he'd been doing, rampaging over the rich farmlands of Samnium and Apulia. Let the wealthy landowners flee to Rome and protest the destruction of the homes, fields, livestock, their elegant, well-stocked warehouses and grainaries, the carefully tended vineyards.

He stared down at the papyrus, the boy bent over it, quill at the ready, watching him "You need to practice those letters, still, Nahatum."

"I will, Sir. I promise. I will work harder on my writing."

Behind them, Jonaz, busy with the broom, took this moment to press his familiar case. "Lord Hannibal, things have not been the same since he began to augur the words and use the quills and somesuch that Solyphos brought into our camp."

What rot. Not again, about the wolf boy. Apparently his stare was not enough to deter the squire's hatred of the servant. Who might rise to be a true scribe at some point. "Lord, if I may speak, Ba'al Shammon, merciful protector of Carthage, is not happy.

Perhaps that is why he is denying us a decisive victory."

He rubbed his hands on the fine pair of cotton pants he was wearing, which came straight out of the Roman landowner's closet in the adjoining bedroom. "With your permission, great General, I will make a sacrifice to the great god to bring the Romans to battle."

"Go ahead, Jonaz. Maybe that will help. And tell our beloved Ba'al Shammon to please tell the citizens of Capua and Napoli to open their gates to us."

"I will, great Lord." And then the humorless man hurried out, leaving just him and the boy, who had watched this exchange with his usual intensity.

"Sir, you were joking about Ba'al, I think. Does the great god not really listen to such prayers?"

"I have no idea who the god listens to, Nahatum. Maybe he does, maybe he doesn't. Regardless, I still want the most favorable ground for battle. And it better be soon."

The boy gestured at the table, the papyrus with the crossed out lines. "I am sorry for this mess. I can do better."

In fact the page was not a mess, even if the story on it just then was one. The boy, incredibly, wrote legibly. Some letters were at odd angles and there were some misspellings, but—Hannibal realized— you would have to be a cold man indeed not to be impressed by what a once- illiterate wolf boy had learned in the time he'd been there.

Yet, still there was a grace and ease to the writing that was missing. More than that: some comfort he felt with the old man, a comfort for which Hannibal seemed to have no words. If only Solyphos were here right now, in his familiar place, the two of them talking, quibbling over words, as he dictated.

Nahatum walked out the villa's great room through the ornate wooden doors graced with carvings of sheep, lambs, vineyards, goblets of wine, pears and appleson to the elegant marble veranda and down the curved stairway to the gardens thateventually led to the meadow where Solyphos lay in his outfitted wagon. The scribe refered to it as his "rolling coffin," a term that distressed Nahatum.

The sun high overhead reflected off the marble of the villa; his eyes demanded time to adjust. Nahatum was in a foul mood, anyway, hardly the spirit of a sunny afternoon. The writing he had just completed weighed on him. The effort of it, trying to remember the curves and slopes and twists of the Punic letters. And more: the strangeness of his sitting there conjuring the same letters that Solyphos used to craft with such ease. His slowness, his stumbles, Hannibal's impatience. His master's unease.

For that matter, who *was* his master now? He was Solyphos' servant still, but also Hannibal's scribe. His unwanted scribe. He could never write like Solyphos. So, who— and what– was he?

He passed through the carefully cultivated gardens, past sleeping soldiers and mules dozing in the sun. In the field just past the prickly rose bushes and grape trellis Jonaz stood with four others, starting their sacrificial fire. He was ripping papyrus into the gathering flames. The pieces glinted in the sunlight as they fluttered into the fire. Around the man's wrist, as a sort of ornament next to the coarse string bracelet signifying piety, wound the deep green and gold ribbon that signified the scroll as the property of the landowner. Nahatum remembered a small collection of papyrus scrolls on a shelf in the great room.

"Stop. That's a scroll." The boy hurried across the alfalfa, recently harvested by the fleeing landowner, perhaps just before the army descended on this part of Samnium. Did the landowner anticipate last spring that his crops would become food for Hannibal's army?

"I know what it is. Ba'al will be pleased by its smoke."

If an auroch could talk, this is how it would sound. A dumb auroch.

Pieces of the burnt papyrus flittered down into the fire like wounded birds. The scroll-stuff twisted, writhed in the grip of the fire. All that remained were a few blackened embers.

Nahatum stepped forward and reached for the remaining scroll still in the squire's hand. Jonaz grabbed his arm and twisted it, hard, bringing back the burning pain that shot up into Nahatum's shoulder that day back in Iberia when he was first captured.

This time Nahatum twisted his arm back, powerfully. Jonaz gave way grudgingly, then his arm was free, and he faced the surprised squire, whose eyes narrowed as he spit curses.

"Be careful. I know what you are doing, casting spells on Hannibal."

The boy ached to punch the man, but what would Hannibal say then if he found him fighting with his squire?

"You are a strange weed, wolf child. I won't let you corrupt Hannibal or my city." He waved the remaining scroll at Nahatum as if shaking a snake. "Get out of here."

Solyphos needed him back in the wagon. Nahatum hurried down the field toward the forest and its meadow, turning for a final look at the squire. The *tine*, the sacrificial fire, roared.

Jonaz shook a metal incense holder and breathed in the smoke. Someone led a goat up and in a moment sliced its throat. The dying animal collapsed into the fire. Jonaz bowed and swayed, reciting prayers. As he did, he wound tighter and tighter the coarse string bracelet at his wrist

When he arrived at Solyphos' wagon, Nahatum checked the water bags on the harnesses of the two mules, then climbed up the uneven wooden steps and pushed past the curtain that protected against the sun. Solyphos was flat on his back on the straw mattress, under a woolen blanket. *Please, do not be dead.*

Solyphos was not even asleep. "Ah, the clouds, Nahatum. Hold the curtains open a moment longer."

As the boy crawled deeper into the dark wagon, a familiar odor engulfed him: thick and low and sickeningly sweet.

Solyphos had soiled himself again. The boy hurried out and returned with a bucket of warm water and some rags, then gently started to bath Solyphos. The boy had never been so close to another man's body.

"Ow." Solyphos' face seemed to shrivel. *Like papyrus in the fire, twisting away into itself.*

"Sorry." He tried to be more careful cleaning around the shattered hip.

"I killed a boy once." Solyphos looked past Nahatum, out the curtain, at the sky. "In a war with the town of Mynos. I lost my wife and son when they burnt my farm so I joined the attack on Mynos, slaughtered a helpless boy in revenge."

The man's bones were like thin tree roots under soft dirt. Where did the muscles go? The boy knew that Lizard Skin was slowly working his way into Solyphos' body.

Even Solyphos—scribe, magician, teacher—could not defend himself againstLizard Skin.

"I've tried to teach you, Nahatum."

"You'll help me with the Greek and Latin, still, won't you? I don't think I scribed very well today for Lord Hannibal."

"As long as I can help you, I will." He winced. "You'll do fine with Hannibal." Again, face conforted. "Something is happening inside me. The humors are very unbalanced; nothing makes them right. Hannibal has sent the doctors, but none of their mixtures or potions have helped. They're about as effective now as when he lost his sight in the eye."

They sat together in silence. Nahatum wanted to move to get more comfortable in the narrow wagon, but then he would have had to take his hand off Solyphos' chest.

"Read the books, the plays equally. Sophocles, Euripides, even though they are Athenians."

"You'll help me."

"Read the books." An urgent look that held Nahatum. "You will learn something very important." Solyphos licked his lips. The wagon was an oven in the noonday August sun. And yet Solyphos insisted on that woolen blanket. The boy brought him a ladle of water and he was back for a moment at the encampment in Iberia kneeling down with The Lady on her pallet. Solyphos drank, slowly and carefully, raised his head just slightly enough to get at the water.

"What will I learn?"

"That when you think you're doing one thing, really you are doing the opposite. I thought I was avenging my son and I killed another boy."

Solyphos struggled to sit up, to clear his throat from a spasm of cough, and the boy put his arm under an ancient shoulder, lifted him up and patted his back until he could breath freely, which only restored the lecture, as if the man had no time to stop, to focus on things like mere breathing. "Maybe that's enough to know—that we don't know ourselves. I wanted revenge and what I got was regret."

The man looked to Nahatum with such desperation that the boy wondered if the old man was pleading with him, except he couldn't imagine Solyphos pleading.

"Please, remember, Nahatum: Do not fall in love with warfare."

The hot, sunbaked small Roman towns in Samnium and Apulia kept their gates closed to the invading polyglot army of tattooed African warriors, half- naked white- skinned Gauls with unkempt red hair flowing down their backs, and white- turbaned Iberians, all equally agitated and hungry for battle.

The Roman army, meanwhile, stayed mainly in the hills, leaving the rich valleys to Hannibal. Fabius Maximus was determined to starve out Hannibal. They called him The Delayer, because he would not fight. Let Hannibal face the impossible task of keeping his army supplied and willing to fight while trapped in a foreign country with no means of re-supply. What Carthaginian general would be capable of that?, Fabius scoffed.

So, they marched—and plundered– along roads lined with tall cypress trees and silvery olive trees. They burnt endless fields of vegetables, overstuffed grainaries, vineyards bursting with purple and green grapes. Soldiers walked along roads with loaves of fresh bread sticking out their cloaks, tunics and coats, and elegant ceramic wine jugs lashed to their backs with leather strips, along with wicker baskets filled with fine meats and cheeses, stolen trinkets.

Two months passed in this manner. The Roman province of Samnium was a ruin, fine villas and farms ablaze.

Then one lovely late summer afternoon, Hannibal stood alone, watching two of his soldiers slowly dig a grave for Solyphos at the edge of a rolling meadow, the sort of spot his old tutor, his advisor, the man he'd hoped would write the history of the invasion, had always preferred to place his tent.

One shovelful, then another. *Hurry up.* How was he to focus his mind on the correct rites and rituals to bury this man in middle of a war? The Romans shadowed his every move, waiting for him to make a misstep and destroy him. His mind raced with plans– march here or there, advance parties, rear guards, best routes—while his heart beat slowly and heavily.

Another shovelful of dirt, then another. The soil had a yeasty smell. *How do you bury a man in a foreign country, not even his own land?* They said the gods were not satisfied if you were buried far from your home, but what of his father, whose body was never found, swept away in a raging Iberian river? There was a Punic saying: you must dig deep to bury your father. *How deep?*

The shovels beat out their rhythm, the thudding dirt on the white shroud, the man disappearing. Hannibal ordered the men to pack the dirt well and watched to the end while they covered it with heavy stones. "Ensure no animal can dig up this grave, defile the body." There would be no gravestone, no marker. What point? The Romans could desecrate it.

Then Hannibal sent the men away. He wanted to be alone.

This war took Solyphos' life, just as war took my father's life. Will it eventually cost me my own? So many costs. His wife and son in Carthage knew nothing of what was happening to him, not even if he was alive or dead. And what of the thousands of men he led, who have put their hopes and confidence in him? Two entire cities— all the men, women, and children—bent to the task of defeating the other. War was a hungry demon that would devour whoever came near it.

And, yet. There's a war to be fought, a war to be won—he must get on with it.

Hannibal bowed before the grave, deeply, lingering there. *Good-bye, my tutor, my counselor. I will miss you greatly.* Then he turned, and walked toward the cavalry fields to check on how much foodstuffs Marhabal's foraging parties had brought back that day.

The boy watched the burial from the edge of the muddy glade, unseen by anyone. Solyphos– the man who had given him so much—was gone. *What is your spirit, young wolf boy?... That is grief. What you saw from the elephants... Those are tears... Come here. Sit in my seat... That is aleph...and that is bet...and that is gimmel.*

The man gave him a language, a voice, a life And what had he warned that day months ago with such urgency in his voice? "Nahatum: Do not fall in love with warfare." He wanted to think more about that, but he could hardly think at all just then. Solyphos was dead. How could this be? Leaning against a tree, alone, Nahatum wept for what he had lost.

Restless, standing by the window of yet another once- sumptuous, now ruined marbled Roman villa, Hannibal imagined that he could see the Roman Consul Fabius, The Delayer, on horseback on the hill in the far distance, watching his army, refusing to come to battle.

They had to keep careful track of their supplies—Fabius wanted to destroy them in pieces, making it hard for Marhabal and his men to forage supplies, picking off their raiding parties, limiting their movements.

Hannibal turned to Gisgo, who was examining a Grecian urn on the finely carved table. "We need a full accounting of our food supplies. Every day. What Marhabal's men bring back. The other foraging parties. All the sheep, cattle, grain, cheese, wine. All of it."

Gisgo nodded, though he could barely count. He was not the one who could do it.

And Solyphos was gone.

A different voice. "I can do that." Nahatum held up the old bag with writing supplies that he now carried everywhere.

"Do what?"

"The last thing Solyphos taught me: how to use a ledger."
That confident tone again. Gisgo scowled.

"Are you sure? We didn't survive the Endless Mountains
to starve here in Italy. All the livestock, all the grain. I want a
complete accounting of the barrels of wine, wheels of cheese,
the number of vegetables, amount of grain. You can do that?"

The boy nodded, holding Hannibal's eyes. As if to say: I
know exactly what you want from me and I can do it.

Why not? Hannibal thought. *Give him a chance.*

By the early fall, they'd become an army of locusts spreading
across the countryside of neat fields, overrunning tidy estates, crisscrossing the Roman provinces, slashing, eating, and
burning. Drunken, angry locusts.

Yet the world was orderly for Nahatum. He came to feel
more comfortable with ledgers. He worried less about making
a mistake, and liked the neat and reliable rows and columns.
The number of head of cattle, the pigs, goats. The wagons of
wheat and corn and barley. The crates of chickens, flocks of
geese. Side of beef, wheels of cheese.

Hardened warriors and slaves and animal herders reported the day's yields from foraging parties. He saw the looks
on their faces as he, a former wolf boy, augured the numbers
and the words.

And he could see that the numbers were barely enough.
The summer was gone. If no city opened its gates soon, they
would all starve before the people of Rome lost patience with
their Consul who would not fight.

Starving, though, was not on Nahatum's mind the day in late fall that he stood in front of a white- columned villa surrounded by grape orchards and fields of olive trees. It was the biggest he'd seen in Apulia. Even after all the looted farms and villas, this one was special. The wealthy family—no fools— must have fled to the safety of Rome in the comfort of their pillowed litters on the shoulders of their slaves.

A tall, white stucco wall surrounded the entire house, which was graced by a string of grated windows, painted a soft, pleasing green. Thick fingers of blacksmoke from the fields across the river rose behind the red- tiled clay roof. Several muscular, large- boned hounds lay dead in the front yard, arrows in their chests. A lifeless slave sprawled face- up across the marble entrance; fresh sword wounds still leaked blood from his chest.

An axe crunched through wood. Tile shattered. Marhabal's voice came from deep inside, along with the clip- clop of horse hooves on marble. Nahatum walked past the fluted white marble columns at the entryway, past the carved oak door, hanging off its hinges, into a shaded courtyard filled with plants and stone sculptures.

On the far side of the courtyard he saw another door. Nahatum crossed the cool open area and walked into a room with soft leather chairs and couches. His sandals hardly made a sound on the polished marble. This house was made for gods. From the outside, he had seen how the white walls shimmered in the sunlight, the house tucked into a slight rise, overlooking the fields.

More voices. Marhabal, Gisgo. He followed the sounds through more elegant rooms, then came upon Marhabal, the red- coated cavalry commander, on horseback in front of a stone fireplace. A horse in a house! The sight still shocked Nahatum, though they'd plundered so many villas that the boy had seen it before– Marhabal often no longer bothered to dismount, just riding in through a broken window or smashed doorway. Gisgo, in a green tunic, stood near him. He was talking to Hannibal, and gesturing around the room.

"This is as beautiful as the villas on the Byrsa in Carthage, Lord, overlooking the Great Sea."

"Almost. Except there is no Great Sea here, and no golden light off the water." Hannibal smiled, then asked Marhabal about the number of heads of cattle they had found at pasture in the low hills out back.

A polished wooden table, honey- colored with thick lines of grain throughout, was surrounded by carved wooden chairs. A window looked out on the leafy interior courtyard, where birds still sang in their cages.

A mosaic covered the entire wall: several people having an outdoor banquet on a veranda, perhaps at this very house. They sat on low couches– a man in a white toga, a woman in a multicolored dress–savoring grapes, holding cups of wine. A bough of delicate leafy branches seemed to float behind the figures. When Nahatum looked more carefully, he found that the leaves were composed of dozens of small tiles. Careful, de- tailed work. Like what he did with the quill. More so: there was a richness of color as he'd seen on the clay amphora jug on the table back in Solyphos' wagon, now his. Glaze, Solyphos had called it.

A family lived here, proud enough to make a mosaic of themselves. There were children, dressed like small versions of the adults, standing near a table.

Outside, the wild call of a trumpet. Shrill and insistent and celebratory. The men had found a cask of wine.

Suddenly, a metal blur ripped through the mosaic tile. Jonaz's axe smashed into the wall. Then again. And again. The brightly colored pieces scattered onto the ground, exposing the soft grout underneath. The fourth time, the axe left a deep trench. The broken remains of the man, woman, their children, lay scrambled around Nahatum's feet.

"Nahatum, over here—take down this report," Hannibal ordered. Then, grimly: "Though there's not much here."

Nahatum removed a quill from the sack, rummaging for some papyrus. Gisgo hesitated, then told him about how many salt legs of lamb and sides of pig they'd found in the store-houses down by the river. Not many. And, the grainery was empty. The cheese house had only one mouse- eaten wheel, when it had the capacity to hold dozens. Somewhere, the rich estate owner had hidden the enormous harvest. Nahatum care-fully wrote down the numbers, which looked small and forlorn on the wide columns he'd created on the papyrus.

"Burn this house to the ground. We move on."

Nahatum hurried to gather up the quills, ink, papyrus. He'd barely gotten his sack open when Jonaz axed the table right in front of him into large chunks of wood. Then he was ripping up an old papyrus scroll to start a fire under the de-stroyed table.

"Where did you get that?"

The papyrus was in flames. Nahtum felt a terrible energy rooting him to the spot.

.Hannibal was already in the next room. "Where did you get that papyrus scroll?" he repeated, his voice rising.

Jonaz jerked his head towards a room off to the side, fur-ther into the villa. The boy turned and walked past the squire reciting prayers over the rising flames through a carved wooden door and into a small, windowless room. The walls were lined with wooden shelves, and each shelf had rolled up scrolls of papyrus, neatly tied with ribbons. Books. Hundreds of them. Solyphos had only a crate of them, and here were twenty, thirty times more.

What men—or was it just one man?– had done all the writing? He unscrolled one. Rows and columns of numbers. A ledger; farm records of crop production, numbers of sales. Another: A history of the man's family. Someone had fought during the firstwar with Carthage, but Nahatum's stumbling Latin made the translating slow. Water stains on some scrolls, others not legible. Some were worn from use, others looked unopened.

He started to run. *Hannibal. I must find him. These are precious.* "Sir," he yelled into the air. Past Jonaz, busy fanning the flames, through the house. Just ahead of Gisgo, Hannibal strode briskly toward the granite marble entry foyer. Marbahal, on his horse, was already in the front yard, yelling orders to his cavalry.

"Wait. Sir. Look." He waved several scrolls in the air, a frantic flapping. Smoke from behind made him cough.

Hannibal, distracted, glared at him. "What is it?"

"Sir, I have found a room full of scrolls." A frown framed Hannibal's grey eyes.

His eyebrows were bushy. Had they always been that way?

Hannibal said nothing. He seemed to be waiting for something more. "Scrolls, Sir. Books. A room full of them."

"So?"

"I request we wait to burn the house until I have removed the scrolls," His voice sounded young and small, though resolute. *He requests?* As if he had such standing.

"Why?"

What to say? Was the general asking why a wolf boy had the rudeness to speak to him that way? Or was Hannibal wondering why some battered scrolls were worth saving?

"To what end? Come on, boy, we have little time."

An unfamiliar, unpleasant thought: *is Hannibal so used to destruction that he can no longer see what's worth saving?*

"We have to go, Sir," Gisgo prompted.

A desperate energy seized Nahatum. "There may be valuable information in these scrolls."

"What sort of information?"

"I need to look through them. They may be of use to us. There may be some maps."

"Maps?"

Maps? Have I caught his attention? "Yes, Sir."

Hannibal sighed. "Scrolls. I'd rather have one head of cattle than all the scrolls in this house. How long do you need?"

How long? "Two or three days."

Hannibal snorted, Gisgo laughed. Hannibal looked at him, a softening in his eyes. "You have till the sun is at its highest today. Noon- high." Then: "See if there are indeed some useful maps." He shouted back into the house. "Jonaz, you and your friend help Nahatum clear the room of scrolls. Bank that fire."

Then he was gone.

Nahatum put a hand on the smashed table to steady himself as he walked back into the room. His voice seemed to shake a little, but somehow he spit out an order. "Hurry, Jonaz, and you too." He pointed at the other man, who wore his long hair piled high on his head. Tantar was his name. He led them into the room of books. "Start bringing the scrolls out in boxes, while I find a wagon."

They both stared down at the floor, like uncomprehending cattle. "Come on!" he barked, jumping slightly at the sound of his own voice. "Didn't you hear Hannibal?"

"These scrolls are….," Jonaz's mouth curled as if to spit.

"Start carrying these boxes of scrolls out to the front." To Nahatum's relief, they obeyed. He tried to flag down a creaky wagon pulled by several long- eared mules, but the driver– in his fancy plumed hat –kept going. So he stepped right in front and grabbed the harness of the lead mules.

"Orders of Lord Hannibal—empty this wagon."

The driver looked at him, then did as he was told. *This is unbelievable: men are obeying my orders.* Was it the purple tunic? Some way he was speaking? No matter, he was going to save those scrolls. Working quickly, they emptied the wagon, then backed it up to the smoking villa. The four of them stacked boxes of the scrolls, some water- stained or ripped or already flaking apart with age.

He made no distinction. "Save all of them."

With the wagon driver's knife he carved the word "scrolls" in Punic into the wagon's worm- chewed back boards. Now that he couldn't burn them, Jonaz seemed scared to touch the scrolls. He held the crates away from his body and dumped them haphazardly into the back of the wagon.

"Be careful with them!"

When Jonaz threw the last crate into the wagon, he looked once at the boy, then hurried back into the villa. Soldiers had gathered around a bonfire in the front yard pawing over the ground for any last gold or silver jewelry or coin or anything else of value. Ordinarily he might have looked too, but now all he wanted was to get the scrolls away from the house.

Flames leapt from the broken roof tile. Jonaz appeared at a window with a burning thatch bundle. Soon flames announced themselves from the front door and windows while men cheered. Jonaz climbed out a low window to the ground and bowed. Soot streaked his face.

The boy climbed up onto the front of the supply wagon, and ordered the plumed driver to move forward. The scrolls would be safe in their wooden boxes. He pictured Solyphos smiling.

As the wagon lurched forward, the boy had no idea— how could he?— of the enormity of what he was to find, nor its consequences.

They wintered in the wretched little Appenine village of Gerontium. Food was so scarce that soldiers swore they'd seen snakes sneak into the barns and drink from the udders of cows. Some days the snow howled like wolves calling to their dead. A pride of lions took two men while they were searching for disappeared goats. A search party went after them and lost another man.

The townspeople, Roman colonists, had resisted when Hannibal's army arrived.

Hannibal barely waited: the wooden village gates were smashed in and the hardened African veterans poured into the town, killing knives glinting in the bright afternoon sunlight.

Taurini, once again.

They lived in the creaky wooden homes of the dead, wore their woolen pants, burlap shirts, and fed themselves from their grainary, which they would soon empty. Ghost people, ghost food.

The snows piled up to the shoulders of the Numidans' horses. They rolled tree trunks through the streets in the bitter cold to pack down the snow. Marhabal's cavalry couldn't scout or forage. Men gambled in their tents, huddled together.

Arguments rocked the rough-hewn wooden house that Hannibal took as his headquarters. Again, a retreat back to

Gaul with their booty was proposed. Some of the chiefs seemed happy that the Romans were still avoiding a fight.

One freezing January afternoon, with Hannibal's roaring fireplace battling to keep the winter winds at bay, Barnabar predicted that "the Romans will only come to battle if they can corner us for a direct attack. No water, no hidden canyons, no attacks from out of the mist."

Silver and gold had replaced the worn bag of teeth the big man used to toss in the air: now he toyed with fine Roman hammered gold rings—officer's jewelry—on each of his fingers as he spoke. Gisgo, Marhabal, and assorted chiefs looked on. When Barnabar gestured, tiny sparkling flames danced on his hands in the candlelight.

I must keep this army together. Forget your own doubt. The plan is a good one.

You cannot fail now, with victory so close. Give these men some hope.

Hannibal could sense it: one more victory would break the Roman Federation. He stared at the gold glittering on Barnabar's hands.

"We are close, great Barnabar. The Romans cannot, will not, let us continue to plunder their lands once spring returns. Consider: you must have half the Roman treasury on your fingers right now. Aren't you hungry for the rest?"

Ah, that produced some cheers from the chiefs. And reminded them how rich they all were, forgetting for the moment that they were trapped in a frozen village in the Appenine mountains with little way to spend all the plunder they'd gained.

The smile soon left Barnabar's face. "You want to force another battle. Yet the Romans, in a direct frontal attack, are unbeatable. With all due respect to our great Commander."

That's what the Romans think, too. And that will be their downfall.

"There is a way to deal with Roman armor, their steel, and greater numbers, even in a direct battle."

Barnabar raised an eyebrow. "And how is that?" All the chiefs bent in to hear Hannibal's plan.

"There is a way." *Yes, indeed.* He had been thinking about this for years, back to those many nights in front of the fireplace in Iberia talking with Solyphos and his father about strategy and military history. They'd expected that in the war to come the Romans would have the advantage in numbers, in steel, in discipline. In a direct confrontation between their two armies, how might Carthage's prevail?

They'd developed a battle plan so audacious, so novel, that it rivaled in inspiration the surprise crossing of the Endless Mountains to invade Italy. "Remember, my son," Hamilcar had emphasized, "take your enemy's greatest advantages, that which gives them the most confidence, and use that against them."

He dared not tell the details to the chiefs in the room. He wanted no chance that foolish talk might find its way to the Romans.

"Hannibal, our food supplies are low, no cities have opened their gates, no uprising among the Roman federation has happened…" Barnabar was counting off the problems on his be-jeweled fingers while the rest of the chiefs nodded…." and here we sit frozen in these useless mountains. The Romans will only fight us if they are certain of victory. And you claim to have a plan?"

"Exactly, great Barnabar." Hannibal could feel the smile forming on his face. He pushed aside his own doubt. "We have the Romans exactly where we want them."

Please, great Ba'al, on the shield of my father, let this be true.

Nahatum wondered which would come first– the end of winter or their own starvation? He slept in his wagon under luxurious, embroidered woolen blankets looted from the finest Roman villas, housed in the spacious barn attached to the house Hannibal used. Who once lived here? Had there been such death in Taurini? Had he not noticed?

His dreams were filled with strange men, women, sad children holding little toy bears and carved lions in their skinny hands. They walked through the barn right into his wagon. He startled awake at the sound of their feet. When he looked in the darkened barn, he could not find them. The dawn was a welcome time, freeing him from his dreams.

The many Roman prisoners they'd accumulated from skirmishes grew more confident and arrogant. They'd heard word of the speech Fabius Maximus had delivered to the Roman Senate: "If this Carthaginian is such a sorcerer, let him conjure up bread for his infantry, oats for his cavalry."

The boy practiced his Latin with them at the house where they were imprisoned, sleeping on beds of straw while they awaited ransom, "if you haven't already surrendered—as Consul Fabius has predicted."

Except for such comments, he liked conversing with them in Latin, entertaining the group with made- up stories about Carthage so good that they were convinced he had grown up there.

Early spring brought hungry bears out of their twilight sleep. Several horses went missing from the stockade, a trail of blood disappearing into the woods. More goats disappeared. It wasn't clear if bears, lions, or their own starving soldiers had taken them.

Nahatum staved off his hunger by translating the most boring scrolls of all—the household ledgers saved from the rich landowner's villa in Apulia. So much smoked meats and winter vegetables sent to be sold in Rome or stored away to be eaten later. He could have chewed on the papyrus. Wine, olives, tomatoes, fattened geese, cattle ready for slaughter. How much yield each field of corn and wheat had given for growing seasons going back dozens of years. There were maps of property scattered all over Italy. The Romans kept track of everything.

All the translating about food stocks made him hungrier still. There were no more moldy turnips hidden in his wagon. Pushing his black raven's feather quill into his hair, he walked into the darkness, confident of finding something from the cooks, even with the extra guards standing watch over the supply wagons.

Halfway down the dark forested trail, a thick burlap bag descended over him.

Blackness. Hands all around. A thick rope binding him in the bag. Men's voices. How many? He kicked out blindly, but was soon hauled up on several shoulders. The burlap muffled his protests.

"Is all ready?" Jonaz's thick voice. *He will pay. I will extract the payment with my own fists.* Thorny branches ripped at Nahatum's coat and pants, even through the burlap.

Was what ready? Someone muttered an oath. The boy cursed back, then heard that word. "Tine." The sacrificial fire, a gift to Ba'als' consort, Tanit.

Then he was on his feet again, the rope loosened, the bag removed, standing in a forest glade illuminated by the light of a roaring fire. There were two others: Tantar, his thick hair piled high, the same dumb look as he had that day at the villa last summer, and another man, equally thick-looking. Plus Jonaz, who for some reason wore his battle armor, which was partly covered by a thick robe such as a priest might wear. The man's eyes seemed to blaze with a fire of their own.

The trail was ahead of him, but he couldn't bolt for it, not with Tantar holding his arms tightly behind his back. The other man, who he had never seen before and had one eye, tied his hands behind his back. The man's hands shook—he was either nervous or sloppy, and he tied the hands loosely.

The boy clenched his fists to make the ropes even looser. The shaky one-eyed man didn't notice. A prayer of gratitude to Ba'al. He had an advantage, a surprise.

Hannibal would say: *use it.*

The heat from the crackling thatch licked at the skin on his legs. There was a sharp taste in the boy's throat. Tantar reached for the raven's feather in his hair.

"No. Leave it." Jonaz' voice broke slightly. *He is afraid of my feather.* "Let the demonic thing be purified in the fire, along with the boy." Nahatum remembered the man's deathly fear of birds, harbingers of death. Another advantage, another surprise.

Use it.

Tantar stoked the fire.

"Are you enchanted by the god of Death, Jonaz? Hannibal will have you tortured for what you are doing."

"Men disappear in an army every day. Through your sacrifice, Merciful Ba'al will see that we have suffered enough."

Jonaz walked up to Nahatum and hit him hard, fist to chin, which concentrated the boy's attention. The raven's feather dug into his skull. Flames leapt into the air. He twisted his hands gently behind him. Not as easy as he'd thought, but they came free. He raised his arms high over his head. All three men moved toward him, and then the raven feather was in his hand and he held it in front of him like a sharp killing knife.

"One more step and I will melt your eyes. They will boil through your cheeks until you choke on the hot, foul mud of your own eyes." He waved the feather in a broad, slow arc, keeping now all three men in front of him.

Jonaz's mouth fell open. The other two looked at the squire. Nahatum hoped that Greek words half- screamed sounded like the most ancient of curses. Jonaz stepped back. The other two moved even further away.

This is the moment: use it.

Avoiding the blaze, Nahatum took a step backward, then turned, took a long stride, and hurled himself deep into the thick forest along the rocky trail.

He knew that no one—certainly not those hyenas—could catch a former Wolf boy in full stride in the forest.

Back in the wagon, pike back at his side, the boy considered his options. He could go to Hannibal, but Jonaz would deny everything and what would happen then? Lots of Jonaz's friends would swear that they had been rolling dice all night with him.

Think about this. The man had treated him like a sack of turnips, like an animal to be sacrificed in the fire, like the Wolf boy he had once been. He would deal with Jonaz himself. At the appropriate time.

Still, there would be no sleep that night. He recognized that familiar feeling inside: his whole chest felt alive as if every caged hummingbird had gotten free, beating against his ribs and his throat.

Calm yourself. You are safe here in your wagon. Hannibal is asleep in the building just through that mud room over there. Here is Solyphos' favorite stylus. The one you used to make notes reading through those endless ledgers.

The ledgers. He lit the candles on his writing desk. There was a scroll open on it, a stone neatly place on each corner. *The very scroll you'd just laid out a few hours ago, before you almost became a sacrificial goat.* He sighed. It's just some old ledger from that villa in Apulia, yet another of dozens that he's been translating to pass the time. *Still, sit, read, calm yourself.*

And so, keeping his pike close, Nahatum began to read, holding Solyphos' old, pitted stylus. Solyphos, who had warned him about the dangers of war, the way it twists men's minds, leads them to do things that they regret the rest of their lives.

"Jovius, the landowner..." He imagined a fat Roman, clothed in a fine toga.

"Three thousand hectare of wheat and hay, two thousand hectare of rice..." *Perhaps this was not a good idea.* His mouth watered and there were now growls from his stomach, the hummingbirds replaced by hungry bears. Skipping down, the scroll didn't look like a ledger anymore. There were too many sentences. He picked his way carefully through the Latin: "... by order of Consul Fabius..." Fabius– The Delayer himself! "...taken by wagon to the grainery in the town of Cannae, for future use, stored there through the winter until needed to feed the army in case of operations against Hannibal of Carthage in that part of Italy."

At the bottom, the scroll was dated and signed, both by Consul Fabius (in asmall, tight, careful handwriting) and the landowner, this rich Jovius. The scroll was dated the past September. That would have been just weeks before they'd arrived and plundered the rich farm, only to find the store houses empty.

Cannae. He'd never heard of it.

Leaning now over the table, the boy went back up the papyrus to read what he had skipped: "The grain is to be hidden in the storehouses in Cannae until needed by the army, or allowed to be distributed to be sold. If taken by the army, the Roman Senate agrees to pay Jovius the sum of one thousand talents of silver." A fortune. A lot of grain. Maybe root vegetables, too. And all the cheese from that empty storehouse on the estate. And wine?

He hurried now, digging through the boxes of scrolls, looking for maps he had seen of the man's vast landholdings. He unfolded the map of the southern section of Italy. His stylus found a little dot in the eastern side of the mountains, on a coastal plain. An odd name: Cannae.

Of course the Romans would want to store grain there through the winter, where we are unlikely to find it. He looked at Gerontium. How far to Cannae?

Then he was all frenzied energy, through the dark mud room, pike in hand, to find Hannibal next door. He concentrated, working to remember that strange name. *Cannae.*

The sand stung the back of Hannibal's neck in the hot morning wind. The theatre of that day had begun. He surveyed the field of battle: a long sandy flat plain, devoid of water, except for a small river on the far end. This is what he wanted, what the plan demanded. In the far distance lay the little town of Cannae.

The Romans were lining up for battle across the plain. Fabius was gone; the Roman Senate tired of Hannibal cutting swathes of destruction across Italy. They'd raised the largest army Rome had ever put in the field and The Delayer had been replaced by two Roman commanders eager to burnish their reputations by defeating the great– and deeply feared– Hannibal. The Consul in command that day was spoiling for a fight; he'd mocked Fabius on the Senate floor for his caution.

Ninety thousand Roman soldiers lay across that plain, facing his polyglot army numbering, maybe, forty thousand. There were so many Roman soldiers it was as if all of Rome itself had come to attention, flags waving, legion upon legion. Hannibal's horse whinnied at the distant sound of trumpets calling units to their place, anticipating what was to come. From the slight rise looking over the dry, sandy plain, Hannibal could just see the river Aufidus coursing through. If all worked according to plan the Roman army will die in sight of all that water, useless to them.

The boy—his lucky charm, his devoted, hard-working scribe– had brought him here, to this: a flat plain on a hot summer day confronting a Roman army finally willing to fight him. Or was it two armies? It was enormous. Brought here to test him, to test the strategy that he had been thinking about since a young boy with his father.

What happens if you intentionally allow the center of your battle line to collapse, retreating slowly and in a controlled fashion? Could you lure your opponent into a position of seeming dominance that then leads to their destruction? The basic principle of warfare was to maintain the integrity of your battle line. The Greek phalanx, the Roman maniple— we fight together as one unit and we do not let the battle line break. If it breaks, then your army can be cut to pieces and destroyed.

So, what if you led your enemy to think that they were about to break through your center, about to cut your army in half, but that was not really so? No, rather what was happening was that a controlled withdrawal led you to enlarge your position slowly on their flanks, eventually almost surrounding them as they advanced. And, if somehow you could find a way to fall upon their rear, your enemy would be encircled and helpless, their large numbers no advantage because the bulk of their army would be trapped in the interior mass of men unable to fight, while your army— attacking now from the center, from the flanks, and from the rear— could destroy the confused mass of supposedly dominant soldiers confronting them.

Or so the plan said.

"Has there ever been an army as large?" Gisgo muttered, adjusting the bridle on his horse. *A good question. The Persians were supposed to have massed a million men to invade Attica, but surely that is simply legend.* Their army at Marathon, Solyphos once claimed, was perhaps fifty thousand. *And Alexander? He took thirty thousand Macedonians in his conquest of the world.*

And here the Romans had massed three times that number. He ought to be honored that they would only fight him when they were certain of victory. Who could defeat such an army?

And the Romans were confident, he was sure of it. A flat plain. No ambushes, no rivers or lakes to die in. No, let's not try to use water to defeat the Romans. Rather, what about thirst? What would it be like to fight on a hot day with little water available? The Romans wanted to avoid fighting him near water? Fine, let them have a dry plain and see what happens. *Let the enemy think he has the advantage and use their advantage to destroy them.*

Hannibal turned to answer Gisgo's question. "Yes, it's a large army. Yet, consider, my friend: in all that enormous number of men there is not a single one named Gisgo." The burly infantry commander laughed. The boy standing slightly behind also laughed. *Good. Most of all we need confidence. And some luck.*

The boy was his luck. He'd known it again when Nahatum had burst in months ago, talking about the ledgers and an enormous storehouse in Cannae, over the time that it'd taken to get there, more fields destroyed, villas burnt, the enormous destruction that finally led the Senate to turn from Consul Fabius, the Delayer, to the Consuls willing to fight.

Hannibal's army was in place, exactly as he wanted it arrayed for battle. Not that it was easy. His commanders were absolutely disbelieving. "Ninety thousand men!" the chiefs had protested at the final strategy meeting the night before in his tent. There were the usual proposals: all of them involved not fighting this army in front of them.

No. "We will defeat this army and the great victory will bring glory to all of you," he reassured the nervous group. And he finally outlined his mysterious strategy. The Gauls and Iberians were to be at the very center of the battle line. "I want the Romans to be facing the very people they hate most."

The Gaulish chiefs started to object; Hannibal interrupted. "All your rebellions and insurrections against the Romans over the years. You've killed their fathers, sons, and brothers at Trasimene and the Trebia. The Romans will be driven mad with the desire for revenge."

One of the Gaulish chiefs realized quicker than most what Hannibal was asking. "You want me and my tribesmen to bear the full wrath of the massive Roman armored infantry charge? Alone?" His eyes narrowed. "While your Carthaginian and African troops wait in reserve on the flanks?"

"Not alone."

"Who else will fight along with us?"

"I will," he'd replied. "Right alongside you."

Hannibal would command the Gauls because they were the key to the whole battle. Their fate would be his. He explained that the center of the battle line would slowly collapse, not in panic or defeat, but yielding as if *about* to collapse. He'd made this point very carefully. They had to draw the Romans in, have them believing that they were on the verge of victory and that their victory hinged on what they did so well— pressing forward, ruthlessly, giving their enemy no quarter.

The overconfident Romans must commit all their reserves, expecting to break his line and smash them. Then the Africans veterans would move forward on their flanks, and destroy them, "like the jaws of a lion tearing apart a dog."

The Gauls had protested that the Romans would then withdraw. Ah, he loved that comment. They wouldn't be able to retreat, he'd explained. Smiling, he'd let Marhabal describe the cavalry strategy: the superb Numidians would for the first time engage the plodding Roman cavalry at the ends of the line of battle, where they were usually placed. The Roman horse would be routed. Then, instead of a cavalry charge into the battle line itself, Marhabal would ride hard to circle around to the Romans' rear— they would then fall upon the Romans, cutting off any hope of escape.

At least that was the plan. And so far the day had cooperated. The sun, high now in the sky, was merciless, the wind direction perfect: the slight breeze sent dry, stinging sand directly into the Romans' faces. He'd already made sure the men had been given plenty of water for what lay ahead.

All around, Gauls shouted, danced, and shook weapons at the assembled Romans across the field. Near Hannibal, three naked Gauls waved their long, thick wooden pikes over their heads at the Roman line as they danced. All had piled their long reddish- blond hair, heavily greased, onto the top of their head. The effect was to make their massive bodies look even taller, more like bear- men.

A Gaul nearby—naked from the waist down– wore only the tunic of a Roman officer, streaked with dried blood, the gold epaulets clearly visible. Past him, several others—red faces bulging– screamed taunts ("your mother is my whore") and threats ("your skull will become my drinking goblet") at the Romans, waving a ripped, bloody battle standard from a legion destroyed at Trasimene.

How amusing, almost comical, if you didn't know what was about to happen. Hannibal could see the looks on the assembled columns of Romans standing watching from across the dry plain, swords and shields at the ready. Legion standards rippled in the breeze. *They hate us. They hate me. All the better: an army that is enraged is an army that is notthinking.*

And then came the peal of Roman trumpets and the enormous line of men across the field started moving toward them, lances extended, armor glistening in the noonday sun.

Behind Hannibal, Nahatum stood transfixed at the sight of the assembled Romans. There was such beauty in the moment. Hannibal's horse whinnied. The golden sun bathed the Roman helmets in light. Once, sitting with Solyphos in his wagon, the old man had told him that there were girls in the lands far north of Attica who had hair that was bright yellow, like golden wildflowers and strawberries. Like the lightest color of the shell of the gall nut.

He hoped someday to see that. Would he see such girls or would he die on this day? He missed Solyphos and all that he had to teach him. There was so much more to learn.

The assembled legions looked so strong, so organized, so well-ordered, but soon they would be a mass of sweating, grunting, stabbing men. The gold would turn to red.

He remembered the water of Lake Trasimene.

He was tired of war, and he hated himself for that. He had seen how excited Hannibal was that day months earlier when he burst in with the scroll and his news of this massive storehouse. He had seen how Hannibal looked at him now: with such love and caring. That very morning Hannibal stood just paces away filled with the energy of battle, confidently waiting for what came next.

And then unexpectedly, Nahatum felt sleepy. He yawned. Was he frightened? No, it was that he wanted to be somewhere else. He wanted to be in the supply wagon talking to Solyphos about why Spartans are superior to Athenians, about the letter "Drie" in Punic, about the girls with golden hair.

How shameful. A bite on the inside of his cheek focused his energies. *You will not think of Solyphos, you will think now only of Hannibal.*

And then they came, on foot, flags unfurled, at a trot, their lances like elongated tusks and for a moment Nahatum grieved the absence of the elephants, now long dead. Then he was no longer thinking but fighting, slashing and hitting with his pike, like all the Gauls surrounding him. He stayed close to Hannibal and Jonaz and the guard of stout Gauls who protected his master.

The sweat running down his back pulled the tunic against his skin. It was so hot. The sharp call of trumpets. Romans were running directly at him. There were so many, as if the earth had sprouted legionnaires.

He missed his quills, papyrus, the quiet of the wagon. All he had wanted to do was fight, to be a warrior in Hannibal's army and now he was and yet… He swung his pike at a Roman, who swerved past him. Several naked Gauls bumped into him. They didn't advance directly, but did so by moving from side-to-side, slowly swaying, as if casting spells as they moved.

Hannibal was just ahead, Jonaz right behind him holding extra shields and swords. All around men pushed, slashed, stabbed. Bursts of red bloomed among splashes of brown leather and sweat-drenched uniforms. A helmeted Roman soldier ran past and slashed his *gladius* at a Gaul who raised his arm—cut off at the elbow. The Gaul's eyes went to the ground, as if searching for something he had dropped. Then an iron- tipped spear shaft emerged from his stomach, like a worm looking for the morning sun. Javelins rained down. Hannibal opened up a long sword wound in the thigh of a Roman soldier, who fell to the ground. Several Gauls killed him with their pikes.

A world of legionnaires advanced toward them. Nahatum swung wildly with his pike, knocking a Roman to the ground. Several other legionnaires slashed at the Gauls around him. Hannibal's voice carried over the noise of battle. He ordered the line to retreat, slowly, his voice strong and relayed all along the line by Gaulish commanders. Then again: retreat!

The world was filled with Romans in their hooded steel helmets, standards flying amidst sounds of trumpets. The sun was at its height. Rivulets of sweat ran down the necks of the Roman soldiers. Again and again, the order to retreat.

The Romans surged forward like a fist. Nahatum held up his pike; someone bounced off it, and he stumbled backwards. He'd been using his pike more to defend himself than to kill anyone. A deep roar; Gauls surged all around, blocking his view. A spray of blood flew into his face from a man with a sword in his chest. He spit to get the blood out of his mouth.

A Roman swung his curved galius at him. He stepped back; the blade hummed as it sailed past his head, like a bird's wing in flight. As the Roman raised his sword over his head in a two-handed grip, the boy thrust forward with his pike, all his might, planting his feet in the ground for force, and found the gap in the man's armor right under his right arm above his ribs. He pushed the sharpened end of his pike deep into the man's body.

The Roman fell over backwards and did not move.

He no longer knew where on the battlefield he was. All was dust and blowing sand and the heat. Ghost-like figures moved around him, the grunt of a sword move, the grunt of a blade piercing flesh. Again—as at Trebia and Trasimene—the low sounds, the quiet, of people killing each other. The thud of pike on a skull. Something wet covered him. He licked his lips. Blood, spurting. Not his. Something fell on him. A Roman with….a part of a Roman. A body without a head, spurting blood from the neck, falling over. He didn't want this, never did.

Where was Hannibal? He could not hear his voice. A blade scratched along his right arm, raising a bloody gash.

Pike in hand, he bent low to confront his attacker: Jonaz, wearing a narrow smile sharper than the galius blade poised in his right hand. *He'd kill me with a Roman knife.*

The air shimmered like the surface of a breezy pond. A long swipe of his pike drove Jonaz back. Then there was a whooshing sound and a flash of sharpened steel. Jonaz's forehead furrowed, then his upper body slid first to the right, then entirely off his lower body. Jonaz was dead, though his legs stood there, then fell forward, revealing a massive legionnaire holding his fearsome broadsword, coated with a pink sheen. Then he too was swallowed up in a mass of fighters. Nahatum hurriedly wiped a spray of blood from his eyes with a sleeve.

Then there was nothing other than more killing. He lost his pike, but there was no time for looking. He—somehow—had a sword, and was quick with it.

There were Romans all around. Screaming Romans. Writhing Romans. Then there were the African veterans, suddenly appearing, killing exhausted Romans, killing stunned Roman soldiers who stood so jammed together in their formation that they couldn't even bring their swords to bear on the soldiers stabbing them.

The Romans were pinned into a mass of hot, exhausted men fighting on all sides.

He cut and sliced and stabbed and killed. The major problem was that the he and the Gauls and the Africans were all slipping on the bloody mass of dead bodies beneath their feet as they thrust forward. He was walking on top of dead and dying men. The sun was so low in the sky. They had been killing all day.

Who was Lizard Skin now? He tripped over a pile of writhing bodies, like dung beatles in the stables. Acqua, acqua.…The dying men wanted water. The Romans had been so careful to avoid the possibility of Hannibal's water traps, only to die calling for water. And, then he heard, too: Mater. Low moans: Mater. The whole world was calling for their mothers.

He was on the edge of a forested area. He ought to have turned around, followed the plain, found the river Aufidus and nosed his way back to Hannibal. But to do that meant to cross the plain of death, to walk over bloody masses of things that had once been men.

He wandered. His mind was not his own. He couldn't think clearly. Was that Solyphos he saw over there in the shadows? Thin, frail, as he was at the Trebia, throwing his sword down in disgust. In his addled mind, Nahatum could hear the man's words as if spoken to him: "I promised myself I would not participate again. Now here I am."

It was night. The funeral pyres blazed so hot and bright that one might imagine the merciless sun had returned. The sliver of a moon rose, a sword blade low in the sky.

He passed a dying Numidian soldier in his djellabah, lying on the ground choking to death in his own gore, nose gone, his face a mask of bone and blood. A dead Roman soldier was sprawled across him, the Numidian's knife sticking out of the Roman's chest. The dead Roman must have gone after the Numidian with his teeth, chewed off his nose and half his face. The man could no longer breathe. Nahatum turned away, but the sight was etched in his mind.

Low moans from the field of the dying. The funeral pyres glowed. Dark silhouettes moved among them, picking through the dead for gold, weapons, trophies.

He was in the Underworld. This was it, it was always around him. He was Lizard Skin. Hannibal was Lizard Skin. Killing everywhere. The stench of the dead bodies.

He had to get away. That was all he could think: *get away. Flee for your life.*

On the edge of the field there were Roman stragglers scattered around. Some ran into the woods, away from the Africans and Gauls busy killing all the survivors they could find. A few Romans were hurrying down a forest trail, trying to get away, anywhere.

The boy walked slowly ahead, swept along, dazed and alone, following the Roman survivors into the forest.

Chapter 6

Alone

Battlefield of Cannae and Southern Italy 216 BC

Something troubled Hannibal as, triumphant, he surveyed the bloody battlefield surrounding him. *What is wrong?*

A great victory: his army sustained only a few thousand casualties while destroying the Romans.

"The Africans crushed them on both flanks. Marhabal routed the Roman cavalry and fell on their rear. There was no escape." Gisgo couldn't seem to stop talking.

Hannibal looked at his burly infantry commander: the man was clothed in blood, on his hands, arms, over the leather on his chest, his leggings. He seemed not to notice. The fiery light of the pyres gave the bloody chest armor an eerie glow. Hannibal looked down at his own arms: *enough of other people's blood there, for that matter. Is that a surprise?*, he asked himself, a bit stunned. *War covers the world in red.*

Yet this was extraordinary. So much red, blood everywhere. The Romans were trapped in their own formations, many died with their arms at their side. It's as if he had created an enormous mill such as the Gauls used for crushing wheat— one that ground the Romans into blood and pulp. *Yes, you are a magician of death, aren't you?*

Well, they had to die so Carthage could survive. The arrogant Romans had given Carthage a choice: surrender up Hannibal or go to war. They'd gotten what they wanted.

"Hannibal's jaws have closed on the Roman army."

He wanted Gisgo to be quiet even a moment so he that could think. *What is wrong here?*

Gisgo complimented Marhabal, standing nearby, which was astounding in itself. Marhabal was also covered in blood and gore. The two of them might as well have come from butchering cattle. Yes. A great victory.

Something is wrong. It was not only the sight on the field in front of him: piles of dead bodies, soldiers searching the dead for gold, clothes, anything they could sell, like versions of Cerebus, the watchdog of the Underworld, inspecting souls arriving in Hades. The stench of the funeral pyres. Sounds of moaning—soft, like animal calls—rose into the warm night air. Even for a warrior this took the breath away.

Still, that's not it. Something else.

Marhabal was claiming that the war was over. Rome will be Hannibal's in a day. "Nothing stands between us and Rome. There's no organized Roman army left anywhere in Italy."

Hannibal nodded. He was not seeing something. Something missing. *Or someone.*

The gold buttons on Marhabal's red vest glinted in the flames of the funeral pyre. "Let me take my cavalry and ride now to the gates of Rome. Follow with the army. You will take the city's surrender on the floor of their Senate in two day's time."

Ah, Marhabal. Impetuous, incautious. Rome still had its formidable city garrison, its well-designed defenses, its stout walls. There would have to be a bloody siege. *Not now. The men are exhausted. We must be careful here.* It was lack of caution that killed his father– drowned, ambushed while trying to withdraw. *We will let Rome become isolated and then surrender.* No more death.

"No, let us now bury the remains of the dead, ours and the Romans," he said to Marhabal. "Let the Capuans—as they have hinted– open their gates to us."

Marhabal shook his head, started to say something, but Hannibal was trying to think. Three resounding victories and Alexander destroyed an empire. Now he had three. "Rome will surrender once the cities of Italy have finally joined with us." Yes, they will now join with him. *Join with him.* That's it!

"Where is the boy?"

"Sir?"

"Nahatum. My scribe. Where is the boy?" He was shouting now. Confused expressions. No one knew. *Calm yourself. Lower your voice.* Jonaz's body had been found, alas, in pieces, but not the boy's. Marhabal returned to his idea of a march on Rome, but Hannibal was not listening.

The boy would never have deserted. He must be dead. Another of the dead. He wanted to see the body. He had an impulse to order a search party, but that made no sense with the pyres and all the dead. Besides, he had to decide: Marhabal would not stop pushing him. Ride to Rome now!

There was comfort in the forest, if not peace. Here Nahatum could find himself. Ancient memories returned. He was again a boy capable of disappearing into a cluster of large rocks, of finding a burrow beneath the pine trees. He was so much bigger, stronger than before, but he collapsed into himself, curling deep in the roots of the tall pines, the ground mossy and soft, smelling of decay.

He stripped off his clothes, those carriers of the sweat, the blood, the killing.

There was a stench of bodies being burnt even in the forest, the dead going up in smoke on the gentle plains of Cannae.

He slept, twitching with nightmares of the dying Numidian on the battlefield, his gasping face just white bone and red blood, calling for Nahatum to help him.

As the sun rose the next day, a war raged within Nahatum. Go back. No.

Was this why Hannibal saved him from the short life of a wolf boy? For a life of killing, of blood, of smashed heads and gore? He had learned to read and write. Solyphos taught him. Him. Why? He might as well have died a hungry, desperate, thieving wolf boy back in Iberia. He wept again for Solyphos, who had died too soon. He wanted the fierce Greek right there in the infernal woods with him, advising him. What were his last words? "Do not fall in love with warfare." Now, finally, collapsed in despair, Nahatum understood: war gets in your blood, you love those you fight alongside, you can't let them go.

He hated himself then. How could he think such thoughts? Hannibal was somewhere back there on the battlefield—the man who gave him life, who trusted him, who needed him. He had to go back there.

Yet he stayed burrowed into the rocky outcropping on a slight hill through therest of that day and the following. He was comfortable in his nakedness, but could not rid himself of the reek of the dried blood on his skin, arms, back. Jonaz's blood? The blood of those he had killed. Gore coated the soles of his feet, the slime of the dead and dying bodies he walked across to get away. The thick odor attacked his nostrils. He wished he could stop breathing.

Elephants marched into his dreams, huge tusked beasts walking through the forest, grazing on leaves, ripping thin branches off the trees, stripping them of their leaves and tender shoots. Chewing in that singular manner, their jaws sliding across, not up and down. Solyphos was there, speaking as he did that day of the awful elephant massacre in Bologna, the village of the Boii: "That is grief. What you saw from the elephant." Then the blood flowed into the dream. First a stream, then a raging river of blood washing away first Solyphos, then the elephants, suddenly panicked and helpless in the thick red torrent. One of them had a face half-chewed away, like the Numidian he'd seen on the battelfield, the elephant with only one tusk, a dark hole where the trunk used to be.

His life seemed unreal, not really his. He was no longer a wolf boy, he knew that. Yet he didn't want to be a soldier anymore. He had languages, but where could he speak them? Who—what—was he? He could not go back to Hannibal. He must go back to Hannibal.

He was not alone in the woods. Stragglers. Desperate men tripped, fell, cried, cursed, called in low tones to each other. Latin. He said nothing, dug deeper into his mossy lair. There was danger out there, everywhere. Humans? Lizard Skin? Was there a difference? The rustling in the woods made the hair on his neck stand up.

The sharp, guttural sound of Latin echoed in his ears, so different from the more musical Punic. He knew them both. Some day, he remembered, he'd hoped to learn Greek. He even had allowed himself to imagine that some day he'd be a father and a husband. There was so much to know and learn in the world. Was he to have it?

Then there was quiet. The darkness of the night of the second day arrived in all its fullness as if there had never been a battle, as if the misery upon misery of that day had never happened. Yet the stench remained in the air; the bonfire of bodies continuing.

The third day brought hunger he could no longer ignore. He knew, finally, what he must do.

Still more scraggly Roman survivors searched in the misty dawn light for a way out of the forest. He followed them, the few lucky—if they could be called that— remainders of what had once been a proud army.

The dead were scattered amidst the trees. Wounded men who'd died in full retreat. He took the clothes of one man—just the pants and ill-fitting shirt, no medals, no armor. No sword. Soon enough a road appeared and the miserable boy joined the stream of bloody, hungry, exhausted soldiers walking toward a villa in the far distance. One foot after another. Every now and then a soldier said something to him, but Nahatum gave no reply. He couldn't even bear talking to himself. He was a deserter. He had abandoned his general.

Hannibal kicked at a rock, watched it tumble quickly down the hill toward the battlefield, still rutted and raw from the fighting, the field churned to mud by the blood. Bodies were still being collected for the funeral pyres, which had been burning nonstop all day. So many dead Romans. Marhabal had almost screamed at him last night, so great was the frustration. There would be no march on Rome. "You know how to achieve a victory, Hannibal, but not how to use one," Marhabal had snapped.

Well, we will see about that. The Roman alliance was already teetering. *Let us use this victory to isolate Rome.* And the first step is the great city of Capua, known throughout Italy as the "second Rome." Two day's ride. *They will open their gates to us. Let us send Marhabal to Capua. Give him something to do rather than yell at me. We will conquer a city without a siege.* What an example that will be to the rest of Italy. And to Marhabal.

Meanwhile, he would wait here, give his exhausted men a chance to rest. Perhaps he would even find time to search for the body of the boy, his scribe.

The villa in the far distance was extraordinary, more beautiful even than the one Nahatum had seen in Apulia the year before, and for a moment he thought of the scrolls and his owl quill back in the supply wagon somewhere in Cannae. Were his tools all still there? Or did Hannibal order the wagon destroyed, burnt to embers, all trace of his disloyal scribe gone?

There was too much pushing and shoving in the mob of soldiers walking across the fields rich with summer wheat and vegetables, trampling everything. He was surrounded by the odor, the sweat of disheveled, disoriented men. He was jostled by someone, pushed back, knocked down a burly soldier who stared at him with crazed eyes. His beleaguered mind was still not his own: the Numidian's half-eaten face, Lizard Skin on the loose, battlefield death everywhere, all pursued him.

The gardens surrounding the villa were filled with men, some sleeping, others dying, some arguing, most sitting and staring, as if trying to see something that they could not get into focus. Horses grazed in a paddock down the hill, next to a barn with cattle. The smell of bread baking drifted in the soft breeze. Tulip leaves waved letters at him as if begging to form sentences.

An argument went on amidst a line of stragglers extending all the way into the house. Some had medals and insignia on their ripped and torn officer uniforms. Nahatum could make out talk of fleeing to Greece. Italy was lost, Rome was doomed. One man in a uniform streaked with dirt and dried gore loudly urged them all to hurry to Athens and plot a return to Rome later, after the war, help her rebuild, rejoin their families. Murmurs of assent.

There was so much yelling and pushing and shoving in the line as it moved into the villa, and Nahatum perceived danger everywhere. He couldn't tell who had a knife and who not. Everyone seemed to be watching him. Running away would be preferable but that wasn't possible in the face of his hunger and besides, his exhausted legs barely obeyed his command to move forward in line.

Then he saw the most elegant woman he had ever seen— *covered in blood?* he wondered– standing on a table in the enormous living room. *No, not blood.* She wore a shimmering light red toga with a soft gray silk Roman stole over her shoulders, draped from neck to ankle. Tall and imposing, she gave orders here and there. Open the storehouses for these men. More flour, more bread. Water to be distributed to everyone. She told her nervous servants to turn no soldier away from the villa.

Her name was Lady Busa. She was the wealthy young widow of the largest landowner in the region. She treated the soldiers like heroes for she was a loyal daughter of Rome. Her parents were one of the first colonists of the region and she was distraught at what had engulfed her house, what she had heard of the slaughter just a few leagues away. The men passed in front of her as if she was the Vestal goddess of home and hearth.

She was so far away that Nahatum worried he would never get to her. A fight broke out behind him, someone calling another a coward for wanting to escape toGreece. A wild-eyed man in an officer's uniform pushed Nahatum. They were all still crazed from the battle, the fleeing, the terror. Nahatum shoved the man away, hard, the man went sprawling. All he could think about then was his lost pike: he wanted to beat the man with his pike, how dare he shove him, and there was all that yelling, he wanted to put his hands over his ears but he had to keep his hands ready at his side, ready to defend, ready to punch any man who came too close to him, why was there no room in the line, everyone bunched up, they were like barnyard animals in a pen, and had he gotten things all wrong– was the line moving toward the slaughter house?

No, think clearly here. Calm your mind. What was he going to do amidst all these Roman soldiers? *You need a plan.*

From outside the villa, someone shouted that Hannibal was approaching the estate. Nahatum's heart raced and there was momentary panic in the room, but Lady Busa stood tall above them and insisted that all reports indicated that the Punic hordes were still leagues away, having not left the battlefield. "They are lingering with their success, likely planning to march on Rome, not here," she announced. "If need be, we will dig fortifications, defend this villa. Remember, you all know how to fight. For now, though, continue to come forward. We have food and drink here."

Then she was in front of him, looking down from the table where she stood. He took the thick bread and the water that the Lady offered him. Ah, he realized, it was wine, not water, even better. The Lady waited politely as he gulped down the bread and wine, as she had done with the other wretched veterans. She wanted to hear his story, asked him his name, what he remembered about the battle, this terrible disaster that had befallen Rome.

Nahatum's calculated. His Latin was not good enough to pass as a Roman soldier, yet he wore the uniform of one. He must not speak and reveal that he was not what he looked like. *Mute. Pretend you are mute, that the gods have taken your speech after what you have seen on the battle field.*

He opened his mouth, moved his jaw, but no words came out.

She stared down at him from her very great height, beautiful in her toga. "And what have we here? A young legionnaire who cannot talk..."

A discussion ensued. No one recognized or claimed him. Was he a simple legionnaire? Perhaps an officer, despite his youth? He looked strong and clearly was big enough to fight, that's for sure, and there were some wounds on him. Still, the Lady hesitated. "There is a trace about him that does not seem like simply a Roman soldier, despite his obvious strength and bearing."

She talked about him as if he was not standing right there. And what, Nahatum wondered, was he to say? Nahatum made his mouth move without words, and this lady could look at him with eyes of concern and speak to him with her soft voice but he knew that nothing would change the fact that he had deserted the very man who took him in. In his misery, Nahatum knew that she should order him taken away and killed.

Lady Busa paused. She looked him up and down. "He certainly is well- formed enough." She leaned forward. With the tips of her fingers—skin soft as rabbit fur—on his chin she moved his head this way and that, admiring him. There was the briefest aroma of fragrant oil. "And not unpleasing to the eye, I imagine, once the blood has been washed off him." Then: "Take him to the kitchen. Feed him, provide him with clean clothes. I am sure we can find some use for him in our home."

A servant led him away. As he followed, he could feel her eyes on him, on his body.

A month passed. There was panic in Rome. First the terrible defeat at the Trebia, then a year later an entire army swallowed up at Lake Trasimene, and now two entire armies annihilated at Cannae. Rome was left without a fighting force to put into the field. Most of Italy had been overrun by the rapacious Punic barbarian. There were reversals in Iberia and the Carthaginian fleet was wreaking havoc along the coast.

Worse, there was an evil portent in Rome: two of the Vestal Virgins of the city— the sacred priestesses who tended the hallowed fire of the Goddess Vesta, protector of home and hearth– were convicted of sexual improprieties. Such behavior could bring even further wrath of the gods down on beleaguered Rome. Unusual rites were called for: a pair of Gauls, male and female, were buried alive in the cattle market. Then, for good measure, the same fate was inflicted on two Greeks.

Rumors were rife: The Punic horde feasts on the bodies of the dead after battle.

Hannibal wants our children for his dark sacrifices. He is marching on the city.

The people of Rome were ordered to stay indoors, silence was mandated on the streets, guards posted at every gate. A Senator proposed that they abandon the city and retreat to a nearby island, as the Athenians had done in the face of the

Persian invasion two hundred years earlier. Mothers called to their children, bringing them running, terrified, into their homes: Hannibal was at the gates!

A draft was instituted: full mobilization

Capua—with its famous marble baths, bronze artisans workshops and marketplace, the large open-air amphitheatre (which regularly produced Greek plays), and grand Temple to the god Mithras– considered itself an equal of Rome. And simple logic dictated that if Rome fell, Capua would become the center of Carthage's Italian empire.

Of course, Hannibal noted, compared to Carthage— with its richly colored mosaics and elegant statues amidst the vast gardens and pools that dotted the city, the wide streets perched above the green-blue waters of the Great Sea, the white citadel of the Byrsa overlooking all, larger than the Acropolis of Athens—well, compared to that, the wonders of this Italian hill city with pretentions of greatness were just that: pretentions. No matter. No matter at all. Carthage and Capua shared the understanding that Italy would be better off out from under Rome's yoke.

"And if Capua wants to become our ally and surrogate city, well, by all means," Hannibal remarked to Gisgo as they rode triumphantly at the head of the army through the city gates and into the town square to receive welcome from the town elders.

Gisgo's laugh rumbled forth, and he told Hannibal what the General already knew: the fact that the city had come over to their side was a major triumph, but—the infantry commander insisted—"we must remember that they will contribute no troops, no cavalry." That had been one of the conditions of the alliance: they would provide no military aid to Hannibal's army. "They insist that Capuans will not kill Romans," Gisgo reminded Hannibal. *Yes: they will just betray them.*

Still, Capua was the second- largest city in Italy, and this alliance was no small coup. As the Capuans cheered and the crowds tossed stalks of fall wheat and freshly harvested apples at the delighted army, Hannibal was only mildly concerned by the fact that Capua was still the only major city to have defected from the Roman confederation, now a month after Cannae.

If one was given to dark speculations, Hannibal knew, one might wonder what more it would take to break the Roman alliance. Trebia. Lake Trasimene. Cannae. What city had ever suffered such a string of horrific losses? *What more, one could ask, would it take?* And there was one who did ask: Marhabal. He had still not forgiven Hannibal for not marching immediately on Rome. Somewhere in the far back he sulked, riding with his cavalry into Capua, thousands of djellaba clad horsemen looking like beings from another world.

Now, though, is not the time for dark thoughts. Capua was not Carthage, but it was a city of delights. Hannibal was given a fine house for his use as long as he wanted. There were minstrels and storytellers who would provide entertainment during the winter months. The city was a wondrous place for a winter encampment. Best of all, the fertile fields around the city, stretching for miles, had provided sufficient wheat and cattle, wine and cheese, so that the army would be well-fed through the winter just arriving, ready to march again in the spring.

Devouring an apple in two large bites, Gisgo remarked that Capuan apples were almost as good as Carthaginian figs, then told Hannibal that he had found a suitable soldier to serve now as his squire, to replace the unfortunate loss of the esteemed Jonaz.

"Yes, that is fine." Hannibal didn't ask more; he trusted Gisgo's judgment in that matter. "And someone to replace Nahatum?" He felt an uncomfortable ache as he spoke the boy's name. The boy's body had not been found. Not a moment to say good-bye before the inevitable funeral pyre must have taken him.

"You mean a servant boy, my Lord? That should not be hard. There are hundreds of Capuan boys who I am sure are eager to be your servant. I will talk to the elders."

That was not really what Hannibal was asking, but he said nothing. The thought of Nahatum– head bent over his papyrus, hands working his quill to form the letters just so as Hannibal dictated— left his heart heavy. Hannibal ignored this. Amidst all this celebration, here at such a moment of triumph, the city elders watching his every movement, every expression, he could not afford sorrow. Wars, after all, bring their losses.

Another freezing Italian winter, but this time Nahatum had the luxury of working in Lady Busa's well- heated villa. He didn't mind doing the laundry or the household chores. That had been the lady's recent idea but it's not where he'd started months earlier.

What he minded was being separated from the animals. All through the winter he had worked in the stables, first bringing in the endless bales of fall hay and then, amidst the winter darkness, feeding the animals, trapping the rats and mice in the hayloft, mucking the mud floor. He liked being amidst the horses, mules, pigs, the cattle, goats, sheep–their simple gratitude at being fed, rubbed down, cleaned. He wished he could talk to them. His voice remained in hiding, burrowed deep in his chest.

The foreman of the farm was a wiry, foul-tempered fellow. He routinely gave Nahatum jobs meant for two men. If the man delighted in using his barbed whip on him, so be it. There was comfort in pain, a comfort that continued when he ran his hand over the jagged slashes on his arms, shoulders, back, alone at night on his straw bed in the stables.

During those busy late fall days, Lady Busa would watch through the windows; he could see her observing him as he went about his chores, sweaty and determined.

Despite himself, he was becoming stronger still. "My mute one," she called him.

And then came the day he had the misfortune of saving the foreman from a bad fate at the hooves of the Lady's favorite riding horse, the powerful stallion, Aquilo.

While the Lady watched, clad in her riding outfit. One thing he'd learned from Jonaz: do not humiliate those who think themselves above you.

"Take the reins, take the reins," the man had yelled that day at Nahatum, from across the paddock next to the barn. There was panic in his voice. No wonder. Aquilo was trying to kill him, probably after one too many flicks of that barbed whip. A well- placed kick was all it would take. Nahatum hurried over to calm the horse. Most of the stable crew called him when they were having trouble with an animal. Something in his touch. When he entered the paddock, the huge horse trotted over to him.

By the time Nahatum had patted and nuzzled him, stroked his mane, given him some oats, the animal had calmed enough for Lady Busa to mount. Nahatum had held the reins and helped her onto the horse, while the foreman stood away, whip twitching in his hand. Who then had he wanted to whip more: Aquilo or Nahatum?

One day soon after that, when the snow was at its highest, the Lady had called him in from the stables and told him that he would now be her houseboy, the one who helped the maids with the heavy chores. He knew this was a position of honor and was not ungrateful. He quickly showed how skilled he was at these activities. Still, he missed the animals.

"You must be from quality, Tacitus," the lady would say, using the name she had given him, the silent one, the mute one, "for some good woman has taught you how to clean and fold clothes, how to care for a person of standing." She would say this as he carried a basket of her clothes right into her bedroom, the lady at her dressing table clad in her sleep tunic, soft linen gently following the contours of her body, while her maid combed out the Lady's thick, black hair. He'd thought to correct her, to tell her that he had learned to work hard at many things while in the company of Hannibal Barca, the same warrior who struck such fear into the hearts of everyone around them. Even as he wanted to shake his head, to exclaim "no, no, you do not know me at all, not even my name," he knew that he must not do so, at pain of his life.

And yet of what value is my life? This was the question always present as he laid in his bed under heavy bearskins. *I who have abandoned everyone.*

He heard about Capua, the news reaching even Lady Busa's house so far away on the other side of the Appenine Mountains. She was distraught, though a woman not given to angry shrieking. She had visited Capua many times, and she talked to him about the golden spires atop the elegant homes of Rome's "brother city," connected to it by a splendid highway of paving stones—the Via Appia– stretching unbroken all the way from there to Rome itself.

"The gate by which my husband and I left the city to journey to Capua is called the Porta Capena," she told her maid, indignant, as the young girl fluttered about trying to comb her mistress' hair. "That is a distinction of honor: it is the only gate in Rome that bears the name of the place to which it leads." She beseeched the gods to bring death and destruction to the dishonored city while Nahatum silently folded her laundry.

She told him to sit near her, rest himself, while she talked of Roman heroism and Punic treachery. He didn't really care, but he listened. She told him of the wonders of Rome, the delights of Capua. He imagined Hannibal in Capua then, spending the winter clad in fine furs, warm to the touch, keeping out the winter's cold, and he dreamt of Grecian urns such as Solyphos had sometimes described to him. He hoped to see a Grecian urn someday, and more mosaics. He imagined mosaics like the one in the villa in Apulia, beautiful mosaics of landscapes and people, magical in their colors, bringing life to ordinary tiles.

Maybe someday he would see another mosaic. It was only a matter of time before more cities defected and the war would end. Then what? He tried not to think about the future.

And, then, one cold evening, the snow driving hard, Lady Busa dismissed her maid after finishing with her hair and turned to Nahatum, who had just brought in a load of wood for the fireplace.

"That is an excellent fire, Tacitus, my mute one." He turned and bowed slightly. "No need to be so formal tonight," she said to him in her soft voice, a playful smile on her lips.

She sat on the upholstered couch, a sort of reclining day bed that she favored, in front of the fireplace. Her eyes were the deepest green—how had he not noticed that before?– and they seemed to sparkle in the reflected fire light. Her hair looked as dark and mysterious as a moonless summer night.

"Here, come sit next to me." Lady Busa patted the finely colored pillows behind her. Her deep blue silk toga—carved ivory broach at the neck– rustled as he sat. His head was light from the scent of her, lotus oil she'd told him, a rich fragrance in the middle of winter! Her black hair cascaded over her shoulders, down her back. When she leaned forward toward the little table beside the couch, her toga rustling again, there was a glimpse of the soft skin above her breasts. He realized she was wearing nothing beneath the long dress. She picked up a delicate clay amphora with a stopper top.

His heart beat so loudly he was sure she could hear it. He wanted to run his hand through her deep black hair, to feel the softness of her skin, to reach for the silk that seemed to barely drape over her. Yet he, a mere servant, dared not.

She removed the stopper from the amphora. "From the baths at the Seplasia, in Capua, the finest perfume market in the world." She sighed, held it toward him. The room was filled with the scent of oranges and jasmine and spices he could not name. She tipped the amphora slightly and then there was delicate oil in the palm of his hand, slippery, like liquid velvet. A warmth seemed to radiate out from his hand toward her.

She looked right at him with those green eyes and extended her arm, the toga dropping away almost up to her shoulders.

Would he rub the oil into her skin, to soften the dryness? No one had ever spoken to him in this way. *Would he?* He could hear himself breathing. She laughed as he nodded, yes,

yes, and had he ever felt anything as soft as the touch of that oil on her downy skin? He worked slowly, carefully, soaking in the feel of her arm, as she looked at him, moving closer, he could feel her breath on his face and then she kissed his ear, murmuring into it, asking if he would like to remove the ivory broach at the neck of her toga…let it drape away. He reached up, his heart beating almost out of his chest. *Yes, yes, he would…*

The Capuan servant boy, brown hair neatly trimmed around his head, looked terrified as he held a tray of especially delicious-looking cheese in front of Hannibal. Hannibal reached for some and gave the boy a smile, which appeared to frighten the poor servant even more. He almost tripped as he backed away, half-bowing.

The cheese was exquisite, with a buttery texture, a rich nutty taste. His hosts told him it was specific to the Campania province, made right there in Capua. "That is mozzarella della buffalo," his host Pacuvius Calavius explained, taking a slice and savoring it, wiping his trimmed white beard with the woven, embroidered napkin.

It had been a long time since Hannibal had sat at a table set with crystal goblets and such fine napkins. Calavius was explaining about the special milk from a strange animal native to Italy, a sort of water buffalo raised for the purpose of the cheese. "We will show you the stables where the beasts are kept, you can have your servants keep some fresh mozarella in your house." The cheese was especially delicious when washed down with the excellent white wine, made from the marvelous grapes of the region.

Calavius was a leading elder of the town, and the man had gone to some efforts to arrange a sumptuous banquet for the conquering general from Carthage, the man who would propel Capua to prominence in Italy. One of his sons was at the table, and the young cavalryman had displayed the reluctant courtesy Hannibal had come to expect from those Capuans whose allegiance to Rome was not so brittle as their fathers. At the father's behest the son had offered Hannibal his loyalty, bending a knee, then embracing him, and finally sitting at the table and joining in the conversation.

Politeness dictated that Calavius ask of his visitor's family, and toasts be then offered to Hannibal's young son and to his wife, Imre. A son was such a source of pride and power. And, yes, also toasts to his father, the great Hamilcar, the terror of Rome's armies. Ah, to be the son of such an accomplished father!

It was as if Hannibal's father was a mountain he stared up at, daunted by the climb. "And your own son, Lord Hannibal?," asked one of the Capuan Nobles. Hannibal stood, wine glass in his hand, and told the assembled banquet that his son would grow up to be a great warrior, in the Barca tradition. He joked that his son would one day visit Capua after Rome had surrendered and had become just a trading town near the Great Sea for the rich merchants of Capua. His son will say, "I visited the great city of Capua and also another little place, what was its name?…A village called Rome."

The Elders chuckled.

There were endless feasts over the winter months, countless goblets of wines hoisted for grandiloquent toasts. Endless pledges of eternal loyalty and goodwill between Hannibal and the Capuans. They toasted him, though, not Carthage, and this did not escape Hannibal's notice.

And then on one particular mid-winter night, he had an excuse to cut the toasts, and the banquet, short. A breathless messenger hurried into the banquet hall with news: a letter had arrived from the Senate at Carthage, carried by several exhausted horseman riding hard from Syracuse, their ally in Sicily, where a Carthaginian naval vessel had brought them.

Hurrying back to his quarters through the cold city streets, surrounded by his bodyguards, Hannibal cautioned himself to keep his expectations in check. Yet this had to mean that the Senate had responded positively to the news he had sent of his victories and would be honoring his request for immediate reinforcements—another army, if possible—to be sent then. Perhaps his brother Hasdrubal would arrive overland with his army from Iberia as soon as the snows melted next spring? More men, cavalry, perhaps even the supplies to lay siege to Rome. Then they could truly isolate it while he turned his attention to weaving alliances with the wavering cities of Italy: particularly Napoli and Tarantum.

He hurried up the wooden stairs and into his house. The letter that awaited was scribed in Carthage—it was a link to home. To Imre, to his son, to all that was back there. Then into the oak-lined study, the thick walls strong against the winter wind and cold, the fireplace roaring, Hannibal settled into his favorite wooden chair near the soft glow of candlelight, holding his wine, and read the letter from the Suffete, the chosen leaders of the Senate.

When he finished, he contemplated the mistakes he must have made in writing as he had. Otherwise, why would the Senate have responded so? He'd written—- or the scribe he was now using had written, that eager son of some noble who took every word he spoke as if it were a pronouncement from the gods– in detail about the accumulated spoils of the great battles: the number of rings, swords, jewels, engraved shields, Roman standards, sitting right now under armed guard in several storehouses in Capua. He'd even sent a chest full of engraved golden rings taken from the bodies of the scores of Roman officers who'd died at Cannae.

Oh, the wine was good in this city, he reflected. Another sip. And what did his descriptions produce in response? Vague encouragement, not reinforcements. In the letter, the Senate praised his "apparent successes" and then went on to say that clearly he did not need reinforcements given the victories he had attained. There was a clear tone of suspicion in the letter, as if he was asking for reinforcements not to bring a final end to the war, but to make up for some unspoken reverses. Why, with such "astonishing"—did they mean to say, "unbelievable"– conquests, would you need reinforcements? "While we, of course, rejoice in your victories and encourage you to continue your efforts, Carthage must devote its resources to the pursuit of operations in Iberia and in Sicily, where Rome continues to instigate trouble against our ally, Syracuse."

The letter ended with the promise of some "possible" reinforcements of cavalry and war elephants, "in due time."

In due time. Of course: anytime between two and five years from now.

Hannibal wondered if perhaps the letter to the Senate was a mistake. *No, not the letter, but the tone and the content. Too much bragging, or perhaps the scale of these victories seemed unbelievable.* He stood, warmed himself by the crackling fire.

Ba'al's breath, what if Solyphos had been here? His tutor would have spotted that, known how to say these things in a way to convince a suspicious Senate more interested in pre-serving its empire in Iberia, sending armies there to protect the mines, the forests, the very stuff that swells the treasuries of the Nobles, than in committing more men and cavalry to fight in Italy. Two long years he had been there now, and he'd received nothing from Carthage. It was indeed him alone against Rome.

Solyphos would have known how to make that argument more clearly: that you kill a snake by cutting off its head, not by swatting at its tail. *Ah, I wish I had said that in the letter.*

Of course the scribes he had now—several, since there are so many letters to be written—all young soldiers well- tutored back in Carthage—did not think about how to phrase words and sentences, how to shape paragraphs. They were too much in awe of him, the great Hannibal, to question anything he said. There they sat, hard and muscled, strung as tight as a bow string, eyes like arrow points. They copied his words carefully but didn't have the spit and fire to suggest an alternative.

Spit and fire. Ah, he'd been down this road before—the road from Solyphos led to Nahatum and sometimes he'd look at the high-born young soldier brought in to scribe for him and he'd send him away, yelling that this was not who he wanted. He'd done that more times than he cared to remember. Through the letters to his brother Hasdrubal, the letters back home to Imre, to his young son. None of which had yet pro-duced a response.

He found all sorts of reasons to dismiss the befuddled scribes, many of which hardly sounded believable even to him: you write slowly, your handwriting cannot be read, you don't listen well. *You may well run through the whole lot of high-born Carthaginians who actually can write.* It must be the wine, be-cause he hardly cared. Of course it wasn't about their ability to form letters or how quickly they wrote—at core, the problem with the whole lot was that not one of them was the one he wanted: Nahatum.

Long-dead.

Hannibal stood, took a final sip of wine, contemplated the goblet. At nights back in Iberia, he and Imre used to have a glass of wine together. He worked to conjure her face in his mind. *How much longer*, he wondered, *before a letter from Imre finds its way to me here?*

The windows of Lady Busa's house were open in the early spring warmth. The squeals and braying echoed even inside the house. Tired as he was, for sleep still plagued him, Nahatum recognized the sound immediately: the wild donkey he'd brought back to the stables. He'd found him almost starved to death in the woods by the frozen pond one day near the end of winter and had led him back, fed and blanketed him. Every day he'd brought him hay and mush.

The Lady, for months by then his occasional lover, had been pleased: a donkey, well- fed and brought back to health would help with the early spring plowing. So many of the horses and pack animals on the farm had been donated to Rome's armies in its time of need.

Looking out the farmhouse window, Nahatum could see that the foreman had taken the long-eared beast out of the stables. The donkey bolted, bucked, bleated as the man tried to break him. "Vitiosi," the foreman snarled. Vicious. Who– the man or the donkey? The foreman retreated back in the face of a sharp backwards kick from the donkey and then for Nahatum it was as if Gisgo was stumbling backwards as Sirius the elephant tried to protect the dead in his herd in Taurini.

The great elephant reared up. Gisgo moved forward long lance in his hand.

Stop him. Now. No, wait, not Gisgo. Something as awful is happening to the donkey outside. It must be stopped.

Nahatum raced out the villa to the paddock, swung open the gate, and walked over to the donkey. Carefully. One kick could kill a man. His chest tensed. There was some connection between them. He, too, knew what it is like to kick in desperation. Their eyes met. He spoke to it as gently as he could. "Calm, little one." He stroked the animal's mane.

The foreman—*that arrogant swine, a cousin of Lizard Skin, if ever there was*– approached, yelling curses. *At the donkey or at me?* The animal started to tremble; the rough skin on his back twitching beneath Nahatum's resting hand.

The air seemed to pulsate. The man had exchanged his whip for a long pitchfork, with its five pointed tines, each a vicious blade. He beat at the donkey's back with the wooden handle, then poked at the terrified beast with the sharp tines. Blood appeared on the animals back.

A darkness gathered inside Nahatum. He picked up a cut piece of fence post leaning against the paddock railing. The foreman moved toward him, brandishing the pitchfork in front, baiting him. With the long post, Nahatum, no longer a boy, knocked aside the pitchfork. The foreman charged at Nahatum, becoming now a bull. Nahatum swung. The heavy fence post smashed into the side of the foreman's head, wood crushing bone. He lay unmoving on his side, blood coursing into the dirt. Dead.

Nahatum looked around quickly. A few workmen stared, speechless, from the barn. *Hurry, think.* He knew it was past time to leave this place. There was nothing here.

He'd killed the foreman. There would be a price to pay. *Leave. Now.*

He moved quickly, leading the donkey by its reins past the stunned workmen, past the villa, out to the empty road, heading south, taking nothing else with him. Leagues from the farm, he carefully lifted the thick rope over the little donkey's bushy neck. They regarded each other. So much smaller than an elephant. And that face, with the ears sticking up and out like stalks of corn and the snout expanding around the nose, a greyish-white against the brown. "Can you smell your way to a forest home, little donkey? Good luck to you." A slap on the rump and the donkey disappeared into the early, budding spring woods.

He watched it go, feeling very alone. Through the chilly night he walked towards whatever town, whatever fate, awaited him.

"My Dear Brother Hannibal:

"Well, you are now the King of Italy! Congratulations on your astonishing victories. It is wonderful to hear that you are alive and well. I want you to know that I, too, have victories to report..."

Hasdrubal—writing from Iberia— went on to detail in the letter some skirmishes and several treaties that he had negotiated with local tribes.

Hannibal read on eagerly, sitting in his familiar leather-covered chair in his Capuan villa. A good day: letters from both Hasdrubal and his wife Imre had finally found their way to him. The Romans were stirring up trouble north of the Ebro river, Hasdrubal wrote, and Carthage had sent reinforcements; he hoped to go on the offensive soon. *He hopes?* There was still the matter of whether some of the other rival Generals from Carthage were conspiring to drain off troops and resources from his own, but he was dealing with that.

"...No matter. I will persevere, and hope that there will soon be two Barca brother praised by all of Carthage, two Barca brothers whose names will strike fear into the hearts of every Roman, two Barca brothers who have made their father proud.
"Your brother, Hasdrubal"

"To my Lord and Husband:
"How I miss you so far away! Thank you for the gift of such a pleasing fragrance from the perfume markets of Capua. And I have had the captured Roman sword—polished and shining– hung in our son's bedroom according to your wishes. How can I tell you about the praise showered on you back here in Carthage? You are our conquering Lion, the Shield of Carthage. Your victories are spoken of with awe. The Senate has minted silver shekels with your likeness in honor of your victories. I include several for you to see. When your messenger showered the floor of the Senate with the golden rings of dead Roman officers, the applause resonated throughout the great building."

However, Hannibal's wife wrote,

"...there are developments here that you should know about. After the cheering in the Senate stopped, vile Hanno the Great rose to make a speech."

She quoted his exact words:

> " 'What, precisely, have we to rejoice over? Hannibal says he has killed whole enemy armies—and then asks for reinforcements. What else would he have asked for if he had been defeated? Sending reinforcements to a victorious army is unnecessary.' "

Her handwriting was sharp and slashing.

> "My love, I can barely restrain myself when I see the foul man at a banquet or some other party among the nobles."

There was more:

> "Hanno had insisted on quizzing your messenger to the Senate: 'Has any member of the Roman Federation besides Capua come over to Carthage's side? Has any citizens of Rome deserted to Hannibal? Has Rome sent any envoys to Hannibal to sue for peace?' The poor man, who had travelled so far with such good news, had to answer No to each question."

Good questions, alas. Hannibal felt the beginning of a headache. *Ones I have asked myself.*

> "Please know, my dear husband, that few were affected by Hanno's speech since everyone knows of his feud with your family. Still he cast a shadow over the debate. Raising and providing you with reinforcements will be a slow process. I am sorry, my love. I wish the news here were better."

Imre closed with some news of their son, his three year birthday, how every night at bedtime she told him a story about his illustrious father.

Hannibal stood up and threw his wine glass into the fire. Shards of shattered glass flew in all directions. *The King of Italy! Sending reinforcements is irrelevant!*

A bodyguard looked into the room, troubled by the sound of smashing glass.

Hannibal waved the man away. Hanno's questions ate at him—he, too, had noticed that so far no other major cities besides Capua had joined him. No Roman deserters fleeing the city, no delegation seeking peace. The Roman alliance had so far held in the face of devastating blows greater, perhaps, than those that brought down the entire Persian Empire.

A servant came in to sweep up the mess, hurrying, nervous under Hannibal's stare. The letters had arrived almost together, an odd coincidence. The first, finally, in three years. He again picked them up again from the table, sat down holding them in his hand. After so long, so hungry for news, he read and re-read what had been written, hoping to wring as much as possible from the marks on the papyrus. And there came a familiar longing, too, the carefully scripted ink inviting a yearning for the person who had written.

Ah, my younger brother. You write that you, too, have victories to report. There was that familiar brotherly competition in the letter. *I wish you were here right now, Hasdrubal, nipping at my heels or whatever. Truth is I've always felt more confident when in your presence.* Hannibal knew that the two of them were bred to destroy Rome. *Perhaps that's all we were to our father: swords to fulfill his dashed dreams.* No matter, he concluded, together we can take on the world—that ancient brotherly feeling.

And Imre, my fiery Iberian princess, you who wanted to accompany me on the invasion? He laughed, thinking of her contemplating revenge on Hanno at some festive event in Carthage. Her tribesmen were adept at close-in knife work; her warrior father taught her a thing or two. He missed her. He picked up the papyrus. She signed the letter, "I await your commands, my husband. Your devoted wife, Imre." He bent towards the words, certain that he found there the slightest hint of her fragrance.

He needed to respond to both letters. Could Hasdrubal be a source of reinforcements, bringing fresh men, fresh horses? Young ponies from Numidia to again outrun the slow Roman horse. Marhabal had been pressing him for more of his own Numidian tribesmen. There had been cavalry losses. Hasdrubal could bring them overland.

Ah, that was the way to bend his brother– you can do what I did. He would write to Hasdrubal about the overland route through the Alps, putting the description in code, lest the letter become captured. No need to call for a scribe, whose work he would likely find unappealing. He would write to his brother himself. And to Imre as well, himself.

Quills! Ink! Papyrus! He was again on his feet, restored, at the door. Where is that nervous servant? Bring me writing materials now.

"Dearest Imre:

I was relieved to receive your letter, with the valuable information about the Senate's decisions. I miss having you with me at my side but am glad you are there to see clearer than I can what is going on in the city. The coins you sent me are yet premature. I have won nothing, really, yet. In that, Hanno is correct. And that is why Carthage needs to send reinforcements to a victorious army, as the devious man must know, so intent on his own grudge.

My dear, we need to win over an Italian city with a fine port so that men, horses, elephants, and supplies can arrive. I sent Gisgo to Napoli with a strong force but they kept their gates—and exceptional harbor– closed and the city is well- fortified. I do not want to become mired in a siege right now. I personally led the army to Nola, near to Naples, where the townspeople were besieging their Senate to ally with me. Their Senate sent a delegation to me appearing to negotiate an alliance but the perfidious officials secretly sent word to Rome asking for help.

Rome raised a force of several thousand and installed it in the city to fortify—really, intimidate– their citizens to oppose me. I was unable to divest it. So, I am not the only one capable of trickery, alas. A lengthy siege there would leave me too vulnerable to a counter-attack from Rome. Even as weak as Rome now is, her martial spirit is still strong. She remains dangerous and Carthage must understand the continued threat.

So, I now march my army from town to town seeking allies— sacking some, negotiating with others– not knowing if I am the vengeful Lion of Carthage or some well-armed supplicant turned away at the gates of my enemies. Still, I persevere and hope to find well-supplied allies soon.

With love to my dear wife, Hannibal Barca"

Summer, 215 BC.

Nahatum stared at the figure in the near distance. *Is it Solyphos come to life? In this strange land?* The man stood across the quay from where Nahatum was unloading cargo. If so, he was a Solyphos dressed better than ever before in his fancy white toga.

And with those strange beads around his neck.

Nahatum lifted a large crate from an Egyptian sailing vessel bringing cotton from Alexandria to the little Italian port of Brindisium, where he had found work far enough from Lady Busa that she would not find him, even if she were looking. Late summer had brought no end to the heat but the blue water of the Great Sea provided a slight cooling breeze. And there were the cormorants all around, every day, fishing in the bay, sunning themselves on the ancient beams of the quay, on the rock outcroppings in the harbor.

There were the occasional fights, particularly when people jostled Nahatum or appeared to making some comment about him, but who, he would reassure himself, wouldn't be enraged at that sort of thing? Still, he knew his mind was not truly his own, ensnared still in memories of the slaughter at Cannae. He was given to quick rages and sudden outbursts if he felt someone standing too close, and he constantly worried that someone was trying to sneak up on him, to run him through with a hidden knife.

He had learned to hire himself out in town for assorted jobs. The fact that he didn't talk was an advantage for him. Many who hired him were relieved at the lack of conversation and others seemed once again impressed at his muteness, as if that gave him some strange touched-by-the-godsquality.

But right then there was the matter of the gaunt, white-haired man in the tailored toga. This merited a closer look. He did not look Roman despite his attire. He couldn't place the man's appearance. Not with the strings of colorful beads of many shapes around his neck, most painted and decorated with all manner of signs. Solyphos would never have worn such a thing.

The man stood in front of a rickety cart, pulled by a tired-looking horse. And what, Nahatum wondered as he drew near, was inside the crate?

"Scrolls!," Nahatum exclaimed, the first word he had spoken since Cannae. He did so in Latin, having listened enough over the past months to speak passably.

The man turned. "Yes." A thick accent. Latin was not his mother tongue. *Good, we share something*, Nahatum realized. And he decided then to keep on speaking— his voice lured from him by his destire to see and hold the scrolls.

The feel of the papyrus in Nahatum's hands awakened him. The heft, the coarse grain that somehow warmed. He had an urge to rub the papyrus up and down, to press his hand into it, to make the scruffy stuff a part of his skin. Something opened up inside Nahatum. He carefully untied one of the scrolls under the man's watchful eyes.

The letters and words seemed to jump out at him. He read aloud, some words about the land of Persia and the great war between the Greeks and a King named Cyrus.

"Ah, so you can read."

"Yes, I can read Punic and a lot of Greek and some Latin… and, maybe Egyptian," which he knew was not true but could not stop himself. "I can write them all, too. I learned a long time ago from a wise Greek man, his name was Solyphos. I wish he was still alive. Would you like me to show you how

I write, would you like to dictate to me? Have you quill and ink?..."

The man stepped backward at the outpouring. Nahatum couldn't stop. The man fingered the beads around his neck. The rush of words was only broken by the sound of the captain of the boat yelling at him.

"Hey, N'tum or whatever your name, come on. We don't have all day. Hannibal is at the gates." At this the gaunt man grabbed the scroll out of Nahatum's hands. "Hannibal! That demon. Here?" He renewed his abuse of the beads around his neck.

"No, Sir. Hannibal is not near here," Nahatum reassured him. "Last we heard his army had moved far east, near Capua." Then: "Do you think those beads will protect you against Hannibal?"

"Of course." The beads, he claimed, had great power against evil forces, hexes, envy and all manner of demonic beings. He spit on the ground, just missing Nahatum's sandals. "Hannibal and all those Punic liars and cheats! Dealing with merchants from Carthage, they are always looking for some advantage, some way to cheat you."

The man was named Tenalakis and he was from the small coastal town of Ierapetra in Crete. He was an itinerant bookseller, one of those men who wandered the Great Sea to bring books to wealthy individuals, and to scribe the books of authors. He had come to Italy hoping to bring Egyptian, Greek, and Persian books to Rome for sale, and to transcribe some books of poets and authors to take back with him, but the war had made all this impossible. He was superstitious and angry and scared and planned now to return to Ierapetra where his prospects were greater. "You claim you can read and write so many languages. A most unlikely assertion. Come with me to the tavern and provethis isso."

The ship's captain appeared with a whip. Before he could use it, Nahatum balled a fist and knocked the man backward.

"Is this man your slave?" Tenalakis asked.

The captain held his jaw, having dropped the whip. Nahatum handed the whip back to him; the man, surprised, took it quickly. "No, but he should be working."

"I am not returning. I am going to the tavern and taking my meal with this man.

You can keep whatever wages I've earned."

The captain stood speechless as his formerly- mute dock laborer and the bookseller walked slowly down the hill to the tavern, leading the weary horse. "I never said anything about a meal. I will buy you a cup of wine if you show me you can truly write as you claim. Can you write as well as you can fight?"

The tavern was ancient, raised by the first Roman settlers who had killed or in- bred with the native Etruscans. Hanging from the wood beams, tallow candles shed light from their iron holders. Barely enough light for the bookseller to take out of his beaded cloth bag, a short scroll of papyrus, a small ink pot with a cork lid, and a quill. What joy!

"Before I write anything, let me see the wine you promised me."

"First, let me see you write something."

Nahatum took up the quill and wrote in Punic: "Hannibal destroyed several Roman armies and soon he will be at the gates of Rome."

The bookseller's eyebrows shot up. "Hmmn. Perhaps. If he does, then I will have to deal with those Punic authors and scribes. Lord. Let me see you write something in Latin."

"First, the wine." What he got was a local sour wine, a wretched mix of fermented grapes, water, and sorry local herbs.

Latin, more Punic, and Nahatum remembered just enough Greek to impress the bookseller. Along the way, he even negotiated a meal from the man. Plus a glass of mulsum, a fine mix of wine and honey that took away the damage from the sour wine.

Finally: "Where have you learned all this?"

"From a learned Greek, like yourself."

"You do not speak like someone who spends his time unloading ships and being whipped. By the way: I am not a Greek, I am from Crete. Can you learn Persian?"

"Yes."

"Well, then come with me to Crete. You will become my scribe, making copies of these books that I have found. I will pay your food and lodgings and a small wage.

You will of course have to leave Italy, this accursed land."

Leave Hannibal behind? Yet for Nahatum all that was left in Italy was his employer's whip and Lizard Skin, who would gladly take him into his dark kingdom when he found him. Which, Nahatum believed on dark days, was perhaps where he belonged.

"Yes. Take me with you. I want to see Crete, I want to scribe books." He thought but didn't say: *I do not want to be Nahatum anymore. Can you change me?*

Summer turned to winter.

"My Dearest Brother Hannibal:

"Alas, I could not read some of the letter you wrote me. I do not know if the ink stains and spots were the result of an unfortunate choice of courier, though when I quizzed the poor man he said he had kept the letter in its waterproof leather sack the whole way and your seal remained unbroken. So perhaps it was some laziness or inattention on the part of your scribe. Or perhaps you wrote the letter yourself?

"I remember how Solyphos would urge you to better your writing skills.

"Well, no matter. Follow the overland route to join you in Italy? I think that is not advised at this point. There are many victories for me to acheive here in Iberia, what with the Romans making such trouble. Let me assure you that I will do my best to make you and our father proud of his Lion's Brood.

"Your Brother, Hasdrubal"

Weeks passed. Another, very different, letter arrived for Hannibal in Capua.

"Come now, boy, do not keep me waiting reading the letter. Do not be nervous in front of the great Hannibal. Your father said you were well- tutored in the Greek language." Hannibal could of course have read the letter himself, but he wanted to test the boy.

The young Capuan scribe's face— Hannibal estimated him be a few years younger than long- dead Nahatum—was tense in concentration, his mouth set—as he sat in his chair bent over the letter—finally!—from the distinguished King Phillip V of Macedonia, across the Great Sea from Italy. *Just read it to me, Ba'al take you, don'tstare down as if you are trying to decipher the letters in each word!*

The letter had arrived only hours earlier, carried by five Macedonian horsemen— well-armed and each well-draped in fur cloaks of royal color. The melting snow and warmer days had renewed the king's ambassadors' courage to make the difficult journey. Now they waited outside his villa for a response from Hannibal to take back to their king. Which he would dictate as soon as the dazed young scribe read to him what Phillip had finally proposed.

"This man is descended from Alexander the Great," Hannibal remarked as much to the empty room as to the scribe. *What joy! What relief! Finally, an ally.*

"Who, Sir, was this Alexander?," responded the scribe, looking up, confusion draped over his face, the latest in a continuing line of servants and scribes Hannibal had found to be inadequate.

Great gods! "Here, give me that letter. Thank you, that will be enough for today, you can leave now."

The boy had scarcely closed the door behind him, relief evident on his face, when Hannibal sat down to read the letter himself.

After the requisite encomiums and other flattery, the King got to the point. He proposed some discussion of their common interests in opposing Rome. The city's expansionist intentions were a threat to all. The King made clear that he wanted to expand his influence in Greece as a counterweight to Roman influence. Would Hannibal be receptive to a joining of their common struggles?

The letter was addressed and sent directly to him, not to the Senate in Carthage. The king wanted to ally himself directly with Hannibal rather than Carthage. How much was the man willing to contribute? The King's interests seemed to be mostly towards the riches of Greece. How cooperative would he be with battles in Italy, further west? *These are matters I must find out, and soon. I must woo this man.*

Then he was up and out of his chair, calling down the hallway for his scribe to return, quickly now, and telling him to bring his quill and ink.

Though Hannibal could not know then how fickle this king would turn out to be.

Summer, 214 B
The Island of Crete

The rough straw mat on which Nahatum tossed and turned made him itch all over. Had the vapors from the Underworld found him on this strange island? Or perhaps it was just bugs.

Even after six months he was not used to sleeping in the ramshackle storage shed behind the bookseller's store, keeping company with the call of a lonely gull from the harbor, the roar of waves smashing on the seawall. He remembered the soft skin of Lady Busa, the feel of her body entwined with his, and wished he were back in that grand bed, covered in plush blankets.

Someone was trying to break in through the rotted wooden door of the shed, he was convinced. Or was it the wind shaking it? He found the rough staff near his bed, checked the door. Nothing. His trickster mind still left him at times confused and unsure.

He held his staff close as he lay back down, trying to sleep. Yet sleep no longer held the promise of pleasure or relief. Sleep was the first step into death, a falling into the giant, black mouth of Lizard Skin. Since Cannae, this had been so.

He stared wide-eyed at the old wooden ceiling, a spider's web woven into thecorner.

Was the boat he took with the bookseller months ago the boat of Charon, the boatman of the dead? Solyphos had told him about Charon during those long nights in Taurini. Perhaps they never crossed the Great Sea to Crete. Maybe he was ferried across Acheron, the lake of the dead that you must cross into the Underworld.

Perhaps this island was the Underworld: the rainy port, the stores clustered around the piers, the boats rowed by weary slaves, the slaves and freemen emptying their cargoes, the tavern with sailors, sellers, farmers, soldiers, Roman traders, merchants from Carthage, Persians, Phoenicians. Perhaps they'd all drunken from the river of…He struggled to remember what Solyphos had called it? …The rivers of Lethe, the waters of oblivion that caused you to forget your past existence. Yet that cannot be, since he remembered. If only he could find the river of Lethe, drink from it. If only he could forget.

He was lost.

One night he dreamt that Hannibal was beating him with a whip. When he angrily rose up and grabbed the whip, Hannibal exclaimed, "how dare you, you are a deserter and have no standing, all you had was me and now you have given that up, you are no one." *Apistode.* A nothing, without a name, a homeland.

Some nights he had to bite into his own skin in order to restore the feeling of being alive, to feel anything at all. He was no longer a wolf boy, he had become a ferret gnawing at himself.

He huddled deeper under the dirty sheepskin blanket, as if there was safety there.

There are bonds that unite people and stretch in unseen ways across all the waves and water and wind that seem to separate them. No amount of Great Sea, Nahatum realized, would break the bond that connected him to those who had saved him, those to whom he owed his life, those whom he'd betrayed.

He'd hoped to be free, but instead he was bound more deeply than he'd ever imagined.

Summer, 214 BC
Capua, Italy

Hannibal was not in a good mood as he left the grand amphitheatre in the center of Capua on a warm summer's night. "Thank you, gracious Calavius, for arranging this entertainment." He meant the first part, but certainly not the second. The entertainer had been a singer of tales, a travelling musician who'd brought his voice and lute to perform the Greek tale, The Odyssey. *What an awful story,* Hannibal thought as he walked the darkened city street, watchful bodyguards at a discrete distance.

He did like the elderly Capuan and the other esteemed nobles. He had even taken to wearing the flowing Capuan hats, which only seemed to increase the summer heat.

There'd been joking about the heat, finally cooling there at night, and Hannibal could amiably say that he'd gotten used to it, having returned now to spend a second summer in Capua.

It was but a short walk back to the same Capuan villa he'd occupied the year earlier. The thought came to Hannibal: *am I visiting or am I marooned in Capua?* He'd hoped to be elsewhere after another year of feints and counter-feints across southern Italy. Tarentum, that rich prize on the heel of Italy, tried to come over to his side but at the last minute a Roman fleet had arrived to prevent the people from throwing off their alliance with Rome. Hannibal had shown great restraint, burning no fields and keeping the army orderly with strict orders against pillaging—all to no avail. He'd almost had the large, renowned city, with its excellent port, in his grasp, along with Capua.

Again: almost. Victory at the edge of his fingertips, still.

And now he'd had to sit through the tale of the Odyssey. He almost couldn't bear it.

Twenty years Odysseus was gone from his family, ten years in that endless siege of Troy and then ten years just getting back home to fair Ithaca. The whole thing started so gloriously, the Greek fleet sailing for Troy, and then they were stuck outside the impregnable Trojan city walls for ten long years.

That shows what sieges will get you, Hannibal thought. Though the part about the wooden horse was excellent. Odysseus was truly a clever trickster, but tricks only get you so far when you are dealing with the whim of fate.

What is really bothering you about the story tonight, though? Hannibal could feel the agitation in his chest as he walked through the quiet, familiar streets. Too familiar. *It was the ending of the story.* Odysseus finally arrived back home in Ithaca, washed up on shore, alone, his army gone, and who did he encounter? His son, now grown. An infant when he left. The son—a strong and powerful young man, a budding warrior– was overcome at seeing his father.

Odysseus' words echoed in Hannibal's mind: "I am this father that your childhood lacked for/ I am he, no other father will come." *Ba'al's breath. There are thoughts that get into your mind and you can't free yourself of them.*

As Hannibal arrived at his villa, his own father came riding to mind on his grand horse holding in his lap his grandson, little Hamilcar. "This is my very grandson," he shouted at Hannibal—"are you raising him to be part of the Lion's Brood?"

Hannibal stormed into his villa and called for a scribe, shouting down the long hallway toward the rooms where the young-people-who-were-not- Nahatum slept. One of them—a stout boy related somehow to a long- retired, once revered Suffete of the Senate, Hannibal could not remember which one— came groggily down the hallway. Hannibal shooed him back to bed. *I will write to my wife myself, I do not need a scribe for this.*

He picked up a quill. *Oh, the hold of memory: if Nahatum were still alive all this time, I would dictate to him.*

"My Dearest Wife:

I sit here in the darkness of night thinking of you and of our son. There is much he needs to learn. This is the time to start with language instruction and the forms of martial training that make young children into adult warriors. When you start young, the sword comes to feel like a part of your hand. We need to start tutoring him in Greek and in military history…"

Perhaps it was the lateness of the night, perhaps it was the glass of fine Capuan wine, perhaps it was that accursed performance of the Odyssey— whatever, Hannibal let his hopes pour out onto the page and included a long list of what he believed his son need learn. Then:

"Forgive me, dear Imre. I have been here too long. Four years. Carthage feels further away now than when I began this invasion. I long to see your face. To hold you. And to hold my son.

Your loving husband, Hannibal"

That summer—the fourth since Hannibal stormed down out of the mountains upon an unsuspecting Italy and Nahatum's second in Crete—was glorious and the small port was bustling.

Tenalakis the bookseller was happy. There was much demand for certain books, including one by Xenophon, the Greek general and historian, about his time with the Persians. Hannibal was savaging Italy, Rome and Carthage were fighting all across the Great Sea, and King Phillip V of Macedonia was making threats against Rhodes and other Greek cities. War, always war, and people wanted to read about that. Business, if not travel, was good.

Nahatum was busy scribing. He now had his own corner in the bookstore, and a rough wooden table that he had sanded smooth to the touch, polished to a shine, where the papyrus could be placed without buckling. The table sat just beneath a window overlooking a fine view of the port, providing abundant light for his scribing.

There was great demand for the books Nahatum copied. "And my talented scribe can translate between three languages!," the bookseller would boast to his customers.

Then he'd add, voice lowered, perhaps thinking Nahatum couldn't hear: "All this just for room and board!" True, sometimes Tenalakis reprimanded Nahatum for yelling at night from his bed in the storage shed, and got angry at him for having "foul moods" during which it was better to keep him from customers. Still, Nahatum had heard the bookseller tell the representatives from the library in Alexandria just the day before that his scribe was "a real bargain."

Now that summer's day, the scrolls of Xenophon's *The March of The Ten Thousand* awaited Nahatum's quill to copy.

In it, the Athenian historian and soldier related his adventures with an army of Greek mercenaires in Persia.

He couldn't wait. He spread out a clean sheet of papyrus, weighting each end down with a stone that he had carefully washed and wiped free of dirt. These were the same polished stones that he used each time he scribed a book. There was a cat on the back of the table, sleeping on the blanket Nahatum had put there for him. He patted the cat; the cat purred. A smart one, it had learned to stay away from the papyrus and ink.

He ran his fingers over the papyrus, felt its grainy-smooth texture, and again he thought of the soft skin of Lady Busa. He had not been with a woman since he'd left her house, and there were still mornings he woke up having dreamt of her. Then the feel of the papyrus would draw him in, calm him, drain away the fatigue from another restless night.

For Nahatum, there was only the quill, the ink, the papyrus. He held the quill properly, familiarly, between his fingers, and moved it gently over the papyrus, oddly soothed by the scratch of the quill on the surface. He would speak to each new scroll, asking the papyrus to please receive the ink and allow the words to form cleanly, beautifully. Nahatum did this because who knew, perhaps the papyrus had a life of its own. He wondered about that when there was an error, a stray line, a malformed letter or entire word. He might be scribing beautifully and just like that the ink would run, there would be a smudge or a river of ink wending its way across the page, destroying what he had done. The papyrus must be treated with great respect.

Nahatum considered the Xenophon scroll in front of him, with its endless list of battles and wars and the glory of victory. It was true what Solyphos had told him in the Endless Mountains: we glorify war to our peril. And there had been so many wars. *You might as well be looking over a precipice without bottom,* Nahatum thought.

Back to work. Focus on the papyrus. There was a familiar, unpleasant odor coming from somewhere in the store, which he ignored. *Tenalakis must be shaving.* He picked up the quill and the black line of ink moved across the papyrus of its own accord, now a snake, now an army moving across a narrow plain, now a broad flowing river, now a narrow chasm that he had to move through and if he could—if he could follow the deep, rich color of that line—perhaps he would find himself in a whole new place. The lines became letters, became words that made sentences that made thoughts, actual, real thoughts. War or no war.

And then… there was no more papyrus for the copying and he crashed back to that narrow, trapped place. He'd used the last blank scroll. *No.* He had to keep going, to hold off the blackness inside.

"Where do you keep extra papyrus? I don't remember seeing more." *Hurry up.*

The bookseller took his time looking up from the little washbasin in the corner of the store. *Hurry up.* Next to the basin was a warm bowl of oil and herbal fragrances— foul-smelling herbs that the man insisted on mixing with the oil when he cleaned himself. He had his *strigli* out—the long curved silver instrument always dangling from his belt that the Cretans used to clean their skin. Sometimes the man insisted on a hot bath loaded with precious oils and herbs in middle of the day if he thought there were evil spirits in the air. Especially if there had been too few customers that week.

The bookseller wiped his face clean, cursed. "Are you writing carefully and with small letters. I told you I want to use as little papyrus as possible."

"I am making my lines so small that no one will be able to read them. You will sell more books if I can write larger. We need more papyrus." The agitation inNahatum's chest strengthened. If he was alone he would have poked at his own arm with the tip of his quill to calm himself.

"You'll have to wait till the next ship arrives later this month from Egypt with more papyrus," Tenalakis announced, sounding irritated. "And I will have to barter with those foul Egyptian merchants who insist on outrageous sums for their papyrus."

"You buy your papyrus?" Nahatum's hand began to twitch. *Wait how long?*

"Of course. When I buy the black and the red ink from the Egyptians. What is wrong with your hand?"

"Nothing. I can make us all the papyrus we need." *I want to do it now. Hurry up.*

The bookseller scoffed, shook his *strigli* at Nahatum. "Do you see any of the papyrus reeds here? Anywhere on Crete?"

"I do not need papyrus, I can use other reeds, such as the ones I've seen in the swamps past the harbor. They are similar."

The bookseller stared at him. "You are serious. You can make papyrus? Where did you learn to do that?"

"From the same person who taught me to read and write." The thought of Solyphos, the prospect of putting his hands in the wooden pans he'd now have to build to make the papyrus, the feel of the soggy reeds as they began to dry into papyrus— all this calmed him. The shaking, the twitching, stopped.

"Who are you, Nahatum? What son of some King or a God are you?" Then the bookseller considered: "Can you also make the fine quality ink the Egyptians charge me an arm and a leg for?"

"Are there gall nuts on this island?"

Then came the day that Archimedes arrived at the bookstore. Not the great mathematician and engineer himself. No, Archimedes was occupied with contributing to the defense of Syracuse, Carthage's ally on Sicily, besieged by Rome. This was a task the brilliant man was carrying out with unbelievable invention, producing an astonishing array of weapons of war that had the Romans back on their heels.

Archimedes arrived, rather, in the form of a scroll Tenalakis dropped on Nahatum's scribing table, as he kept a careful eye on the wasps gathered around a nearby clay jar of gall nuts, newly collected.

"'The Essays of Archimedes,' written by the great man himself," the bookseller announced to Nahatum. "Real demand for this book—they want it in the library at Alexandria so their engineers and generals can study it. Get to this one fast." On his way out, he made a detour around the gall nuts, though the wasps were hardly interested in an overly fragrant old Cretan.

Unrolling the papyrus, Nahatum read about catapults that could hurl enormous boulders of such weight as to sink Roman ships assaulting the city, about artillery that launched vicious stone missiles, about city walls designed with small, unseen loopholes for surprising attackers with deadly-accurate fusillades of arrows. Archimedes designed all this through careful calculations made on his sand table, which Nahatum came to understand was like papyrus you could use over and over again, the great man writing out his formulas and designs with a large quill-like stick.

How wonderous! From that sand tablet had emerged such amazing machines, including enormous swing beams with grappling hooks that protruded from the sea walls of Syracuse and—through the calculated use of metal chains and heavy weights—had lifted Roman war vessels right out of the water and overturned them into the sea!

Nahatum was fascinated with the ideas. Even without understanding what Archimedes called "mathematics" and "geometry", Nahatum saw that it was the formulas written on the sand tablet—and copied on the scrolls right in front of him—that could lift the warships out of the water, scattering sailors like falling leaves.

"Give me a place to stand and with a lever I will move the whole world." As Nahatum copied those words onto the papyrus, they seemed to come alive. The man could move the world entire? The Endless Mountains they had crossed? The Snow- Capped mountains of Iberia? The whole of Italy, Taurini, Cannae? All this, Archimedies could move with a giant wooden lever? And he figured that out with the marks he made—numbers and symbols—on his sand tray in his garden in Syracuse?

Nahatum stared out the window of the bookstore, heart beating, then returned to his work, breathless at the power held in his hand as he moved the quill quickly and effortlessly, so gracefully, over the papyrus.

Summer, 211 BC

Several years passed.

"To The Illustrious King Phillip V of Macedon:
"Great King, I understand your desire to bend Rhodes and the other Greek cities to your will, but I must urge you to focus your energies on the war with Rome."

King Phillip has the attention of a distractible puppy. Ah, maybe that's what I really need, Hannibal thought: *a dog. A loyal companion who will obey me.* He sighed. The Capuan scribe waited for his dictation, quill in mid-air. *Focus: what to say to the King, to rouse him to action?*

"Your illustrious predecessor, Alexander…"

Who truly deserved the title, Great….

"…knew that he had to strike hard and relentlessly at his true enemy, Cyrus of Persia. His victories are legend. Today Rome is your real enemy, not Rhodes or the little city states of Greece. An invasion of Italy, joining with me, will seal your reputation for bold action. Act now and together we will toast victory on the floor of the Senate in a few short months."

Now I'm beginning to sound like Marhabal at Cannae. "All right, you can go." He instructed the scribe to seal the letter and send it off with the King's messengers.

Hopefully this will get through to the King and the man will finally act.

As the oak door in his Capuan villa closed behind the scribe, Hannibal suddenly called him back. He needed to reply to a recent letter from his brother, in Iberia, so full of hope and pride. He dictated:

"My dearest Brother:

"Congratulations on your successes in Iberia. I was overjoyed to learn that you recently enjoyed a resounding victory over a large Roman army at the Baetis river, killing both commanders, Publius and Gnaeus Scipio. I gather that all of Iberia south of the Ebro river is under Carthage's control. That is wonderful news. Here in Italy, I control much of Calabria and Bruttium. With the help of some townspeople who opened their gates in the dark of night to my army, I occupy rich Tarentum, though the Romans still retain the well-fortified citadel of the city with its access to the harbor."

Almost, still, Hannibal thinks as he dictates. *I am close.*

"However, I caution you against your plans for further conquests to the north in Iberia. Rome is clearly reeling now from these losses in Iberia— the news from traders coming from Rome is that their Senate has had trouble finding a Consul willing to go to Iberia at all, considering that a death sentence. The Romans do not want to face you in battle! This is the time for decisive action: join me now in Italy, so that we together can bring this war to an end... Now!"

As the scribe sealed the letter and quietly left, Hannibal could not rid himself of an urgency working at his chest. There was something he didn't say to his brother. Yes, the Roman Senate had trouble finding a new Consul in Iberia, but one person had in the end come forward: the 25-year-old son of Publius Scipio, the general who'd just died in battle with Hasdrubal's army. His name: Publius Cornelius Scipo.

When the trader from Rome had told him this news a few days earlier, the man had asked: "Do you know of the new Consul, great general?" The trader had asked with a slight hesitation, as if the question made him uncomfortable.

"No, should I?" Hannibal had replied.

"He is said as a young officer to have survived the battles with you at the Ticinious, the Trebia, and at Cannae. How odd that he would have survivedsuch onslaughts of yours...."

The new Consul Scipio was the same age Hannibal had been when he took command in Iberia. And he, too, was doing so after the death of his father in battle. In Iberia.

Odd, indeed. As was the fact that the man had had three opportunities to die at Hannibal's hands and somehow had survived them all. *You're not really a superstitious fellow.* Still, he was on edge. *The fates conspire to crush your dreams.*

He felt then an added urgency to move to victory, as if fate had set in motion through this young, far-away Scipio the very instrument of his doom.

Winter, 211 BC

Already at work at his table, Nahatum could see that Tenalakis was upset from the moment he came into the store and took off his winter coat. He stroked those beads around his neck so intently Nahatum could hear them clacking.

"It's the wasps," the bookseller finally said. "They congregate around the storeroom and the store, right at the front door now, keeping customers from coming in." Gloomily, he reported, "There is gossip that something accursed happens in here."

Nahatum slammed his fist down, startling the cats, angered by the distraction from his quill, the ink, the book he was copying; he worried he'd miss a word or make an error—ink running across a scroll– and mess up his day's work: another copy of the Works of Archimedes, that wondrous mathematician who claimed he could move the entire world. The bookseller had been hurrying him to finish. There were representatives from the great library in Alexandria waiting to take a copy back with them.

"Wasps? Gossip? I hadn't noticed."

"Ever since you started making the ink, years ago. The wasps have gotten worse and worse."

"Ah, yes, they love the gall nuts."

"There is one now right on your shoulder." Nahatum shrugged.

"What strange powers do you possess?"

If he keeps at those beads, he's going to wear them out. Nahatum wondered if perhaps he, himself, should get some, considering his dreams, at night, alone in the shed. Will Hannibal never stop pursuing him, judging him? "The only power I possess is the ability to make papyrus and ink and to use them to write, to tell stories, histories, all the things I have been copying." Solyphos couldn't have said it better.

Tenalakis sighed, keeping an eye on a nearby wasp. "Well, I need what you can do. You are saving me a fortune by what you are doing...." He coughed. "Though all these pans and supplies are very expensive, of course, so I can't, as I said, pay you anything...And these wasps are costing me customers, as are the rumors about you."

Nahatum didn't care how much he was paid. He knew he was not worth money and, anyway, all he wanted was the feel of the grainy papyrus forming itself in the wooden pans, the feel of the quill as it ran a river of dark ink across the papyrus. He had long ago given up the hope that all the ink in the world could cover up the stain that covered him.

"Tenalakis, Have you ever visited Syracuse?"

The man sat down near him, eyes still on the offending wasp. "Of course. A great city, the one place in Sicily that I always visit when travelling. I haven't been able to visit for over a year, though. The war, you know. The Romans have been beseiging it. Their army is now commanded by the illustrious Consul Marcus Claudius Marcellus who put down the Northern Italian Gaulish revolt decades ago, killing their leader himself in hand-to-hand combat. In Syracuse, though, he hasn't had much success, what with the defenses Archimedes has invented."

Nahatum tried to talk about Archimedes, but the old man only wanted to know about his progress scribing. "The Egyptians are waiting. They represent King Ptolemy IV himself." The boy interrupted him, read him Archimedes' claim that with a lever he could move the whole world.

"Tenalakis, I sometimes wonder if words can do that."

"What?"

"Move the world."

The wasp lifted off his shoulder and headed for the bookseller, who leapt from his seat, almost knocking the bowl of ink onto the floor. Nahatum barely saved it from spilling.

"These wasps! You will have to do something. Today."

What I have to do is get away from these pointless interruptions from the bookseller. He wanted to be alone with his work. And the wasps. He'd live among the wasps. "I may have a solution to the problem of the wasps."

"Yes? As long as it doesn't cost me too many drachma."

"Hardly. You know the meadow that you own on the edge of town, the one by the stream, just over the hill with the Temple to Athena on it. Out of sight of everyone?"

A nod. "Go on."

"Let me put a tent there—a hardy one that can withstand this winter. I'll move all these supplies there. The wasps will follow me and the townspeople will not have towalk past either me or my friends here"—he gestured at the wasps—"to get to your store."

He would be blessedly alone with the furrows of ink on the papyrus, watching the black lines, all else dropping away, a sort of nothingness, only the quill and the ink and the papyrus and his hand and they would all be one.

Summer, 210 BC

"Dear Hasdrubal:

"I hope my scribe's word craft is more pleasing to your eye than my last letter, dear brother. I have had a terrible time with scribes since the victory at Cannae took my best one. First I lost Solyphos, who succumbed to the rigors of the invasion in our first year here.

Then I lost his student, an odd young boy, completely untutored yet one who mastered the arts of writing very quickly. Truly amazing. You had such advantages it's no surprise you have become such a talented writer, but this boy had a special ability. Alas, he died at Cannae and somehow I have scarcely been able to replace him. There are no lack of candidates, of course. Some of the noblest families of Capua have put forward their eldest sons for the position, but I can't find someone truly suitable. I use several and the one I am dictating to now is the best of the lot."

The boy scribing at the polished table smiled. Hannibal reminded him not to smudge the ink.

"So, the summer of my eighth year in Italy. I might as well have joined clever Odysseus in his endless siege of Troy. I lack simply for the Trojan horse to bring Rome to its knees. While I was engaged in operations elsewhere, the Romans broke out of the Citadel at Tarentum and regained control of the city. Ah, brother, I cannot be everywhere at once.

"I miss the sea breezes at our Iberian home in New Carthage. They are lovelier even than the winds of Carthage itself. Do you agree? I miss our laughter together. I would like to hear your laughter. You were always the one who had something funny to say when things at dinner with father became too serious. Perhaps you have written and letters have been lost. It is the not knowing that is the hardest part.

"Write to me and let me know how the war in Iberia is progressing. I hope for news of your success. Hopefully you will deliver a sound defeat to this young Consul Scipio, then march north immediately to join me so we could finally put an end to this seemingly endless war."

Ok, enough. Close it with my seal, he instructed his hapless scribe.

I do not need this interruption. Nahatum could hear Tenalakis coming up the forest path toward his tent in the meadow. He looked down at the papyrus in front him, the words he had been scribing—the black lines finally bringing some relief after an awful night tormented by yet another dream of Hannibal, this time his former master himself dying, his face slowly being chewed upon by a terrible Lizard Skin, snout-like mouth with rows of bloody ferret- teeth…

Tenalakis was at the tent entrance, the old man humming to himself, so happy his beads seemed to be singing.

"This new arrangement is a gift from the gods. You are are gift from Zeus himself."

I don't need such enthusiasm, such praise. What I really need is a gift from Morpheus, the god of sleep.

"Making the papyrus and ink here, bringing the completed books into town…. you have revived my business."

The man rambled on in praise of the blooming of the spring wildflowers, predicting a summer of warmth and plentiful rain. And the look on the faces of the Egyptian merchants, Tenalakis said, when he told them he no longer had need of their papyrus! Clearly the man was making money, hand over fist.

"Of course money is still short, I mean we are barely making ends meet, but still…."

And then he coughed up a strange suggestion: "I do owe you something and since you will not take any payment at all, let me take you into town to the tavern, buy you dinner and wine."

There will be so many people in the tavern. Too many, too noisy. Nahatum had come to hate crowds; he did whatever he could to stay hidden and alone. That was the whole point of his pasture, high on the forested hill, so difficult to reach. He tried to become invisible, but his treachery lived clearly on his skin, visible in the burn mark, the lacerations of his own making, the sword wounds from Cannae.

As Tenalakis stood waiting at the tent entrance, Nahatum looked down at the burn mark on his wrist—that gesture that had once expressed his deepest bond to Hannibal and now was a mark of his treachery and disloyalty. He'd just been scribing a word that day. *Perfidy.*

Some excuse, any excuse. "But I need to work on this book. There is plenty more light for scribing today."

"Nonsense. You can take an evening to relax with friends at the tavern."

Friends?

All the way down the hillside trail and into the small port, the man bubbled with advice, as if they were going to a party at the Acropolis. *Did they have parties at the Acropolis?*, Nahatum wondered and wished Tenalakis would stop talking, so he could ask him. *What about the great library at Alexandria: Is it truly the biggest in the world?*

"Come now, let the townspeople actually see you. Try to laugh." They walked through the little forest, past retreating pockets of winter snow, barely noticeable in the evening twilight. The two of them could have been Roman survivors of Cannae on their way to Lady Busa's house. Nahatum's cheeks felt hot at the thought. *No, try not to think about that.* What forced itself upon him then was an image of the Numidian soldier on the battlefield at Cannae with the chewed- up face, blood bubbling from what remained of his nose and mouth.

"Listen, Nahatum. Eventually someone will need to help me with managing my store, particularly when I travel. You, I trust. But I can't leave you in charge if no one will come into the store when you are there. Or if you are always hiding away in the meadow." Tenalakis produced a sort of choking laugh, as if he had said the funniest, cleverest thing.

Tenalakis pushed open the heavy oak tavern door. Their arrival in the busy, wood- beamed place was met with silence, but the bookseller worked hard at being merry and he was, after all, a prosperous and well- regarded member of the community.

Everyone kept a wary eye on Nahatum who was himself nearly overcome by the thick, acrid smell of alcohol, garlic, and sweat, an odor of rot and decay which hurled him back to the smell of the dug pits where men relieved themselves in the army, the impossible stench, the smell of butchered elephants that day in Taurini, the air in the forest after Cannae, filled with the stink of the funeral pyres.

So many people were talking, he couldn't get his bearings. And then, to his shock, Tenalakis started making toasts and people were returning the toasts, handing him glasses of wine, of retsina. Soon enough Tenalakis was even telling the crowd about his assistant.

"Yes, Nahatum here does have special powers, but they are not of the evilspirit, or the evil eye. He has learned to make papyrus from a very learned Greek, a great man named, um,..."

Everyone clustered around the long wooden bar seemed to be staring at his burn mark. Nahatum's eyes started to itch. The bookseller lumbered ahead. "...Solyphos."

I can't breathe. Too many people.

"Yes, this Solyphos was a learned Greek who tutored Nahatum as a child in Thrace. This man's father"— here a hearty if overwrought slap on Nahatum's shoulder— "was an advisor to the King there—I forget his name—..."

Who? Tenalakis was making up a story about his father, who was unknown even to Nahatum. Worse, he couldn't even rub his itchy eyes, he was so hemmed in.

" who, ah...died tragically during a raid by King Phillip of Macedon. Nahatum fought well alongside his father and.... Solyphos...but to no avail, they were outnumbered and betrayed..."

Nahatum tried to recall how much Tenalakis had had to drink. How much longer could he keep this made-up story going? He was slowing down, but calling for more retsina. The man took another long draught of the sharp stuff, wiping his lips in a surprising, savage manner. "....Yes, betrayed by trusted guides in an ambush, guides who had been bribed by Phillip of Macedon. Nahatum's beloved father and the brave king, both among the massacred...."

A pause here for another hand on Nahatum's shoulder, a look of immense sympathy on the bookseller's face, so moved was he...."in just such a trap as that murderous Punic, Hannibal, sprung on the Romans at Cannae."

A searing pain shot through Nahatum's chest. All the sad faces, the looks of sympathy. For him. *What a liar and fraud I am.* All he wanted was to get away, back to his tent in the meadow.

"...and so young Nahatum was forced to make his way south with just his strength—and you can see that is considerable—and his wits to survive." More murmurs of intolerable sympathy. Raised glasses, nods of condolence.

"And his wits may be even greater than his physical strength. He eventually made his way to me, as he had heard of my reputation as a scholar and a merchant, so wide has my renown spread. And, I am happy to have given him shelter and a new life, for he can make papyrus better than the Egyptians, he can outwit the wasps to make ink on his own, and he can read and write in five languages."

Five?!

"Such was his instruction by his earlier tutor and the careful schooling I have given him in my employ."

Nahatum ignored the nausea, ignored the fire spreading across his cheeks. He bit down hard on his tongue, letting the pain flood through him. *Just keep nodding with that smile on your face. Fine: you wanted to be someone else, anyone else, and now you are.*

Barely two days had passed since his evening in the tavern. All the toasts and the laughter, the stares of the faceless collection of townspeople, the lies told by Tenalakis, all were still fresh in his mind. Including the stench of Cannae.

He was at his refuge, his scribing table, concentrating hard on the Archimedies scroll he was copying, when he heard a rustling from the trail, bushes being pushed aside, the scrape of boots on the dirt, then a timid call from outside the tent.

"Hello? Is anyone in there?"

He reached for his staff, which was really a version of his old combat pike. He had taken to calling the thick carved stick a staff to hide its real use: to protect him from whatever, whoever might appear. Then he heard a mangled, tortured version of hisname, in that foul island accent. Tentative, then louder.

When he pulled apart the tent flaps, he found a young man standing in the late afternoon haze.

"Yes. What is it? You've interrupted my work." He shook his quill at the intruder.

The man stepped back. "I am so sorry, sir." Though clearly stout enough to defend himself, the poor man looked like he wanted to run away down the trail. *Please do. And take those infernal Cretan beads around your neck with you.*

The man managed to stammer out that he had been in the tavern the other night– "proud sir"– and heard Tenalakis saying that Nahatum could read and write, "that you do the scribing."

Oh, by the ears of Ba'al, I don't want this interruption.

The man explained that there was a letter he needed written. "Might you kind, Sir, be willing?"

I don't have time for this. And, besides, this man stands too close when he talks.

Still... "What kind of letter?"

"My brother is in Tyre, three days sail from here. Our mother is near to the Underworld, very sick, and the priests say there is little to be done. I must write him and tell him to return home. Can you do that? I can pay you what you want."

"Your mother?"

"She is dying, kind sir. I must reach my brother."

Something opened inside Nahatum then, some softness, nearly forgotten. A dying mother. A mournful son.

"No money, you need not pay me. Come in. Sit. Ignore the wasps they will not hurt you."

Nahatum scribed while the man dictated the sad news for his brother, urging him to return home as quickly as he could. The man had hopes of seeing his brother soon.

Nahatum had never scribed anything so personal. He started scribing on one of his carefully dried fish skins, but stopped and told the man he would use fine papyrus for a letter such as this.

Before the grateful man left, rolled papyrus tied with string in his hand, he insisted Nahatum take the two drachma he had brought. Finally, Nahtum told him he would take one. Nahatum advised the man to use the same captain down at the port that Tenalakis used for his correspondence with book buyers in Tyre, wishing the man well, telling him that he hoped the letter—and his brother—arrived in time.

So started new gossip: There is a wise man in the meadow. He needs no money to survive. He is a Sofos: an Old Soul, a man with great knowledge in a strong body. He is frightening, he charms wasps, and....he is kind.

Here we go again. Now for the third time:

"Most Distinguished and Powerful King Phillip V of Macedonia:

"Oh, Great King, it is with anticipation I write to you once again requesting that you now send military commanders with your mighty troops here to Italy. I suggest, nay, even request, this because of confusing news that comes to me. The traders who come through this part of Italy tell me that you have invaded Illyria, near to Greek- Land.

"I can understand your desire to exert your benevolent powers over a land near your own, but I remind you that Rome is your real enemy and needs to occupy your full attention.

"If you—in alliance with me, as we have negotiated—do not stop Rome, whatever claims you have to Illyria will be washed away by their lust for empire. Now is the time for you to step forth boldly—Great King!—perhaps at the head of the army yourself. Imagine joining me in triumph as we stride into the Roman Senate chambers.

"You may have heard rumors that Capua has fallen to the Romans. There is no truth to that. Yes, they are besieging the city. However, I am undertaking several operations in Italy that will draw off their troops and force them to end the siege. Meanwhile, Rome and Napoli are swollen with peasants who have fled into the city; life there has become

more and more unmanageable. Seers and sooth-
sayers abound, selling their prescriptions for purifi-
cation and salvation from the death and destruction
that I, the great Hannibal, am prophesized to bring
to them. The Senate has banned public demonstra-
tions of superstition and foreign rites.

"Meanwhile, I await reinforcements as promised
by our treaty signed nearly five years ago. Please accept the gift of this ceremonial headdress adorned
with the very peacock plumage traditionally wornby
the Suffette, the leader of our Senate in Carthage.
Hopefully your helmet will be so adored when you
take your proper place alongside me at the head of
the victory parade the day—soon—when we enter
the city of Rome.

"Respectfully,
"Hannibal Barca, Commander of Carthage's Army
in Italy"

The scribe withdrew and Hannibal settled into his folding
wooden camp chair inside his tent in the fields outside the
ancient Italian city of Lanusium, twenty miles from Rome. He
had hopes of turning the townspeople's allegiance to Carthage.
What he most wanted, though, was the pleasure of reading a
recently- arrived letter from his wife Imre, at long last.

"My Dear Lord and Protector:

"I hope this letter finds you in Italy. I think you
have not received some letters I have written, nor I
yours, since I have not had the satisfaction of reading

your words in over a year. How sad to think that some of our dearest sentiments lie in a sunken ship at the bottom of the Great Sea or, worse, in the hands of the Romans.

"You should know of some news that may not yet have reached you in Italy. Your dear brother Hasdrubal has been fighting valiantly in Iberia but has encountered great difficulty. Hasdrubal is one of three generals commanding armies in Iberia— the Senate, goaded by Hanno, not willing to put complete command under one he calls "'yet another Barca general.'"

"My Lord, you would know better than I the problems of cooperation and morale among three competing armies. As you might expect, the Romans—commanded by this troublesome young Consul Scipio– have delivered several decisive defeats to Hasdrubal. He has withdrawn to New Carthage and is now attempting to rebuild his army there. The Senate has agreed to send substantial reinforcements to him and we are all hopeful. We do feel the weight of the war now, though. Taxes have increased here in Carthage and the price of food is shocking.

"There is good news, though. The Roman siege of mighty Syracuse has stalled and we are all hopeful that soon Carthage will have regained its lost colonies in Sicily. From Sicily we are now able to buy some of the winter melons from the slopes of Mt Aetna that are especially rich and tasty and which are a favorite of young Hamilcar, who continues to grow into a fine young boy.

"I am worried about Iberia, though. I know it is much too dangerous to travel there now, but I hope to see my father and my family back there before too many months have passed. And, my beloved, I yearn to see your face again, to hold you in my arms.

Your Loving Wife, Imre"

Hannibal's dog, Molussus, wandered into the tent and sprawled down next to him without a care in the world. Hannibal sighed, patting the big, muscular dog, bred by the Capuans to fight wolves. *Good boy. Patting your midsection is like beating on a drum. Very satisfying.*

Molussus was a gift from his Capuan hosts before he launched his summer campaign, before the Romans seized on his absence to suddenly besiege the city. *That is bad news from Iberia. I had hoped, dear Hasdrubal, that you would have destroyed this young Scipio by now.* Hannibal felt the dread of something awful coming closer, of time getting shorter. He patted Molussus, who nuzzled into the palm of his hand.

Scipio. Again.

Early Fall, 210 BC

Someone had been watching him for several days from the meadow. Nahatum was sure of it. There was movement from behind the trees when he went out for sun, and when he would unexpectedly peek out from his tent. At first he had thought it was a deer or bear. No, it was a person. Or several. How many? He kept his pike close.

I never should have written that mournful letter for that man to his brother two weeks ago, Nahatum concluded. Ever since, others have come, a steady trickle. More interruptions, less scribing. Still, he could not turn people away. "Please, Sir, can you write to my son working on a ship in Alexandria?"

"Wise One, I beg: a letter to some oil merchants in Athens."

"Sophos, I want to leave my house to my daughter, who lives now in Rhodes. Can you scribe that for us?"

And then this. Being watched. Danger.

Then, just like that, two people emerged from behind the largest tree near themouth of the trail. A man and a woman. And then they were at the entrance to his tent. She was a young woman. Perhaps sixteen, two years or so younger than he. The man, whom she would introduce as her brother, carried in front of him rather effortlessly a large clay amphora sealed at the top. Her name, she told the Wise One, was Sappho.

The brother stood away from the tent, eyes on the wasps. A scarf covered her head, but Nahatum could see the deep brown eyes, dark hair, strong face. Tall. In a light blue blouse with her long flowing skirt, she seemed to glow in the warm summer sun as she stood there at the entrance to his tent. She appeared undaunted by the wasps, who circled curiously around her. The effect was to leave him wondering: *Have there been other women as lovely on this island? Why have I not noticed her before?*

"May I enter?" A soft husky voice that excited a desire deep inside him.

"Yes, please do. By all means. And your brother as well, of course. The wasps will not bother you."

But she seemed to know that already. The brother, however, clearly did not and only reluctantly accompanied his sister into this evidently demonic place because propriety demanded it.

"Here, I will clear a space." Nahatum moved aside some inkpots and scrolls. The watchful brother put the tall clay pot on the writing table with a thud.

Sappho looked lovingly at the jar and then reached over to the mottled clay top, sealed with ancient wax, faded dark black. The brother took his knife and carefully, skillfully, cut away that seal. Sappho looked to be holding her breath. The brother reached into the amphora, but his sister put out her arm to stop him.

"I will do that, dear brother."

She carefully reached in with her delicate hands and slowly pulled out a long, thick scroll of dusty, faded papyrus. The three stared at it, Sappho and her brother with a look of reverence and, perhaps, sadness.

Nahatum could hear his own heart beating. Sappho unrolled the scrolled papyrus, which crinkled with the sound of years. Nahatum placed one of his writing stones on two corners; the scroll too thick and long to be completely unrolled. Sappho had her hand to her mouth and looked about to cry. The brother didn't take his eyes off the wasps lolling drunkenly around a cup of gall nut meat.

What is on this scroll?, Nahatum wondered. The writing was different from any he'd seen. And the lines were very uneven, unlike any of the books he has copied. Short lines, long lines, lots of wasted space on the papyrus, now aged and brown. Whoever did this was clearly untutored at scribing, wasting so much good papyrus.

"The entire scroll is poetry, written by my aunt Sappho, years ago," the young woman explained.

"I have heard of 'poetry' but never seen any," Nahatum confessed, bemused. "Why are the lines so disorganized? This is such a waste of papyrus." He added, "… and it's not easy to make papyrus."

She smiled in a way that left him suddenly feeling much younger than her. He did not like that, though the loveliness of her smile removed some of the sting. She explained that poetry was a way of saying something very differently from what he probably was used to scribing. More from the heart. And here she touched the palm of her hand to her breast, a movement that made him thick with desire.

The scroll she had brought was comprised entirely of poems from her namesake. "She is related to my mother, many generations ago, a great-great- great Aunt, I'm not sure how many 'greats' there are." A hint of laughter. "I just call her, Aunt Sappho." Long-dead. Her aunt Sappho had lived on the far- away island of Lesbos, and the urn had made it—through various wars and turmoil— to her family on Crete years earlier.

"My mother sometimes recites Aunt Sappho's poetry from memory, but no one has thought to open the urn as none of us can read. You are a magician and I hoped, perhaps, kind sir, you would be able to read it to me, so I can know more of what my aunt wrote." Her eyes—a lustrous golden- brown, like the summer thrush that visited his meadow— were on the papyrus. Then they moved to him: "they say you are strange, but you do not seem so to me. When I heard you are wise, I hoped you could tell me of the words of this great woman."

Wise? It remains to be seen who here is the wise one. All Nahatum wanted to do was to keep talking to this lovely girl-woman with the penetrating eyes and a voice like warm July mist. Her hands, smooth and delicate– he wanted to hold her hand.

"Come, sit here next to me and let us look at what is written on this papyrus, what your great- great....your aunt Sappho wrote in her poetry." She slid onto the bench next to him, bringing a scent of honey. "Did your aunt scribe this herself?"

"I believe so. She could read and write. She was herself a wise woman."

"So we are looking at her own handwriting, right here before us on this table, a piece of her that has survived and come to you."

Her eyes widened and she touched her hand to the edge of the papyrus. Was that the trace of a tear?

"Let us see what she wrote." He took his eyes off her and studied what was spread out on the table. Then he read it aloud:

> "You lay in wait/ behind a laurel tree
>
> and everything/was sweeter
>
> women/ wandering
>
> I barely heard/ darling soul
>
> Such as I now am/ you came
>
> Beautiful/in your garments."

Something softened in his chest. She asked him if he would read the poem again to her. Yes. He read slower this time, letting the words tumble and flow around and through him. The words sparkled, glowed with.... with the spirit-stuff of the fish- rock his mother had brought him when he was a young boy back in the Iberian forest. Words that were themselves deep and mossy. Unexpectedly, his eyes teared.

"She loved women, my aunt, but what she writes of love is for all of us."

Deep breath. He felt a bit dizzy. "Would you like to learn how to read, so you can know your aunt's words yourself?"

"Oh, yes, Sir." A big smile, eyes widening again, with their own glow. "And to write, so you could make words yourself?"

The smile seemed to get bigger even. "Very much."

"I can teach you."

From across the tent, the brother, who had sat staring at the wooden pans of soaking reeds, as if in search of inspiration, came to life. "It is late. We don't want to return from here through the forest in the dark." He spoke as if planning an escape from the Underworld.

She stood, tall and willowy. Her flowing skirt rustled, talking to him. *Beautiful/ in your garments.* Nahatum told her he would like to make a copy of her aunt's poetry. And would she like a first lesson in reading?

"Yes, sir." Her eyes looked down, shyly. She would return in two days.

Your aunt loved women. Can you love men?

Two days. He could barely wait.

Chapter 7

Levers To Move The World

"Shoo." Tenalakis appeared at the tent door, waving the wasps away. The bookseller's arrival had been announced already by the overpowering stench of the peppermint oil he used to protect himself from the insects.

Sappho welcomed the man in as Nahatum bent over a scroll, working on another copy of the Archimedes manuscript. Nahatum noticed that Tenalakis once again barely nodded at the woman who had become his constant companion. And lover. He remained rude, even months after Nahatum and Sappho had begun living together in the meadow. Nahatum suspected that the old Cretan didn't like an unmarried woman living there with his scribe. Or perhaps he wished he could share a bed with such a beauty.

Whatever it was, his pleasure at having Nahatum in the meadow, far away from the bookstore, had disappeared.

"Over a year I have trudged out here to pick up the scrolls. Perhaps you'd like to consider moving back into town."

He made it sound as if he walked the entire way up the hill to the meadow and back down, all alone, struggling with crates of rolled scrolls draped over his weary back. In truth, the bookseller always rode his old donkey, who in turn pulled a cart hauling the boxes of scrolls down to the bookstore. More scrolls than ever, now that Sappho had taken to her lessons in scribing. And, her aunt Sappho's poems had also attracted attention. The copies they have made sell well.

"Move back to town? No," Nahatum replied. "Why would we want to live amidst that gossip-mongering group of superstitious farmers? Besides, no one in town would have us living near them. They consider us outcasts."

Sappho smiled at him, he smiled back.

"Well...." Tenalakis scratched his beard. Nahatum took pleasure at watching their smiles register on Tenalakis' face. He contemplated asking the bookseller if he'd like Sappho to brew them some tea just to watch the man squirm.

"Besides, who knows what Sappho's brother would do to me, if I were to move into town, without my wasps to protect us."

Sappho gave out a hearty laugh. "You are bigger than my brother and you are a warrior, too, though you will not admit that. When will you talk to me about what happened in Italy?" She smiled, and the lilt in her voice raised his heart. The bookseller coughed, possibly from the cloud of peppermint oil choking him or perhaps from the sweetness that had grown between his scribe and his scribe's scribe. *This beautiful woman, the scribe's scribe. Ah, how did I ever become so lucky?*

"Well, I must be on my way. The two of you will stay outcasts, then." He was in a hurry because the boat to Athens was soon to depart. He was eager to sell these scrolls there. Then on to Tyre, Alexandria, and likely even to Carthage, if the war allowed.

"Remember, Nahatum, you can voyage with me to help with the selling."

"No, thank you."

Tenalakis and his donkey, and the creaking wagon heavy with crates of new scrolls, had barely disappeared down the tree-lined trail, when Sappho asked him why he didn't want to see those cities. He had repeatedly turned down Tenalakis' offers to take him along. "Not that I want you to go, but still…"

"I've seen enough of things. I like being here, with you, scribing….our life."

She smiled. "Well, speaking of here and our life, there is something else we might think of between us." She looked at him, then away, moving strands of her lovely black hair out of her eyes with the gesture that upended his ability to think clearly. And he could see her shyness again, too, the shyness that accompanied deeply heldy earnings.

She did not have to speak; he knew her unspoken wish: *she wants a child.*

To be a father. Nahatum had never thought before of the possibility. To bring a life into the world with this woman he loved. Walking to the bookstore, he considered the men he'd pass in the narrow streets of Ierapetra and wondered if each was a father. That tall, bearded man there outside the tavern— did he go home to children? The sea captains and sailors who docked at the port—did they have sons and daughters waiting for them in distant places? Did they miss them?

One day he spent most of an hour watching a man, hardly older than Nahatum himself, fishing off the long wooden pier with two young boys. "Father, here, look! I caught a fish." The pole jumped and bucked as the boy struggled to bring in the treasure. The man put down his own pole and hurried over, put his arms over his son's arms and steadied the boy as he wrestled the fish—a large seabass, silver scales glistening in the sunlight–up onto the pier. The boy was overjoyed, as was the father.

"This will feed us all tonight," the man told the boy. "Your mother will be so proud of you."

Nahatum was stunned. He couldn't take his eyes off the scene—the warmth between them all, the two boys so eager to take in all that their father had to show them. The boys watched their father with such devotion, his ease baiting their hooks, the laughter and excitement between them all. How did the man feel such calm and confidence being a father? There seemed some unknown quality or endowment, a reservoir of feeling and action, that made a father. Nahatum wondered if he had it.

The question of children remained unspoken between Sappho and Nahatum, even after Tenalakis had returned from his travels, even after another winter, a new year, and the arrival of spring. Perhaps it was just that: the arrival of spring, with all the new buds and new life.

Sappho had become quite proficient at scribing and even helped Nahatum with the making of papyrus and the ink. Her handwriting may even have become better than his, though neither of them said that. He'd redoubled his efforts at teaching her the art of scribing, varying the kind of quills, grinding the most perfect black ink; amidst the business of their life the question of a child had faded from his mind. And then one night, when they were alone in bed in the tent, she turned to him and observed, clearly, with all her courage evident: "We have never talked of children."

He nodded. "Perhaps it is time, my love."

She smiled. "I want to bear you many children."

He placed his hands on both her cheeks and held her close, imagining little children running through their meadow. He pictured a boy and a girl, the four of them playing in the tall grass, teaching them to read while sitting in the sunlight under the trees, he and Sappho scribing while their little babies slept nearby.

Sappho fell asleep in his arms, Nahatum drowsy with the possibilities of life. He knew now that something had changed between them, and for him. A light rain filled the warm night with dappled music. He imagined their children in the meadow running toward him out of the rain, laughing, clustering around him as he dried them with a towel. Then that vision dissolved and a dark, shrouded image appeared in Nahatum's mind. Hannibal. Nahatum's body tensed. Hannibal in far- away Italy.

What was Hannibal doing at that very moment while Nahatum slept in such warm comfort in his lover's arms? He imagined the great commander alone in a tent, on the march, studying a map, in pursuit of some strategic advantage while thousands of Romans were arrayed against him.

The rain became more intense, insistent. Sappho opened her eyes and looked up at him, her sleepy eyes filled with love. She smiled dreamily and returned to her sleep. They were still entwined, and even in sleep a smile remained on her lovely lips. He tried to calm himself by imagining that Hannibal would be happy at all the good fortune that had befallen Nahatum— his life filled with books, with the love of a women, soon to be with children of his own— but he could not. Instead he was filled with remorse at his disloyalty to the very man who had given him life. What kind of father comes from such betrayal?

He clung to Sappho, gently breathing in her slumber, and finally fell into a fitful sleep himself.

The next day, Nahatum worked hard to forget the darkness that had invaded his mind the night before. Such forgetting was not hard when Sappho was near to him. She sat at her desk beside him and completed scribing her copy of the poems of Acindous— already bought by the library in Athens– and left him fragments in her elegant handwriting, fragments that made his heart sing…and doubt.

"From all the offspring/Of the Earth and Heaven/Love is most precious."

Yes, he wondered, *but can I be trusted with something so precious?*

Strange how wars can confound you, Hannibal thought, sitting in his tent contemplating the walls of Rome barely a mile away. *You enter into them anticipating a quick victory. And why not? Your battle plans are brilliant, your overall strategy guarantees that you will win. Why else would you go to war?*

It was Hannibal's tenth year in Italy. His army was camped along the river Arno, just outside Rome. He sat in his tent at his writing table amidst a torrential downpour, the second in two days. *And if there is any question about your strategy, there is always the belief in your own sacred, special power. A power that comes from somewhere unseen but is rooted in the specialness of your history and the sacredness of all that has come before, all that separates you from your enemy, who is somehow less than you.*

He'd been perched there for over two weeks, after marching on the city in an attempt to frighten the Romans into leaving their siege of Capua. Soon after arriving, he'd ridden with Marhabal and two thousand of his best Numidian horsemen right up to Rome's majestic Porta Collina to personally survey the city's defenses.

As anticipated, there was panic in the streets. Hannibal is at the gates! Rome was already a mess as peasants and countrymen had surged into the already overburdened city with their families and cattle the closer Hannibal came.

Despite that, the city remained well-defended. He did have the satisfaction that day at the Porta Collina of throwing a spear over the city walls, but he had to do something far more than symbolic. So he had crossed the Arno two days earlier and drawn up his army for battle right outside the city—a direct challenge. To his delight the commander, Consul Flavius, had then drawn up his own army opposite his own in the fields outside the city gates. They faced each other in what would be a single battle for control of the city. Finally. The war hinged on that day.

And then the rains started. Torrential. No one could see anything. The ground turned to mud. Both sides withdrew. The next day dawned miraculously bright and again both armies drew up for a decisive battle, but again the rains came to pummel both armies, so intense that men could not even hold their weapons. Both armies withdrew.

The Romans took the rains as divine intervention, a portent that battle with Hannibal would have disastrous consequence. It was hard enough to entice the Romans to fight him—the catastrophe of Cannae marked every year by a day of mourning– without the gods advising the Romans to beware.

Hannibal sighed. *Are we but playthings of the gods? Are they amused at tantalizing me?*

Rain pounding his tent, he put quill to papyrus.

"My Dear Imre:

"I sit here writing you outside the very walls of Rome, listening to a thunderous torrent soaking everything. The rains have put an end to my chance to bring the Romans to battle. I will soon have to break camp—Marhabal's foraging parties return with less and less of the grain and hay we need– and move on without having broken their siege of Capua.

"Have I now twice lost the chance to capture Rome?– once after Cannae when perhaps I should have acted and now again when I did act but the rains came.

"To make it worse, my dear wife, messengers have arrived here from Sicily with news of the fall of Syracuse and the death of Archimedes. Ah, how I could have used that genius. He had such a mind– worth at least an entire Roman army. Now dead, and of no use to anyone. I'd have given the man whatever he needed to produce some marvelous creation that would breech the walls of Rome. Now gone. At the hands of Marcellus, that wily Roman Consul. Well, in fairness, the Consul had ordered that Archimedes be captured alive and left alone. And then what happened? An ignorant soldier finds the master at home in his garden working out formulae at his sand table (amidst the final battle for the city!) and thinks the genius is conjuring evil spirits, so runs him through with his sword."

Hannibal re-read the letter, satisfied, then decided to add one more thought: "Is there no end to human stupidity, my dear?"

Crete and Southern Italy 208 BC.

The following year brought storms never before seen on Crete. They began in the winter and rolled through all summer. A turbulent summer during which Nahatum and Sappho waited for a child, enjoying their love-making, wondering when fate would grant a pregnancy. The sun hid behind the blackest of clouds, Zeus unleashed his endless arsenal of thunderbolts, and the water was churned to a froth from Athens to Alexandria.

Perhaps it was one of those storms that took the sleek ship carrying the bookseller back to Crete, though there was talk that the boat was seized by the Romans and destroyed soon after it left Carthage. What was known was that the boat carrying Tenalakis and a number of other prosperous merchants disappeared at sea. And so, to his surprise, Nahatum became the owner and proprietor of the little bookstore, increasingly well-known, near the wharf at Ierepetra.

Crete pulsated with stories about Hannibal and there were always sailors on the wharf or in the small wooden tavern willing to talk about the news they had heard.

Nahatum became a familiar figure at the town harbor whenever a ship arrived. The first question he'd demand of the arriving captain: any news of Hannibal and the war in Italy?

Rome's armies now controlled all of Sicily. On the other hand, a number of Italian towns told Rome they had no more men or money to contribute to the war effort. Carthage was recruiting thousands of Numidian cavalry and infantry to reinforce Hannibal's brother Hasdrubal in Iberia. Traders and sailors brought vague rumors of big Carthaginian plans afoot in Iberia. There were fewer Carthaginian merchant ships docking at Crete, more of the Romans. Still any Roman would freely admit that as long as Hannibal was ravaging Italy, the war held in the balance. There was no telling what surprise, what trap, that man could spring.

"Why do you always ask about Hannibal?" Sappho asked one day as they rode back to their meadow with a shipment of scrolls that needed copying from the library at Alexandria.

"I want to know what is happening in Italy, so we can think about sending scrolls there. As soon as the war is over there will be rich men—either Punic or Roman—who will want to show their wealth by investing in a fine library."

"True, but..." The cloth covering above their heads flapped in the breeze and Nahatum leaned in to listen to her. He was very proud of that cloth cover: he'd had it made especially to provide shade and protection from the rain when they drove their wagon pulled by the fine set of horses he'd bought. He insisted it be dyed purple. A lovely addition to the wagon indeed. "Still, you ask specifically about Hannibal andyour whole aspect changes when there is information."

"Yes, interesting about Carthage's defeats in Sicily, their sending men andhorses to Hannibal's brother in Iberia. Very interesting."

"Just interesting? That's all." She looked at him with those rich brown eyes, that penetrating gaze. He wished he could hide himself behind the purple covering above their heads.

"Yes, that's it. Just business curiosity and an unfortunate preoccupation with warfare."

"Hmmn." A trace of a smile. "Perhaps that is why you so often go into the meadow to practice with that pike of yours."

They had hardly finished unloading the wagon when she asked him if he had heard the news. News?

"About the death of Archimedes? Word just arrived, though it happened last year. When Syracuse fell."

The crate of scrolls in his hands fell to the ground, cracking open, and spilling scrolls onto the wet ground. "Archimedes, dead? How?"

"I am so sorry, my love, I know how much you admired the man."

Death, again. His head felt light, like a bubble in water. He pictured Archimedes' bloody body, Lizard Skin oozing into the great man, squeezing the life out. Sappho quickly gathered up the scrolls and handed the crate back to Nahatum.

Put the new box of scrolls down there. Find the ink, the quill. Papyrus, quickly.

Get to work. Nahatum hurried to keep from his mind the picture of Lizard Skin eating the great man's face. Spreading out one of the papyrus scrolls, placing his familiar rocks, one in each corner. *Does anything survive?*

He sat, took the quill in hand. *What is the text to be copied? Ah, Archimedes himself, a theory of levers. Scribe this book, now.* As he worked, Nahatum thought of all the books he had copied going out into the world. All of the books that were being written only existed because someone made copies of them. *Maybe something will survive. Ideas, books. Scribing a book is like creating a life.* The ink ran so smoothly from his quill. The beauty—and safety—of those lines. When he was done with that one, he would scribe another copy, this time for the library in Athens. *They should have a copy. We will donate it.*

"Here, let me help you." came a voice from behind him. A calming voice. Gentle, soothing. There was a hand on his shoulder. Sappho sat next to him, her skirt rustling. "In fact," she said, "you know if there were more of us to scribe, we could make more books to sell. They will survive, as my aunt Sappho has survived."

She held up a copy of the collected poems.

More of us to scribe? Sappho would not drop the idea. When she was determined, Nahatum had come to see, the woman was unstoppable. The young children of the town, the boys and girls who needed work, those from desperate families, soon appeared in the meadow. She helped him to find the smartest ones, and, most importantly, those with curiosity. Over the long winter when the fields were asleep under a cover of snow, they taught five boys near to manhood to read and to write. Capably. He liked the teaching, sitting next to the boys, showing them what words were, letters, sentences, how to hold the quill.

He loved to see the power that holding the quill and doing the scribing brought to the boys. To make a book. He could see it in their eyes when the black lines flowed onto their papyrus. Who cared how much papyrus it took? For a time they were back to writing on dried fish skins. He had to send the boys out in boats when the weather permitted to catch fish to hang in the sun to dry. The boys could not believe it. Go fishing? Yes, today we go fishing. Why, Sir? For a fine dinner. And: to have something for you to practice your writing on. He loved the looks on their faces when he said that. They brought the fish back and before he cooked them, he showed them how to skin the fish so as to dry and preserve the papery coverings. He was, indeed, a magician.

"And...," one day Sappho said to him as they watched the boys go about their work—if each had a part of a book to scribe, they could produce a single book so much faster with five young, nimble hands working on it—"....you will of course next winter include some girls, yes?" She looked at him with those dark, burnished eyes. *Girls? Yes, surely– if girls can write poetry, they can scribe books.* Then she said: "I will make sure the townspeople understand that this is good."

By the end of the second winter and arrival of the summer trading season the little bookstore was crammed with scrolls to sell and with traders and merchants seeking to buy them. Nahatum sent young men to Alexandria, to Athens, to Babylon, with their books. He wanted to copy everything. We must make copies of Hippocrates, of theGreek playwrights, what of the Persians, their mystics and poets? Let us learn what they know. The library in Alexandria, the greatest on earth, regularly sentemissaries.

The young were everywhere– around their cabin in the meadow, warmed by the hearth fire in the winter, playing in the meadow in the wondrous Cretan summer, most of all sitting at special desks fitted to their size to scribe and copy the elegant scrolls demanded now by the rich of Athens, Sparta, Jerusalem, Tyre, Babylon, Alexandria.

Some were close to manhood or womanhood, their hands quick and agile with the quill, others still children—eight, nine, ten years old— eager to help making papyrus, intent on their task when grinding the ink with mortar and pestle.

Other people's children. Sappho saw his abilities as a father everywhere. "I love to think of the father you will become. Children listen to you."

As the summer wore on, she stopped mentioning it, though Nahatum didn't notice, busy as he was.

The older ones brought their younger brothers and sisters. They sat around the bookstore, the braver ones coming up to the meadow, where there were now several tents and sturdy well-built workshops, all protected by wasps. The Wasps of the Gall Nuts, the children called them. He joked that the wasps were sent by the God of the Gall Nuts; he claimed the wasps were the god's representatives. The children giggled and laughed and he could see that they more believed him than not.

Then one warm summer night Sappho turned to him in bed after their love- making and burst into tears.

"My love, what is wrong?"

He pulled her close, felt the heat of her body against his. She was inconsolable, burying her head into his chest. He gently stroked her dark hair, murmuring to her, while she wept.

Once, while scribing, Sappho had read aloud to him from one of her great- aunt's poems: "What cannot be said, will be wept."

Now he worried: *what cannot be said between us?*

Finally, Sappho sat up and looked directly at him. "Two years since we talked of children and I am still unable to give you a child, no matter that I burn the sacred incense, that I mix honey with cinammon and wine as the midwife advised me. ..."

He loved her even more then, embraced her, whispering: "We have our love, my dear."

"What if I am barren?"

"If the gods favor us, you will become of child. If not, that is fate. I love you none the less."

She slept in his arms that night, holding tightly to him.

A darkness returned then for Nahatum as he lay next to sleeping Sappho. Perhaps he was the barren one to be denied children. Perhaps there was a curse on him, for his disloyalty. For his desertions. For the first time in years, thoughts of his mother returned to him that night, shocking him. She had died alone, in the dark woods after she left him with the wolf pack. No burial, her shade left to wander unhonored as he abandoned his homeland.

Then Hannibal walked into his midnight thoughts, staring, imperious, accusing, the very man who had given him life and the man he had deserted—this clearly had displeased the gods, who saw that Nahatum's own seed was corrupt, defective. Was it his own worthlessness that was bringing this misery down upon the woman that he loved?

He began to shiver, even under the warm blankets.

Oh, Archimedes, is there a lever that will move dread from this world?

"My Dear Husband:

"The war takes such a toll on life here in Carthage. A shekel buys so much less. So many people are truly hungry. Last year a barrel of olive oil cost me 10 shekels and yesterday I spent 15 for the same amount.

The Senate has reduced the amount of gold in the shekel; some say there is less than a third gold, the rest is bronze.

"I dearly hope you can soon bring matters in Italy to a successful conclusion. More and more people talk about you since the news from Iberia continues to be gloomy despite your brother's best efforts and the loss of Sicily again has left the city's walls draped in black cloth.

"And now, my Lord, I must confess painful news: my father has died. News of his death reached me yesterday. I worry for the fate of my family as the Roman Consul Scipio continues to have success in Iberia. And the worst of this is that I cannot be at his funeral since of course travel there is far too dangerous at this point. If only our fleet had been able to regain domination of the Great Sea! I miss him greatly. As I miss you. I can see your face in our sturdy Hamilcar, who also one day will grow up to be a great soldier, worthy of his father.

"Your devoted wife, Imre"

"My beloved wife:

"I am so saddened to hear of your father's death. He was a good man. He was always loyal to Carthage and gave me personally the greatest of gifts—your hand in marriage—to seal our alliance. I have ordered a sacrifice of several sows in honor of your father and will make a funeral oration for him this evening. Many of the Iberians in my army will attend, to honor him.

More painful is my knowledge that you cannot be present at your father's burial. Please take heart in the hope that we will return soon to your place of birth, the land where your father died, as did mine, and together we will visit his grave.

Please write me again as soon as you are able."

Your Loving Husband,
Hannibal Barca"

A noise from outside the tent set Mollusus to fierce barking. He stroked the fine beast. The Captain of his guard appeared.

"My Lord, I have news. Roman Consul Marcellus has marched within three miles of our army."

Hannibal considered this welcome news. A hero after his success against Syracuse, Marcellus had been called north by the Senate to defend Rome against Hannibal. Three Roman armies were now arrayed against him; they were back to their strategy of attrition. Marcellus had been cautious, marching only during the daylight and mainly through open fields. The man wanted to avoid any of Hannibal's traps.

Ah, the pleasure of having a smart opponent. Hannibal reached down to quiet Mollusus. *I wonder if the Romans are thankful to me for teaching them how to fighta war.*

"Find Marhabal," he instructed the officer. "Tell him to have a thousand of our best cavalry mounted and ready to ride at tomorrow's first light. Let us see what we can learn about Consul Marcellus' intentions."

"News of Hannibal?"

In the dim light of the little tavern's candles, Nahatum considered the quizzical face of the sea captain, his skin almost elephantine in its wrinkles. "Yes, what have you heard?"

The sea captain nodded, stroking his bushy Athenian beard. Based in Piraeus, the man traded all around the Great Sea, including Italy, and often stopped into Irepetra.

Nahatum had vaguely recognized him when he came into the tavern— he often expressed sympathy for Carthage's cause— and so had engaged him in idle conversation. Yet the man had clearly had more than a few glasses of the fine retsina; he stared at his cup, as if his memory were stored there.

"Well, what is it?" Nahatum slapped the man harder on the shoulder than he intended. Which seemed to rouse the man. Oh, yes, the captain told him, a Roman sailor in Syracuse had all the news: Hannibal had ambushed and killed the Roman Consul Marcellus, commander of the army opposing him. "The Consul had been out scouting for Hannibal, but Hannibal found him first."

He lifted his cup. Empty. Nahatum ordered him another. The grizzled captain nodded.

"Here's the strange thing: you may know that the estimable Marcellus, victor at Syracuse, had two sons. Well, Hannibal had appropriate prayers said over Marcellus' body and then had his cloak and sword and shield sent back to Rome to be returned to the man's sons. 'No son should have nothing of his father's uniform,' Hannibal said."

Fathers, sons. Hannibal's loyalty to his father, the great Hamilcar. And his loyalty to his son—he had even ordered Nahatum to pack up that little stick construction for the journey into the Endless Mountains, a reminder of his son that Nahatum retrieved from the supply wagon and brought to him that dark day Hannibal had seemed so discouraged. Loyalty and devotion.

This was not what Nahatum wanted to think about.

"I have heard that King Phillip has yet to send reinforcements to Hannibal...", Nahatum started to say.

The captain was roused by the mention of King Phillip. "That bag of wind? All he does is threaten wars in Greece; he ruins my shipping trade. The man will never send help to Hannibal. He has the spine of a worm, and less attention. He has made threatsand offers of allegiance to half the countries around the Great Sea…No, Hannibal's truly on his own now."

So that makes two of us, Nahatum thought as he walked back home from the sleepy town through the dark woods to Sappho and their meadow. *We are both on our own now.* Or is that true? Nahatum considered: He had Sappho, his meadow, his bookstore, his books. And Hannibal was alone in Italy wrestling to—somehow– defeat the might of Rome.

Life is so strange: I once had nothing and Hannibal had everything. Now I have so much while Hannibal has so little.

Strange, too, to find so many candles burning in their house. And to find Sappho awake and waiting for him, despite the hour, standing by their fireplace. She seemed to glow in the reflected light of the flames, her nightgown shimmering with its soft folds. She smiled as she walked toward him, putting both her hands out in a gesture of embrace.

"I am with child, my love."

"Dear Brother Hasdrubal:

"The loss of New Carthage to the Romans, along with our family home in Iberia, is a terrible blow. I am stunned and hardly know what to write. The news had reached me here on the march in Bruttium even before your letter arrived; such was the talk of celebration among the Romans brought by local traders.

"A clever move by Consul Scipio to gain access to the city with his army while you were campaigning further north. He is indeed a spectre who seems to haunt me, as he does you.

"The Romans have become more clever, more resolute, less impetuous. Capua is gone. I could not break the siege there and eventually the city was forced to capitulate. You can imagine the revenge the Romans took on the very people who threw their lot in with our cause.

"King Phillip has written me yet again, his letter filled with compliments and deference, telling me that until he has conquered Illyium he cannot reinforce me with troops, and then he suggested that after Rome has surrendered I consider sending him parts of my army to extend Carthage's reach all the way to Athens!

"I seem to have become admired everywhere by everyone who is not Roman, but no one will send me reinforcements. Does the world think that I can defeat Rome while they go about creating their own empires elsewhere?

"I confess, brother, to being tired. So many have died. Last week in the town of Salsipa turncoats betrayed the cavalry garrison I had stationed there, and, worse, it was captained by my dear friend Marhabal. He died along with hundreds of his Numidians, who were there to protect the town from the Romans. I can't replace that cavalry. Such horsemen! Such a friend! I am even more alone.

"Have I mentioned that Gisgo is gone? You remember my infantry commander, he was already a formidable fighter when we were young. He fought alongside our father. The coughing sickness just a few months ago. Gisgo, Marhabal, Solyphos so long ago, Jonaz at Cannae. The best scribe I ever had died there, too. A clever boy named Nahatum. That battle was so long ago and still the Romans fight on.

"So many people are gone. What is the value of remembering them? Excuse my writing about this. And I hope this letter does not fall in to the hands of the Romans. Who cares? Let them know I am tired. I am no less ready for battle than I ever have been.

"So it is up to you: I urge you to elude this Scipio, turn away from him and from Iberia and bring your army to me—let us join forces here in Italy. A second Hannibal descending down upon Italy from the Endless Mountains! It is time that we again strike terror in the hearts of the Romans, bring the fire of Carthage—of our father, whose shade must be looking with pride at his sons—down onto the very floor of the Roman Senate!

"Your Loving Brother, Hannibal Barca,
Governor of Carthage's Territories in Italy"

I am to be a father.

This was no longer simply an idea, a possibility, it was now to become a reality.

So a new, troubling question was born: who was his own father? Nahatum had hardly thought about that, certainly never in the past years. His mother never talked of him. He imagined a soldier from the army camp back in Iberia, the very place he had left so long, long ago. He tried to picture this father, but the form of the man remained blank. Any one of the thousands of soldiers he had run away from, walked by, stolen from, could have been his father, but the one fact is that his father was never there. How do you be like a person you never knew?

Sitting at his writing desk in his cabin in the meadow, Nahatum closed his eyes and tried to will himself to picture his father. The form slowly filled in as he saw....Hannibal. Hannibal was clearly not truly his father, but in another way he was, certainly the closest thing he had to a father.

But if Hannibal was his father, what sort of faithless son was Nahatum? That night, as Sappho softly slept beside him and wove a baby in her womb, Nahatum dreamt of Hannibal staring at him, accusing him, with those eyes that could loose thunder bolts.

Sleep, dreams were no longer his friends. Some nights he dreamt of holding their baby as it died of the coughing disease, as his mother had. Coughing, retching, the little swaddled infant of his dreams bucked violently in his arms, gasping for spasms of breath as it slowly suffocated, face contorted, lips blue. One horrible night he dreamt that the baby's face had been eaten away by Lizard Skin and he woke in a sweat, remembering the dying Numidian on the battlefield of Cannae. He dreamt of his mother walking away from him, a sad, stooped figure, coughing. He'd call out to her: Mother! Mother! Yet she kept walking and he'd run after her but could never catch up. No matter how desperately he tried, in his nightmares she was always out of reach, disappearing into the thick, unforgiving woods.

He awoke yelling, startling Sappho out of her deepest sleep. He lashed out in nightmares trying to keep Lizard Skin away from their sleeping baby, Lizard Skin creeping up as Nahatum desperately swung at the demon with his pike. Once he almost hit Sappho as he swung his arms violently during a nightmare. He worried about injuring her. The life growing inside her seemed so vulnerable, so fragile, how could it ever survive? Would he possibly lose—could he even think of that?—Sappho. Would she die in childbirth as happened so often in the village?

Watching her playing with the scribing children in the meadow he yelled at her to be more careful. Don't run so much, he cautioned, you might fall. As she laughed and chased after the happy children all he was aware of was her big belly. She told him not to worry, she felt very healthy, but some days he stayed at his scribing desk rather than go outside and watch the children and his wife at play.

He knew that he was doomed to fail at becoming a father, a father who could protect and defend his baby. The baby would die and he would be unable to bear that.

He woke in the mornings trying to calm himself, his bed-clothes wet with the sweat of his black dreams. He had not expected this, the flood of feelings and memories from so long ago. *This is worse than the battlefield, fighting ghosts and shadows of the mind. Courage, Nahatum. There is room for courage in the bedroom as on the battlefield.*

He tried. He imagined this beautiful woman who lay beside him at night, who scribed beside him during the day, as the healthy and grateful mother of his children. He spent two days converting one of the long wooden papyrus-making pans into a cradle for their baby. From making papyrus to making babies.

"What are you doing?" Sappho asked, reminding him that they had an order from Babylon for several copies of the Archimedes. "You need to make sure the boys are copying it correctly." She seemed almost to waddle rather than walk now, her belly so big. This unnerved him even more, the changes in her body.

"Yes, yes," he replied, pounding nails with his hammer. "I just want to finish making this cradle."

He wanted it so strong that he could be sure that their infant was safe in it. He made the cradle out of thick oak, double- nailed the sides, a baby could have sailed safely in it through the Santorini volcano that the traders talked about. But was that enough? He wanted a cradle that could withstand even the arrival of Lizard Skin.

He didn't speak to Sappho of any of this. Not of his fear for their baby, his mistrust of himself, how much after all these years he missed his mother, nor his shame about Hannibal.

What cannot be said/Will get wept.

One morning soon after, Nahatum looked up from his scribing, glanced overat the impressive wooden cradle now waiting in the corner, and said to Sappho, sitting in the desk next to him, "I wonder how my mother cradled me."

There had been no cradle, of course. His mother's life had been too hard and brutal for such comforts, and his life with Sappho was so rich that it made plain how hard his mother's had been. Still, that morning he allowed himself to imagine he had been cradled in his mother's arms. He pictured her singing softly to him when he was an infant. He could feel her love in his very bones, so it must have been there. He remembered the wondrous night she had brought the glowing spirit rock to him from out of the army camp, and he remembered the light he so often saw in his mother's eyes.

How fiercely she loved him.

Sappho looked up, moved a strand of hair off her forehead. "I hardly know of your mother, you so rarely speak of her." She looked more closely at him, seeming to see something in his face, her own face changing, softening.

"What are these tears?"

Her arms opened to him, and he yielded, pressing up against her and their unborn baby. There Sappho was again, asking him to talk to her, and now this was a relief and a good thing because suddenly all the world seemed wet. He had not realized the violent thunderstorm that grief could become, but it overtook him as he talked to the woman he loved about the mother he loved and had lost, his wish to somehow honor her memory and her suffering.

She listened so patiently, until he had finished. She moved slightly, momentarily uncomfortable in her abundant body. Then she observed:

"You speak of Iberia and your mother, but you came here from Italy. There is more to the story, isn't there? Does it have something to do with Hannibal? With Rome?"

What cannot be said/Will get wept.

"My love, I cannot talk of all that now. I am exhausted."

She nodded, clearly disappointed, but gratefully she did not press him. Then.

Early Spring, 207 BC

"My Dear Brother Hasdrubal:

"Your letter brought tears of joy to my eyes. Yes! You are indeed embarking on a great journey. Eleven long years since we have seen each other. Finally we will be united in the fight against Rome. This is our last, best chance to turn the tides of this war in our favor.

"You will bring forty thousand infantry and twenty thousand cavalry, a large number of them Numidian, plus forty war elephants. The Romans will not be able to oppose our combined armies.

"Now, listen well, brother: I insist that we respond to each other only in code now. You will send me a coded letter the day you arrive in Northern Italy. Your riders will find me by staying close to the Southern Italian cities allied with me, in Bruttium and in Lucania. Remember, the Romans again patrol the roads carefully. Letters from Imre in Carthage are less and less; too many I am sure have wound up in sunken boats or couriers intercepted. Rome regains strength and their conquest of Iberia will only add to their treasury.

"So, may your journey be easy and quick. Be careful when you enter the territory of the Allobrodge—they are a terrible people. Trust none of them. However, the Gauls of Northern Italy will welcome you. If King Magalus still reigns, he will provide men and arms for our cause.

"I eagerly await news of your arrival. We shall sit here in my tent and take our wine and talk of Carthage and the old days. We will toast our father, and we will lay out the final strategy that will bring Rome to sue for peace. If she has not already by then, once she hears that 'a second Hannibal' is storming down upon them from the mountains of the north!
"With Anticipation,

"Your Loving Brother, Hannibal"

Chapter 8

Devotion

Ierapetra, Crete and Hannibal's encampment,
Southern Italy Fall, 207 BC

For Nahatum, the haggling over the price of his Archimedes book with the pompous man who represented a wealthy
landowner in Athens was actually fun. *He can afford what I'm*
asking for my work.

Nahatum had gotten so much better at negotiating,
mainly because of Sappho, who sat across the room in their
bookstore, with her very round belly, hunched over a manuscript—a collection of Persian love poetry she was copying.
He looked at her, how lovely she looked, and felt a deep satisfaction. The sea was high; he could hear the waves running
through the thick pilings of the old wharf down the street.

The Athenian book buyer seemed barely able to bear the
fact that he—an Athenian—had to come all the way to this
little town in Crete to buy the books his master wanted. That's
what made the haggling so much fun for Nahatum.

"Scribe Nahatum, you drive a hard bargain, but there are none like your copies of these books."

"The one you are buying was scribed mainly by Sappho, my companion." He nodded toward her, so intent on her scribing that she didn't hear his words. He repeated them more loudly and she looked over, her quill carefully poised above the papyrus, and smiled at him.

She had turned to him last night in bed and asked what he would like to name their baby. "Do we know if it's a boy or girl?" he'd asked, confused, wondering of some female knowledge known only to his Sappho. Which apparently there was, since she confidently claimed to have intuited that their baby was a girl.

"What was your mother's name?" she'd wanted to know. "Mother."

She laughed then. "Mothers also have names."

He thought hard then, forcing himself through sadness and the dark fear that he might not know, and remembered finally what he had heard others call her: *Alazne.*

He spoke her name aloud, to Sappho, for the first time in his life. Alazne.

She smiled. "That will be the name of our daughter. Alazne. Your mother will survive through our daughter."

Even in the greatest darkness, something will survive.

Finally, the Athenian bookseller agreed to his price. That wetness again.

Not now, not with this Athenian talking to him, saying something about....what? "What I said was: if you are busy now, wait till next year when the Romans come begging for copies of the great works to fill their libraries."

"The Romans?"

"After that great victory of theirs last month, the war will not be going on much longer. Thank goodness. I have had to submit too long to Roman ships stopping my own, even near Piraeus. They are polite, but always arrogant, searching for anything that might be of aid to the Carthaginians. They even smashed once a beautiful urn I brought back from Carthage."

The man prattled on. Nahatum fought to get his mind under control. "Indeed. Now, what was that about a great victory that Rome achieved last month– what victory? Did Hannibal….?"

"No, Hannibal was not defeated. He suffered a worse fate…"

"What?" He wanted to throttle the man, who was now going on about Hannibal's brother, Hasdrubal, whose successful crossing of the Alps earlier in the year was well known even on Crete.

"Hasdrubal was not as clever as his older brother. The Romans got wind of his plans to unite with Hannibal in southern Italy. They set a trap and Hasdrubal's army was annihilated by two Roman armies, the brother killed."

All the air was suddenly sucked out of Nahatum's lungs. The room felt very, very cold.

"The Romans delivered the news of the defeat and death of his brother to unsuspecting Hannibal in a most creative fashion: they cut off Hasdrubal's head and threw it into Hannibal's encampment for him to find."

Then the man was saying something more, but Nahatum was no longer listening.

"Excuse me. Sir, where are you going? Illustrious Scribe, have I offended you in some way?

The long wharf near the old tavern looked out in which direction? If he climbed the hill up the road, Nahatum wondered, all the way past the meadow, could he see Italy? *Strange that I've never thought about which direction Irepetra faced, and where Italy is in relation to it.* That thought soon gave way to the image of guards bringing the severed head to Hannibal. *How did he react?*

Nahatum remembered that he'd seen Hasdrubal but once, that day in Iberia before Hannibal had broken camp to begin the march to Italy, when the man had appeared riding hard with his guards. So long ago. Handsome. Not quite as tall as Hannibal. Clearly they were brothers, you could tell the way they moved, the way they acted around each other. They'd embraced. Even now he could remember the momentary tenderness, maybe only now he could understand what he saw.

He'd wanted to turn away from the warmth between the brothers because it had been so foreign to him. No, not foreign, rather because it had been so *desired* by him, to feel that warmth. Now he knew what it was like to feel so connected to another person. He knew it then because of Sappho. Hers was the deepest embrace he had known. He had wanted a lever to move the world and she was that lever, their love had rescued him.

And then there was Hannibal holding the head of his brother in his hands. And holding more: the death of all hope of winning the war. Such darkness. *Ah, Lizard Skin you must be laughing today. You couldn't take Hannibal but you took his brother. And, have you destroyed the man in the process?*

When Sappho arrived at the wharf, Nahatum was still sitting there, staring out to sea, bent over, one arm on his knee. The tide was going out. She hadn't heard the Athenian's story, but had seen Nahatum leave abruptly, so she had taken the man's money, bound up the book, and had gone in search of Nahatum.

As he told her about Hannibal and the grisly death of his brother Hasdrubal, she looked dazed. Her hand went to the bump in her belly, as if she felt the Roman savagery in her very body; an instinct to protect what you valued the most.

The sun was a fireball dousing itself in the Great Sea as he finally told her all that he had never spoken of: about Hannibal, about his past. About Solyphos, Cannae, Lady Busa. Through the darkness, she listened, sitting beside him on the raw wood of the wharf, looking up at him, reaching out and taking his hand. Occasionally she asked a question, needing him to explain, but mainly she listened.

At some points he imagined she was going to cry, and hoped not because if she started, then he might also. And right then he had to keep his thoughts clear, given what he knew he had to do. He wanted to prolong the story, to keep talking about the past so as not to have to tell Sappho his intentions.

Finally, in the gathering darkness of the mid-summer's night, it spilled out. "My dear, I must go to him."

At first she didn't understand, then she shook her head in disbelief. "What are you proposing? Why?"

How to explain? "I left. I ran away, I abandoned him." He wanted to say what he was thinking– *I cannot become a father knowing I have not made this right*—but he didn't know yet what that really meant. "You once asked me where is my courage. Well, it is here. In what I must do."

She misunderstood, of course. "You want to join his army again, to leave mehere...to go...fight?"

"No. I want to go and see him, not to rejoin his army."

"Why?" Her voice was so low that he could hear the quiet evening waves lapping at the pier. A pale moon rose high in the nighttime sky.

"I must see him." That was the best he could do.

She raged over the next days. Back in their bookstore, she threw a precious decorated amphora against the table, shattering it into a thousand pieces. She said he was being selfish and cruel. He stayed resolute. He must do this. Finally, tearfully, she spoke her fear:

"My love, you will be killed. If not by Hannibal, somewhere along the way trying to get there. How can you possibly cross all that land and find him?"

I am the wolf boy. "I know how to live in the forest. That I know. And I know how to disguise myself. It will not be so hard to find where he is encamped." So many tears had flowed that it was surprising to see there were some left, barely below her eyes. "Will you at least take some of the men from here with you, to guard you?"

"My dearest Sappho, I will be safer on my own. I always have been. Until I met you."

Her eyes seemed to float in a pond of tears. "You must promise to come back to me."

Yes. Yes. And: *please may this be a promise I can keep, for once.*

Hiring a ship to take him to Italy was too risky; he'd stand out if they encountered Romans. So, he took a simple merchant ship from Athens to Tarentum, the port city on the heel of Italy, where there were many sympathizers to Hannibal's cause. There had been Roman vessels patrolling. He had brought his scrolls and crates and to the Roman officers he was simply a prosperous Cretan merchant looking for business, selling his books. He restrained himself when questioned shipboard by the imperious Romans, made his face a mask. Arrogant, self- assured, rummaging carelessly through his crates of books. He could have swung freely with his thick staff, smashing Roman heads.

Then to find Hannibal. A few discreet inquiries in Tarentum. All his books and crates left behind with a friendly merchant in the town. He would be back for them in a few days. Where was he going?, the merchant asked. To visit family north of here, he explained. In the province of Lucanium. Be careful, that is where Hannibal is camped. Romans patrol as well.

All he took was his staff and a small pack with food in it. He traveled lightly, able to disappear into a copse when necessary. Three days of hiking. He'd avoided the Romans. Highwaymen were another matter. Even in the woods there were those all too happy to murder a man for a light pack. Who knew what gold he might carry with him? There had been several scuffles but his pike work was still excellent, thanks to all his practice over the years. He slept one whole day deep in the roots of a cypress tree, exhausted after the rigors of the trip. And, finally, after another two days of hiking, he spied from the woods a cluster of Carthaginian cavalry riding into what had to be an enormous army encampment. So, he emerged from the forest, not knowing if he would live to see it again, and walked alone down the road toward a suspicious group of well- armed guards watching him approach…

The weight of his brother's head had surprised Hannibal. The heaviness of it. When the stunned guards had brought it to him, his hands had tightened around the cold, matted hair, the dried blood pressing into his palms.

The eyes were shut. Someone—his guards?—had the decency to close them. Hannibal recalled that the Romans preferred to leave the eyes of their dead enemies open as further evidence of the man's shame. Hasdrubal, in death, had not looked ashamed—he looked determined.

Weeks ago, yet still so vivid, Hannibal had been encamped in Lucaniumso long now that the tent had the look of a villa. His brother had died fighting, that was clear. *You always looked so determined on the one hand and yet unsure on the other, my brother.* There was an aspect of their father Hamilcar in the thick beard and sharp eye brows.

Truly, he couldn't stop thinking about it. He had felt so overwhelmed holding the head. Still, his hands had gripped the skull so tightly, as if the pressure of his tired muscles could have brought his brother back to life.

Shall I raise the matter of the codes, Hasdrubal, that I told you to use? His brother hadn't used any sort of code in his letter proposing where they were to meet. The horseman had been intercepted; the Romans knew his exact marching plans. *Ah, who am I angrier at: myself for sitting ignorantly with my army in the luxury of Lucanium or Hasdrubal for being so arrogant and lazy as to send such a letter?*

Frankly, he was too weary for anger, though he tried to rouse himself to it.

I see the death of us all in this catastrophe, a prophecy of the death of Carthage. The war is lost.

He'd buried his brother's head outside his tent, in this temporary encampment, wrapped in a silk cloth. Gisgo's burial—so many years ago—had been a hasty affair, amidst some military maneuvers. Where in Italy was that grave? There had been no burial for Marhabal, slaughtered with his men in the middle of the night by that turncoat garrison, in…what was the town? And, his father, swept away by a river amidst a retreat in Iberia.

We are all swept away, aren't we? Carthage will be swept away. Perhaps, though, he would see it again. Walk among the orange trees with Imre. See his son.

Would he? These days every dusk felt like his last, the setting sun a sort of final light that deepened the gloom all around him.

Such dark thoughts. Get ahold of yourself. There is an army here that depends on you. Thousands of men and cavalry, allies, an ancient, venerable homeland…they all depend on you. *Gather yourself. If you can.*

An awkward cough came from the tent entrance. He wouldn't have heard if not for Mollusus's deep growl, the way he sprang toward the interruption, teeth bared. What did the dog know? He was more protective than ever.

For a moment, he imagined it was Hasdrubal, finally arrived, but that reverie quickly dissolved into a guard, standing there, looking as if his chest armor was way too tight, as if all he wanted was to be out of the tent. "Well, what is it, soldier?"

"There is a man here, Sire. He looks well-born, though he carries only a pack, and our perimeter guards said that he came down the road from out of the forest. The strange thing is that he claims to be your scribe. Or was. I checked with the Captain of the guards and he is not now your scribe….We were going to send him away, but he produced this and said to please give it to you."

He held something rolled up in his hand, and stumbled on. "We searched him carefully and he carries no weapons. He refused to surrender his pike, but let us search it for any hidden blades. Anyway, My Lord, there's this."

The guard held out a piece of papyrus. Written on it in a reminiscent hand: "There once was a wolf boy who was your scribe. I am he, returned."

I have to sit down. Where is the dog? His brother's head had rested right over there on the bed, on its blanket of silk.

Beyond the tent's entrance shadowy figures stood in the misty afternoon light. Several guards surrounded whoever he was. A broad- shouldered tree of a man.

Certainly not a boy. Still there was something in the way he stood.

Another Roman trick? What you want to do in warfare is to demoralize your enemy. You want them to feel that it is useless to fight on. Hannibal felt so tired.

Nahatum died at Cannae. *Or so I have believed all these years. We shall see. If the Romans are again toying with me, I will have this man flayed, then crucified and left to be eaten alive by wild dogs.*

"Bring him in."

He was scared that he would lose his voice, that he would become dizzy and fall to his knees right between the two guards holding his arms, that he would slide helplessly into tears.

The dog concentrated Nahatum's attention. A fine, lean muscular beast who rustled over to him and sniffed at his hands, then sat on its haunches, as if granting him permission to be there.

And then, Hannibal was in front of him. Hannibal, but different. Still the flash of lightening in the look, that penetrating gaze, the lupine eyes. But older. His hair was gray and his face marked with lines. The skin around the dead eye had hardened.

And he used to be taller. It was hard to think; Nahatum's heart beat against his chest.

Hannibal was staring at him. Then spoke: "Let me see your wrist."

Nahatum tried to put out his arm, but a guard restrained him. Hannibal gestured. Nahatum put his right wrist forward. The burn mark was clearly visible.

Hannibal nodded, taking the wrist in his hand. The touch was firm. "You said once that you wanted to be like me, to show your loyalty."

Now the tears came. He was on one knee. He could not speak.

"Stand. There is no need for such tears." Was Hannibal speaking to him or to himself?"

The guards had disappeared. They were alone, with the dog sitting quietly on the old carpet. Could it have been the same carpet he had swept so many times all those years ago?

"I thought you died at Cannae. Here, come sit."

"I deserted you, My Lord."

"Deserted?" There was a hush in the tent, which now felt close and hot.

Hannibal repeated the word and Nahatum couldn't tell if it was a question or an indictment.

Then: "Why?"

"I don't know, Sir."

"I want to know what happened." Hannibal said.

What was the use in not telling the truth? So, Nahatum spoke of the moments on the battlefield at Cannae when his mind was addled, he couldn't remember all that much about it, really, there was smoke and blood, Jonaz sliced in two right before his eyes, the smell of burning bodies, someone had chewed off another man's nose, and the next thing he knew he was in the forest. Then he was starving and then he was at Lady Busa's where he could remember more after that. Brindisium, Tenalakis, "a man like Solyphos only really not, but a good man nonetheless," the bookstore, and now there was a woman, his dear Sappho, with a child on the way.

As he spoke Nahatum wished that Hannibal would interrupt him but instead the man just listened, sitting still in that wooden chair of his, watching him, occasionally resting a hand on the big dog sprawled out next to them. Finally: "And your loyalty to me, what happened to that?"

"I thought you would kill me."

"Kill you? Your return is the first bright moment in this darkness that surrounds me." Then: "That is what kept you from coming back?"

"I thought so once, but…." He paused, stared at the carpet as if some truth was buried there. "I discovered a different life. The world. Words. I've become a bookmaker. A scribe. One who makes books."

"You deserted from my army because you wanted to scribe scrolls?"

"Now they're called 'books,' Sir." *Why am I going on about this? Gather yourself.* "Yes, scribe scrolls. I own a bookstore. I copy books and sell them."

"Books."

"They are precious to me, Sir. They have saved my life, many times over."

"And you travelled all the way back here, risked everything, including my wrath, to see me."

"I had to, Sir….when I learned what had happened."

"Yes, of course. That." A single tear—the rear guard— escaped down Hannibal's lined face. The man slumped in his chair, a hawk crashed to earth, the energy drained out of him. "All lost. Everyone…"

All but me…

"I am not myself, Nahatum." Hannibal patted the dog on the head tenderly then rubbed its chin. "A bitter, cheerless cloud has overtaken me…"

"Sometimes sorrow saps our strength," Nahatum murmured. How odd, he noted, to be saying this, he who had never been able to outrun his terror of Lizard Skin, who had nightmares about becoming a father. And, yet, something had shifted there, too. There was Sappho, the baby. "We are thinking of naming our baby, Alazne. If it is a girl."

Hannibal smiled. "A beautiful name."

Then, shockingly, Hannibal asked: "So, what am I to do? I am in a terrible strategic position. I can trouble the Romans, but Carthage can no longer defeat them. Scipio is in Iberia now, but he will strike directly at Carthage next, I'm sure. That's what I would do. It seems I have been their tutor all these years, teaching the Romans how to create an empire. Solyphos, Gisgo, Marhabal, all gone. I'm not sure I can bear defeat."

Nahatum slowly drew in his breath. Was he to speak? "Sir, your father."

"My father– what of him?"

"He too knew defeat, despite his best efforts."

"My father never lost hope. He never surrendered, really. He said to me once right after he arrived back in Carthage from the defeat in Sicily: 'now we must rebuild.'"

"Well, now *you* must rebuild," Nahatum ventured.

Hannibal was looking right at him and it was that look that moved Nahatum to find more words.

"That is what you must do, Sir. Rebuild. This war is not over. Your army is intact and the Romans fear you still. They always will. You have become a part of their very language: In times of fear, the Romans exclaim, 'Hannibal is at the gates!'"

That produced a brief smile from the General.

"You will rebuild, Sir— yourself, your confidence, then your city."

"With your help, Nahatum, with you here to scribe for me."

There was silence. They were looking over an abyss.

"My Lord, I cannot. I promised I would return home. I have a child coming."

Hannibal's eyes grew dark. He stood up, toyed with a dagger on his writing desk, balancing the point, digging it into the wood. "And what makes you think I will let you go? You were once my scribe and you can be again."

It had been years since Nahatum felt this rising in his stomach, threatening to come up his throat and right out his mouth. The tone in Hannibal's voice was both menacing and hopeful: the man had not lost his steel. Even the dog had sat upright, ears alert. *Take a deep breath, Nahatum, you are a man now. Act like one.*

"My Lord, you will let me return to my life, my wife, the family I hope for, for one reason: I have something I can offer you in return."

"And that is?"

"To tell your tale. To write the story of Hannibal's War with Rome."

"You can write of me here. While I dictate to you."

"Here? While Rome blocks communication? How much better if I am free, back in Crete, with access to Athens and Alexandria, free to write the story and to sell it from my bookstore, to make the tale of this war known to all the world."

Hannibal sighed, sat down in his chair. "I do not really wish to keep you here against your will, Nahatum. You have already given me a great gift by returning." Then, a sharp glance, a piercing look that held his eyes: "You will write the story, as Solyphos would have, the story of what happened, what I have done?"

"Yes, with pleasure, my lord. And we will copy the story into books for the world to know."

The day was fading. An early evening chill. Nahatum looked at the coal brazier. "Let me restore the fire so we can be more comfortable."

In the warmth of the fire, Hannibal said, "Ah, it is hard to let you go again. When do you plan to leave?"

"Tomorrow, my Lord. I must return to the very worried woman I dearly love."

"So soon. I am a bit envious. Come, let us have dinner tonight and talk of those who are not here. I have a story to tell you about Hasdrubal, when he and I were young....And, what of this little girl you await, this Alazne?"

Endpage

**Nahatum, Sappho, and Daughter Scribers
and Booksellers of Crete**

Books for sale by Herodotus, Thucydides, Polybius,
Archimedes, the plays of Euripides, Sophocles, Aesychlus
and others, the poetry of Sappho of Lesbos

And: Nahatum of Crete, *Hannibal's War With Rome*

Postscript

"….I hardly know whether Hannibal was not more wonderful when fortune was against him than in his hours of success. Fighting for thirteen years in enemy territory, far from home, with varying fortunes and an army composed not of native troops but of a hotch- potch of the riff-raff of all nationalities, men who shared neither law nor custom nor language, who differed in manner, in dress, in equipment, who had in common neither the forms of religious observance nor even the gods they served, he yet was able, somehow or other, to wield this motley crowd so firmly together that they never quarreled amongst themselves nor mutinied against their general…"

– Livy, *The War With Hannibal,* p. 512

Epilogue

Hannibal fought on in Italy for four more years. He retreated into the rugged province of Bruttium, the heel of Italy, where he continued to occupy the Romans. Such was their fear that Rome arrayed four legions against him but again refrained from open battle. Bruttium is a hilly province not given to farming and it is further testament to Hannibal's leadership that he was able to feed and supply his army over this time without mutiny or rebellion. His army stayed intact and active in southern Italy, which served the strategic function of diverting Rome's resources from an attack on Carthage.

In 204 BC Scipio landed an army on the coast of North Africa and put increasing pressure on Carthage. In 203 BC Hannibal was recalled to defend the city. He had spent fifteen years in Italy, a longer period than he had ever lived in Carthage. Upon his return, Hannibal worked feverishly to cobble together an army of mercenaries to face Scipio's large force of well- trained and experienced soldiers. At Scipio's invitation, the two generals met near the town of Zama. Hannibal implored Scipio to negotiate a just peace without further bloodshed. He spoke as a wise, older man to a respected, younger opponent. Scipio refused, blaming Carthage for all the years of war. At the battle of Zama, in 202 BC, Hannibal's overmatched army was defeated by Scipio's forces, who dominated the field of battle with—ironically—far superior cavalry than was available to the Carthaginians.

After the war, Hannibal returned to Carthage and—following a period of some turmoil and accusation against him—eventually became a leader of the city, rising at one point to become Suffette (chief magistrate) of the Senate. He pushed hard for Carthage to rebuild. He worked for reform of the Carthaginian constitution to lessen the power of the ruling elites, he reorganized the state finances, and even engaged in urban planning and a rebuilding of the vital port area. Despite the losses of the war and indemnity being paid to Rome, Carthage was again a prosperous and thriving city.

Eventually, these efforts also brought Hannibal again into conflict with the anti- Barca elements of the ruling aristocracy in Carthage, who joined with Rome to trump up charges that Hannibal was secretly plotting another war. Scipio, his former opponent, now greatly honored in Rome and given the esteemed title of Scipio Africanus for his victory at Zama, spoke in the Roman Senate to defend Hannibal against the false accusations, to no avail.

A Roman delegation was sent to Carthage demanding that Hannibal be brought to trial. In 195 BC, Hannibal, now in his early fifties, fled Carthage and began years of wandering. His fame throughout the Mediterranean world was such that he became a rallying point for those trying to resist the growing expansion of Rome. In Tyre, where his family traced its roots, he advised Antiochus III in his resistance to Roman expansion. He eventually wound up at the Court of King Prusias of Bithynia (part of modern Turkey), advising the king in his anti- Roman efforts. According to Cicero, Hannibal's "name was held in great honour among all men." One oft-repeated story of Hannibal's military cleverness was his strategy, while commanding Prusias' fleet in battle, of lanching ceramic pots filled with poisonous snakes onto the decks of enemy ships. The smashing pots were first met with enemy laughter, then with panic as their occupants created havoc amidst the enemy, who finally surrendered.

While the Romans eventually won the war against Prusias, they remained terrified of Hannibal. One requirement of Prusias' surrender was that he surrender Hannibal to them. Rather than submit, Hannibal is rumored to have committed suicide in the small seaside house he occupied, taking poison that he always carried with him for that eventuality. He died at age sixty- five in 183 BC, the same year as his adversary and nemesis, Scipio Africanus.

And the fate of Carthage? The war with Hannibal endured in Roman memory through the generations and created a vengeful preoccupation with Carthage. Despite the fact that after the second war the balance of power had firmly shifted to Rome, the Roman Senator Cato ended many of his speeches with the famous phrase, "Carthago Delenda Est" (Carthage must be destroyed). Finally in 146 BC, Cato got his wish. After a two- year siege– and ingenious and heroic resistance by the eventually overwhelmed citizens of Carthage– the city was razed and all survivors were sold into slavery. The legend is that the orders to the Roman commander were to destroy the city so completely that a plow could make a furrow unimpeded from one end to the other.

Author's Note

Most of the background characters in this novel are real, though I have created their lives beyond what is known in the historical record. The figures of Gisgo, Marhabal, Imre, Soly-phos, Lady Busa, all exist in fragmentary ways in accounts of the Punic Wars. The historical accounts, however, are written exclusively from the Roman point of view. The great historian Titus Livy wrote at the time of enormous Roman power and influence. His magisterial account, *The War With Hannibal*, reflects the presumption of Roman exceptionalism. When Rome razed the city, almost all record of a great civilization was lost, including Carthage's accounts of the wars that led to its destruction.

The story of Hannibal has excited me since I was a child and read historian and naturalist Sir Gavin de Beer's accounts of his tramps through the Alps to re-trace the exact route Hannibal took. Hannibal's life has fascinated people to the present day. Freud identified with Hannibal and claimed him as his favorite childhood hero. Hannibal's "Cannae strategy" (also known as the double envelopement, or pincer, movement) has influenced military leaders through history. Dwight Eisenhower wrote that every military commander "tries to duplicate in modern war the classic example of Cannae," and historian

Will Durant declared it, the "supreme example of generalship, never bettered in history..."

As a graduate student in psychology in the late 1960s, I went to Tunisia to complete some cross-cultural research and while there had an opportunity to visit Carthage, now a suburb of the capital city, Tunis. I was disappointed to see that what exists is mostly Roman Carthage, established as a Roman colony by Julius Caesar. Little of the original city remained to be seen. What is it like, I wondered, to have your history disappear from the human record? What is lost, what is forgotten?

The scholarship on Hannibal and the Punic Wars is voluminous. Sir Gavin de Beer's books, *Hannibal: Challenging Rome's Supremacy* and *Hannibal's March: Of Alps And Elephants* are entertaining introductions, if a bit outdated. More contemporary overviews include Adrian Goldsworthy's *The Punic Wars* and *The Fall of Carthage*. Eve MacDonald's *Hannibal: A Hellenistic Life* in particular explores the human dimensions of Hannibal's life and sets the man in the context of his historical time. As for the historical record, Livy's *The War With Hannibal* and Polybius' *Histories* offer the most reliable accounts closer in time to the actual events, though, again, both—while often laudatory of Hannibal– are seen through the lens of the victors. I am indebted to all of these works, and the scholarship and scholars they represent.

Acknowledgements

I've been lucky to have worked with a number of talented editors and writers over the years as this novel developed from an idea into a reality. Many thanks to Abigail DeWitt, Jane Rosenman, Susan Leon, and Sophie Powell for helping me craft this story. Many thanks as well to my friends and family who have encouraged me to keep going through numerous drafts, in particular my son Toby, my daughter Emily-- and of course and always, my dear wife Julie, who provided essential optimism and great editorial suggestions at crucial moments.

Alejandra Oliva and Sophie Wolfe were two superb, unflappable research assistants.

I am very grateful to my late mother, who modeled for me how to be a writer, and my late father for passing on his love of history and for keeping well- stocked bookshelves in the living room that fed this child's imagination and curiosity about the world.

The scholarship on Hannibal and the Punic Wars is voluminous. Sir Gavin de Beer's books, *Hannibal: Challenging Rome's Supremacy* and *Hannibal's March: Of Alps And Elephants* are entertaining introductions, if a bit outdated. More contemporary overviews include Adrian Goldsworthy's *The Punic Wars* and *The Fall of Carthage*. Eve MacDonald's *Hannibal: A*

Hellenistic Life in particular explores the human dimensions of Hannibal's life and sets the man in the context of his historical time. As for the historical record, Livy's *The War With Hannibal* and Polybius' *Histories* offer the most reliable accounts closer in time to the actual events, though both—while often laudatory of Hannibal– are seen through the lens of the victors. I am indebted to all of these works, and the scholarship and scholars they represent.

And, of course, no book gets written without the invaluable support of the many people an author counts on through the inevitable dark times that accompany the writing process. For me, these people include my wife, Julie Snow Osherson, my children. Toby and Emily Osherson, Steven Krugman, Stephanie Rambler, Malcolm Slavin, Paula Chu, Roland Davis, Sandy Drob, Jane Rosenman, and Susan Leon.

About the Author

 In both his fiction and non-fiction, Sam Osherson has explored the complexities of men's lives—their love for and fear of women and the feminine, their attraction to war and the thrill of battle, their desire for family, and their yearning for the hero's quest. Of particular interest to Osherson has been the complex relationship between father and son.

The story of Hannibal's heroic efforts to redeem his father's legacy and secure the future of his doomed city has fascinated Osherson since high school when he first came across a book in his town library about the Alps, elephants, and an extraordinary army leader rolling the dice in a most unexpected way. He has spent time in Tunisia, site of the ancient city of Carthage, and visited parts of what may have been Hannibal's route crossing the Alps.

He has taught at the Harvard Medical School, University of Massachusetts, Harvard University, MIT, as well as the Fielding Graduate University.